Me~

LORDS ~~~

COLLECTION

*When courageous knights risked all
to win the hand of their lady!*

Don't miss any of this stunning collection!

July 2007 – Volume 1
Conquest Brides
He took her lands – but can he capture her heart?

August 2007 – Volume 2
Blackmail & Betrayal
Forgive and forget…or take her revenge?

September 2007 – Volume 3
The War of the Roses
Brought together by passion, torn apart by war!

October 2007 – Volume 4
Christmas Knights
Spend a medieval Yuletide with a perfect knight!

November 2007 – Volume 5
Exotic East
All the heat and spice of the desert…

December 2007 – Volume 6
Mediterranean Heroes
These men have a passion as fiercely hot as
their homelands!

Medieval
LORDS & LADIES
COLLECTION

Conquest Brides

Julia Byrne & Elizabeth Henshall

*M&B™ and M&B™ with the Rose Device
are trademarks of the publisher.
Harlequin Mills & Boon Limited, Eton House,
18-24 Paradise Road, Richmond, Surrey TW9 1SR*

MEDIEVAL LORDS & LADIES COLLECTION
© Harlequin Books S.A. 2007

The publisher acknowledges the copyright holders of the
individual works as follows:

Gentle Conqueror © Julia Byrne 1992
Madselin's Choice © Elizabeth Henshall 1997

ISBN: 978 0 263 85881 5

53-0707

*Printed and bound in Spain
by Litografia Rosés S.A., Barcelona*

Gentle Conqueror

by

Julia Byrne

Julia Byrne lives in Australia with her husband, daughter and a cat who thinks he's a person. She started her working career as a secretary, taught ballroom dancing after several successful years as a competitor and, while working in the History Department of a Melbourne university, decided to try her hand at writing historical romance. She enjoys a game of cards or Mah Jong, usually has several cross-stitch projects on the go and is a keen preserver of family history.

Historical Note

In the autumn of 1068 William the Conqueror had been King of England for almost two years, but another three years were to pass before William conquered the entire country. Several uprisings centred around the Saxon Prince Edgar, last of the old English royalty. However, he was merely a boy, a figurehead, whose supporters alternately sided with William or rebelled against him, according to their fluctuating ambitions.

These rebellions effectively wiped out the Saxon nobility. Prince Edgar fled, with his mother and sisters, to Scotland, and by 1071 there was only one Saxon Earl remaining in England, the Court spoke Norman French, and, though the common folk remained relatively unaffected, the ruling minority became more Anglo-Norman than Anglo-Saxon.

The Atheling Edgar eventually returned to England and was sent to William's father-in-law in Flanders for several years. He spent the remainder of his life drifting between England and Scotland, apparently lacking the strong personality necessary to make a bid to regain his family's throne. However, the ancient royal line continued through a woman.

Prince Henry, the only child of William and Matilda to be born in England, was crowned Henry I in August 1100. He married Edith of Scotland, Edgar's niece, thereby uniting his family with the last Saxon princess.

Prologue

Romsey Abbey, near Winchester, September 1068

"'Tis of no use to argue further. I cannot help you." The black-robed woman standing by the window folded her hands over the intricately carved wooden rosary at her waist with a gesture of finality.

Her visitor's grim expression showed his intention of ignoring this remark, but the nun's face, framed by the white wimple and black veil of the Benedictine Order, remained steadfast.

"If they may not seek shelter here, Reverend Mother, where else can they go? You are their only family remaining, and you know the alternative."

"A fate shared by many," the nun answered implacably. "They could fare worse."

"Marriage to men my ladies regard as enemies?"

"Enemies," she scoffed. "The late Confessor's Queen—Harold's own sister, I would remind you—herself handed over the royal town of Winchester to William of Normandy; which proves her opinion of her brother's ambitions. When I advise my nieces to obey the King I but

follow the example of a pious and noble lady. Naturally we
welcome any girl who has the King's permission to dedi-
cate her life to God. However, such true brides of Christ
bring with them a dowry. Worldly goods though they are,
even a large house such as ours cannot exist without
funds.''

"A dowry!" the visitor exclaimed, frowning at her. He
took a hasty turn about the room, the glimpse of chainmail
beneath his mantle and the dagger at his waist jarringly
alien in the peaceful simplicity of Reverend Mother's
chamber. "My Lady Enide, what dowry can they possibly
bring now their heritage has been taken from them? In
truth, they are as poor as the lowliest serf.''

The nun gestured slightly with one hand. "In that case
there is no more to be said. And I am no longer the Lady
Enide, as you well know.''

The elderly soldier regarded her sombrely. He had not
really expected the request to be granted; but he had promised to deliver it, and he would never break a promise to
his lady. Even if he did happen to agree with the Prioress
that continuing to treat the Normans as enemies was futile.

"Then I shall not impose on your time any longer, my
Lady Prioress," he said, giving subtle emphasis to her title.
"My apologies for disturbing you.''

He turned to open the door, not staying for her blessing.

"Wait!" The nun looked away, through the open window. She was silent for a long moment.

Though autumn was upon them, the leaves outside were
still green here in the sheltered cloister, but her eyes were
blind to the summer verdure. She saw instead the trees
surrounding her girlhood home, already beginning their
transformation to red, gold, and amber, fed by the cool air
blowing across from the Welsh mountains.

"I cannot act against the King's orders," the Prioress

said at last, "but…we do not refuse shelter to those desperate enough to arrive at our gates with nothing."

There was another long silence. Then she added, "God go with you, Bertrand." It was dismissal.

The nun heard the door close softly, but remained by the window. A faint breeze rustled through the leafy branches, touching her face with a warm caress.

Had she done right? Her own kin, and she'd had to refuse them. But, with only four other nunneries in the whole of England, they could not take in every Saxon widow or bereft daughter who objected to the likelihood of having a Norman husband foisted upon them. Already her resources were dangerously stretched to the limit.

The wily old warrior had tried an appeal to memories of her life before the cloister by using her former title, and it had almost succeeded. But if she offered shelter to three penniless girls of her own family the Abbot would have plenty to say when he arrived for his next visit of inspection; and she had no intention of ceding her place to one of the ambitious Norman ladies who coveted her high position.

The bell tolled for Prime, recalling the Prioress to her duties. She could only pray for her nieces. Pray that they had the courage to face whatever future had been ordained by the will of God.

Or rather, she amended with wry pragmatism, by the will of the Conqueror.

Chapter One

The late afternoon sun, shining through the narrow windows set high in the walls of the great hall, sent dancing rays of golden light across the rush-strewn floor, enveloping the three girls seated near the huge stone fireplace in a soft luminous haze. Bertrand, coming in through the main door and rounding the corner from the screen passage, paused to watch them for a moment.

They presented a peaceful tableau, a little apart as they were from the bustle elsewhere in the hall as the house carls set up trestles for the evening meal. Two of the girls sat close together on a wooden bench, the fair head of the elder bent over the sewing of her younger sister and guiding a hand still unskilled and impatient.

A smile crossed Bertrand's lined and weathered face. Young Catherine would much rather be out in the stables or running through the orchard on this warm autumn day than confined indoors, wielding a needle.

Then the smile faded as his gaze rested longest on the middle sister, Lisette, who sat curled up on the floor at her sisters' feet, a large black mastiff stretched out by her side, his head in her lap. She, too, had been stitching, but her hands were now resting in the thick fur of the dog's ruff,

Gentle Conqueror

and she sat gazing into the fire, where a small flame flickered into life against the oncoming chill of evening.

Bertrand, gazing at the pure outline of her profile etched against the dark stone, considered her the loveliest of his late master's daughters. Although they all had the fine-boned, delicate features of their Celtic mother, Lisette was the only one who had inherited that lady's dark colouring, Enide and Catherine having the fair skin and hair of their father's Saxon forebears.

"She looks at ease for the first time in months," murmured Bertrand to his companion, a brawny youth garbed in the leather apron of the blacksmith.

"A fragile peace at best, my friend," the younger man answered, drawing Bertrand back into the passage. "She's been worried about you travelling alone, and now 'tis all for nought. You should have taken them with you, as I suggested."

"They were safer here," said Bertrand mildly. He and Siward had had this argument before, and it was irrelevant now.

"Do you still say so now the Norman usurper has thrown his shadow over them?" Siward's voice grew angry. "We can still fight."

"You hotheaded young fool," retorted Bertrand. "There are at least forty soldiers about to arrive against eight of us—apart from the serfs. You might be willing to throw away your life for nothing, but my lady would never permit it. You can serve her best by accepting what we've always known would happen."

Siward swore softly. Aye, they had known, he thought. Since William of Normandy had conquered England, Norman overlordship was becoming more and more the rule as the King rewarded his followers by granting them the lands and manors previously held by the Saxon Thegns who had died with King Harold in the bloody battle at Hastings. Or in the uprisings since that date. But knowing didn't make acceptance any easier.

"I was my Lord Alaric's man," he said sullenly, turning away to the door. "And I don't intend to serve his enemies."

"My lord admired William," Bertrand called after him, hoping the reminder would hold Siward's hot temper in check for a while. It was the truth, after all.

Alaric, Thegn of Ambray, had accepted the Witan's decision to crown Harold Godwinson King of England, despite the claim by William of Normandy that the English crown had been promised to him by his cousin, King Edward, known as the Confessor. Edward had no true right to will his crown away, English Kings being elected; and Harold was Saxon, the most powerful man in the land, and the late King's brother-in-law, three circumstances which made his claim a good one. But Alaric had had doubts.

He had travelled extensively in his young days, staying some considerable time in Normandy, where he had remote family connections dating back to Viking days, and had considered William to be a strong ruler. Ruthless certainly, but fair, and possibly better able to unite England under one leader than the old Cerdic line, where bitter fighting between factions and brothers divided the Saxons, weakening the country.

In fact, on Alaric's return to England years earlier, King Edward, who was half-Norman himself by birth, and had plenty of his mother's countrymen in his service, had besought Alaric to settle on his land-holdings in the west, promising him aid in building the Norman stronghold of Alaric's ambition in exchange for helping to maintain the peace on the Welsh border.

However, King Edward's death had caused more than

one claimant to the English throne to come forward. Harold Godwinson might have managed to have himself elected and crowned, but his position was not secure. When the Norwegian King, Harald Hardrada, had mounted an attack in the north, Alaric, considering himself more Saxon than anything else, had finally sworn fealty to Harold and marched with the fyrd to a resounding victory at Stamford Bridge. The Norwegians had been utterly routed, limping home in only twenty-four of the three hundred ships in which they had arrived.

But then news had come of William's landing at Pevensey on the south coast, and Alaric had found himself in the forced march back through England and in the thick of the fighting at Hastings.

The Saxons had fought bravely, but an army weakened by two long marches with a battle between, in the space of thirteen days, was no match for the disciplined Normans. Alaric had been taken prisoner, and, before being given the opportunity to transfer his allegiance to William, had died of his wounds, leaving his three daughters without the male protection needed in these troubled times, and an estate upon which more than one Norman knight had cast an acquisitive eye.

Nestling in the rolling green pasturelands of the Wye Valley, with a prosperous village clustered around a stone church, and many acres of farmland bordered by dense forest, it was a fair estate indeed. And crowned by the small though solid castle, built after the Norman style which Alaric had so admired on his travels, and which was easier to defend than the usual simple wooden dwellings favoured by the Saxons. The castle, in its still unfinished state, was more a fortified manor-house, but a tower had been added to the hall, from which an excellent view could be had of the countryside, and a stone wall protected the manor and outbuildings, replacing the original wooden palisade.

Three smaller compounds, once occupied by Alaric's retainers, completed the estate. A comfortable prize for an enterprising man with ambition.

Well, thought Bertrand, recalled to his mission, if change must come, at least the terms the King had laid down would ensure that Lord Alaric's daughters would be cared for; and the estate had been given to a man who looked as if he could be one Bertrand could come to respect, and even admire. Still, he sighed, Lisette would not take kindly to handing over her family home to a stranger, and a Norman stranger at that.

Bertrand knew well her opinion of illegitimate Dukes of Normandy who decided that a kingdom would suit them and rode roughshod over any who stood in their way, and he would not place much dependence on her meekly accepting the terms the King had ordered him to deliver. She had already been given plenty of reason to hate and fear any Norman, let alone one who now had absolute control over her future, and Bertrand was conscious of extreme reluctance to be the bearer of such tidings. But, as the subject of his message was at this very moment only about a mile behind him, he had best get on with it.

As he strode forward the sun slid further towards the western horizon, plunging the hall into sudden dimness, and he hoped it wasn't an ill omen. Then all other thoughts were forgotten as Lisette heard him and turned her head, a smile of welcome lighting up her lovely face.

"Bertrand!" She sprang to her feet with a light, graceful movement, disturbing the dog from his slumber. He rose also, whining and coming forward to snuffle at the familiar figure before flopping down again before the fire, knowing his mistress had no need of defence.

Lisette held out her hands in greeting. "I didn't look to see you so soon. What news from Winchester? Did you see my lady aunt? Will she take us into sanctuary? Has she heard any talk of the manor?"

The spate of questions tripped over each other in a breathless rush as the cares she had tried to forget in day-dreaming for a few moments flooded back, causing a frown to appear on her smooth brow.

Bertrand sank to one knee at her feet. "Lady, dear, news indeed. And you must quickly prepare to meet it in the flesh, for the new lord would have me travel with him when he learned from whence I came, and is only a few minutes behind."

Lisette's face paled suddenly as she listened, Bertrand's voice seeming to come from a great distance.

"New lord?" The question was a horrified whisper.

After nearly a year of peace she had forgotten, Lisette thought. Had forgotten how sickening fear could be. But she must not give in to the numbing feeling of helplessness. Too many people depended on her. The churls...her sisters...

"Then Enide and Catherine must be got away. Hidden in the village until you can take them to my aunt..." Lisette faltered to a stop as Bertrand shook his head.

"Hear me out, mistress." His voice was grave. "I wish I could have spared you this, but the King has granted all your father's lands to one of his young officers, Alain of Raverre, a younger son of a noble family, I am told. And that is not all. He has also granted him the wardship of yourself and your sisters, so you are under his protection and not destitute or a charge on the royal household."

"You saw the King himself?" Lisette asked. "He knows of us?"

"Aye," confirmed Bertrand, rising stiffly to his feet. "I

came upon him and some of his knights the instant I set foot inside the town walls, and was promptly seized.''

''Oh, Bertrand!''

'''Twas not so bad. I had thought to mingle with the beggars, and slip unnoticed through the city gates at dawn, but there were soldiers everywhere, interrogating all who passed.''

Bertrand grimaced at the memory, but his tone held reluctant admiration for such Norman efficiency. ''There is no time to tell it all now, but William remembered me from the time I asked his permission to bring your father's body home for burial. The next thing I knew, he ordered me to the palace so I could meet my new liege lord.''

''Then I left it too late to send to my aunt.'' Lisette's voice held such despair that Bertrand felt compelled to steady her with a sustaining grip on her arm.

''You mustn't blame yourself, my lady. Even had I gone earlier—''

He hesitated, trying to find the right words. He knew Lisette's concern was all for her sisters; that, despite the many tales noised abroad of manors and villeins deserted by their Thegns, she had not once considered the personal consequences of remaining in her home until the inevitable arrival of a Norman master.

''I did have some speech with the Lady Prioress, and, though she sends you her blessings, she bids you obey the King. Although she did say she would shelter any who came.''

He stopped, not wishing to add to her worries. He could not bring himself to tell Lisette of the Prioress's offer of shelter on the condition of a dowry, or unless they came alone, practically as beggars.

His news had brought the other girls to their feet, their sewing falling unheeded to the floor, and the servants crowding around, asking questions, fearful of the future. Catherine clung to Lisette's hand and Enide, although the eldest, also looked to her sister for guidance.

The load was too great for a young girl, thought Bertrand, wishing he had the power to lift some of it from her slender shoulders. Her face was so pale that he feared she might swoon. And she looked tired, as well she might, having had the running of the estate since her father's death, as well as the ordering of the household.

"A Saxon woman may hold land in her own right," she murmured, as though in puzzled denial of Bertrand's words. "The Witan would have named Enide as our father's heiress before Hastings. Do you tell me that now we own nothing, and are dependent upon a stranger and an enemy?"

A flash of anger suddenly went through her, pushing the fear aside for the moment, but there was no time now to rail against fate. Without waiting for an answer, Lisette squared her shoulders and, gently putting aside Bertrand's supporting hand, set about quieting the servants.

"Hush, all of you," she commanded firmly. "Go about your business. You are in no danger, and I am here to speak for you. When I know more, so will you, but for now we will not show frightened faces to these Normans."

Hoping that the familiar preparations for the arrival of visitors might occupy the serfs enough to keep them from panicking, she turned to old Wat, who ruled the kitchen slaves with a stern hand.

"Wat, you had best prepare plenty of food; no doubt our—" she hesitated, then took a deep, steadying breath and went on "—our guests will be hungry. The rest of you, go back to your work."

As some of the serfs scurried away to the kitchens, murmuring among themselves, Lisette turned back to the man who had served her family faithfully for so many years.

"Bertrand, can you manage? You will know what to do. How many men should be housed here in the bailey or elsewhere…"

Her voice trailed off, and Bertrand knew she was re-membering the last time Norman soldiers had been in the castle and the terrible damage that had been done. He could at least set her mind at ease on this question, however.

"Lady, see to your household and don't worry your head about the soldiers. Raverre has not brought many men. Three of his own knights with their retainers, the rest merely as escort on the road, and he has them well disci-plined. You need not fear for yourselves or your people. Indeed, from what speech I had with him as we travelled, Raverre intends things to go on much as before."

He paused. There was a lot more to say but it would have to wait. Bertrand, knowing of his late lord's high opin-ion of Duke William, had also been impressed by the young man he must now call master, and was willing to co-operate with him, but he wanted Lisette to judge for herself. He knew she was prepared to see nothing good in any Norman from the King down, but he hoped in time she would come to accept this change in her life, and not become bitter and angry.

Bertrand remembered the carefree, innocent child she had been two years before. Afraid of nothing. Facing life with happy anticipation. Eager, loving, she had seemed to carry light and laughter within her. He knew the child could never return, but he hoped the woman who emerged from the years of uncertainty and loss would still have that gift of happiness and love.

Hearing the jingling of harness and voices raised in com-mand coming faintly through the unglazed windows, Bertrand left the hall swiftly, and Lisette sank back on to the settle for a moment to gather her strength and courage. She had to think. There was so much to do. But of the myriad thoughts jostling themselves about in her head, only one stood out clearly.

He has come.

As if sensing the tension in the air, the dog rose again, ears pricked towards the sounds outside, and would have investigated, but Lisette held him back.

"Stay, Finn," she commanded, and felt slightly comforted at the touch of the big animal under her restraining hand. Her eyes flew to her sisters.

Enide had the mindless, vacant look in her eyes that Lisette dreaded to see there, but Catherine was now looking ready to do battle with any amount of Normans, her little fists clenched and a pugnacious tilt to her chin. The sight of her made Lisette smile slightly and she quickly rallied, kneeling to gather up the forgotten threads and cloths.

"Come," she said, striving for a brisk tone, "we will show these Normans that we are not disturbed by their arrival. Fear will only make us appear weak. Sit down and at least pretend to be calm. Catherine, as soon as you can, take Enide up to our chamber and wait for me there. Whatever this Norman Baron intends, we must surely be allowed some privacy."

Catherine only had time to nod her understanding with a quick glance at the still silent Enide when firm footsteps sounded at the head of the outside stairway and a man strode into the hall. Taking in the servants huddled in one corner and the three girls seated by the fire, without breaking stride, he advanced towards them.

Tension gripped Lisette's body instantly. The Norman's quiet entrance, unattended by any soldiers, had not been at all threatening, but she felt herself brace as though about to confront an unknown, unseen danger. Her mouth went dry, and her heart beat so fast that she could scarcely catch her breath.

He was so big.

Standing well over six feet tall with broad shoulders and a deeply muscled chest, tapering to more slender but still strongly muscled hips and thighs, he was the most powerful-looking man Lisette had ever seen. And, though the power was contained, leashed by the lithe, controlled grace with which he moved, the aura of physical strength about him was palpable.

He was dressed all in dark blue, including the ankle-length mantle he wore, which seemed to add to his height, and his tunic and trousers were of fine woollen cloth, obviously the best quality and weave. Although he wore no mailcoat, a deadly-looking sword was buckled at his hip, and a visored helmet of black metal concealed his eyes, making him appear even more formidable.

This, however, he pulled off as he approached, revealing a head of thick fair hair and a strong handsome face, tanned from long campaigning in all weathers, with broad, high cheekbones, an aquiline nose, and piercing ice-blue eyes, whose cool, hard gaze clashed with Lisette's and held. For a heart-stopping moment she was aware of nothing else but him.

She rose swiftly and immediately cursed herself for doing so, remembering that she had meant to remain seated, refusing to offer this invader the courteous greeting normally given to any guest. It was as though his compelling eyes had brought her to her feet before she had had time to think about it. As he reached them Lisette lifted her chin, staring him in the face. But her widened eyes and the pulse fluttering in her throat betrayed the sudden fear his intimidating presence had aroused.

His firm mouth quirked a little at the defiant picture she made, but after a sweeping glance which took in all three girls, making Lisette feel as if a lightning bolt had shot through them, he bent his head a little in her direction and addressed her directly in fluent English.

"Lady, I am Alain of Raverre, lately Captain in the army of William, King of England and Duke of Normandy, now, by the King's grace, Baron of this manor and its lands. You are—?" He paused interrogatively.

"Lisette of Ambray," she informed him briefly, surprised at the cultured note in his deep, slightly husky, voice. "These ladies are my sisters, Enide and Catherine." Her own voice wavered a little when she saw her fear mirrored on the faces of the other girls as they gazed up at Raverre in awe, but she forced herself to go on firmly.

"I ask your permission for us to retire to our private chamber and for me to reassure our serfs that no harm will come to them, and that they may continue to go about their business until any further order from you."

Raverre watched Lisette as she spoke, hearing the breathless catch in a voice he deemed would be low and sweet when she wasn't frightened almost out of her wits. And the fear was there in her eyes, despite the defiant tilt to her chin and the determined way she looked him in the face. He couldn't remember ever seeing eyes so deep and dark a blue, so full of violet shadows. She has known suffering, he thought, as he gazed down at a face so lovely that he found himself unable to look away.

Framed by silken masses of hair the colour of bronze, her delicate facial bones were slightly more defined than they should have been, given her youth, but neither meagre food nor strain could detract from the beauty of those dark long-lashed eyes set beneath finely arched brows, or the sweet, full-lipped mouth, closed now in a firm, determined line. He noticed the faintest hint of dimples at the corners of her mouth and wondered irresistibly what the serious little face looked like when she smiled.

Colour had suddenly come into her cheeks as he continued to stare at her, and Raverre belatedly realised she was waiting for his answer. His own wits seemed to have gone a-begging, he thought, impatient with himself for staring like any callow youth. He had seen beautiful women before, for God's sake.

Seeing his quick frown, Lisette prepared to argue. She and her sisters would not sit here to be ogled or accosted by Norman barbarians, and so she would tell him. Raverre saved her the trouble.

"You may retire for the moment, my lady. However, I want you all to sup with me here in the hall tonight."

As Lisette drew in breath to speak Raverre continued quickly, forestalling the protest he knew was about to be uttered, "It will reassure the serfs. If they see you accepting this change in your state without fuss and rebellion they will do likewise, and it will make life easier for all concerned. I have no desire to be forever disciplining unruly serfs, made so by the example set them by their late masters. Or mistresses, as the case may be."

He added briskly, "You and they need have nothing to fear from me. I have had a surfeit of fighting and am heartily tired of it, but nor will I tolerate any insurrection among my serfs or in my household. I trust you understand me?"

Lisette bristled. *His* household? *His* serfs? Did he perhaps expect a speech of welcome from her? she wondered rebelliously. He hadn't even paid her the courtesy of asking her to surrender the manor, but had calmly walked in and taken possession with typical Norman arrogance.

But, as Raverre's brows rose in challenge at her continued silence, Lisette forced herself to be calm. He might speak as though he owned the place, but the unpalatable truth was that he did, and standing here arguing the finer points of conquest and surrender would be useless.

She needed some time alone to marshal her thoughts and prepare for the more important battle. Because battle it would be if this cool, self-possessed Norman Baron thought the three of them were going to remain to watch their home taken over, and acquiesce in the disposal of their persons without so much as a by-your-leave.

Lisette looked up into Raverre's stern face and spoke with icy control. "I understand you, my lord."

She gestured to Catherine and Enide, and her sisters crossed towards the screen passage where a flight of stone stairs led to the upper gallery and the tower room. As they turned the corner a young man entering the hall quickly almost collided with them. He stood back with a startled apology, looking admiringly after them as they passed, but then recollected himself and hurried forward.

Lisette started towards the servants while Raverre was distracted by the newcomer, but she had only taken two steps before he moved in front of her and laid a restraining hand on her arm. His grip was firm, though not unduly so, and she pulled away immediately, startled by the warmth of his touch.

Raverre's mouth curled in a sardonic smile at her recoil. "I will address the serfs myself, lady; it will be better so."

He glanced at the other man, who had by this time taken in Lisette's beauty and was watching her, a deeply appreciative look on his face. Raverre grimly resolved to keep the girls from causing trouble among his men at his earliest opportunity, and his voice became curt.

"You may retire, my lady. I will send for you when we dine. And until I have seen to the placement of such men as I intend to keep here, and the despatching of the others

back to the army, you and your sisters will keep to the
manor and not wander outside.''

"I might have known you would treat us as prisoners,''
Lisette retorted in angry resentment at this abrupt order.
"I'm only surprised that we are not to be confined to the
dungeon.''

"I doubt if you have any idea of the treatment of prisoners,'' Raverre replied coldly. 'But you'll find out soon
enough if you give me any trouble. I don't issue empty
orders, girl, and this one is for your own safety, so you
would do well to obey me.''

He sensed, rather than saw, the look of surprise that
crossed the face of the young soldier next to him, and didn't
wonder at it. The girls were perfectly safe and both men
knew it, but Raverre, surprised at his sudden feeling of
distaste at the thought of Lisette being the subject of the
speculative looks and coarse jests of his men, could hardly
explain that this was the real reason for his order.

God's blood! Why was he even thinking of explaining?
He *never* explained his orders—except occasionally to his
knights. Had those shadowed eyes, now flashing daggers
of scorn, cast some spell over him?

"'Tis a shameful thing when a lady is not safe in her
own home,'' she said bitterly. "But I forget. Ambray is no
longer my home, is it, my lord? Nor will be, as long as
Normans are here.''

"You still have a home, lady. Just remember that I am
now master here, and we will deal well enough.''

A quiver of distress crossed Lisette's face for the merest
instant, but Raverre saw it. His eyes lost a little of their
hard glitter.

"Don't make this more difficult for yourself,'' he advised in a softer tone. "There's no need. When you know
me better you'll find I mean you no harm.''

"I would rather not know you at all," Lisette snapped back, angry at having betrayed herself. Turning abruptly on her heel and summoning Finn, she left the hall with what dignity she could muster, sped on her way by the entrance of several more men, who shoved each other good-naturedly through the doorway and filled the hall with their noisy laughter.

Raverre watched her thoughtfully until she was out of sight, then turned his attention to his companion.

"You may remove that grin from your face, de Rohan," were his first words, but the corners of his own mouth curled in the beginnings of an answering smile.

"Spirited little armful," remarked his friend judiciously. "And beautiful enough to make taming her an extremely pleasant occupation. I know you said you mean her no harm, but if she proves troublesome, what *do* you intend to do with the wench?"

"Marry her," said Raverre succinctly. He ignored de Rohan's dropped jaw. "So keep a civil tongue in your head when you mention her."

"Aye, sir! A civil tongue, sir!" De Rohan came smartly to attention.

"Idiot," returned Raverre, cuffing him across the back. A thick cloud of dust immediately rose about them.

"Mother of God, Gilbert, you need a bath," Raverre informed his henchman. "We both do. Let's get this place sorted out, and the men settled. Then we can turn our attention to William's little problem."

"I don't know whether I'd refer to an object needing twelve men to lift it as 'little'," argued Gilbert. "But you're right about the bath. Do you want me to speak to those goggle-eyed serfs? They're looking at you as if you might spit them on the end of your sword."

"Then the sooner they learn I won't, the better," replied

Raverre, advancing on the silent group in the corner with grim determination.

Gilbert shook his head, a rueful smile on his lips at his friend's forceful methods, then turned and started bellowing orders. In less than a minute the efficient machinery of Norman occupation was set in motion.

Raverre found the main solar to be a goodly sized room at the end of the hall. It had once been comfortably furnished, and even had a fireplace with an outlet set into the wall, which didn't smoke too much unless the wind happened to blow from the wrong direction. However, a band of marauding Norman soldiers had stripped the castle of everything they could carry away, leaving a trail of devastation and death in their wake, and the room was now bare.

As Raverre stood by the empty fireplace, watching two serfs pour hot water into a big wooden tub, he sent a brief mental thanks to William for allowing him to retrieve his personal belongings from Normandy before taking possession of his new lands.

His mother, obviously believing him to be settling in a heathen land with scant amenities and fewer luxuries, had loaded his baggage wagon with such diverse objects as a sheepskin rug, a tall iron candle spike, and an illuminated psalter. Not to mention his great-grandfather's raven sword, which really should have gone to one of his older brothers.

In vain had he told his over-zealous parent that Saxon learning and craftsmanship far outstripped anything Norman. She had brought out a wall tapestry for good measure.

Raverre had laughed at her, but hadn't had the heart to unload it all again, and now he was glad. Thanks to his mother's endeavours, the lord's solar would soon be properly furnished as it should be.

The manor itself would probably take several months to bring into order, having been without a master for two years, but on the whole, Raverre considered, his plans were moving along very nicely. He had a title, his own estate and, as soon as he could arrange it, a wife.

Raverre smiled slightly as he remembered Gilbert's description of Lisette. A spirited little armful, indeed. She obviously deeply resented his arrival and made no secret of it, despite her fear. But instead of feeling anger at the way she had spoken to him in front of the serfs, Raverre had been intrigued. In his experience, such outright honesty was rare in a woman. Most would have played the obedient martyr while wanting to stab him in the back, or cowered away, treating him to female weepings and wailings.

And she was exquisite. A man could drown in those deep iris-blue eyes. Had it been her fragile beauty which had compelled him to declare his intentions to Gilbert so quickly? Or had it been the unpleasant jolt that had gone through him at the idea of Gilbert, or anyone else, taming her proud spirit?

At that moment Raverre suddenly realised, with another more violent jolt of awareness, that he'd had no thought of taming Lisette himself. She had aroused some other, until now unknown, emotion within him. He tried to recall the strange feeling that had instinctively made him want to keep her away from his men, but was distracted as another serf entered the room, carrying straw to cushion the hard wooden pallet on the floor.

Raverre shrugged, dismissing the question from his mind. Not a man who was accustomed to pondering over-much about his own emotions, he turned his thoughts to more practical matters. One of which was making the cold, bare solar more habitable. He wondered briefly if the tower room was as cheerless, and if the ladies had retired there thinking it was safer.

Lisette had not really considered safety. Since the tower had been built its small solar had been used as a sleeping chamber by the girls, and it was to this familiar haven that she had sped after leaving the hall.

The tower was the usual example of its kind. Square and rather squat-looking, the lower level housed the guard-room and opened directly into the bailey. Then came the solar and, above that, reached by a treacherously narrow stairway in the thick castle wall, the rooftop battlements.

As Lisette had hurried along the gallery she remembered how minstrels had once played there, that fine silks had covered the walls, the sconce lights gleaming on rich gold thread. Remembered how lavish had been Alaric's hospitality whenever guests came to the castle.

Those days of extravagance were past, however, the minstrels long gone, and what few household comforts Lisette had managed to salvage from the raid now furnished the room where her sisters and their old nurse waited.

Anxious faces turned to the door as she entered, beginning to feel her trembling reaction to the encounter below. Her mind felt more confused than ever—anger, distress and fear now warring with the memory of glittering blue eyes in a handsome face, and an impression of invincible strength.

Seeing her mistress's tense, pale face, Marjory bustled forward, taking Lisette's hands and murmuring soothingly. She drew her towards the brazier in the centre of the floor, where a small fire sent a cheerful glow into the room, and hushed Catherine, who obviously had a hundred questions ready to tumble off her tongue. By contrast, Enide sat quietly on a chest by the window embrasure, her hands folded gracefully in her lap and her face as serene as a madonna's.

Only the empty look in her grey eyes as she gazed into an invisible distance betrayed the fact that her calm was not natural.

Lisette sank on to a stool by the brazier with a sigh, while Marjory fetched a comb and set about smoothing the tangles out of her hair before braiding it into two thick plaits which fell to her waist. Eventually those gentle ministrations did their work, and Lisette sat up straighter, gesturing to the others to sit also.

"We are bidden to supper this evening," she began. "And, even though I dare say the smallest morsel of food eaten at the same table as a Norman Baron will be hard to swallow, swallow it we must, along with the loss of our freedom and status."

"Are we to be slaves, then?" asked Catherine, appalled, and obviously remembering every rumour of Norman brutality that had ever been spread about.

"No, of course not," Lisette hastened to reassure her, hoping devoutly that she was right. "After all, we are daughters of Saxon nobility. Even if we don't look it," she added, glancing ruefully at their shabby homespun gowns and mantles, bare of any ornamentation.

"I intend to tell his lordship 'tis our earnest desire to enter the cloister," she went on after a moment. "I can't see why he should object. He would be rid of us, for one thing. After all, our presence will be a constant reminder to our people of one who was a fair and generous master."

"Aye," put in Marjory sceptically, who had been a shrewd witness to Raverre's long scrutiny of Lisette, "but will he wish to be rid of you, sweeting?"

She went on with the acknowledged freedom of an old servant who had nurtured her mistress from babyhood and was now her right hand in managing the household.

"He doesn't appear to be penniless, I grant you, but the

wardship of three marriageable girls is still profitable, and he would not be here accepting lands from the King if he had enough back in Normandy. As for the cloister…'' Marjory's wrinkled old face beneath her linen wimple looked rather like that of an enquiring brown wren. ''Are you so sure 'tis what you wish for? I cannot see that life for you, my dearest lady, nor for Catherine, come to that. You should both be out in the world, with husbands and children.''

Lisette jumped up violently, upsetting the stool, as her emotions broke through the restraints she had placed on herself in the hall.

''Are you suggesting we allow ourselves to be given in marriage to further the mercenary ambition of a Norman?'' she demanded angrily. ''You know that is what will happen if we stay. Is that what you wish for us? To be at the beck and call of our enemies, meekly submitting to any rough treatment they mete out to us? You saw what happened to our mother, God rest her gentle soul. Is that what we must now look towards? I will never do so, *never,* I tell you! I would rather choose the cloister!''

''You may not be given the choice, my love, and 'tis of no use to frown and toss your head at me as you did when you were a wilful child. That will not serve you now. As for enemies—well, the fighting is over. William is King, the Normans are now our masters, and surely they are not all evil. The young man below appears reasonable enough.''

''*Reasonable!*''

''Bertrand seems to think so, and I would trust his judgement against any man's. Your father did also, remember—''

She was interrupted again as mention of Alaric fired Lisette's temper afresh.

''Marjory, I cannot believe I am hearing you aright!''

she cried, amazed at this change in one whom she had considered to be an implacable enemy of the Norman invaders. "Have you forgotten so quickly? Did my mother's torment mean nothing to you? Must we submit to the same? I would rather take my chances in the forest with the wolves! At least I wouldn't be tortured before I died."

"Oh, Lisette, do not speak so, I beg of you," cried Catherine, distressed, and crossing herself hastily against her sister's words. "Perhaps it will not be so bad. Raverre might be pleased to see us gone, as you said." She stopped, not knowing what else to say to placate the older girl, and Marjory patted her hand.

"It shall be as Our Lord wills it," she said, firmly. But she cast a worried glance at Lisette, who was pacing restlessly about the room.

The strain of the past months is beginning to tell, Marjory thought. The child is as taut as a drawn bowstring, ready to snap at any moment, and not in the mood to listen to rational arguments, or to exercise her usual good sense. And what will become of us if she enrages the Baron? What do we know of him, after all?

Then Marjory remembered the fleeting expression on Raverre's face when he had first seen Lisette. Perhaps the future would not be as bleak as they all feared. This thought, however, Marjory kept to herself. She quietly crossed the room to rouse Enide from her reverie in preparation for supper.

"At least we may sleep soundly in our beds tonight," she said placidly. "We are unlikely to be raided, with soldiers running about all over the place."

This calm observation had its effect and the angry colour faded from Lisette's cheeks, although she gave a short laugh and said ironically, "A comfort, to be sure."

However, she bent to give Catherine a quick embrace.

"Fear not, little sister. I am not about to throw myself off the tower roof, or do anything without a deal of thought." She straightened, her eyes fiercely determined. "I intend to see this through to whatever end may be in store."

Catherine looked cheered, but inwardly felt extremely uncomfortable for harbouring the thought that a cloister wouldn't suit her in the least, and that marriage, even to a Norman, would be preferable. Especially if he was young and good-looking, like Raverre. Guiltily realising what Lisette would have to say to such a rebellious idea, she set about helping Marjory tidy the room while they waited for the summons to supper.

Darkness had fallen before the knock came at the door and Lisette had long since tired of being shut away, not knowing what was happening below. She desperately wanted to find out more from Bertrand, but, much as she was tempted to slip out, she was more afraid of encountering a Norman soldier in the dark gallery and being marched ignominiously back to the solar.

She tried to comfort herself with the reflection that, until she had further speech with Raverre, it was useless to speculate about his intentions. But on one point Lisette was determined: that Enide, with her fragile hold on reality, should not be married off to a man who would never understand or sympathise with the reason for her mental withdrawal from a world that had become too brutal for her to bear.

Marjory had opened the door to the young man who had accompanied Raverre. He smiled and bowed slightly.

"I wish you good even, ladies, and am come to escort you to supper. I am Gilbert de Rohan, at your service."

He looked so young, no more than a year or so older than her own sixteen years, Lisette judged. And so pleasant, his cheerful smile lighting his dark eyes and lending boyish appeal to his frank, open countenance, that she was disarmed in spite of herself. Smiling faintly in response and taking Enide's hand, she preceded him into the gallery, leaving him to offer a gallant arm to Catherine.

The gallery was now well-lit, every sconce holding rushes bound together and dipped in mutton fat. Remembering how they had been forced to grope their way along the gallery in near-darkness for the past several months, Lisette could not help but appreciate the difference. My Lord Raverre was obviously used to living with a good deal of comfort, she reflected, and, as if her thoughts had conjured him up, he appeared at the foot of the stairs, waiting to take them into supper.

From the seeming chaos of the Normans' arrival, order had been restored. The hall was bright with the light of many sconces and the fire blazed merrily. Trestles had been set up along both sides of the great room, with wooden trenchers and drinking horns upon them, and men were taking their places on the benches as the servants waited for the signal to bring in the food.

Lisette barely glanced at Raverre as she entered, but as a sudden hush fell over the room his hand closed around her own, his grip sure and strong.

Tingling warmth raced up Lisette's arm. Her fingers quivered in his. Startled by such an intense sensation, she instinctively pulled back, only to find herself unable to free her hand without a futile struggle.

She was forced to suffer his bruisingly possessive hold across a hall that suddenly appeared endless. Forced to suffer being seated next to him at the high table on its dais across the end of the room. Forced to suffer the bold scrutiny of what seemed to be innumerable eyes.

"Must you behave like a conqueror parading his captives

before his men?'' she demanded in a goaded voice, casting a resentful look up at him.

Raverre returned her look with a faintly challenging expression, his fingers tightening briefly before he released her.

"Would you rather have walked across the room alone, giving my men an opportunity to do more than just look?'' he asked mockingly, wondering with some amusement what her reaction would be if he told her that, by taking her hand, he was indicating to his men that he claimed her for his own.

Then as Lisette tossed her head and looked away, refusing to answer, he added, "Maybe some food and wine will sweeten your temper.''

"I would rather starve,'' she muttered, but he had turned to seat Enide at his other side and her remark went unheard.

Gilbert, who appeared to be Raverre's lieutenant, politely handed Catherine to her place, seating himself next to her, and looking very much amused at her flushed face and downcast eyes.

Lisette noticed that Bertrand had been placed at the high table, and he gave her a reassuring nod as she struggled to regain her composure. In reality, after that first interested silence, Raverre's men had quickly gone back to their talk, but Lisette was too embarrassed and angry to realise this, and her own face felt as fiery as Catherine's. Her hand still smarted from the compelling pressure of Raverre's fingers, and she told herself that rage had caused that powerful reaction to his touch. She felt as if she had just been branded as his property. As though I were a slave, she thought furiously.

Then, as Raverre signalled to the serfs, sudden memory distracted her. With the hall echoing to the sound of Norman voices, Lisette almost felt like a stranger in her own home, and yet in another way all seemed so normal. As if she had gone back to a time when the hall was full of people she knew, sitting down to a good meal with the promise of entertainment to come.

As bread was laid before her and the noise of conversation rose again Lisette imagined that if she turned her head there would be her father sitting in his great carved chair, jovially calling to some neighbouring Thegn, or arguing with Bertrand about where the best hunting could be had on the morrow.

She felt unaccustomed tears prick her eyelids at the recollection, and blinked them furiously away. Never would she show her enemies any sign of feminine weakness, and to divert her mind she glanced around at the assembled company.

Four or five men were seated above the salt, and these, Lisette assumed, were knights, although their dress was as plain and functional as those of their men-at-arms. Only Raverre and Gilbert wore tunics of finer wool, and even these were without braid or fur.

My father wore garments more richly ornamented and of finer quality, she thought with scornful satisfaction. These creatures dress like the barbarians they are.

There were other differences. Used to the long hair and full beards of her countrymen, Lisette found the bare faces and close-cropped heads of the Normans a strange contrast. Most of the men were dark and stocky in build, unlike the fairer, taller Saxons; although there was the occasional reddish tint in the colouring of both races.

She found herself wondering if Raverre's unusual height and almost silvery-blond hair had their origins in a Norse ancestor, and was instantly annoyed with herself for feeling curious about him. What difference did it make where his forefathers came from? The Devil himself, probably.

These profitless ruminations were interrupted as Raverre began carving meat from the chunks of venison roasted and brought to the table on spits. Spearing several slices on the point of his dagger, he piled the meat on to their shared trencher. Lisette's brows rose. Was he such a favourite of William's that he could hunt the King's deer with impunity?

Raverre saw the question on her face and said conversationally, "We hunted quite successfully on our way here, my lady, as you see. Not knowing what supplies you might have had, and with so many of us, it seemed prudent to make sure of our first meal under this roof. William has granted me free warren—leave to hunt game in the forest—so tomorrow I'll send some of my men out to replenish the stocks of meat. With winter coming on, it will be needed, and you appear to have little in the way of livestock. That, too, shall be remedied."

Lisette, still smarting from her embarrassment, decided he was being critical. "Our stocks are low because 'tis hardly safe for anyone to go out into the forest," she said hotly. "Let alone a woman with no one to defend her should she meet a party of Norman soldiers. They seem to be everywhere," she finished bitterly, looking about her.

"Times change, my lady, and men must therefore change with them if they would survive," Raverre answered lightly, taking a hearty bite of the venison with strong white teeth, and gesturing for her to do likewise.

She felt as if the food would choke her, but, despite her earlier angry remark, Lisette knew no good would come from starving herself. With a few helpful swallows of wine she managed to eat a little of the roasted meat. Catherine seemed to be having no trouble, she thought forlornly, and was even beginning to shyly respond to Gilbert's gentle efforts to encourage her to talk to him. On Raverre's other side Bertrand was coaxing Enide to eat also, but, though her sister complied, it was as if she were a puppet, and he pulling her strings.

After watching them for a moment Raverre turned back to Lisette.

"Indulge my curiosity, madam. Your sister Enide, I am informed, is the eldest of you all; indeed she must be at least twenty years, by my reckoning. You are very much younger but are clearly in command here. In fact I could not imagine the Lady Enide in charge of such a household. How is this?"

Gladly seizing an opportunity to put him in his place, Lisette turned flashing dark eyes on him. "My sister once was as capable as any one of us until you Normans came ravaging and killing through this part of the country," she said fiercely. "She saw our home invaded and stripped of anything they deemed of value, but even that was not enough for them. They sacked the village, killing our bailiff, though he was an old man who was no threat to them, and attacking my mother and the priest when they tried to defend him!

"My mother was beaten and used like some common street harlot! By more than one of the vile brutes. She died from her injuries when they were through with her, and my sister witnessed it all. Enide was fortunate that in the end she had swooned away, and they thought her dead. They had no respect for the fact that we were women and defenceless."

Lisette's voice shook with the memory of that terrible day, and despite herself her lovely eyes filled with tears again. She no longer cared; let him see them and know what his countrymen had done.

Raverre watched her expressive little face closely, but

whatever pity or shame she had hoped to arouse did not show on his own.

"You speak as if you were not here when this befell."

"No. Catherine and I had been driving the swine out of the forest. When we came back—" She shuddered, unable to continue.

"*You* were herding swine?" His eyes narrowed intently. "In other words, there were no men here to do such work. What was your father about, to leave his family so unprotected?"

"King Harold needed all our warriors to stand against your Duke," she replied shortly, stubbornly refusing to give William the title of King.

Raverre looked rather sceptical at this explanation, but merely asked, "Did anyone hear a name spoken that could identify the attackers?"

Lisette was surprised into looking up at him. "What difference does a name make? They were Norman wolves. Savages! What else is there to know?"

"William is not in the habit of making war on defenceless women," he answered curtly. "I do not speak of the casualties that must occur in the taking of a town or castle when the occupants will not surrender without a fight, but from what you say this was not an attack sanctioned by the King. You must know he has spared every town which has opened its gates and acknowledged him Sovereign. When, pray, did this raid occur?"

"Last winter," she admitted reluctantly, knowing full well William had been back in Normandy at the time, leaving England to the joint stewardship of his half-brother, Odo, and William fitzOsbern, Earl of Hereford.

But, rallying quickly before he could pounce on this, she added sternly, "We are not the only family to be so bereaved. There are many such. As to towns spared, what of

the villages burned to the ground, the people driven from
their homes or killed? And you speak lightly about innocent
lives taken in battle. Soldiers at least have chosen their
manner of death. Do we women have such a choice?''

Deep down Lisette knew this was unreasonable. She herself would have been willing to fight to the death in defence
of her home and people, and Raverre knew it. He smiled
suddenly in genuine amusement, an unexpectedly boyish
grin which completely banished the stern expression his
face usually wore in repose.

''Lady, I think you would be a fierce opponent indeed,
whether you were given the choice or not,'' he told her, a
hint of laughter in his voice.

Lisette blinked up at him. Her comfortable conviction
that anger had caused her acute awareness of Raverre was
shattered. His smile was devastating.

His strong features could never look soft; though handsome, he also looked tough and rather dangerous, but the
smile made him appear younger and more approachable.
Lisette found herself so fascinated with the question of how
eyes which had seemed forbiddingly cold could now hold
so much warmth that she completely forgot to be incensed
by his teasing comment.

Then a burst of laughter from a nearby group of soldiers
broke the spell. Lisette flushed, glaring down at her unfinished meat, which had rapidly gone cold. Say something,
she told herself. Don't let that Norman predator make such
a fool of you with just one smile. But, before she could
think of a reply which might convince Raverre that he
hadn't managed to addle her wits, Gilbert decided to enter
the lists.

''Why, my lady, Raverre speaks truly. You Saxon
women are no mean fighters when pushed to it. Don't you
know 'twas none other than a woman who stirred up the

good townsfolk of Exeter to defiance of the King earlier this year? Earl Harold's mother, no less. And, though the nobles came out to surrender to William, she rallied the common folk and held out a further eighteen days.''

"Aye, I do know," Lisette retorted, venting her frustrated anger on de Rohan's unsuspecting head. "I also know that your so honourable King ordered a man's eyes put out before the town gates in an attempt to break their spirit!''

Gilbert retired, discomfited, with a rueful look at Raverre.

"Never argue with a woman unless you have all the answers," recommended his lord, and turned back to Lisette, who was seething again at this deliberately provocative remark.

"William regretted that action, you know," he told her quietly while she was still speechless. "When the town finally surrendered he not only spared the rest, but also refused to collect the tribute owing to him."

Lisette digested this statement. She wasn't sure of her reasons, but she didn't think Raverre was lying.

"And the Lady Gytha?" she asked after a moment, her interest in the fate of Harold's mother overcoming her wrath.

Raverre shrugged. "She managed to escape to Ireland with Harold's sons by his mistress, Edith of the Swan-neck. But she need not have fled. William would have treated her with courtesy."

"Perhaps she was thinking rather of what he might do to his rival's sons," remarked Lisette shrewdly. "They are her grandchildren, after all."

"Grandchildren or not, Gytha knew the risks she was taking, and still decided to make a stand against William, though there was little chance of success. She was willing to face death if necessary. And you, my lady, though you look like a fragile little rose, would have done the same. Even today, had you the manpower to back you.''

Lisette was reduced to fuming silence again. Fragile little rose, indeed! How dared he sound so patronising? Fortunately she was spared the effort of having to think of a scathing reply to this broadside by Gilbert, who, directing a question to Raverre across her as to the activities for the following day, unwittingly gave her the chance to catch her breath and calm down. Letting this enormous oaf of a Norman goad her into arguing with him would not help her cause in the least, she reminded herself sternly.

Catherine caught her sister's eye and gave a faintly guilty smile. Lisette smiled reassuringly back. It was no use chiding Catherine just for allowing Gilbert to coax her into talking to him. At thirteen, she was still young enough to make the best of the situation now that her immediate fears for their safety had been allayed.

Maybe life would be easier for me if I could do that also, thought Lisette, but I am not made like that. I have not chosen that my home be taken away from my family, and I and my sisters perhaps married off to men of whom we know nothing, except that they are our conquerors. This thought reminded her of her resolve to speak with Raverre about sending them off to a convent, but, looking at his preoccupied expression, she decided now was not the time.

Coward, she scolded herself. But, on the other hand, there was no need to antagonise him and spoil her plans. So, fragile or not, he thought her a worthy opponent, did he? Well, she might not be capable of bearing arms, but how many times had she heard Marjory say that a woman had more powerful weapons that could be used?

The only difficulty was, Lisette felt very conscious of her inexperience in the subtle mysteries between men and women, and she had an uneasy suspicion that using such weapons against Raverre would be rather like playing with fire. Just because he hadn't had them all killed, it didn't make him any less a barbarian in other ways.

Taking another sip of wine from the plain wooden beaker reminded her of the finely crafted glass goblets her mother had prized so highly, and which had been found needlessly smashed after the raid she had spoken of. The delicate brows met in another frown as Lisette cast a glaring look at Raverre from under her lashes.

She found that he had now abandoned Gilbert, and was watching her with a light in his blue eyes which instinctively put her on guard.

"Am I wrong?" he asked, returning to their sparring and wondering if she would deny his charge. "Although the battle is over and the English crown on William's head these past two years come Christmas Day, you would still fight if you could. Tell me why."

But, instead of the feminine prevarication he had half expected, Lisette leaned forward, gripping her hands together and looking him straight in the eyes. Her voice was low, trembling with the intensity of her emotions.

"Aye, the battles are over. You have conquered our land and taken our homes. You can even make us bow our heads to Norman rule. But know this! You will *never* conquer our hearts, our minds or our souls!"

The strange light in his eyes seemed to blaze with sudden fierceness. "Lady," he instantly replied, his voice soft so that only she could hear, "your soul belongs to God, and your mind is your own. But your heart—" his voice deepened to a note that made Lisette think of darkest night "—that indeed would be a prize worth winning."

Raverre held her gaze for a deliberate minute, before Lisette managed to wrench her eyes from his, breathless and shaken. What had he meant by such an answer? Win her heart? He could never do so.

"Never," she whispered, as if trying to convince herself, unaware that she had spoken aloud.

"Never is a dangerous word," Raverre murmured, still watching her closely, "when it becomes a challenge."

Ignoring the pounding of the heart in question, Lisette steeled herself to meet his eyes again. If Raverre meant to mock or torment her she would not give him the satisfaction of seeing how easily he had reduced her defiance to trembling confusion.

"I meant no challenge, sir," she said with spirit. "But you may amuse yourself by thinking so if you wish. There is no other entertainment to be had at present."

He smiled faintly, but surprised her by saying, "Then perhaps, if you have finished your supper, you and your sisters should retire again. My men have sat down to their first civilised meal for some time and I dare say some will drink far more than is good for them. You will be more comfortable elsewhere. We shall have plenty of time to speak further tomorrow."

Lisette rose at once, glad of the respite until morning, but her docility fled when Raverre also stood. She was tremblingly aware of him, tall and powerful by her side.

"Bertrand can escort us to our chamber," she said hurriedly. "I wish to speak with him before I retire."

"Tomorrow," Raverre answered with dictatorial brevity. And, giving Lisette no time to argue, he propelled her across the hall by the simple expedient of an unbreakable grip on her arm. They were followed meekly by Enide and Catherine.

"And to think I was beginning to wonder if you might not be such a tyrant after all," she muttered furiously as soon as they were out of sight and hearing of his men.

"Oh, did you not wish to leave?" he asked, mockery in the look he slanted down at her. "I thought you seemed somewhat eager to quit the hall."

"I was *not* running away!" she enunciated through gritted teeth, trying to free herself. Raverre didn't even appear to notice her struggles.

"No." The mocking gleam disappeared. "I think there would be little you would run from, my lady," he said thoughtfully, almost to himself.

Lisette stopped fighting him. It was useless, and she was only hurting herself anyway. The man was infuriating. Arrogant, domineering, mocking. And then, when she least expected it, disturbingly perceptive.

She was glad when he said nothing further, seeming to be deep in thought, but the silence only served to make her senses more acute. Why had she never before noticed the strangely fantastic patterns in the flickering shadows of the vaulted roof above her? Or the way the voices below seemed to echo off the walls in hollow cadences?

And why did her arm tingle from shoulder to wrist? A tingle that wasn't caused by pain, for Raverre was not hurting her, but by a rapidly uncoiling heat.

Lisette was relieved when they reached the doorway to the tower room. Now he would release her. But, as her sisters entered, Raverre held Lisette back a moment, casting that quick all-seeing glance around the room as he did so.

Like those of the hall and solar, the walls were bare stone, the floor wood, the single window narrow and unglazed. But the contrast between the empty chamber where he was housed and the small comforts of table, chests and bearskin-covered bed in this room was immediately apparent. Raverre made no comment, however, merely lifting an expressive eyebrow before returning his gaze to Lisette.

She looked small and defenceless, framed in the doorway. Her eyes were cast down, watching his fingers curled around her arm. Against her slenderness Raverre thought his hand seemed large, threatening. His hold slackened as a long-forgotten instinct, buried by years of fighting, stirred within him.

"Did I hurt you?" he asked softly.

"I probably don't have a drop of blood left in that arm," Lisette complained crossly, then looked up in startled indignation when he laughed. "You think that amusing?"

Raverre smiled. "One day I'll share the jest with you," he said, the warmth in his eyes seeming to reach out and enfold her.

Lisette had a sudden vision of herself out in the freezing winter snows with Raverre, and still feeling warm. She must be afflicted by moon madness. A sane woman did not have such thoughts about her enemy.

Then, as she stepped back, his expression changed. Became serious.

"You are safely guarded now, my lady," he said very low. "Sleep well." And, sliding his hand down to her own, he raised it to his lips, with a caress so brief that afterwards Lisette wondered if she had imagined it in her flustered state.

Then Raverre was gone, gently shutting the door behind him before she had a chance to answer, even had she known what to say.

Chapter Two

The morning dawned, with the promise of bright autumn sunshine and a good day for the hunt. Lisette rose early after a night spent in puzzling about Raverre's behaviour towards her.

His arrogant possession of her home notwithstanding, she had to admit they had been treated with more consideration than she'd expected from a Norman Baron. He had even permitted Bertrand to ride ahead yesterday to warn them of his arrival, when he could just as easily have taken the manor by sheer force of arms alone, precipitating the sort of panic that could quickly lead to disaster.

And there had been his unexpected gallantry when he had left her last night. Remembering the beautifully shaped, long-fingered hand wrapped about her arm, and the unexpectedly gentle note in his deep voice, Lisette had spent hours alternately hoping that Raverre was not the barbarian she had been convinced he would be, and worrying about his plans for herself and her sisters.

Feeling the need for some fresh air after such a restless night, she dressed in her worn homespun gown, and braided her hair. Then, quietly leaving the solar, she climbed the stairs at the end of the gallery, and opened the wooden trapdoor which led to the roof of the tower.

Lisette had often sought this retreat to be alone, and to look with pride over the green fields of her father's manors, although in recent months she had usually spent the time gazing anxiously along the empty road to the east for any signs of Norman activity. There was bustle aplenty now, however, as she watched the hunting party set out, with young de Rohan in the lead.

Full of early-morning high spirits, the horses paced through the gates, heads tossing, tails pluming; made even more skittish by the gambolling of several deer-hounds between their hoofs. They were making for the woods, west of the manor, but before the riders were out of sight among the trees Lisette saw them branch off on to the path she knew would lead them around the perimeter of the manor wood to the river and greater forest beyond.

Bertrand has given them directions, she thought, and was comforted to know that he was still within the castle.

Leaning over the battlements, Lisette could see one of the kitchen girls throwing grain to the hens as they clucked and pecked busily about her feet, while across the stream outside the stone wall of the bailey the smoky haze rising in the still air from the cluster of cottages indicated that the villagers were stirring, and would soon be about their daily business.

Despite the disagreeable sight of sunlight flashing on the mailcoats of the Norman soldiers moving about the bailey, the peaceful scene tempted Lisette to linger and enjoy the rare moment of quiet solitude. Then a movement from the kitchen shed caught her eye, and, seeing two maidservants emerge bearing a covered tray, she hurriedly returned to the solar, determined to learn as much as possible before she had to face Raverre again.

She found the wooden shutters flung open to let in the light, her sisters dressed, and Marjory directing the servants to lay flat wheaten loaves and ale on the table so they could break their fast. Lisette immediately pounced on the elder of the girls for news.

''Edgith! Tell me what is happening below? You have not been ill-treated, I hope?''

''Oh, no, mistress. Those of us in the kitchen have been left to our work. But there are soldiers everywhere, so Wat refused to send me alone with your bread and ale. And as we crossed the bailey I heard the Baron send more men into the village. I think Bertrand may have been with them, but I can't be sure. We didn't want to stay longer to watch in case they noticed us.''

The girl looked worried, as though she had done wrong, and Lisette hastened to reassure her.

''No, of course you must not linger outside while so many soldiers are about. My Lord Raverre has said that no one will be harmed, but we can never be sure. I warrant you, he would soon change his orders if we put up even the slightest resistance.'' She frowned. ''And we have not. So why would he send soldiers into the village?''

''If Bertrand is with them,'' soothed Marjory, ''you need not worry, my love.''

''How can I not?'' Lisette began to pace, agitatedly waving away the morning ale Catherine was offering her. Her voice rose. ''I have been given no chance to speak to the village folk, and you know Siward's temper. What if there is some misunderstanding and the soldiers use force? Oh, why did I not send Bertrand with a message last night? I should have insisted.''

She started impulsively for the door, but Marjory, seeing her intention, grasped her mistress's arm, holding her back.

''And where, pray, do you think you are going, child?

Not to the village, if that is in your mind. You will sit down and break your fast like a sensible girl, and wait for Bertrand. What? Would you go rushing out heedlessly, only to be stopped at the gate, and that none too gently if my lord is not by. 'Tis why he asked you to keep to the manor, after all.''

''It sounded more like an order to me, and I will not be treated as a prisoner in my own home!'' retorted Lisette stormily, shaking Marjory off.

She was interrupted by a knock on the door and they all froze.

''Bertrand!'' uttered Lisette, recovering first and darting forward.

She flung wide the door. ''Thank the Saints—you've—''

The words were choked off as her heart leapt into her throat. Raverre stood before her, filling the doorway.

His brows lifted quizzically at her greeting, but when Lisette said nothing further he strode past her into the room, the impact of his size immediately causing much the same effect on its occupants as a predatory fox in the dovecote. Enide paled and retreated to the window. Catherine and Marjory both dropped rather nervous curtsies. While the two maids, seeing him at close quarters for the first time, gaped up at him in mesmerised dread.

Acutely conscious of the unmade bed, and the various articles of intimate female apparel scattered about the room, Lisette turned in time to see open amusement on Raverre's face—due as much to the fact that he was conscious of looking singularly out of place in such an atmosphere of flustered femininity as to the paralysing effect his entrance had caused—and felt temper promptly replace her nervousness.

Kicking a flimsy shift out of sight under the bed, she

demanded, "Why have you sent soldiers into the village? Surely force is unnecessary when there is no resistance?"

Raverre's brows rose again at her belligerent tone. "'Tis not a matter that needs concern you, my lady," he dismissed curtly. Deliberately ignoring her outraged gasp, he turned to address Marjory with courteous deference.

"Mistress Marjory, please don't disturb yourself," he began, with a smile Lisette angrily considered was calculated to disarm the most ferocious guardian of innocent maidens. "I am merely come to ask your lady if she will accompany me while I acquaint myself with the manor. She will come to no harm, I assure you, and—" determined to try forbearance, he turned the smile on Lisette "—I believe she is the best person to advise me on what is needed to see the household through the winter."

Lisette could think of quite a number of people who had tried charm on Marjory when they wanted something—to their subsequent discomfort. Raverre was obviously not one of them. In stunned disbelief she watched as Marjory not only dropped another curtsy, but also smiled back as she assured Raverre that she trusted him to care for her lady's safety, and that she and Lisette would be only too glad to have the fast-dwindling stores replenished.

Lisette glared at her. So the man had charm. Hadn't she felt it herself last night when he had smiled at her for the first time, practically making her forget her own name? Oh, she had no doubt at all that he had melted many a female heart, but did Marjory have to be quite so—?

"Well, my lady?"

Lisette shifted the glare to Raverre. He knew he had managed to disarm Marjory, she realised as she saw the devilish gleam he directed at her. Well, she was not about to fall a victim to his smile a second time.

"*I* am not so easily distracted, my lord," she told him

scornfully, watching a lowering frown replace the gleam with immense satisfaction.

She added emphatically, "They are my people. I have a right to know. What have they done to be guarded and constrained? They will not resist you." A bitter sound of resignation escaped her. "We have learned that lesson well, I assure you."

Raverre felt his hold on his patience slip. Lisette might have admitted defeat last night, he thought with some exasperation, but she was still far from showing him the meek, unquestioning obedience that he would have expected from any other unprotected girl in her position.

He had been hoping that this morning she might begin to see him in a different light. Since he was more annoyed that Lisette apparently hadn't changed her opinion of him than by her determination to know what was going on, his answer came out more harshly than he intended.

"Very well, my lady. I have sent Bertrand with a message to the villages, to summon all the men of the estate here today to swear fealty to me as their overlord. The soldiers are there to make sure some do not think it worth their while to disobey."

No one replied to this concise statement for a moment. Indeed, Raverre's action was only to be expected, but Lisette's temper was not placated in the least by his high-handed methods. Were all her villeins and cottars to be herded to the manor like so much cattle?

"You certainly don't waste any time," she accused.

"To what purpose, madam?" Raverre frowned down at her. To hell with patience, he thought as he caught the full force of the hostile expression in Lisette's eyes. How could he be expected to cause her as little distress as possible, when she was looking at him as if he'd crawled out from under a maggoty log?

"And I want you and your sisters to attend me in the hall this afternoon also," he ordered brusquely, adding the final goad to her temper.

They had both forgotten the others in the room.

"Why? Do we have to swear allegiance to you also, my lord?" Lisette challenged. "You'll have to imprison and torture me first, and I still would not do so!"

"That could no doubt be arranged," he countered immediately, "but it won't be necessary. You hold no land or wealth under my protection."

This brutal reminder that Raverre now held the land, and that she was totally dependent upon him, struck Lisette like a bolt from a crossbow. Every muscle in her body clenched against the pain.

"Then you had best have your soldiers accompany you about the manor this morning," she lashed back blindly. "They will be more protection for you against your unwilling slaves than a woman!"

The moment the words were out Lisette regretted them. She did not need to see Catherine's look of shocked dismay at this blatant insult to bring her back to an awareness of her surroundings. Or to know that she might have jeopardised their chances of leaving for the safety of Romsey Abbey.

And, by the expression on Raverre's face, it was useless to hope that he had not understood her. He strode forward, his eyes threatening. Grasping Lisette's wrist without another word, he yanked her out of the room with breathtaking speed, slamming the door shut behind them.

"How dare you?" Lisette fumed, refusing to give in to the quick fear churning inside her at the thought of the punishment he might inflict.

Struggling to free herself from a hold that felt like an iron shackle, she demanded, "Loose me at once! I am not some slave girl whom you can handle in any way you choose! Let me go, or—''

She found herself pushed hard against the stone wall of the gallery and released, but before she could escape Raverre placed his hands on the wall on either side of her, bending until he could look her in the face. Lisette scowled furiously back at him, unconsciously rubbing her wrist, where his fingers had gripped her.

''Be still and listen to me!'' he snapped, now as angry as she. ''I had no intention, this morning, of doing more than coming to a better understanding between us, but make another remark like that and I'll take my whip to you first to teach you some manners.''

''A Norman, teach a Saxon manners?'' she scorned recklessly. ''Impossible!''

''Try me,'' he said with dangerous quiet. The eyes boring into hers were like chips of ice.

Lisette was silenced.

Raverre watched defiance and doubt chase each other across her face, before adding in a forceful voice, ''It will be to your advantage also if we are not continually at loggerheads.''

For a moment longer they glared at each other. Then, just as Lisette was sure she was about to swoon through lack of air, Raverre straightened abruptly. With a surprisingly jerky movement he turned away to gaze down into the hall.

Lisette released her pent-up breath in a soundless gasp of relief. But it had not been Raverre's threat to beat her that had caused the constriction in her chest, or her pulse to flutter so wildly.

She had been completely dazed by the unexpected tremors Raverre's nearness had caused her to feel, hardly able to listen to what he had said for the sudden thundering of her heart in her ears. He had been so close that Lisette could see that his thick lashes were a darker gold than his hair, and how his eyes had deepened to slate with anger, before lightening again to their usual vivid blue as he controlled the emotion.

Like his men, he was clean-shaven, and her eyes had wandered in helpless fascination from the strong line of his jaw to the beautifully drawn mouth, saved from unrelenting toughness by the slightly fuller lower lip. Lisette had felt her own lips, only inches from his, part slightly as a wild unbidden urge to know the touch of his firm mouth on hers had swept over her, shocking her into mindless immobility that held her against the wall until Raverre was several paces away.

What was the matter with her? She was behaving like a witless fool. A *wanton* fool, she corrected herself savagely. How could she have wanted a Norman to kiss her? Lisette trembled. Did he know? Had he seen? How could she ever face his scorn? she thought despairingly, not daring to raise her eyes.

Her turmoil was unnecessary. Totally preoccupied with his own reaction to Lisette, Raverre had no idea of the emotions seething in his companion's breast. For in those few brief moments when they had been standing so close, glaring aggressively at each other, he had known with a sudden gut-wrenching flash of insight that this girl, this member of an alien and only recently conquered race, had to belong to him, was the other half of himself. As necessary to him as the very air he breathed.

Oh, yes, he had been aroused enough by her beauty and pride to decide coolly that she was the one he would marry. And he had admired her courage in defying him, despite the threat of punishment. But these feelings were wholly overshadowed, eclipsed, by the blinding knowledge that now he would kill for her. Give his own life for her. Even, should her rash hostility put her in any danger from William, defy his King and liege lord for her.

There was no gain in questioning why he should feel this way or how it had occurred so quickly. Used to sizing up the unexpected, Raverre recognised what had happened and as swiftly accepted it. But straight on the heels of this acknowledgement came the realisation that Lisette's own feelings were another matter entirely.

As he turned around at the precise moment that Lisette looked up at him, their eyes met and held. Raverre could see that she was still angry, but behind the anger in her wide gaze there was a startled new awareness of him as a man. It was enough for now. First, she had to learn to trust him.

Raverre held out his hand.

"Come, my lady. Let us cry a truce. You may not want me here, but surely your people's welfare comes first? I am told your store-rooms are almost empty, and I have the means to remedy that—with your help."

Whether knowingly or not, he had made the one appeal that would reach her. Lisette could not bring herself to apologise for implying that Raverre had wanted her to accompany him for his own safety. However, drawing on every ounce of dignity she possessed, she allowed her hand to lie in his for a brief moment.

"Then I will accompany you, my lord." Profoundly thankful that he seemed not to have noticed anything amiss in her demeanour, she gestured towards the stairway. "The store-room lies beneath the hall."

Raverre stood back, allowing Lisette to precede him down to the screen passage and the outer stairs. He had to resist the temptation to take her hand again as she swept past him. The large open area in front of the hall seemed at first sight to be full of men and equipment, but this soon resolved itself into piles of weaponry, and other trappings of war, being sorted and stored under the keen supervision of a weather-beaten sergeant-at-arms who had made short entries on a piece of parchment. Lisette heard his murmured voice as she passed.

"Heavy crossbow with one hundred bolts, eight ordinary crossbows with five hundred bolts, forty lances…"

The list seemed endless.

Sternly repressing the thought of the use to which the weapons had been put, Lisette refrained from comment, and produced the key to the store-room from the girdle about her slim waist. Pushing the big wooden door wide to let in as much light as possible, she entered the cool, dim interior of the room and stood back to let Raverre pass her.

The store-room was huge. Ambray Castle having been built for defence, the hall and solar were situated on the upper floor, reached by the narrow outer stairway. The more vulnerable area at ground level was used for storing goods needed by the estate and its dependants and stretched the whole length of the building. A wooden platform, half-way up one end wall, held the table and chair at which the manor steward did his tallying and issuing of supplies. Its dusty emptiness bore grim witness to the absence of both steward and stores.

Raverre wandered around in silence for a few minutes, lifting a barrel lid here and there, and looking into the recesses formed by the buttresses of the thick stone walls, while Lisette stood waiting. Then, as she made no move to follow him, he looked back questioningly.

"I already know of what we stand in need," she explained. She hesitated, but then decided to elaborate, hoping that cool civility would prove safer than other more heated emotions.

"We are not usually so ill-provisioned. Our land is fertile
and well-farmed, but last season's crops barely survived
destruction by your army, and the winter which followed
was the hardest for many years. Then there were the home-
less, and the hungry. I couldn't turn them away and so…"

Lisette looked about the echoing space and made a resigned encompassing gesture that went to his heart.

"Were there many strangers passing through?"

"Not many." She wondered if the question was quite as
offhand as it seemed.

"No bands of men, returning to their homes perhaps?"
Raverre persisted.

Lisette shook her head. "The nearer towns are north of
here. South there is only the forest for mile upon mile, and
few manors. Those who came were mostly women and
children, or old folk seeking shelter for a night on their
way to find kin in the villages that were not burned. And
we had to feed them." She sounded slightly defensive.

"As I would," he assured softly, coming back to lean
against a large barrel near her. He lifted the lid of another
smaller keg and peered into it, drawing back immediately
as the pungent smell of sheep fat and wood ash assailed
his nostrils.

"What the hell—?"

A mischievous dimple appeared and was ruthlessly banished.

"'Tis soap," Lisette informed him in her briskest housewifely manner. "But don't worry, we scent it with herbs
before we use it."

Raverre gave her a look from under his brows and replaced the lid of the keg firmly. "I'll make sure herbs are
on your list," he remarked wryly, hoping to draw the fugitive smile from her, but Lisette considered his remark
quite seriously.

"There's no need, I grow them in the garden here. Well," she amended, "most of what we use. But we'll need pepper, cloves, ginger, cinnamon, almonds." She ticked them off on her fingers, warming to the task. "And then candles; I should think three pounds each of large and small—"

"Stop! No more!" he begged laughingly, holding up an imploring hand. "You may order anything you please, but no more lists."

He thought he saw an answering flash of laughter in her eyes before she quickly moved out of the light, turning her head away to indicate the small block of salt in a dark corner.

"The salterer usually calls before now, so we may cure meat for the winter when the pigs are slaughtered, but he may not come this year, if the roads are not safe."

"I think he will. Now that William is back in England, travel is becoming safer, even for a wealthy man, let alone a humble salterer. And, speaking of William…" Raverre looked at Lisette gravely. "I want to know the true reason why this place was left so undefended that fitzOsbern's men could overrun it without hindrance, causing the destruction they did. If it happened last year, as you say, your men weren't still fighting for Godwinson."

This unexpected change from light-hearted banter to serious questioning threw Lisette mentally off balance.

"I…I don't know what you mean," she stammered, desperately searching for an answer that would satisfy him.

"This isn't the usual little wooden hall," he insisted, rapping his knuckles against the stone wall for emphasis. "You could have held off a raid easily, and renegade bands of mercenaries are not equipped for a long siege. What happened?"

Lisette looked down at the floor for inspiration. Finding none, she stayed silent.

"Your mother had allowed the men to leave to help in some uprising or another, hadn't she?" Raverre prompted gently.

That brought her head up again. "If you know that much, you know that I won't tell you where or who with," she replied shortly, confirming his suspicions. "Do you think I would betray my people? Besides, 'tis finished. They were beaten yet again. Isn't that enough for you?"

"Not quite," he answered coolly. At her dismayed look, he continued, "I don't intend to punish your churls for rebellions a year old, but after today you and they had better understand that, no matter what is going on elsewhere in the country, this is where they stay unless I order otherwise."

"*Is* there something going on elsewhere?"

"Don't sound so eager," Raverre commented sardonically. "I'm not about to be displaced. I merely referred to riotings of the kind that crazy forester stirred up last year. Edric the Wild, they called him, or some such heroic name."

A betraying flush crept up Lisette's face before she could look away again.

"So!" he exclaimed. "That's where they were. Miles away to the north. Do you realise your mother signed her own death warrant by her actions, and put you all in danger? Now you have no guard and barely enough men to work the fields."

At the thought of what might have happened to the delicate girl before him at the hands of some of the commanders with whom he was only too well acquainted, Raverre's voice became harsh. "My God! Anyone could have ridden in here and killed the lot of you before you'd had time to realise you were under attack!''

"Oh, do forgive us for wishing to be rid of a plundering army of butchers and murderers,'' Lisette retorted sarcastically, her eyes flashing at his criticism. "I suppose we should have permitted them to do as they pleased without raising a hand in our own defence. 'Tis not enough for the Duke of Normandy to kill or dispossess most of the Saxon nobles, wiping out an ancient and honourable race. Now he must destroy the lesser folk as well!''

"Don't judge the *King* by his brother or his friend,'' Raverre advised, emphasising William's proper title. "He has not returned to England only to quell rebellions, but to repair some of the damage done by Odo and fitzOsbern. 'Tis why he is quick to pardon. He is no tyrant, nor does he allow his men to loot and kill needlessly as they did.''

"Bishop Odo of Bayeux was still considered suitable to be left in charge,'' Lisette argued, unconvinced by this speech. "He is supposed to be a man of the Church, and yet I have heard that he leads his men into battle himself, and—''

The rest of her sentence was abruptly drowned out by sounds of violent altercation coming from the bailey. Raverre swung round immediately, but Lisette, recognising a familiar voice through the din, darted past him.

"Oh, dear God, no,'' she uttered, halting in the doorway at the scene before her.

In the gateway three of Raverre's soldiers were engaged in a fierce struggle to subdue the Saxon on that ground beneath them. Curses and the sound of blows rent the air as one of the soldiers was sent sprawling by a well-placed kick, and the victim leapt to his feet, his muscular arms brushing the other two off like bothersome flies. They circled warily around him, waiting for an opening, egged on by their fellows, who had gathered to watch the fight.

In silent contrast, several Saxons watched uneasily from the kitchen, casting angry glares at the Normans but too afraid to venture nearer.

"Siward, no!" Lisette cried out as she saw the young blacksmith advance towards the nearer of the Normans. She started forward, but Raverre's arm shot out and circled her waist, pulling her back against him.

She briefly felt the hard strength of his body against her side before he released her, ordering, "Get back inside," as he strode forward.

Ignoring this terse command, Lisette followed.

Siward had turned at the sound of her voice, and, ignoring the Normans at his back, stood proudly defiant, waiting for the order that would send him to his death. He expected no less.

Raverre didn't even glance at him.

"What in God's name happened here, Arnulf?" he demanded, addressing the sergeant Lisette had noticed earlier. At the note of impatience in his voice, the Norman contingent of spectators began to sidle unobtrusively back to their duties.

"I don't rightly know, sir," admitted Arnulf uncomfortably. "This young fellow came through the gates and the next thing I knew, Will there was lying in the dust and a fight had broken out."

Raverre shifted his cold gaze to the soldier who had felt the toe of Siward's boot.

"The smith started it, my lord," Will accused sullenly. "He came in and asked to see the Lady Lisette, and, when I told her she was engaged with you, he went for me." He sent a furious glance in Siward's direction. "Saxon scum!"

"That's enough!"

Raverre looked at Siward, who remained silent, not bothering to hide the contempt in his eyes.

"Oh, Siward, if you have any defence you must speak," cried Lisette, wondering at the blacksmith's silence. Siward usually had plenty to say for himself.

Raverre turned, frowning even more ominously.

"I told you—"

"Let her be, Norman," rasped Siward. As Raverre swung back to him, eyes narrowing, he added quickly, "I have only obeyed my lord, and now his daughter, but I will speak if I may talk to you alone." His eyes shifted briefly to Lisette and back to Raverre's face, which was suddenly intent.

"Your loyalty does you credit, even if your methods are somewhat foolhardy," Raverre remarked evenly. "But if you have anything to say I will hear it now. And so will the lady." His face was coldly implacable.

Lisette glanced from one man to the other as they eyed each other measuringly. One fair, possessing the natural arrogance of his class and the assurance of years of command; the other darker, pride blazing from clear grey eyes. Both big men. Equal in size, if not in status. And if Siward felt any awareness of their difference in station during the silent battle of wills he did not betray it, although a flicker of respect showed in his face for a moment.

"I came to see my lady," he finally answered. "To know she was safe. That dolt at the gate said you were amusing yourself with her, and asked if I wanted to wager how long I'd have to wait until you'd taken your pleasure. I hit him to shut his foul mouth."

Something dangerous blazed in Raverre's eyes for the merest instant, but it was enough to make Siward begin to look wary.

"'Tis the truth," he said.

"Holy Saints, Siward!" exclaimed Lisette, borrowing one of her father's favourite expressions. "What were you thinking of, to risk your life for such a trifle?"

Both men looked at her in surprise. She flared back at them, annoyed at their apparent lack of comprehension.

"Well? Do you expect me to fall into a swoon because of the boorish comments of an uncivilised Norman?" she demanded impatiently, momentarily forgetting that Raverre was one of them.

"No doubt you consider we're not worth the trouble," he snapped with heavy sarcasm.

Lisette felt a sickening chill. She must not anger Raverre now, when Siward was in danger. When that danger was acute. Though Lisette might consider Siward a freeman, to the Normans he was a serf who had struck a superior, and such a crime exacted severe penalties.

Raverre gestured to Arnulf, hovering near by. "Bind this man and put him in the guard-room. Use chains if he gives you any trouble. I'll speak to him later."

Siward's hands clenched into fists at this order, but something in Raverre's expression—a flash of acknowledgement perhaps, one male to another, of his defence of a lady's honour—gave him pause. He allowed himself to be led off, ignoring his recent adversary's triumphant smile.

Raverre turned as though to speak to Lisette, then, in a lightning-swift reversal of movement, whirled and swung his arm around, backhanding Will across the mouth with a blow that nearly broke the man's jaw.

Will crumpled to the ground, dazed, but still sensible enough to obey instantly when Raverre grated, "Get back to your post until I'm ready to deal with you."

He's a barbarian, after all, Lisette thought, dismayed to find how upset she felt. A fine tremor vibrated through her limbs as Raverre turned to look down at her. If he struck his own man, what would be Siward's fate? Or hers? She stepped back a pace, eyeing him warily.

His expression gentled instantly.

"You shouldn't have had to witness that," he said, so calmly that Lisette suddenly realised his violence had been coolly deliberate. Controlled. She began to feel less frightened.

"What do you intend doing with Siward?" she ventured huskily.

"I'm not going to have the fellow killed, if that's what is worrying you," he said at once. "But his insolence can't go unpunished. He answers to me now, and I won't have divided loyalties on my estate."

"Siward loved my father." Lisette's voice was low, and soft with memory. "He was found abandoned as a child after a battle against the Welsh. My father brought him here and had him taught the trade of blacksmith. No one else cared. Siward would have died for him."

"A touching tale, my lady. But he'll find himself dying for a lot less if he doesn't learn to curb that temper."

"He was only trying to defend my honour. Against *your* men."

"I'm aware of that," he told her sternly. "However, from now on the only person with the right to defend your honour is myself. Your people have already been told that if they have any complaints against my men they must come to me to have such disputes settled properly, and I intend to be obeyed."

Lisette opened her mouth to deny that Raverre had any rights at all where she was concerned, but he swept on regardless.

"And I have just bethought me of the priest you mentioned last night. You said he had been attacked. Is he dead also?"

"No," she said, worried again. What did he want with a priest if Siward was to live? "But he is old and ill abed at this moment."

"No matter. In the hearing of disputes he should also be present, and I wanted him to attend this afternoon's ceremony. However, I have no intention of dragging a sick man from his bed. Your presence should be reassurance enough for the serfs."

Raverre paused, watching Lisette intently, and, seeing her concern, reached out to take her hand. She was so small that it was like holding some precious, fragile ornament, he thought, trying to ignore the sensations that shot through him at the feel of her soft little palm against his rougher one.

"That is why I want you there this afternoon," he explained more gently. "I would not willingly cause you distress, but it will be better for your people. 'Twould also help if I had the deeds of land so I may easily match the men to their manors."

Better for you, too, thought Lisette resentfully, but unable to refute his statement. The last part of it registered and her faced paled. Her father's deeds, granted to their family almost two hundred years before by the great King Alfred himself, to be handed over to this intruder! This foreigner!

Raverre saw Lisette's face tense with suppressed emotion and tightened his hold, drawing her attention to the fact that he still possessed her hand. Trying unavailingly to free herself, Lisette glanced quickly around the bailey, further upset by the thought of how they must appear, standing close together in deep conversation, her hand clasped warmly in his, in full view of his soldiers and her serfs. And after what had just happened.

She got her hand free at last, fighting back tears of frustrated rage.

"You may have your deeds," she informed him bitterly, taking refuge in chilly courtesy.

"I'll need a list of the goods we lack also," Raverre reminded her. "I expect you would prefer to make it up yourself than have one of my men do it for you. And don't forget to include whatever feminine gewgaws you and your sisters may lack."

"That will take some time," she managed to say through the lump in her throat. "So I ask that I may be excused from dining in the hall." If she had to witness her erstwhile free churls becoming the bondmen of a Norman Baron then she would not willingly sit at table with him as well.

Raverre's keen gaze searched her face. There was a betraying shimmer in her eyes, a tender, vulnerable curve to her mouth. He saw her throat move as she swallowed hard. She had obviously endured enough for one morning.

"Very well." He tipped her face up to his with one long finger under her chin. "But you must promise to eat something. I believe I interrupted your breakfast." He smiled.

Lisette felt her knees shake. She forgot her distress. She forgot Siward. She forgot everything, except the need to escape from an abrupt premonition of danger.

"I have no intention of starving myself," she retorted, jerking her head aside.

Turning, she walked away. Quickly. Before she succumbed to an utterly perplexing temptation to change her mind and stay with him.

"Lisette! At last. We've been worried."

Catherine hailed her sister as Lisette stepped into the screen passage, forcing her to stop.

So much seemed to have happened since her earlier confrontation with Raverre that Lisette gazed at Catherine's anxious face for several blank seconds. When she did remember, however, she found herself recalling, in shameful detail, her disturbing reaction to Raverre in the gallery. She prayed Catherine wouldn't notice the heated flush staining her cheeks.

"'Twas no cause for worry," she assured the younger girl.

"You mean Raverre didn't punish you at all? But he looked furious."

Lisette waved a hand airily. "Aye...well...he issued a few warnings. But, as you see, I'm quite unscathed."

"Marjory said she didn't think Raverre would hurt you, but I wouldn't have been in your shoes for anything. Please be careful, Lisette."

"Marjory sometimes thinks she knows a great deal more than the rest of us," Lisette retorted, unaccountably annoyed.

Catherine's eyes widened in surprise at her sister's waspish tone. Lisette was immediately contrite. Really, what *was* the matter with her? First she had forgotten Raverre was an enemy to be kept at a safe distance. Now she was snapping at her innocent sister.

"Oh, Catherine, I'm sorry. I didn't mean to speak so sharply. It's been a difficult morning."

This vague excuse sounded lame indeed, but Lisette was reluctant to go into detail. The others would find out about Siward soon enough. At the moment she simply wasn't capable of dealing with the barrage of questions and worried conjecture that would arise as soon as it was known that Siward was being held prisoner.

Fortunately, Catherine accepted the apology at its face value.

"I'm going to help Marjory take an inventory of the

linen,'' she announced, moving towards the hall. ''If Raverre is set upon bringing the manor into order we can burn
the sheets that are beyond mending.''

Lisette nodded, smiling absently at her sister as she
started up the stairs. She had to hastily erase a sharp mental
picture of Raverre's large body sprawled between fine linen
sheets. What had the man done to her that she had such
unsettling thoughts about him? Never before had she been
so conscious of a man that he seemed to have taken up
residence in her head. Wasn't taking over her home enough
for him?

By the time she reached the empty tower room Lisette
had concluded that it would be far better for her sanity if
she spent as little time as possible in Raverre's company.
Poised to defend her rights, and those of her people, from
the moment of his arrival, she found it rather difficult to
maintain this aggressive stance when her disordered brain
couldn't decide what to make of him.

The words ''arrogant'' and ''intimidating'' sprang immediately to mind, but she also had to admit that she trusted
him to give Siward a fair hearing. Lisette knew she should
be thankful that Raverre hadn't ordered Siward's tongue
cut out for his defiance, but, perversely, she decided that
the overbearing, loutish Baron of her imaginings would
have been easier to deal with.

She only had to look at her flustered reflection in the
polished copper plate which served as a mirror to see she
was a mass of conflicting emotions. No wonder she felt
worn out. And the day had scarce begun.

Indulging in a fit of temper rather than useless feminine
tears, Lisette relieved her feelings somewhat by slamming
the door, marching across the room, and flinging open the
chest which contained her father's documents with such

violence that the lid hit the wall and promptly fell down again.

So much for temper. Lifting the lid more carefully, Lisette began to pull out the parchments bearing the ancient royal seal of Alfred, firmly suppressing the strange tearing feeling in her heart.

The number of churls and villeins in the bailey increased as the day wore on. They stood in wary, sullen groups, speaking occasionally to each other, greeting new arrivals, but on the whole silent and suspicious.

Despite their rough homespun clothing and generally unkempt appearance, Raverre thought they looked healthy enough. He leaned negligently against the store-room door, his alert gaze moving over his new domain.

The compound formed a large square, with the hall occupying the centre. Raverre considered the stone structure thoughtfully, having no difficulty in recognising the clean, austere lines of its architecture. Somewhere in the not too distant past there had been a marked Norman influence here at Ambray. A mystery he intended to solve.

The kitchen sheds, to the right of the hall, were definitely Saxon. Built of wood and thatch, they were snug and in good repair. As were the ovens, if the smell of freshly baked bread was anything to go by.

Raverre wondered if the tempting aroma would entice Lisette to eat more than she had last night. In the clear morning sunlight she had looked so damn fragile. And, though her spirit belied her delicate appearance, Raverre knew that even the most courageous spirit could not survive forever against poor food, little rest and constant fear. The lady would never admit it, but the truth was he had arrived not a moment too soon.

Raverre moved his eyes on to the well, making a mental note to replace the fraying rope with a chain.

He had frightened Lisette when he'd struck Will. Raverre grimaced at the memory of huge eyes looking at him as though their owner expected to be struck also. But after threatening to use his whip on her he could hardly blame Lisette for being wary of him. She was not to know the threat was now an empty one. After all, when he'd uttered it Raverre himself hadn't fully realised he would do anything to protect her from such treatment.

He'd backed himself neatly into a corner there, from which only time would extricate him. And, if the rumours of strife in the north became a reality, time might be short.

Determinedly bringing his mind back to the manor yet again, Raverre mentally retraced his recent inspection. Behind the hall lay the midden, and in the opposite corner the small garden Lisette had mentioned, abutting on to a vacant dovecote. The cote would make a passable mews if he ever found the time to indulge in a little hawking.

The only other building in the compound was the stable, also standing empty, its roof looking badly in need of thatching, and the interior musty with the odour of disuse. It needed to be repaired immediately so the horses would have shelter for the winter.

Raverre's eyes completed their circuit of the bailey, returning to the gate as Gilbert rode in with his men.

The Saxons gave way before the advancing horses, some of their dour expressions lightening at the sight of the heavy game bags hanging from the Normans' saddles.

''A successful chase, my lord,'' murmured Bertrand, who had come to report that all were present. ''In my Lord Alaric's day that usually meant a feast.''

Raverre looked at him, humour in his steady gaze. ''Then

let them feast by all means. Perhaps it will sweeten their oaths of allegiance.''

''There'll be no trouble, my lord. They already know you have treated the ladies with respect, and that you upheld Siward this morning against your own man.''

''Though he still languishes in the guard-room, and Will goes free?''

''It might encourage the hothead to use his brain instead of his brawn,'' remarked Bertrand unexpectedly.

As Raverre lifted a brow in half-startled enquiry he added, ''We are not all rebels, sir. Don't be misled by the people's wariness. After two years of savage defeats they only want to be left in peace, to lick their wounds and rebuild their lives.''

Raverre nodded thoughtfully. ''They share that ambition with the King. He wants England and her people to prosper. So do I.''

''And my ladies?''

''You refer especially to Lisette, I think,'' remarked Raverre shrewdly.

''Aye.'' The furrowed face of the old warrior softened. ''I can't help but love her most. You might think her rebellious, but—''

''She will come to no harm with me, Bertrand,'' Raverre interposed quietly.

Bertrand looked up at his new master searchingly. Raverre's words could mean anything, but there was something in that level regard which said more than mere words.

Bertrand inclined his head. ''I see de Rohan giving orders to have the meat smoked and stored,'' he said, his tone businesslike again. ''I'll make sure that rogue Wat keeps some aside for tonight.''

He moved off, nodding civilly to Gilbert, who was strolling towards them. Gilbert's eyes went to the open door of the store-room.

"Anything?"

Raverre knew Gilbert was not referring to food. He shook his head.

"Nothing. Not here, at any rate. I've just been all over the place and there's nowhere an object of that size could be hidden." He made an impatient gesture. "I didn't expect to find anything. Whatever William's spies might have told him, I don't believe the ingot was ever this far west; certainly not here, where the local people are all well known to each other. We can search the villages and other manors, but I'm damned if I'm going to search the whole forest."

Gilbert nodded gloomily. "Perhaps it's been taken out of the country," he suggested. "To Wales."

Raverre shrugged. "I don't think there's been enough time since the robbery, but if you're right the Saxons could have taken it by any route. Why come all this way? When you consider the problems in moving it at all, let alone any great distance, I'd wager 'tis still close to Winchester."

Gilbert nodded agreement. "No wonder the fools couldn't run the country with any accord. They can't even pull off a robbery efficiently. Imagine taking Hardrada's gold ingot, and leaving a chest full of smaller, more easily managed treasures."

"Whoever was responsible obviously decided to take the gold, not realising the value of the other pieces. That ingot must be worth a King's ransom, and even a peasant knows the value of gold."

"Are you suggesting a serf is the culprit? It doesn't seem likely." Gilbert sounded sceptical in the extreme.

"Why not?" argued Raverre seriously. "We know the guards were drugged. Who else had access to their food and wine? Saxon serfs. But I didn't mean they were acting alone. Someone with more authority ordered that robbery. And it had to be someone who knew that Godwinson seized the ingot for his treasury after Harald of Norway was killed.''

"And that William then took over the treasury after Hastings,'' concurred Gilbert thoughtfully. "It all comes down to wealth, doesn't it? The Saxons need it to finance their rebellions, and William needs it to pay off his mercenaries.''

"Well, he can't parcel out land to that lawless scum he recruited from all over Christendom. Can you picture them setting up in baronial grandeur? They'd be at each other's throats in no time.''

"Aye, by God,'' said Gilbert feelingly. "'Twould be Normandy ten years past, all over again.''

Raverre looked grim. His uncle and two of his brothers had died in the constant battles of Baron against Baron, Knight against Knight, until William had finally brought unity and law to his warlike race.

Gilbert's eyes drifted casually across the bailey. "Speaking of fighting, the fellow at the gate is nursing a swollen jaw,'' he observed, only the faintest hint of a question in his voice.

"He can thank the Saints that's all he's nursing,'' growled Raverre, reminded that he had enough problems of his own.

Gilbert looked amused. "You sound annoyed. Your little Saxon causing trouble already?'' he enquired.

"No, damn it! 'Twas one of her churls exercising a misguided sense of chivalry in her defence. All *she's* done is throw out insults, argue with me and disobey my orders! Why should I be annoyed?''

Gilbert laughed outright, and Raverre gave a reluctant grin.

"I wonder if William is having as much trouble with his policy of diplomacy and conciliation?" he asked ruefully.

"He's probably not dealing with a female," suggested Gilbert. "You'd better marry the girl tomorrow. I've noticed you never have any problems with a woman once you've bedded her." He saw Raverre's face change, and flung up a hand.

"I meant no disrespect," he added hurriedly. "For God's sake, don't hit me too—I wouldn't wake up for a week."

"How tempting," said Raverre silkily.

Gilbert hastened to change the subject.

"What have you done with the churl?" he asked. 'I don't see a corpse hanging from the tower."

"Nor will you. Diplomacy and conciliation, remember. Beside, the fellow meant well. I'm leaving him to cool his temper in the guard-room for a while. After that, we'll see. The manor needs a strong reeve, and he seems intelligent enough. Loyal, too, if I can win him over."

"Aye, but a Saxon," murmured Gilbert doubtfully.

"All the better. You've seen the results on other manors where Norman bailiffs and reeves have been appointed. The word 'churlish' is taking on a whole new meaning, and I don't want that happening here."

"It might work, I suppose, but what if the fellow uses his position against you?"

"Then you'll see a corpse hanging from the tower. But I don't think he will. If I'm right about him he might use his position to argue a decision, but not to incite outright rebellion."

Gilbert looked even more doubtful. Used to the instant and implicit obedience given to a Norman Knight from those below him—an obedience the Saxons seemed most reluctant to grant—he could only hope that Raverre knew what he was doing.

Raverre did know. But he waited until the last Saxon had knelt, placed his hands between those of his new master, and vowed to become Raverre's man for life and limb and earthly worship.

None of the Englishmen looked particularly happy with the situation, but there was no overt dissension. When all were done the villeins were ushered out to the bailey, where food and ale awaited them.

Lisette prepared to follow as inconspicuously as possible. Worried by Siward's continued absence, she was hoping to find out what had befallen him. She should have known better than to think she would escape Raverre's notice.

He halted her at the screen passage, his eyes scanning the list of goods handed to him earlier by Marjory. Despite his instructions to the contrary, Lisette had not included any personal requirements.

Raverre glanced over the shabby russet gown she wore, noticing for the first time the thinness of her homespun mantle, and the roughly made bone clasp holding it together at her throat. He wondered if she'd had anything new to wear since her father's departure two years earlier.

"I see you did not avail yourself of my offer to provide whatever you might need," he said, thinking of his mother's overflowing chests back in Normandy and mentally adding their contents to the list.

"My sisters and I need nothing from you," Lisette replied shortly. Then added with some reluctance, "Although I thank you for providing the feast tonight when food is still short."

Raverre regarded her somewhat ironically. "You Saxons are a stubborn lot," he informed her. "I'm not a tyrant, you know, and I see nothing to be gained by inflicting further hardship on a community that has already suffered enough. Although anyone seeing all these sour faces would be pardoned for thinking I had done just that!''

"Giving a feast is all very well," she flashed back, springing to her people's defence, "but you have taken something far more important to them. Their freedom!"

"Freedom to do what?" he demanded impatiently. "To run about the country like disorganised rabble, leaving their families to starve and perish at home?"

"But some of them were freeman farmers, or skilled tradesmen, like Cuthred, the carpenter. They attended the shire courts with my father, and could even attain the rank of Thegn if they acquired enough land or riches."

Lisette sighed, looking up at the uncompromising expression on Raverre's face. There was no hint now of the easy charm he had shown her earlier.

"Under Norman law they'll be no better than serfs," she finished dejectedly. "That is what they were fighting to avoid."

"They are *all* serfs," Raverre answered sternly. "Whether they paid rent for their land or did week work is irrelevant. They are now united in equal status and will be protected and provided for."

"Aye, little more than slaves!" she cried, knowing the argument was useless, but unable to stop. "Answerable to you for everything, no longer to have any say in their own lives!"

"Don't exaggerate," he remonstrated. "King, Baron or serf, none of us is truly free. Aye, the serfs will have to answer to me, but I then must answer to William, and he in turn to his conscience and to God for the repose of his soul.

"Besides," he continued, trying to make her understand, "even the free churls had obligations to your father while living on his estate. The only difference for those men is

that they cannot leave without my permission, which is no
bad thing. I have little sympathy for a system which allowed vassals to leave their master's family defenceless."

Lisette glared at him in baffled fury. She could not in all
honesty deny this claim, but determined not to let Raverre
have the last word, she seized on another grievance.

"You must still regard them as slaves," she accused.
"Why else would they not be eating with you here in the
hall?"

Raverre parried this shift in the argument without a blink.

"I know better, at this stage, than to mix Normans and
Saxons at the same table while ale is being freely imbibed," he retorted. "There'll be time enough for that
when—" He stopped dead.

"When we're all cowered into obedience?" Lisette spat,
her voice shaking with anger.

"No, I was *not* going to say that, you little shrew."

Lisette turned away, struggling to hold her temper in
check. "Whatever the words, the meaning is the same,"
she said bitterly.

Raverre took a quick step towards her.

"Sweet lady!"

Lisette glanced back, startled, not quite sure if she had
heard the softly spoken endearment. Raverre was watching
her. The blue flames in his eyes burned so intensely that
the breath caught in her throat.

"You *will* know me better," he stated with a calm certainty that shook her to the core. "And when you do you
will know I never want to see you cowed. I would not
demean you so."

The silence following this pronouncement seemed to Lisette to be fraught with promise. Or was it warning? She
was incapable of answering. Incapable even of movement.

Pinned by Raverre's compelling gaze until he turned away, disappearing through the door into the gathering twilight.

Lisette slowly climbed the stairs, unaware of her surroundings until she found herself outside the solar door. There she hesitated, not wanting to face the others in her bemused state.

Walking to the end of the gallery, she sat down on the bottom step of the narrow staircase. Faint grey light still showed through the cracks in the trapdoor above her, but the sconces had not yet been lit and the gallery was growing dark. Wrapping her arms about her knees, Lisette gazed broodingly into the shadows.

Did Raverre really mean to know her better? Or had he deliberately diverted her because he had changed his mind about sparing Siward? If Siward had refused to swear allegiance with the other churls Raverre could well make an example of him. Lisette doubted that two instances of defiance would go unpunished. And yet, knowing this, she had weakly allowed herself to be distracted.

She sat up straighter. Where was her fighting spirit? Was she a spineless female who mindlessly allowed others to rule her life and dictate her actions? No, she was not! She would discover why Siward was still imprisoned, and would calmly demand an explanation from Raverre, instead of wasting her energy in useless arguments with him.

Lisette jumped up, full of determination. Then abruptly sat down again. If she ventured outside immediately she would probably meet Raverre before she got halfway to the guard-room. And the bailey would be full of men, Saxon and Norman. She didn't want a repeat of this morning's scene.

There was an alternative, however. At this end of the gallery, beside the stairs leading to the roof, there was a small alcove. To the casual eye it seemed no more than that, but closer inspection revealed a steep flight of stairs leading off at a sharp angle, descending into darkness.

A prudent man, Alaric had not relied totally on the almost impregnable position of the hall. At the foot of the stone staircase a small door had been cut into the castle wall. Barely four feet high and narrow, almost concealed by a solid buttress, it opened out to the rear of the bailey. It had been intended as an escape route for the family should one ever be needed, but it would serve Lisette's purpose as well.

Her hand was seeking out the postern key before the plan was fully formed. It wasn't late. She would not be missed for another half-hour or so. And it was extremely unlikely that she would encounter anyone in the garden or dovecote at this hour.

Feeling defiantly pleased with herself, Lisette waited until the glow in the hall brightened as more sconces were lit. Night was not far away, but there would still be enough light to see her way to the guard-room.

Trying not to think of the repercussions should she be caught, she groped her way carefully down the stairs. Something small skittered out of her path. Mice, Lisette told herself firmly as she descended further. Dense blackness pressed about her, and she shuddered as her hand encountered a clinging spider's web. The staircase hadn't been used in years, and she was glad to reach the last step and open the door.

Slipping easily through the narrow opening, Lisette straightened and glanced cautiously about. She was outside. Now all she had to do was reach the guard-room unseen. Not too difficult, surely, in the half-dark? And if Siward was still bound there might not be a guard to contend with.

She had reached the corner of the tower safely, when a distant footfall sounded. Heart pounding, Lisette strained to listen, trying to determine its direction. Glancing over her shoulder, she saw a light at the far corner, and held her breath. The glow flared, then dimmed, and Lisette heard the faint closing of a door.

A soldier visiting the privy, she thought, relieved. But there was still the possibility of his returning to his post in her direction. She couldn't stand here forever, gathering courage. The knowledge that she was still afraid underneath her bravado spurred Lisette to action.

As the light flared brightly again she darted quickly around the corner. And ran straight into a large, solid object.

Lisette gave a startled squeak, the impact almost knocking her off her feet, but the object reached out to grasp her arms, holding her upright. It was obviously human.

"Do I have to bind you hand and foot to keep you inside?" demanded Raverre.

The resigned amusement in his voice carried a clear message to Lisette's brain. She recovered from her fright in a hurry.

"You knew I was going to come this way," she cried indignantly. "How?"

"Never mind how," he commanded, releasing one of her arms and marching her back to the small postern so fast that her feet barely touched the ground. He held out his hand imperatively. "The key, if you please, my lady."

"I'm going to have another bruise on this arm," she accused, trying to delay the inevitable.

His punishing grip didn't slacken this time. "The key!"

Lisette glared at him, but the effort was wasted in the darkness. Fumbling with her free hand, she extracted the key and slapped it into Raverre's open palm. His fingers closed over hers.

Then, before Lisette could object to his familiarity, she was abruptly pulled into his arms.

There was one second of frozen amazement, then Lisette began to struggle. Raverre's arms tightened immediately. One large hand pressed her face into the soft expanse of wool covering his chest, effectively stifling her instinctive protest; the other arm became an iron band across her back, holding her clamped against him. She could feel the steady rhythm of his heart. In spite of her helpless position, it was oddly reassuring.

"Is all secure, sir? I thought I heard—"

The moment Lisette identified the soldier's voice her rigid muscles eased. She felt Raverre draw a breath to speak as he turned his head slightly.

"It's all right, Arnulf. I was just checking here myself. All's well."

"Aye, sir."

Lisette heard the privy door close. Another one, she thought. It must be all that ale. A giggle rose in her throat at the notion, and she wondered if she was becoming hysterical.

Then her unexpected flash of levity died away as Lisette realised that Raverre's swift action had shielded her from the disparaging gossip which would have ensued had the sergeant seen them together in this dark, secluded corner.

At the same moment she also realised that she was still clasped against Raverre's broad chest, and that he showed no inclination to release her. The wool caressing her cheek was the only soft thing about that chest, she mused vaguely. Beneath the smooth fabric was solid muscle and bone. His arms were hard also, but a subtle change seemed to have occurred. Lisette still felt their strength, but now they cradled her.

She shivered, wondering how it was possible to feel both protected and threatened at the same time.

"You see what may happen when you wander about after dark," he murmured above her as she stirred against him. "I was here to protect you from Arnulf, but who is going to protect you from me?"

Lisette's hands came up instantly to push against Raverre's unyielding frame.

He released her slowly. "I'm glad you now understand why I asked you to remain indoors," he growled. But he was unable to summon up real anger. She had felt so right in his arms. If they hadn't been out in the open—

Mortified heat swept through Lisette's entire body. Dear God, she had willingly remained nestled in Raverre's embrace, when he had only been intent on punishing her. She had even been thankful for him. It was ten times worse than this morning in the gallery. At least then he hadn't known of her feelings.

And she had forgotten poor Siward *again*. Although now, Lisette suddenly discovered, her fears for Siward had been laid to rest while she had been held fast in Raverre's arms. She decided not to question this startling conclusion.

"What if you'd run into some yokel with a skinful of ale under his belt?" Raverre continued, unlocking the postern. "Little fool."

Shame and gratitude vanished.

"I have no reason to fear my people," she declared loftily. "Besides, 'tis your own fault! I was concerned for Siward, and you wouldn't tell me anything."

"You didn't ask," he stated irrefutably. "But, as a matter of fact, I was coming to tell you what had passed. 'Twas how I knew you weren't in the castle. After seeing this door earlier, it didn't take long to realise what you were up to." His voice held amusement again.

"Very clever," she muttered.

Raverre opened the door, bending almost double to peer up the stairs. "Ingenious. I was up on the tower roof this morning, and I didn't even notice this stairway when I returned."

He glanced down at Lisette, unable to see her face clearly, but sensing the unspoken question hovering in the air. "Well?"

"Well, what?" She sounded extremely grumpy.

Raverre grinned. "Aren't you going to ask me about Siward? Nicely, I hope," he couldn't resist adding.

She ground her teeth.

"Tell me what you've done with Siward, *please*."

"I've appointed him manor reeve."

"What?" Lisette gasped, instantly forgetting her wrath. "Then he must have sworn fealty to you. How did you manage it?"

"By giving him a choice. Become my man or leave the estate. Without a safe conduct, however, he would have had to remain free for a year and a day before he could seek out work in a town. I told him I didn't think that feat beyond his capabilities."

"Merciful Saints!" uttered Lisette faintly. "What did he say to that?"

"He didn't believe me at first. He thought I'd have him killed if he refused to swear allegiance."

"Many would."

"Whether he was dead or merely gone, I would still have been without a blacksmith," Raverre explained with calm practicality. "And I also needed a reeve whom I could trust to speak as fairly for me as for the Saxons. Your Siward struck me as a man of his word, once he gave it."

"Aye," Lisette said quietly. Of all the actions she

thought Raverre might have taken, she had never considered this one.

But his leniency didn't make him less dangerous, she reminded herself. Siward was no doubt trying to make sense of the fact that, though he was no longer free, he had been given a position of some authority, but Lisette knew the blacksmith had been shrewdly manipulated. In fact she was beginning to realise that, despite his daunting appearance, Raverre was no uncivilised savage relying on brute force to attain his goals. There was a shrewd, far-sighted intelligence at work behind that cool, tough façade.

"Where is Siward now?" she enquired.

"Feasting with the others, I expect. And, as your own supper is probably growing cold, you had best return to your chamber before Marjory sends out a search party."

"Very well," she acquiesced guilelessly. "May I have my key back?"

Raverre threw back his head and laughed, startling Lisette again. She had not thought him capable of such a light-hearted gesture.

"No, you may not have your key back, my little innocent," he chuckled. "But it was a nice try."

"Ohhh! You…"

Rendered speechless, Lisette spun about and stalked to the doorway. Her pose of injured dignity was rather impaired by the fact that she had to bend considerably to negotiate the low entry.

As Raverre closed the door after her the muttered words "overgrown bully" floated down the stairway. He grinned back, pocketing the key as he walked away.

Life in England certainly promised to be entertaining.

Chapter Three

From her perch in the window embrasure Lisette could see the serfs making their way through the wasteland on the far side of the manor fields. It was the time of gathering bracken and acorns to see the swine through the winter months, and she thought wistfully of days spent roaming the woods, enjoying the last of the mild weather before winter's icy gales swept down from the north, blanketing the countryside with snow.

Surely it couldn't hurt to venture into the garden, if only for an hour. After Raverre's swift discipline of Will yesterday Lisette doubted if she would be accosted by any soldiers, and she would take Finn with her.

She stepped down into the room in time to hear Catherine complaining that if she had to set another stitch her fingers would well nigh fall from her hands.

Obviously restlessness was becoming a problem here, too.

''And how will you fare when you have a family to mend for, if you don't mind your stitching now?'' scolded Marjory, brandishing a torn gown belonging to her obstinate charge.

"I shall give it to my faithful old nurse, of course," said Catherine airily, skipping nimbly out of Marjory's reach.

"Let me mend the gown, Marjory," interposed Enide's soft voice.

They all jumped, as if a ghost had suddenly addressed them.

Enide smiled gently at them and took the gown from Marjory's limp hold. "You know Catherine will make it look worse, and you will have to do it all over again. 'Tis not good for your eyes, such close work." She sat down on the stone seat in the window embrasure recently vacated by her sister, and took up her needle.

This assumption that life was going on as usual sent a shiver down Lisette's spine. Was it possible that Enide really didn't comprehend what had happened? If so, the sooner she was safely in her aunt's charge, the better. Lisette resolved to speak to Raverre about the matter that same day.

"Come, Catherine," she said firmly, turning to her rebellious younger sister. "If you scorn to sew, perhaps you would like to help gather some herbs. 'Tis time I should be making simples for the winter ills that will no doubt beset some of us. You should learn how to mix a soothing salve for chapped hands, or your faithful old nurse won't be able to wield a needle."

Armed with this innocent excuse to be out about her business, Lisette ignored a sharp look from Marjory, and cautiously opened the door. An empty gallery greeted her, but sounds from below indicated that preparations were well in hand for the main meal of the day, and she could see Raverre conferring with a number of his men. He was standing before a table covered with parchments, which, even at that distance, she had no trouble in recognising as her father's deeds of land.

"Dividing the spoils of war already," she muttered to herself. "We shall be next, no doubt."

Raverre could not have heard her, but, as if sensing her presence, he raised his head and saw Lisette watching him. Murmuring an excuse to the others, he crossed the hall to intercept her as she and Catherine reached the door to the outer stairway.

"You are going out, my lady?" he asked, politely enough, but Lisette heard the underlying steel in his voice.

"Not far, my lord," she answered with deceptive sweetness. "Just to the garden to gather some herbs. For tisanes and salves, you know." As he considered this she added, "Who knows, you may even need one yourself some day?"

Raverre's hard eyes lit with appreciation at this sally, but before he could answer his attention was diverted by the appearance in the doorway of the village priest.

Father Edwin was meant to be a fat, jolly little soul, comfortable in his faith and a comfort to his flock, but the tensions of the past few months had made him a thin, nervous creature, who devoutly hoped he would not be called upon to do anything more courageous than give solace to the womenfolk of the castle in the face of this latest invasion.

The last time he had overcome his fear of violence to intervene on behalf of those in his care he had been rendered unconscious, and had lain senseless for three days. On returning to consciousness and learning of the tragedy which had overtaken Lord Alaric's family he had been almost as much in need of consolation and gentle treatment as Enide.

There was no help to be looked for here, Lisette knew, but she was fond of the old man, and greeted him warmly,

enquiring about the ague which had kept him in his bed
for the past week.

"'Tis nearly cured, my lady," he answered, plucking
nervously at his coarse woollen gown as he glanced up at
Raverre's imposing figure. "I am only sorry that I have not
been able to conduct the Mass for you, but I will do so
tomorrow, you may be sure. 'Twould never do for you not
to receive such comfort on the Sabbath. No, no. You may
come to worship with an easy mind."

"We shall be glad of it, Father," said Lisette gravely,
"and will give thanks for your recovery."

An awkward silence fell, and she turned reluctantly towards Raverre, feeling as if somehow she betrayed the
memory of her father by making Raverre known to Father
Edwin as the new lord of the manor. Nor, she realised, was
Raverre going to make it any easier for her by introducing
himself. As her eyes met the relentless expression in his
Lisette knew that he was aware of her feelings, and was
going to force her to acknowledge aloud his baronetcy, or
appear ignoble in defeat. And that she would never be.

Her head lifted, and her voice was steady as she said,
"Father, you will not have met Baron Alain de Raverre.
He is the Lord of Ambray now." She deliberately used the
Norman pronunciation of Raverre's name, and had the sat-
isfaction of seeing a flash of surprise in his eyes before he
greeted Father Edwin courteously.

"Your arrival is most opportune, Father. I would be
pleased if you would join us at dinner so I may have speech
with you. I am sure you will be most helpful in reassuring
your people that I am not the Devil incarnate, and that their
lives will be disrupted as little as possible, the times being
what they are."

The little priest's worried expression lightened somewhat
at these words, and he happily nodded his acceptance. Lis-

ette, meanwhile, seeing that Raverre would be occupied for the moment, seized Catherine's hand and made good her escape into the bailey.

The garden in its sheltered corner was warm in the morning sun. As the girls gathered herbs in the fragrant air Catherine, with a sidelong look at her sister, observed carefully, "You seem not to be so angry this morning, Lisette. Did the night bring good counsel?"

Lisette looked up with a rueful smile, remembering how she had stormed into the solar last night, still reviling Normans in general, and Raverre in particular.

"Have I indeed been so bear-like, sweet? I am sorry. 'Tis not that I am angry so much as afraid, I think, and the anger keeps the fear at bay. But I should not be speaking of such things." She squeezed Catherine's hand. "Here I am, trying to be a good example to my little sister, and all I can do is bleat about fear like a frightened lamb."

"I was afraid, too, Lisette," admitted Catherine, her round blue eyes solemn. "The other day, I mean. When Raverre first came into the hall he made me think of a great, fierce warrior. But later, when I saw his face clearly, I was no longer afraid. I don't know why exactly, because he *is* a Norman. But he has been kind to us, after all. He reminded me a little of the master mason King Edward sent to our father when he was planning the manor. Don't you remember? He carved a little wooden horse for me; I think I have it still. He and Raverre are not like those others who came, are they?"

Lisette warmed to her sister. She had become so used to being the strong one—taking care of everything and trying not to worry the others by letting her own fears show. And all the time she had overlooked the strength and quaint woman-child wisdom that Catherine possessed beneath her urchin behaviour.

"You must try to forget those others, Catkin," she said, reverting to her sister's childish pet name with quick affection. "They were evil men, and will meet their punishment in death, even if they escape it in life. Marjory was right. The fighting is over and we must learn to make the best of our lives while we still have them."

She belatedly realised that this sound advice could as well apply to herself, and hastily dismissed the thought. 'Tis different for me, Lisette told herself stubbornly. She still had an uneasy feeling that somehow, in some way as yet unknown, Raverre posed a threat to her.

"Will we make the best of our lives in a convent?" asked Catherine doubtfully. "Would it not be better to stay here?"

"Oh, Catherine, I wish we could with all my heart. But even if we were to be married, we would have to leave. As soon as Raverre is settled he will be looking to make alliances with powerful families, with us as pawns."

"He might not," said Catherine hopefully. "You'll be needed here, Lisette. No one knows the estate as you do. Why, you've even been presiding at the manor court."

Lisette jumped up. "Blessed Saint Catherine, for sending that thought to your head!" she exclaimed. "I'd forgotten all about the court. No wonder Father Edwin is here—'tis Saturday. And we'll be lucky to finish dinner before Edric and Wulf are upon us."

"Are they still squabbling over that strip of land? I thought—"

"What else? Here, take these herbs to the store-room, sweet. I must think what to say to Raverre.

"If he lets me speak," she added to herself as Catherine left the garden, her willow basket laden with the sweet-smelling harvest.

The fact that she had been holding the weekly court hearings for two years might not impress Raverre at all, Lisette suspected, and she began to consider the best way of convincing him to let her speak for the two contentious churls.

It was Finn's low growl of warning that first alerted Lisette to danger. Glancing up, she was startled to find Siward's foe of yesterday standing a few yards away. The garden was enclosed by a low stone wall, and Will was effectively blocking the way out. They were also, Lisette saw, quite alone on this side of the compound.

Unable to think why the Norman would seek her out, she ventured a careful question.

"Have you come to summon me to dinner? I didn't mean to linger so long, but the garden was so pleasant, and—"

"I'm no serf to be sent on such footling errands," he interrupted. His voice was rough, the English heavily accented but understandable.

"Well…even so, it must be quite late. I should return to the hall."

Lisette took a step forward, but her resolve faltered when Will stood his ground, scowling at her under heavy black brows.

Even if he'd worn a more amiable expression, Lisette thought he would not be an attractive specimen of Norman manhood. His blunt-featured face was coarse, almost brutish, his eyes small and malevolent. The ugly bruise across his jaw didn't improve an overall impression of viciousness. He was only of average height, but still bigger and stronger than her. Lisette felt a swift stab of fear, and struggled to control it, as Will spoke again.

"Not so fast, wench. Because of you I'm to be sent back to the army. I don't like that."

He moved closer. Lisette backed away, watching him. She wondered if she could manage to scramble over the wall before Will caught her, but, at the moment, he seemed

more interested in talking. Perhaps he was only trying to
frighten her. Surely the man wouldn't risk actually hurting
a woman who was under his lord's protection?

"I thought I'd have a nice little post here," he went on.
"Some guard duty, plenty of ale and women. No more
chasing after you Saxon vermin through sodden, overgrown
forests." His eyes narrowed speculatively, and a vindictive
smile crossed his face. "You owe me something for ruining
my plans, and I intend to see you pay up."

"Don't you come near me!" Lisette said fiercely. "I'll
scream!"

Will chuckled. "A wrench with spirit. All the better.
Scream all you like. I'll enjoy it. Everyone's in the hall at
their dinner. You won't be heard."

Lisette felt the blood drain from her face as a helpless,
nauseating weakness seemed to grip her limbs. Her nerves
felt stripped raw by the menace in the Norman's slow advance.

She continued to retreat before it until she came up
against the dovecote.

Will laughed evilly, but halted, still some feet away. He
was relishing her fear, Lisette realised. He licked his lips.
His little coal-black eyes glistened. Fingers tipped with dirt-
encrusted nails reached for her.

"Raverre will punish you again," she cried desperately,
shrinking back. If that filthy hand touched her she would
be sick.

Finn stirred restlessly at the tense note in her voice. His
low continuous growling became a full-throated snarl, his
lips drawn back over fangs that could tear a man's throat
out as easily as a deer's.

Will's eyes turned ugly.

"We'll get rid of that cur first," he snapped, drawing his
sword and coming forward in a rush.

Lisette screamed. She flung herself to her knees, throwing her arms around the wildly barking dog. Her action stopped Will in his tracks. Unfortunately, it also prevented Finn from attacking.

"Raverre will kill you if you touch us," Lisette cried over the commotion Finn was making.

"Are you going to tell him after you've been despoiled, bitch?" Will shouted back. "I think not. Even if he does have some crazy idea of handling you Saxons with velvet gloves, you'll have no value to him after I've had you. He'll hand you over to his men."

"I don't believe you," she retorted bravely. "Raverre would never do such a thing."

She didn't have time to wonder at his confident judgement of a man she had known for scarcely two days under less than ideal circumstances.

"You're absolutely right, sweetheart," said Raverre's cool voice from behind Will.

As Will slewed around Lisette slumped to the ground in relief, her head drooping against the dog's bristling fur. Dimly she realised he was still barking deafeningly, but she couldn't seem to find enough energy to calm the animal.

"Finn, sit!" commanded Raverre quietly. The clamour subsided instantly. Finn sat.

Lisette raised her head, staring at Raverre in amazement. He stood with legs braced apart, his sword drawn, its point resting lightly on the ground between his feet. He looked relaxed, but his glittering eyes never left Will's face.

At the same moment Will broke into a torrent of Norman abuse directed at his commander, and Lisette's amazement became horror as the enraged man suddenly turned and lunged at her, sword out-thrust.

Raverre leapt to intercept him, bringing his sword around in a widely swinging arc. His swing deflected Will's attack, and, carried by the fierce momentum of Raverre's powerful arms, the blade sliced through mail and flesh, straight to the heart.

A silence that could be heard fell over the garden. Lisette rose shakily to her feet, her horrified gaze fixed on the shapeless bundle that, only seconds ago, had been a man. She wished she could look away, but she seemed to have lost control of her senses.

Raverre wiped his sword on the grass and sheathed it. Stepping over Will's body and blocking it from Lisette's view, he took her hands. They were ice-cold and trembling. Her eyes lifted to his, wide and fearful. He deliberately made his voice hard.

"Take Finn and return to your chamber. Don't speak of this to anyone. No one at all, do you understand? Go back inside and act as though nothing has happened. Here, use the postern."

He produced the key and folded her fingers over it. Lisette barely registered its presence.

"But—"

At her faltering protest, Raverre's control snapped. If he hadn't just saved her life Lisette would have shrunk from the rage blazing in his eyes. She didn't notice how pale he was beneath his tan.

"Damn it, girl, just do what you're told for once!" he grated harshly. "I don't want you involved in this. Isn't it enough that I've had to kill one of my men because you wilfully disobey my orders?"

Hot tears sprang into Lisette's eyes. "I didn't mean...I didn't know..." Her voice broke.

"Don't bother with lame excuses. Go!"

The tower room was quiet. Marjory and Enide sewed, Catherine was reading, and Lisette sat by the brazier, her

outward composure giving no hint of the turmoil within.
She had even managed to eat her dinner, while pretending
an interest in Father Edwin's gossipy conversation. Although, after one look at Raverre's forbidding expression,
she had been glad to retire immediately after the meal.

Now, however, her first shock at the violent events in
the garden had worn off, and righteous anger was beginning
to take its place. It was hardly her fault Will had decided
she was to blame for his banishment to the army. But even
if she had been the innocent cause of the man's resentment,
her mere presence in the garden didn't justify his wild attack on her life.

Lisette had just reached this conclusion when Bertrand
entered through the open door. She looked up enquiringly.

"You are summoned to the hall, my lady. And my lord
wishes you to hand over to him any documents you hold
pertaining to the manor."

Lisette rose. "He has the deeds of land. What more does
the man need?" she demanded, not disposed to be cooperative.

Bertrand gave her a straight look. "I think you would be
well-advised to accede to this request, my lady. Raverre
has already had enough to deal with today, and he's in no
mood for more."

"Why, whatever do you mean, Bertrand?" queried Catherine idly from the floor, where she was turning the pages
of a book borrowed from Gilbert.

Lisette had been too preoccupied to enquire how her sister and young de Rohan had arrived at such good terms so
quickly.

"Nothing out of the way," Bertrand replied, neatly side-
stepping the issue of Will's untimely demise. "Merely that
he told Siward he would hear petitions today from those

who had suffered losses in the past two years.'' He turned
to Lisette.

"He'll need your help with that, my lady. Father Edwin
knows the men, but he hasn't been running the estate. Raverre seems bent on learning the life story of every serf who
has ever been born on the place, from what I can make
out.''

These words reminded Lisette of Edric and Wulf. Loath
though she was to face Raverre again so soon, she could
not abandon her people. Delving into a chest, she produced
the household accounts and manor rolls, which she had kept
for her father since well before his death at Hastings.

The memory of his pride in her ability to manage the
estate whenever he was absent gave her courage.

"Then let us help, by all means,'' she told Bertrand.

He gave her an approving smile. Marjory beamed.

Curbing an impulse to tell them that their attitude bordered on traitorous, Lisette marched out of the room.

Raverre sat at the high table, flanked by Father Edwin.
As Lisette laid the rolls of parchment before him he glanced
up, his face hard.

"Thank you, my lady. You may return to the solar.''

Lisette's eyes widened in surprise. "But—''

"I doubt if you can help with these matters, and I have
no time to further indulge your taste for discord.''

Lisette flinched at this merciless reference to the morning's catastrophe, but recovered quickly.

"How do you expect to—?''

"My God, are you still arguing?'' Raverre demanded
angrily, coming menacingly to his feet. He had looked less
dangerous when facing Will. "Get back to your proper
place!''

Lisette gasped, recoiling as if Raverre had struck her.
Even knowing he was still angry, she had not expected to

be dismissed so cruelly, as if she were of no account, a
mere woman, incapable of doing more than run a household.

She barely noticed Bertrand's look of consternation as a
tremor of rage shot through her at the full significance of
Raverre's words. But as Bertrand would have spoken out
Lisette made a savage gesture, silencing him. With shaking
hands she unfastened the girdle of plaited silks at her waist,
which held her keys.

Wrenching it from her gown, she flung girdle and keys
across the table with such force that Raverre had to stop
them from tumbling to the rushes on the other side. He
immediately looked thunderous, but Lisette forestalled any
outburst.

"There, my lord," she bit out. "Now you have it all!"

Not waiting for a reply, she turned and walked swiftly
out of the hall.

Her rigid control lasted along the gallery and up the stairs
to the tower roof. Not until the trapdoor was safely shut on
any pursuit did Lisette's façade of composure crumble, and,
trembling violently, she allowed herself to fully realise
what had happened.

After her struggle to keep the estate well managed she
was not to be consulted, not to be permitted to speak for
her people. Dismissed. Rendered powerless. All taken from
her in less time than it took to think about it.

Oh, it was lost indeed. Her home, the happy life she had
known with her parents gone forever. Swept out of her
reach by circumstances over which she had no control; by
people who, until several months ago, had not even known
of her existence.

Already strained to breaking-point, the dam holding back
her turbulent emotions crumbled. The green and gold view
of meadow and forest blurred before Lisette's eyes as the

tears she had never allowed to show fell in an uncontrollable stream, and she sank to the ground against the sunwarmed stone parapet, sobbing out her heartbreak.

The distant sound of the trapdoor slamming echoed through the hall. Father Edwin was obviously trying to find the right words to smooth over the incident, but Bertrand turned to Raverre, letting his disapproval show.

"That was ill done of you, my lord," he said roundly.

Raverre already irritated, flashed a frowning look at him. "What the hell does that mean?" he asked impatiently. "God's blood, this is not a woman's business. The household, aye, but not all these records of tithes, bond days and such. How could a young girl hope to fathom them? And without a steward, or even a bailiff to aid her? Has she bewitched you all into thinking her the master here?"

"Not master, no, my lord. But more than capable of husbanding such an estate while the master is absent. Do you think I can be of help to you here? I have been away more often than not, and am a soldier besides. What do I know of lands, villeins and the rest? Who do you think has struggled to keep the estate together these long months? Not I, nor the good Father here, but yonder maid."

The frown didn't lighten, but Raverre looked thoughtful.

"I think my lady would have explained all to you fairly had she been given the chance," went on Bertrand. At a sceptical look, he insisted, "Whatever she may feel, she has been taught to value justice and honest dealing."

"You think Lisette would deal fairly with me? she would be glad rather to see a sword in my heart, I think. Your lady has not yet laid down her arms."

Father Edwin tut-tutted deprecatingly at this, and shook his head. He was ignored.

"Had she been asked she would have surrendered the

castle to ensure peace for her people," argued Bertrand. "Believe me, I know her well. 'Tis being given no choice that she cannot stomach. As to these documents—" he fanned them out on the table "—see for yourself. They mean nought to me, but you can say if they are well kept or not. Even so, you will still need her to explain those small day-to-day matters that must arise on any large estate."

At this inauspicious moment a commotion at the door heralded the arrival of the claimants for the contended strip of land. Wulf, a choleric fellow with an air of self-importance, had brought along two of his fellows for support, all of them well primed with ale imbibed at their noon meal. And, not to be outdone, young Edric, a fair boy of tender years but stubborn will, had dragged his shrinking mother and sister along.

Various uncomplimentary exchanges had taken place as they had made their way from the village, and Wulf's temper was already running hot. He had been prepared to listen tolerantly to the lad before putting his own case. After all, the boy's father had fought by his side at Hastings and the two families were long-time friends, but the accusations of unfair claims had worn his patience thin.

Dishevelled beard bristling, he strode forward, already launching into a belligerent speech, hoping he would win his case before the new lord quite caught the gist of the matter.

Wulf was not to know, however, of Raverre's preoccupation with Lisette. Before he had completed the first sentence he was silenced with an imperious gesture. Raverre rose to his feet again, his awesome height and build also silencing Edric, who was protesting as volubly.

"Is this how your lady conducts the manor court?" Raverre enquired disparagingly. "Or am I especially privileged?"

Even Wulf looked somewhat shamefaced at this. His whiskers quivered as he chomped his jaws up and down, but he prudently remained silent. Seeing his foe effectively subdued, Edric eyed Raverre with cautious approval.

Satisfied that order had been restored, Raverre turned to Bertrand.

"Tell these people to wait," he instructed. "If they have a case it had better be put to their mistress as well as myself. And, Father, I would like you to stay. I may have a further request to make of you."

Bertrand looked very thoughtful at this cryptic remark as he seated both parties at a safe distance from each other while Raverre disappeared up the stairs after Lisette. It looked as if the new master intended the girls to continue here for a while. Of course, the manor needed a mistress, and who better than a daughter of the house, but exactly what position did Raverre have in mind for her?

Lisette had not thought she could have cried so many tears as the pent-up emotions of the past year seemed to flood out in an unending, hopeless stream. It was only when she heard the trapdoor open that she made an effort to stem the flow, but she didn't look around.

"Go away, Marjory," she choked. "I must be by myself for a while more."

The only answer was the closing of the door and a firm tread. Startled, Lisette looked up to see Raverre watching her, his brows coming together in a quick frown as he saw how upset she was. Springing to her feet, she turned her back again, taking a few steps away from him. The tower roof seemed suddenly to have become very small.

"Come to gloat over your conquest, my lord?" she attacked huskily, brushing a hand across her eyes in an attempt to hide the evidence of her distress.

"No, my lady," he said seriously. Then a hint of laughter came into his voice. "Rather, 'tis your conquest. I have just been taken most soundly to task by Bertrand for my brutal treatment of you. And straight after we were interrupted by two quarrelling parties who, no doubt, will expect you to amend all, even though 'tis I who passes judgement. What else was I to do but come in search of you?"

Forgetting her reddened eyes and damp lashes, Lisette turned to face him.

Raverre leaned carelessly against the battlements, swinging her girdle in one hand. The sun glinted on his fair hair, turning it to gold, and his eyes held an expression of mingled laughter and appeal.

Lisette eyed him uncertainly, not quite trusting this sudden light-hearted manner after his biting anger.

"Are you asking for my help?" she queried hesitantly.

His expression sobered as quickly as it had lightened before, and he regarded her with a strangely considering look.

"Not only help," Raverre said slowly, knowing he must tread carefully. If his lady once suspected that he had become her slave when they had looked into each other's eyes yesterday, Raverre knew he would have lost any hope of winning her love. She would use his own feelings against him at every turn, and he could not fight them both.

Under his steady gaze, Lisette began to feel very wary. "What is your meaning, then?"

"An estate must have a strong master," he began. "I could bend the serfs to my will, but 'twould not serve my purpose to have hateful looks and rebellious mutterings follow me every time I go about my own lands. 'Twas not for conquest and loot that I came into England with William.''

As a look of disbelief crossed her face he said vehemently, "I speak truth, lady! William did not win himself a crown merely for the love of conquest. He wishes to make England a great part of his lands, to have some of his sons settle here and call their line English. 'Tis what I want also, and to this end, on learning that Lord Alaric had left three daughters orphaned and still unwed, I formed the intention of taking one of you to wife, that the estate would have a mistress known to the people, that our children would unite Norman and Saxon, and mayhap the period of reconciliation be reached sooner.''

"Oh, did you so intend?" Lisette interrupted indignantly, unable to keep silent any longer. "And no doubt we were to have no say in the matter at all. Take one of us to wife, indeed! Just to make your way easier! I could wish we were all ill-favoured or…or already betrothed, if only to confound you. Or did you think we might be willing to fall in with these careful plans?"

"Before I came here I knew nothing of you, lady, except what Bertrand let fall on our journey, which was little enough, God knows. In truth, I'm surprised you and Enide are still unwed. You must have had suitors aplenty, being the daughters of a landed Thegn and beautiful into the bargain.''

This last was said with a caressing look that swept Lisette from head to toe and back, making her colour rise with renewed indignation at his frank appraisal. Then, as Raverre's eyes lifted to her face, she glimpsed a flash of hot desire, swiftly veiled, and her heart lurched.

Men had looked at her before now with warm appreciation, but never had Lisette felt as though her flesh had been seared wherever their eyes touched. She felt hot all over.

"Enide was betrothed years ago," she said hurriedly, despising the nervous quiver in her voice. "To the son of one of my father's friends, but he was never heard of after Hastings."

"And yourself?" Raverre persisted, having seen the quick fear in her eyes and deciding her temper was the best cure for it. She would certainly reject the other remedies he had in mind. "Don't tell me men weren't falling over themselves to court you."

Lisette's eyes flashed fire again at this. "My father needed me here to oversee the manor. He was often absent. He said I was as good as any son would have been."

"So I have just been told," Raverre answered, smiling slightly at her vehemence and the obvious implication. "I did not mean to belittle your work, my lady. At home my father has many sons to fill his shoes; my mother and sisters would not be able to manage without them."

This mention of a home and family made Lisette look at him searchingly. "So you have sisters, my lord," she said slowly. "How would you feel, I wonder, if they were in the position I and *my* sisters now find ourselves?"

He looked taken aback for a moment at this unexpected challenge, then shrugged.

"'Tis the fate of all women, I suppose, to be under the authority of one man or another—a father, a husband." The caressing gleam came back. "If it must be a husband my sisters would soon become reconciled, even to an invader, if he treated them well. A woman thinks only of her home and family, after all."

"Not all of us are so compliant," Lisette answered hotly, too annoyed at this sweeping statement to notice his expression. "We Saxon women are used to more respect and independence, even under the law. We may inherit land, a widow cannot be made to remarry against her will—'' She stopped abruptly.

"None of you is a widow," Raverre pointed out gently.

"I suppose you think that will make it easier for you?" Lisette challenged. "And which one of us did you have in mind, pray tell?"

Raverre smiled teasingly again. "Which one? Well, let us consider a moment. By rights I should choose the Lady Enide, being the eldest, and your father's heiress—"

He got no further.

"You could not!" Lisette exclaimed, missing the lighter note in his voice in her sudden anxiety. "Oh, my lord, you must see how it is with her. After what she has suffered she could not become any man's wife. Oh, how can I make you understand? She could not endure it; I think her mind would be lost forever. And Catherine is but a babe, a child."

Forgetting her pride and her resolve never to yield in her fear for her sisters, Lisette impulsively flung herself on to her knees before Raverre in a sudden, graceful movement which caused her loose gown to billow about his feet. Her dark blue eyes, the long lashes still wet from weeping, pleaded with him as her hands clasped unconsciously.

"Oh, my lord, I beg of you, of your kindness, let us retire to the cloister. We could go to my aunt at Romsey Abbey. She would take us, I know."

As he looked down into the sweet face upturned to him Raverre had to repress an almost overwhelming desire to sweep Lisette up into his arms and hold her close. Ardent words rose in his throat. *Trust me. Let me care for you. Let me love you.*

What was he thinking? He'd frighten her away completely.

His hand clenched on Lisette's keys in abrupt impatience at having to move so slowly with her, and he cast the girdle aside. Then, leaning down from this great height and gently grasping her arms, he drew her to her feet, releasing her immediately, but retaining the memory of the feel of silken hair against his hands.

He had to clear his throat before he could speak.

"So," he said gruffly, "you would go on your knees before me, if only for your sisters' sake. But consider. Do you truly believe the Prioress would take all three of you without a dowry to enrich Holy Church? I do not; maybe you know her better."

Lisette looked away, unable to deny this assumption, but a ray of hope gleamed. "She would at least take Enide without a dowry, I think. My sister was named for her; she is her godchild. If my aunt knew how Enide has suffered she would be glad to accept her into the Order." She turned solemn eyes on Raverre again. "I ask nothing for myself; and for Catherine only that you wait until she is full grown before giving her in marriage. But for Enide, I beg you, send her to my aunt."

The opportunity to make her his own was there, and Raverre seized it without hesitation. "And if I grant this, would *you* come to me, a willing wife?"

Chapter Four

"*Me?*" Lisette squeaked in horror, aghast at the trap she had set for herself.

"Well, if Enide is to be cloistered, and Catherine too young, who else is there?" Raverre asked, not quite able to keep the note of satisfaction out of his voice. "Besides, you would retain your position as mistress of your home, which any fool can see means a great deal to you. Your sister would be safe under your care until she reaches marriageable age, and—I promise not to beat you if you behave yourself," he finished with a wicked grin.

That grin laid the flint to Lisette's temper.

The frustrations of the past two days rushed forcibly to her mind, mingling explosively with the fact that she could not see another way out of the dilemma facing her.

Her home had been taken. Her life had been threatened. She had been lashed by a tempest of rage and grief. And, as if that were not enough, she was now conscious of a *frisson* of excitement deep inside which, illogically, upset her more than all the rest. And the cause of this tumultuous storm of emotion stood there grinning at her! It was too much.

Lisette launched herself at Raverre like a spitting wildcat, aiming a blow at his face with her open hand.

"How dare you smile like that and mock me so?" she cried furiously. "How dare you?"

As swift as a hawk striking, Raverre captured her hands. Holding them behind her back with one of his own, he imprisoned Lisette in a close embrace which lifted her easily from the ground. His other hand encircled her slender neck, forcing her head up. But, though rendered helpless, she stared defiantly into those blue eyes not six inches from her own.

The teasing light slowly died out of Raverre's eyes as they gazed at each other, to be replaced by that intense, steady flame. Lisette was suddenly acutely aware of her heart racing wildly against the strong beat of his, and the feel of his hand on her throat. And heat. The wind blew coldly up here on the tower, but she felt surrounded by his warmth. She wanted to struggle...she wanted to melt...

She could not utter a word.

"What now, my fierce little Saxon warrior?" he asked softly. "If I loose you, will you stay quietly by my side, or try to scratch out my eyes?"

His gaze lowered to her mouth. Her lips parted, and Raverre felt her tremble in his arms. He managed to resist temptation. "Well, what shall it be?"

Lisette finally located her voice again. "Would you force me to wed you?" she asked shakily.

Raverre at once lowered her to the ground, setting her free except for the grip he kept on her hands.

"I would rather not drag you before a priest," he answered with a slightly crooked smile. "But you will be my wife. And, though you know but little of me, you can see the advantages as well as I."

"Aye, but marriage..." she faltered. How could she tell

him that the very word conjured up a frightening vision of
the power Raverre would hold over her? And yet he already
held that power, she thought confusedly.

But marriage! She would belong to him. Would have to
lie with him. A man she hardly knew. An enemy.

Desperately casting about in her mind for some alternative, Lisette had to acknowledge that she had very little
choice. True, she could refuse him, but what then would
become of them all? Even if, by some miracle, they managed to escape from the manor and discover the way to the
Abbey, Lisette had seen enough of Raverre to know they
would not get far before he caught them. And what if he
took revenge on her people?

On the other hand, if she married Raverre Enide would
be safe, and Catherine also, for a time. Besides, these things
could not be arranged in a hurry. Some other idea might
yet occur to her, but for now...

Lisette bent her head. "Very well, my lord." Her voice
was so low that Raverre barely heard the words. "I will
marry you."

He felt her hands quiver in his, and tightened his hold.
"I swear you will have no cause to regret that decision,
sweet lady," he said gently and, releasing her, stepped
away.

As Raverre stooped to retrieve her mistreated girdle Lisette tried to still her shaking limbs. Not regret her decision?
She was already regretting it. By what ill-begotten quirk of
fate was she now committed to marrying a Norman? She
must have been mad to agree. Hasty words of repeal hovered on her tongue.

They died unspoken as Raverre straightened and smiled
down into her eyes. He held out her girdle, but as Lisette
would have taken it Raverre suddenly captured her in the

circle of his arms and Lisette felt his hands, warm about her waist, as he fastened the silks.

He seemed to be taking an inordinate amount of time to replace the girdle. Why did his nearness disturb her so? She could hardly breathe. This close, he seemed enormous. She felt overwhelmed by his size and intimidating strength.

As the familiar weight of her keys settled at her side Lisette stepped back nervously, bumping into the parapet. Raverre quickly closed the distance between them, lightly clasping her arm.

"Careful," he murmured. "I don't want you falling over the battlements." He felt her tense under his hand, and added softly, "Don't fear me, little warrior."

Lisette glanced up. Those ice-blue eyes held so much warmth. She could almost believe there was nothing to fear from him. Almost.

"Did you have to kill that man?" she blurted out, surprising herself. She had sworn to herself never to broach the subject.

Raverre also looked surprised, but he didn't appear disturbed by her question.

"Of course. Didn't you hear what Will was saying?"

Lisette shook her head. "He spoke too quickly for me to follow."

So, my little dyed-in-the-wool Saxon speaks some Norman, thought Raverre. He let this go for the moment.

"Will accused you of luring him into the garden by witchcraft," he told her. "'Twas why he attacked you, trying to redeem himself with me."

Lisette stared at Raverre in sudden dismay, realising the extent of the danger Will had posed.

"Aye, you see now, don't you? Had I merely prevented Will from killing you he would have publicly accused you to explain away his actions."

"But you didn't believe him. Did you?" she asked tremulously.

"Of course I didn't," he answered gently. "But some of my men might have been more superstitious. They'd have been within their rights to demand your trial; something your people would have protested violently against, I'm sure. We don't need such a disaster."

"Oh." Lisette's voice was very subdued. Well, what other answer had she expected?

Raverre grinned. "And I didn't fancy seeing you drowned to prove your innocence, troublesome wench though you are," he added teasingly.

Lisette flushed. He hadn't read her mind, had he? She hurried into speech again.

"Then how did you explain…?"

"Will's death? My men thought he'd attacked me in anger at losing his post. It helped that we'd clashed previously over his attitude to the Saxons, even before we arrived. But he'd sworn to obey me, and was a good fighter—"

Raverre broke off and shrugged. "The best thing you can do now is to forget the whole incident."

Good advice, he thought wryly, knowing he'd never forget the chill that had gone through him when Lisette had screamed. Or the sight of her crouched at Will's feet, trying to protect her dog. That sight alone had nearly made him strangle Will with his bare hands.

"Come," he said. "'Tis cold up here. We had best return to the hall. I fear our combatants will not have wearied of the delay; however it may have cooled their ardour somewhat. Tell me what it's about."

Lisette gathered her scattered wits, trying not to feel too grateful for Raverre's sudden businesslike approach.

"Last month Edric's father died and he laid claim to the land, as was his right. But Wulf has been accusing Edric of neglect. His land adjoins Edric's strip, so 'twould be convenient for him to add it to his own holding.'' She looked up at Raverre appealingly. "But Edric has no other skill with which he can support his mother and sister. He doesn't want them reduced to landless slaves, and Wulf has enough for his needs.''

"From that explanation, I presume you've allowed Edric to keep the land. You realise, of course, that can't continue. I remember his record of bond work from yesterday. He's no more than a child. He'll never be able to plough three acres in spring, haul a load of wood and work two days each week as well as tend his own land. No doubt it *is* neglected. And did he pay the merchet due on taking up his inheritance?''

"Do you Normans ever think of anything but money?'' Lisette demanded, immediately put on the defensive. "Edric will grow older and stronger, and his family can help him.''

Raverre ignored this. "The sister looks of marriageable age,'' he said thoughtfully. "Her mother could come here to the manor. All we have to do is find something suitable for the boy.''

"But they'll own nothing if they lose the land.''

Lisette began to worry. This was exactly what she had feared. She saw the serfs as separate beings, part of the estate, yet individuals. But would Raverre? "Edric has his pride, you know.''

"His pride won't feed and clothe his mother and sister,'' Raverre retorted grimly. Then, as Lisette turned her head away to gaze frowningly into the distance, he gave a reluctant smile.

"I think we've argued every time we've had a conversation,'' he remarked, trying to lighten the atmosphere. Lisette didn't respond.

The smile reached Raverre's eyes and he stretched out a hand to cup her cheek, gently forcing her to face him again.

"Won't you trust me to come to a fair decision in this?" he questioned softly, his voice deepening to a husky caress as his hand savoured the silky texture of her skin. Not daring to test his control by moving a step closer, he murmured, "You can, you know."

Lisette's heart seemed to stop beating the moment Raverre touched her face. Unable to move away, she gazed up into his eyes, held captive by the warm understanding she saw there. A most unaccountable urge to let him take over the burden of command swept over her.

She was barely conscious of her agreement to support whatever decision he made. The staggering idea invading her head that Raverre was just the strong, protective male her intensely feminine little heart had once dreamed of drowned out everything.

She was only distantly aware of Raverre lifting the trapdoor, of descending the stairs, of returning to the hall. But, when Wulf and Edric stood before the high table, Lisette began to worry that she had let her people down rather badly.

Fortunately for her conscience, this feeling was short-lived. Further upsetting her preconceived notions about him, Raverre decreed that Edric must relinquish his claim, but would be taken into the household as a page, to be eventually trained as a squire should he prove loyal and diligent. Astonished delight replaced the shock on the boy's face, and he turned glowing eyes on Lisette, obviously thinking he had her to thank for this unlooked-for elevation in status.

Sobered by the lengthy delay in presenting his case, Wulf was equally amenable to the edict that the land would become his on condition that a marriage be arranged between Edric's sister and one of Wulf's brawny sons. In this way

Alfrida and her mother would be provided for, without being regarded as objects of charity.

So thankful was Lisette for a solution which seemed to please everyone, and which, she admitted privately, would not have occurred to her, that she had a sudden flash of understanding of the more positive side to Norman feudalism.

Then her emotional seesaw dipped the other way again as she heard Raverre announce their betrothal. Taking her hand, he led her up to Father Edwin.

"Father, your lady has done me the honour of granting me her hand in marriage. Would you hear our betrothal vows?"

"God save you, my son. 'Tis a day for betrothals, I vow. A happy day for Ambray."

But, despite these transports of delight, the little priest avoided Lisette's eyes. Under the sconce lights a light film of sweat gleamed on his tonsure.

Father Edwin can no more refuse Raverre than I can, she thought. And who can blame him?

She started nervously as Raverre took her hand. He looked into her eyes.

"I, Alain of Raverre, plight thee, Lisette of Ambray, my troth, as God is my witness." He crossed himself.

Steadying herself with a deep breath, Lisette repeated the vow. But her voice faltered at the end, suddenly aware, as she saw the various speculative glances from those present, that a way out might not be so easy to find after all.

She was further dismayed to hear Raverre ask a startled Father Edwin to prepare for their marriage the following week. The priest drew Raverre aside.

"Next week, my lord? Surely such haste is unseemly."

"Of course 'tis unseemly," protested Lisette, following them. She glanced up at Raverre. His eyes held a strangely wary expression, but it was gone so quickly that Lisette thought she must have been mistaken. "Please, my lord. We don't...I hardly know...I need more time," she stammered.

"This is not the time for long betrothals, my lady," Raverre said curtly. "Neither of us needs approval or consent by another party, and I see no reason to wait."

"The King?" she questioned faintly, grasping at any straw.

"I had his consent before I left Winchester," he answered, putting an end to this hope for a delay. "Indeed, William will be sure to visit us before long. He is no idle ruler, but one who travels constantly, overseeing all for himself. And I would have you safely wed before he gets here," Raverre finished grimly.

The tone of voice left no doubt as to his meaning. Father Edwin looked shocked.

"Surely the King would not..." He broke off, glancing worriedly at Lisette.

"Not William, no. But he does not travel alone, and his soldiers are men like any others. Men, moreover, who have been without their wives for some time. And I don't need the added trouble of defending an unmarried girl from their attentions."

"Indeed?" asked Lisette, incensed. She turned to Father Edwin. "Go ahead and arrange for the wedding, Father," she instructed imperiously. "We certainly don't wish to cause my lord any *more* trouble."

Head high, she swept both men a regal curtsy. Ignoring Raverre's amused expression, she brushed past him and went to sit by the fire with her sisters, realising too late that she had just played into her tormentor's hands.

Catherine's artless excitement over this turn of events inwardly enraged her further. After supper that night Lisette had to bite her tongue to keep from berating her sister for gazing up at Raverre with childish hero-worship. All the way through the meal.

"And, what's more, he is not above encouraging her," Lisette said furiously to Marjory the next afternoon as they scattered fresh rushes over the floor of the hall. "She is in positive thrall that Raverre has promised her a new mare of her own to ride. 'Tis bribery, no less!"

The rushes flew about in all directions under Lisette's agitated hand, and Marjory gave her a shrewd look.

"Mayhap Catherine sees further than yourself, my sweet," she said. "You see a Norman Baron who knows what he wants and takes it. An enemy, you say, and hate him accordingly. But some of us see a man who has been fair in victory. A man who can be gentle and generous when he chooses, though fierce in anger, I have no doubt. Why, did you know that the serfs no longer have to pay to use the manor ovens? They may bake their own bread, which will mean less coin in Raverre's coffers."

Lisette remembered her gibe at Raverre about money. "They still have to bring their corn to the manor mill to have it ground," she argued perversely.

Marjory clucked impatiently, waving an admonishing finger at Lisette. "They've been doing that since your grandfather's time. And did Raverre punish Siward? Has he been harsh with you and your sisters? Is he milking the estate of what little is left? Quite the contrary!

"Besides," she added, with purely feminine satisfaction, "He is young and strong, and handsome enough to assail any maid's heart and win it. You may be sure there were many such across the sea in Normandy."

"Well, he can go back there and marry one of *them*," was the tart response to this remark. Flinging the last of the rushes down, Lisette marched outside, hoping to find some much needed solitude.

The bailey was sunny and peaceful. Two soldiers lounged idly in the gateway. A half-dozen more were gathered in the field across the stream, engaged in archery practice. The steady plunk of arrows hitting the butts was oddly soothing. Occasionally a cheer went up as one of the Normans aimed true.

At least they're practising on targets and not Saxons, thought Lisette as she wandered aimlessly towards the stables. She wondered why she felt so low.

"My lady!"

At the muffled exclamation Lisette jumped, almost tripping over a deerhound, sunning itself in the stable doorway.

"Siward? Holy Saints, how you startled me."

"Hush, my lady." Siward beckoned from the stable. "In here, where we may speak without being heard."

Lisette obeyed. "Why, what is it?" She glanced about as she spoke. The roof had been newly thatched and fresh straw laid in the stalls. This evidence of Raverre's outlay on the manor made her feel worse.

Siward was engaged in checking the hoofs of a powerful grey mare. Several other horses looked on curiously.

"Are these the only horses in the stable?" asked Lisette, surprised. "Where are the others? For that matter, where are the soldiers?"

"Out hunting, supposedly," answered Siward with a significant look.

"Supposedly? What does that mean? Are you talking in riddles, Siward? Let me tell you, I'm in no mood for them. The Normans have been hunting every day."

"Have they?"

"There you go again. What else would they be doing?"

"I'd like to know, my lady. They've ridden out each day,

118 *Gentle Conqueror*

'tis true. But have you noticed the number of empty game bags for so many men? Methinks 'tis unlikely they hunt game every time.''

Lisette looked up at the young giant in consternation. "What, then?"

Siward shrugged. "I know not. But I thought you should be warned. Perhaps they look for runaway slaves, or masterless men who've left the army and are still free."

"Here?"

"Such men are everywhere, my lady. And in the forest could stay undetected and free for a long time. But I'm not saying 'tis so." The blacksmith's usually sombre face lightened unexpectedly in a rare smile. "Perhaps the Normans are poor hunters."

Lisette gave him a sceptical look. "In this forest? Even Enide could hit something if it stayed still long enough. Do you know, Siward, I think I shall go riding?"

Siward looked alarmed at this thoughtful remark. "I didn't mean for you to go probing into this, my lady. 'Tis enough that you be warned. My Lord Raverre is a just man. Perhaps you could ask him what is going on."

"Ask *him?*" she queried incredulously, forgetting that she was referring to her future husband. "The wretch is not likely to tell me anything. Here, Siward, saddle up this horse for me."

"Now, my lady," Siward began, in the minatory tones he had used when a very young Lisette had demanded to handle the bellows in the forge. "You can't just ride out of here as though on a jaunt. What of the soldiers? Besides, the horse needs shoeing."

"Good. We'll take her to the forge, and I'll leave from there. Simple."

"Simple? Raverre would have my head on a pike. And I wouldn't blame him," added Siward objectively.

Lisette looked thoughtful. "You're right," she said at last. "But at least let me walk to the forge with you, Siward. I need some exercise, and we can put our heads together and see if we can find some answers."

Siward agreeing to this, they set off. The guards at the gate, seeing her with the blacksmith, gave Lisette no more than a cursory glance, and the archers were too busy arguing about increasing the distance of the targets to pay them much heed.

Lisette wondered if Raverre would allow her to shoot at the butts some day. No wonder she felt so unlike herself. She was not used to being confined indoors with little to do.

"Things have come to a pretty pass when a short walk along this rutted track cheers me so," she commented.

Siward sent her a sympathetic glance over the horse's withers as the mare clip-clopped between them.

"Soon there won't be so many soldiers here, my lady," he assured her. "And it will be safe for you to venture out. Raverre's knights will be settled at the other villages and their men will rotate the guard duty here, I'm told. The others return to the army when they escort Lady Enide to Romsey."

"You sound content to have it so, Siward."

"'Tis difficult to despise a man as just as Raverre," commented Siward thoughtfully. "And if you can marry him to benefit the estate, my lady, then I can serve him for the same cause."

Four blasts from a horn resounded faintly from the forest.

"Well, some of the soldiers are hunting," remarked Lisette, noting the direction of the sound. "They've brought down a hart."

She thought guiltily of the scheme she was hatching. If the men really were hunting she might be courting trouble for no reason. Then determination took hold. The Normans were up to something, and she was going to find out what it was.

The day was growing cloudy, a forerunner of the colder autumn weather to come. Leaves fluttered to the ground in gently eddying circles, those still clinging to their branches creating a fiery blaze of red and amber, a brilliant contrast of colour against the brown fields and misty blue-green of the distant hills.

The grey mare pranced nervously along a well-worn forest path, unaccustomed to the light weight on her back and the strange guidance of a rope. Lisette was kept so busy preventing the horse from shying at every floating leaf that she didn't see the huge black destrier emerge from a side-path until she was nearly on top of him. The mare plunged to an abrupt stop, almost unseating her rider.

Lisette stared guiltily into angry ice-blue eyes.

"What in God's name are you doing on that horse?" Raverre thundered incredulously.

The mare side-stepped, on edge and tossing her head. Lisette grabbed a handful of mane and hung on. Raverre grabbed the rope halter and hung on.

"Sweet Jesus! You haven't even bridled Phantom, let alone saddled her. Just what do you think you're doing?" he demanded, still angry but lowering his voice. Despite his shock at seeing Lisette on the most nervous horse in the stable, sudden admiration flashed into Raverre's eyes.

"Trying to find out what *you're* doing," she retorted crossly. Why did the man have to turn up whenever she didn't want him?

"I've been inspecting the village at Wiford," he said mildly. "You knew that."

"Do you think we're all blind?" Lisette demanded.

"Your men are out hunting every day, but 'tis not game they hunt, is it, my lord?"

Raverre eyed her thoughtfully. "Siward was supposed to be shoeing this horse. Perhaps you can explain why he apparently saw fit to allow you to ride her instead." He laid one arm across his saddle, leaning forward to pin Lisette with a narrow-eyed stare. "And did my men turn their backs while you rode through the gates?" he asked in ominous tones.

Lisette tossed her head. "They were too busy showing off their marksmanship," she derided, consigning the Normans to Raverre's retribution without a qualm.

"And Siward?" he prompted forebodingly.

"'Twas not his fault. The mare was at the forge and I...I borrowed her while Siward was busy stoking the fire," she explained defiantly. "You could hardly expect him to give chase on foot."

"Borrowed?" he repeated. Then he grinned unexpectedly. "Why don't I have any trouble believing that? I can only praise the Saints that I'm on Lanzelet, or no doubt you would have borrowed *him.*"

Lisette breathed a sigh of relief. "Is that his name? What does it mean?"

"'Tis Norman for Lancelot, and aye, I've heard the legend. Come on."

"Where are we going?" she asked, curious.

"Back to the manor. Where else?" Raverre nudged Lanzelet to a walk. Phantom fell in beside him. "If you think I'm going to permit you to continue with this foolish idea of yours you can think again."

Lisette subsided into frustrated silence. Not only had she been defeated, she still didn't know what the Normans were doing out in the forest every day. Raverre had ignored her challenge about his men's activities as though it had never been uttered. Resentment drew her brows together.

Raverre glanced sideways at Lisette's frowning countenance, remembering that he had wanted to see what she looked like when she smiled. She hadn't really had a lot to smile about in the past few days, he reflected.

"I suppose you know that Bertrand set off for Winchester this morning," he remarked. "Along with your shopping list, he is carrying a message to your aunt to inform her that Lady Enide has permission to enter the cloister."

Lisette glared at him. "You're not going to tell me, are you?"

Raverre reined in at the edge of the wasteland. A distant grove of trees separated the manor fields from this rough open area, where logs and dead branches lay in scattered profusion. Hillocks of grass concealed numerous rabbit holes, and stunted bushes and brushwood abounded.

"Do *you* trust *me?*" Raverre challenged quietly.

Lisette searched his face. Did she trust him?

His mouth curled sardonically at her long silence. "No. I didn't think so."

Sensing the tension in the rider on her back, Phantom moved restlessly, and Raverre reached out a quieting hand.

"I want your promise that you won't ride my horses again," he said severely. "I've asked Bertrand to keep an eye out for good mounts. He knows what you can handle. Phantom is safe while I'm with you, but she is a strong horse and still easily startled; you couldn't hold her if she bolted."

To confusion and a strange regret that she had not answered Raverre immediately was added fiery resentment.

"Oh, you think so?" Lisette demanded, haughtily. "Watch this!" And before Raverre could stop her she wheeled the big mare, put her at the solid log immediately in front of them, clearing it with feet to spare, and took off towards the trees at a headlong gallop.

Cursing, Raverre followed suit, thundering after her. Even carrying the greater weight, Lanzelet would have caught Phantom, but Raverre had to consider the dangers of rabbit holes to his horse's legs, whereas Lisette knew the rough terrain. She bent low over Phantom's withers, revelling in the power and speed of the big horse as they seemed to fly over the ground, clearing every obstacle as if it did not exist. The wind rushed past her face, whipping colour into her cheeks, and her hair flew out behind her.

The small wood came nearer, and she pulled on the rope to slow the mare. Phantom, however, was enjoying herself. Without a bridle Lisette only just managed to pull her in to a canter before she found herself among the trees, guiding her mount unerringly until she finally succeeded in halting on the other side.

Raverre, seeing his quarry disappear into the trees, swore violently as a hideous picture of Lisette dashed against a solid oak sprang into his mind. He emerged into the field still at a gallop, almost overshooting Lisette, who sat calmly waiting, while Phantom lipped the ground as if she'd never had anything further on her equine mind.

Relief that Lisette was safe inevitably gave way to blazing anger at her recklessness. Dismounting, Raverre strode back to her, looking furious. Grabbing her arm, he yanked her off the mare's back, shaking her until her hair, already loosened by her wild ride, swirled about her face.

"You stupid little idiot!" he roared. "Don't you know better than to ride through trees at that speed? What were you trying to do, kill yourself?"

But Lisette was too elated to be chastened. Shaking her hair back out of her face, she laughed up at him. Suddenly she felt more alive than she had for months, and Raverre's fury had no power to subdue her.

Phantom, however, startled by the angry voice, flung up her head nervously, dancing away as Raverre, hurriedly releasing Lisette, made a lunge for the halter. Then, with a defiant series of snorts at him as he tried to catch her, she cantered off in the direction of her stable.

Raverre turned back to Lisette, who had collapsed in helpless mirth at the horse's antics. He eyed her ominously for a moment. Then, as she looked back at him, her eyes dancing, hair tumbled about her shoulders, and those two mischievous dimples hovering near her mouth, Raverre felt his anger melt away.

She had been lovely before, he thought, but, lit up now with the sudden glow of happiness, her radiant beauty shone so brightly that everything around her seemed to pale into insignificance.

Blind to his surroundings, forgetting every other emotion save the longing to have her love him, Raverre slowly walked back to Lisette, to stand so close that she had to tilt her head right back to look up at him. His hand lifted to lightly touch the vulnerable line of her throat.

"Well," he said, his voice husky with repressed desire, "I wanted to see you smile, and now I have. You are indeed fair, sweet mistress."

His hand fell to his side and he stepped back, before the temptation to tumble her down into the soft meadow grass grew any stronger. He couldn't destroy the faint beginnings of trust behind the questions in her eyes.

So absorbed were they in each other that both failed to sense the presence of a third. In the shadows at the edge of the wood a darker shadow stirred. So close to the protective bole of an oak that the form of a man was barely discernible. The shadow lengthened slowly as the man moved back towards the wasteland, drawing his bow.

"Can Saxon and Norman trust each other?" Raverre asked.

"I...I'm going to marry you," she stammered, wondering if that was really an answer.

Raverre heard the shaky breath she drew in. By marrying him she was going to trust him in the most intimate way a woman could trust a man, and he knew that sudden realisation had frightened her.

"My men are searching for a gold ingot," he said abruptly. "Stolen from the treasury at Winchester several weeks ago."

Lisette's eyes widened in surprise, but Raverre saw her quickly grasp the issue.

"You think this ingot will be taken to safety in Wales? No. 'Twould be there by now."

Raverre nodded. "We've orders to search the manors and villages along the border. But 'tis such an unwieldy thing that I think it unlikely to be far from Winchester. Gold is heavy. 'Twould need at least twelve men to lift it, and to transport it out of the country would be well nigh impossible. You've heard nothing of such a robbery?"

"Nothing. And we surely would if such a large group of travellers had passed through any of the villages. They'd have a wagon and horses, too. No, we've heard nothing. Nor seen any—"

A swift rush of wind was the only warning Raverre had. It was barely enough. Acting from instinct rather than knowledge, he shoved Lisette to one side.

The arrow whizzed past his left shoulder as she fell, and Raverre swung round, sword drawn, his narrowed gaze keenly searching the trees. There was no movement, and he couldn't leave Lisette to go after the sniper. Reaching

Lanzelet in three strides, Raverre grabbed his hunting horn from the saddle and blew a single deafening blast. A moment later an answering blast echoed from the forest about half a mile away.

Slinging the horn back over the saddle, Raverre turned to help Lisette to her feet. His blood froze.

She still lay where his thrust had sent her, the arrow protruding from her upper arm. Then, even as he saw that she was not fatally hit, Lisette stirred. He was beside her in seconds, tearing away the sleeve of her gown.

"Lie still, sweetheart. I'll have to get this out before the shock wears off and the pain starts."

He flicked a glance at her face. She looked dazed, but this time her eyes held utter trust.

Still speaking, Raverre laid his hand over Lisette's shoulder, bearing down strongly. She felt her arm go numb.

"Thank your Saint, whoever she is, that 'tis only a flesh wound," he said through his teeth. "The arrow was nearly spent. Only the tip of the barb broke the skin."

Grasping the shaft with his other hand, he pulled swiftly. Lisette gasped. Her face went white, but her lips parted in a shaky smile.

"'Tis St Elizabeth," she said faintly.

Raverre made a rough sound in his throat and pulled her into his arms, holding her tightly. She should object, Lisette thought, but instead she turned her face into his shoulder. Her hand came up to grip his tunic. She could feel his fingers, warm against the soft skin at her nape, stroking gently. Strange, he seemed to be shaking slightly. No, 'twas the ground shaking.

Lisette raised her head as several Normans rode across the field at the gallop. It must have been the vibration of so many hoofs causing the strange tremor she'd felt. Raverre would not tremble. The man was unshakeable. Look at him. As cool as a summer rain shower as he released her and bound her arm with her torn sleeve.

Lifting her into his arms, Raverre rose to his feet as horses slithered to a stop all around them.

"My God, sir!" exclaimed Gilbert, taking in Lisette's pale face and bloodstained gown. "What happened?"

"A sniper," said Raverre briefly, jerking his head at the arrow on the ground. "You can tell your men to search the forest, but he'll be long gone."

"I'm all right, Gilbert," assured Lisette as the young Norman turned a shocked countenance to her. "'Tis only a scratch."

Raverre growled something under his breath. It didn't sound very agreeable, but he was gentle enough as he lifted her on to Lanzelet's back. Swinging up behind her, he settled Lisette in the crook of his arm and gathered up the reins.

"There's little time before sunset," he advised Gilbert. "But see if you can find any tracks nearer the wasteland. He fired from quite a distance."

"Sir!"

With a flourish Gilbert wheeled his horse and was off. Lisette saw him raise an arm in a sweeping gesture, signalling his men to spread out, before Raverre turned Lanzelet and started at a sedate walk back to the manor.

She was glad to rest her head on his shoulder when he drew her back against him.

"All right?" he murmured. His lips brushed her hair, but Lisette was too comfortable to protest. She nodded silently, and his arm tightened. She felt safe.

That was strange. Safe with an enemy? Lisette thought drowsily of trust again. Why hadn't she felt able to tell Raverre she trusted him, when in many ways she did? She trusted him to keep his word about Enide. She would trust him with her life. But what of her heart?

Lisette shivered. Why had that thought intruded? She didn't have to trust Raverre with her heart. It was perfectly safe from him.

"Easy, little warrior," he soothed, feeling her movement. "I know your arm is probably stinging like the Devil."

"'Tis not that," she denied. "I scarce feel it."

"What, then? You tremble. Are you cold?" He drew her closer.

"No, no," she said, becoming more agitated as his warmth enfolded her. "I...I just wondered who..."

"Someone whose aim is dangerously bad. 'Twas more likely meant for me than you."

"Even so, if you hadn't pushed me..." She turned her head to look up at him. "You were so quick."

Raverre slanted an amused glance down at her. "I've had enough arrows whistling about my head to recognise one coming when I hear it," he said. "You'll always be safe with me, little warrior."

"Why do you call me that?"

He chuckled. "It suits you. But if you don't like it you'll have to lay down your arms, and obey me."

She liked him in this mood, thought Lisette. Even though he was a Norman. Her enemy. But she was too tired to worry about that now. She could be a warrior tomorrow.

"I don't want to fight any more," she said wearily, resting against his shoulder again. "I feel safe with you today."

"Considering that's what I wanted, I find myself extremely inconsistent," Raverre muttered. There was no response.

He glanced down at the dark head against his shoulder

and smiled ruefully. If he had to undergo the tortures of the damned to have Lisette as warm and trusting in his arms when she wasn't hurt, then he'd do it.

This praiseworthy intention lasted until they rode into the bailey to find Phantom standing peacefully outside the stable. Recalling his fear for Lisette's safety, Raverre fixed his men with an intimidating glare.

Siward was already exhorting the soldiers to search for Lisette, but he broke off when he saw her.

"My lady! What have you done to yourself now?" He sounded more resigned than worried. "My lord, please believe that had I—"

Raverre dismounted. "Spare me, Siward. I'm quite sure you, along with everyone else at Ambray, have absolutely no control over your lady. That situation, however, is about to change."

He lifted Lisette to the ground, smiling at her affronted expression. She was obviously starting to feel better.

But the glare returned twofold when Raverre turned on his men. "Dolts!" he began furiously.

"'Twas not their fault," admitted Lisette reluctantly. "They thought I was merely walking to the forge with Siward."

Raverre gave her a hard stare. "'Tis more than time someone took you in hand," he said grimly, picking her up.

"Put me down!" Lisette protested, annoyed at this arrogant treatment. "I can walk. My arm is not even bleeding any more."

"Go shoe the horse, Siward," instructed Raverre, ignoring Lisette. "And don't turn your back on your mistress again."

"Aye, my lord," responded Siward, grinning at Lisette's indignant face.

"And if you ever do anything so reckless again," Raverre threatened softly, carrying his betrothed up the stairs, "you won't escape so lightly. Now, do I have your pledge that you won't borrow my horses?"

Lisette studied the determined set of Raverre's mouth. "Aye, my lord," she said demurely as he set her down outside the tower room.

Marjory hurried forward, exclaiming in startled concern. Then, as she urged her mistress into the room, Lisette looked back at Raverre with an impish smile.

"But you will at least admit that I can ride."

The door shut on Raverre's resigned face.

A few miles away to the south, deep in the forest, the watcher in the trees hurried towards his secret haven. He smiled grimly to himself. He knew this forest like his own hand, and had left those thick-headed Normans going around in circles like dogs in a bear-pit.

'Twas a pity his arrow had struck the girl instead of its intended victim, but her wound had been slight. And why had she been so snug with a Norman Baron anyway? Oh, yes. He had much to tell his master of what he had seen this day.

Chapter Five

"'Tis as well you mend quickly, my love," remarked Marjory two days later. She rolled up the linen bandage in her hand. "You have no more need of this."

Lisette glanced down at her arm. She had been more stunned at being hit than badly hurt by the arrow, and only a faint puckering of the skin showed where the barb had entered. Even that would fade in time.

Lisette donned her gown. "Does this mean I may now walk farther than the hall?" she asked with gentle raillery.

"Now, sweeting, you know 'twas for your own good that my lord confined you to the manor. He was concerned for you."

"Hah! He was concerned that I'd find out he was interrogating every man on the estate. As if one of our serfs could lay his hand on a bow. The only good that has come of it is the delay of an indecently hasty wedding while he hunts further afield."

"And how do you know that, pray?"

"Oswy told me."

"That half-wit!" scoffed Marjory, beginning to braid Lisette's hair. "What does he know of weddings?"

"Hush, Marjory. Oswy can't help being simple. Why,

even Raverre saw immediately that the poor boy is harmless. He said such people are usually good with animals,
and put him to work in the stable.''

"Raverre sees a lot," cautioned Marjory. "So 'ware how
you flout his orders."

"I am still mistress of this manor," flashed Lisette.
"And I have every right to be in the stable talking to Oswy.
Catherine spends half her days there and Raverre doesn't
object."

Marjory tied the end of Lisette's braid with a faded ribbon, giving a rather more vigorous tug than was strictly
necessary. "Catherine wasn't hit by an arrow," she pointed
out grimly.

"Tush! A scratch. I feel perfectly well, and am off to
the village before the serfs begin to think I'm the weakling
Raverre considers me." This last was said rather defiantly.

"As you wish, my love," was the soothing reply.

Expecting an argument, Lisette stared at her old nurse
suspiciously. Marjory returned the stare with a bland smile.

Of course, as she paid a visit to the cottars every week,
perhaps Marjory had thought better of protesting the performance of this duty, Lisette decided. But as she started
for the village, she puzzled, nevertheless, over her nurse's
calm acceptance. And, now she thought about it, the guards,
too, had not seemed particularly worried about her being
outside the gates, and alone. Glancing back, Lisette soon
discovered why.

She was being followed.

Several yards back, a Norman soldier trod resignedly
along the road after her. Wrapping her thin mantle more
securely around herself against the cool wind, Lisette
waited, tapping an impatient foot.

"My lady," the man greeted her politely when he
reached her.

She had noticed him at table, Lisette remembered. He was considerably older than Raverre, a stocky, grizzled Knight who had seen many years of hard service in William's army.

"You are following me," she accused.

"Escorting you, my lady," he corrected stolidly. "My lord's orders."

"Indeed?" Lisette's voice was icy. "Your name, sir?"

"Richard de Somery, mistress."

"Well, Sir Richard, you may tell your lord that I declined your escort to the village. 'Tis not needed."

"That's a matter of opinion, my lady," de Somery argued gruffly. "My lord thinks of your safety. 'Tis not known for sure whom that arrow was meant to strike."

"That is foolish talk," said Lisette scornfully. "Why would anyone wish to harm me?"

"You are marrying a Norman Baron, madam. Some might think that cause enough."

"But my people here are pleased." Lisette was indignant. "'Twould be as easy to suspect one of you Normans."

De Somery seemed unmoved by this charge. His expressionless face studied Lisette dispassionately. Rather as though she were a cockroach which had suddenly crawled on to his trencher, she thought.

"*You* seem to disapprove," she added pointedly.

"'Tis not my place to approve or not, lady. The marriage is necessary. You'll learn to respect Baron de Raverre."

De Somery didn't waste his time wondering if love was involved in the match his lord was planning. Of course, the Lady Lisette was strikingly beautiful with her delicate features, dark hair and deep iris-blue eyes, framed by those impossibly long lashes. However, a man merely considered himself fortunate if his wife was physically attractive, and

closed his eyes to her imperfections or, more likely, took
a mistress if she was not.

De Somery knew that Raverre would have married one
of the girls to further his plans, regardless of their looks.
He understood such practicalities. What he couldn't fathom
was why his lord had chosen this argumentative wench instead of the more docile Enide.

"That may be," retorted Lisette, "but he will also learn
to respect me. Where is he? Still hunting for your missing
gold?"

"He rides the fields, my lady," explained de Somery,
stoically polite. "He would have the serfs know him, and
he them."

"Well, I also have business to attend to," Lisette stated
firmly, determined to continue with her plans for the morning.

Voicing no objection, de Somery fell into step beside
her. And remained at her side all the while she exchanged
greetings and gossip with the village women.

He didn't speak to her again, but while she was occupied
with the bee-keeper Lisette noticed him chatting pleasantly
with Siward in the doorway of the forge. It seemed everyone was welcoming the Normans with open arms. Even the
bees were producing more honeycomb, she was told with
pride. Feeling strangely bereft of support, Lisette turned her
footsteps homeward.

Still silent, de Somery accompanied her, leaving her with
a brusque nod when they re-entered the bailey.

"Accursed soldiers," she muttered as she reached the
empty stable, intending to challenge Raverre the instant he
returned. "Respect Baron de Raverre indeed. How dare he
have me followed, and on such a weak pretext? More likely
he thinks I might run away."

Lisette found herself so hurt that Raverre might mistrust

her to the extent of having her followed that uneasiness rippled through her. It was not the first time she had felt that icy finger of warning whenever she thought of him. She had even come dangerously close to liking the man the other day, and made haste to remind herself that he was arrogant, annoyingly dictatorial and obviously thought her a weak creature in constant need of safeguarding, if de Somery's explanation had been truthful.

An insidious suspicion that she didn't altogether dislike Raverre's protectiveness sent Lisette hurrying out of the stable again. To emerge straight under the nose of Lanzelet, who, fortunately, had halted and seemed to be looking down at her enquiringly with his great brown eyes.

Raverre dismounted, running a hand down the satiny neck of his destrier.

Thinking Lisette might have been startled by almost colliding with the huge animal, he commented, "Don't be fooled by Lanzelet's size, my lady. Fearless though he must be in battle, he has no meanness in his nature. He would carry you as safely as any lady's palfrey, though he would be too strong for you if anything upset him."

Like his master, thought Lisette, so instantly that she hoped Raverre couldn't read her mind.

He led Lanzelet into the stable as he spoke, taking off the heavy saddle.

"Why are you having me followed?" she demanded, his preoccupation with the horse steadying her nervousness.

She regretted this impulsive question immediately. Raverre turned his full attention on her, his face very serious. Lisette felt her heartbeat quicken. Those light, glittering eyes seemed to look straight into her soul.

"I would not keep you imprisoned, sweetheart, but I will protect my own."

Lisette occupied herself with stroking Lanzelet's black

velvet muzzle. It was better than looking into eyes that
made her want to forget who and what—

"I stand in no danger from my own people," she managed to say. Indeed, she felt more endangered at this very
moment. She should leave the stable. If only her heart
would not beat so fast she would be able to think, to protest
at Raverre's orders.

Raverre watched Lisette murmur to Lanzelet, the big
horse bending his head to her caressing hand.

Lucky devil, he thought, and a pang of longing to feel
the touch of her hand himself made him move restlessly,
sending a broom skidding across the floor. Lanzelet, startled by the loud clatter, threw up his head, knocking Lisette
off balance. She would have fallen, but Raverre grasped
her around the waist to steady her then, unable to help
himself, gently drew her into his arms.

Lisette looked up in startled enquiry, her hands coming
to rest against the solid wall of his chest.

"What—?"

"Hush," he murmured, holding her eyes with his. He
slowly lowered his mouth to hers. "I would not have you
entirely ignorant of me before we're wed, little maid."

The moment Lisette realised Raverre's intent she stiffened in alarm, but, though part of her wanted to resist,
another part, deeper, hidden, was strangely reassured by his
words. She remembered the warm sense of safety she had
known in his arms before, and as his lips brushed hers
Lisette gave in to the sudden questioning in her mind, relaxing against him. And unleashing a storm.

Raverre was lost. As he felt her slender body suddenly
pliant in his arms, when he had expected resistance, his
control splintered. Crushing Lisette against him in an iron
hold that made her gasp, he covered her mouth with his,
kissing her so deeply and fiercely that she grew faint with

the waves of half-frightened excitement shaking her body. Where had safety gone? There was none in the yielding weakness seeping through her limbs. She couldn't even fight, but only cling desperately to him in an attempt to hold on to her shattered senses.

Raverre broke the kiss at last, breathing hard and staring down into her face with such naked desire blazing in his eyes that Lisette was overwhelmed with dismay. How had her innocent curiosity unleashed such barely controlled passion? How had she submitted so easily? And to a Norman. He would think her wanton, shameless.

"Don't look at me like that," he ordered hoarsely. "By the Saints, sweetheart, I'm only human."

"I'm sorry…" she faltered, only wanting to escape. He was blaming her already.

Wrenching her eyes from Raverre's with an effort, she became aware that she was still clinging to his tunic for balance, and, releasing the fabric as if it carried the plague, she whirled about and fled from the stable.

Raverre took a quick step after her, but paused, knowing reassurance would be useless. Not realising that Lisette had been more shocked by her own behaviour than his, he thought he had frightened her with the unrestrained ardour of his embrace.

He cursed as he remembered that her normal girlish apprehension of men had probably been exaggerated by the attack on her mother. But when she had remained so willingly in his arms his intention to be gentle until he had overcome her mistrust had shattered along with his control.

As he remembered how soft and yielding her body had felt against the hardness of his own an impatient groan of frustration escaped him, and he struck the stable wall with his clenched fist, making Lanzelet snort in disapproval of such foolish human behaviour.

"What is it about her?" Raverre asked the great war-horse. "She's wilful, stubborn, and argues with me whenever she gets the chance. Yet I could no more leave her to marry some frivolous Norman wench than fly through the air." He eyed Lanzelet in sudden wry amusement. "And now she's got me talking to my horse.

"Well," he continued, after a thoughtful pause, "every man has his weakness, and that tormenting little mixture of Saxon and Celtic womanhood is mine." Lanzelet flicked an ear forward in agreement. "But one thing I know well," Raverre told the horse. "She is a woman after my own heart, and if I can win hers I will win more than a meek female who would run my household, produce my children, and would bore me in less than a se'nnight."

The memory of her helpless submission in Raverre's arms haunted Lisette constantly the next day, and she avoided him as much as possible. It wasn't difficult. Whether the Normans were searching for gold or snipers, Lisette only saw Raverre at mealtimes, where the presence of others provided a shield against any advances he might have been inclined to make.

When he seemed more disposed to ignore her Lisette was torn between relief and a strange feeling of pique. She knew Raverre was only marrying her for convenience, but did he have to make it quite so plain? The disturbing idea that he might consider her passivity to be a sign of surrender was enough to goad Lisette into lingering with him after supper during the following evenings, to prove that she wasn't afraid of him.

Which was precisely what Raverre intended.

He encouraged her to question him about his plans for the land, the castle, and anything else that came to mind. Whenever a dispute arose among the serfs or villagers, though Lisette admitted to herself that Raverre's judge-

ments were fair and sound, she took a perverse delight in
challenging them and arguing with him later.

Raverre let her argue and even once or twice agreed with
her, lounging back in his chair with careless male grace
and watching Lisette under lowered lids as she paced back
and forth, propounding her father's pet theories for the
management of vast land-holdings and the treatment of
serfs.

However, when the disputes involved Saxons against
Raverre's men, he would order Lisette to the tower room,
where she had to continue her pacing, frustrated at not
knowing what was going on below.

She was engaged in this fruitless exercise three days
later, when Enide answered a knock on the door to find a
scared-looking cook demanding entrance.

"Save you, Wat," greeted Lisette. "You look as though
the very fiends of hell are on your tail."

"Worse, my lady," cried the wizened little serf agitatedly. "You must go down to the hall. They've dragged
Edgith from the kitchen, accusing her of stealing food. And
knocking me over the head with my own soup ladle when
I protested," he added, aggrieved.

"Edgith, stealing food? By our Lady, why? You must
have got it wrong, Wat."

"Not I, mistress. Go see for yourself. That de Somery
fellow is foaming at the mouth, demanding trials, and—"

Lisette did not wait for more. She flew down the stairs
and across the hall to find Richard de Somery standing over
a ragged Saxon in shepherd's garb. Edgith was on her knees
before Raverre, sobbing into her hands.

Lisette put her arms around the girl, drawing her to her
feet. "What is happening here?" she demanded angrily.

Raverre flicked her a frowning glance, but said nothing.

"Your stupid slave here has been passing food and who

knows what else to this felon,'' de Somery stated abruptly. He turned back to Raverre. "I demand that they be punished, my lord. Their lives forfeit, or we'll have every peasant in the area walking in and taking whatever they please.''

Edgith gave vent to a shriek at this and started wailing. Lisette glared at de Somery. "How dare you threaten—?''

"Wait!'' Raverre interrupted her tersely. "How do you know this, Richard?''

"The wench confessed to one of my men, sir. Out of concern for your lady, she would have had him believe, but more likely in fear for her own miserable skin.''

"We've always given food to those in need,'' protested Lisette, determined to be heard. "If that's a crime under Norman law you'll have to kill all of us.''

Raverre ignored her. "Speak, girl,'' he ordered Edgith. "If you are truthful you need not fear for your life.''

Edgith glanced at Lisette, who nodded. "I was in the wasteland, gathering kindling,'' the girl quavered. "The shepherd came from the forest. He had been without food for days, he said, and begged me to fetch some for him. I saw no wrong.''

"Then why didn't he come openly to the gates, girl?'' questioned de Somery impatiently.

"I didn't think of that 'til later, and then I remembered he had a bow, not a crook. 'Tis why I went to Geoffrey.'' She turned to Lisette pleadingly. "Oh, my lady, forgive me. I thought he would understand. He's not like some… I…we…''

"You have committed no crime, Edgith,'' assured Lisette, her expression daring Raverre to contradict this statement.

But his attention was now on the shepherd who glared back at him. "What have you to say, fellow?''

"What matters it?" the man spat, getting to his feet. "You will kill me anyway, though that wench deserves to die also for betraying me." He turned a look of hatred on Lisette. "As does this one for becoming a Norman's wh—"

He didn't get a chance to finish. Raverre's clenched fist shot out, landing with sickening impact on the Saxon's jaw. The force of the blow lifted him several inches off the floor before he fell heavily among the rushes, spitting out a tooth but still defiant.

"Aye, you have the upper hand now, Norman swine, but not for long. Your King can't pay his army without gold, and soon his wealth will be in other hands."

Three pairs of eyes stared at him intently. The shepherd laughed scornfully. "Hah! Mention gold and you Normans stiffen like dogs after a bitch's scent."

Lisette turned impetuously to Raverre. "Do you think he means—?"

"Keep silent!" Raverre snapped. His cold gaze returned to the Saxon. "A bow?" he queried softly. "Now why would a simple shepherd need a bow? And what do you know of gold?"

The shepherd sneered. "Do you think I'll tell you anything, Norman dog? I am dead away. Why should you get more from me?"

"There is more than one way of dying," snarled de Somery, advancing towards his captive. Fastening his hand around the neck of the Saxon's sheepskin mantle, he forced him to his knees. "Let me choke it out of him, my lord."

"I claim justice," the shepherd gasped. "'Tis only that fool girl's word about the bow. Do you see one now? I demand Saxon justice. Trial by iron."

Raverre frowned at Lisette. "I've heard of this trial. What is it exactly?"

Lisette felt slightly sick. Her father had never permitted such brutal methods of judgement.

"'Tis meant to show proof of guilt or innocence," she explained quickly. "An iron rod is placed in the fire until white hot. The accused must take it in his hand and walk ten paces, then the hand is wrapped for three days. When uncovered, if 'tis not blistered he is innocent."

"Superstitious savages," growled de Somery, giving another twist to the Saxon's cloak. "Are we living in the Dark Ages? It will be Norman justice for you, robber, with proper witness and judgement. And for the girl also."

"Is that what you call justice?" Lisette cried. "After Edgith warned—"

She quailed as Raverre turned on her menacingly, but held her ground. "Edgith was loyal."

A look of admiration, albeit unwilling, crossed de Somery's rugged features as Lisette faced Raverre. Something not many of his men would have cared to do in his present mood.

"Your lady speaks truly," he conceded reluctantly, his usual sense of justice overcoming his wrath. "The girl can think herself lucky to escape with a warning. As for this scum, maybe that hot iron wasn't such a bad idea. It might help him talk."

Lisette opened her mouth, but before she could protest Raverre grabbed her arms with bruising strength. "If I have to force you back to your chamber you'll regret it," he growled through clenched teeth. "Now take that snivelling girl and get upstairs. This is no sight for you."

Holy Mother, he's going to do as de Somery suggests, she thought, appalled. Stricken, she grabbed Edgith's hand and almost ran from the hall.

"My lady, wait," panted Edgith, catching sight of her Norman soldier hovering outside. "Geoffrey will take me back to the kitchen.'' She flushed. ''You are not angry with me for going to him? That shepherd frightened me and—''

''I'm not angry, Edgith. But tell me quickly, did you only speak to him the once? Did he say where he came from? Are you sure about the bow?''

Edgith looked more flustered than ever at his spate of questions. ''I only saw it from a distance, my lady. The man laid it down before he approached, but 'twas not a crook, I swear.''

''And you remember nothing else? Think, Edgith! He must have come from somewhere.''

''I don't think— Stay, he wanted a light, too, my lady. Perhaps for his shepherd's hut.''

''Perhaps,'' murmured Lisette. ''Go now, Edgith. You are safe enough, I think.''

She barely heard Edgith's fervent thanks through the clamour of her thoughts. She needed time to sort them out, but it was not to be granted her.

Lisette had scarcely closed the tower room door when it was flung open again without ceremony and Raverre strode purposefully into the room. He didn't waste words.

''Out!'' he ordered the others, his voice so commanding that even Catherine, whom he always treated with affectionate indulgence, obeyed in a hurry, scurrying through the door he held open. It was immediately slammed after them.

''If you ever again question my authority before one of my men,'' he began in a quiet voice that nevertheless sent a quiver of alarm through Lisette, ''you'll wish 'twas you in that convent and not your sister. I will not have any woman, even my wife, interfering in matters of which she knows nothing. Your father might have allowed you a free rein, but he is dead and you would do well to remember that.''

This brutal reminder stung. "I didn't question—"

"Do you think me so incapable of justice?" he overrode her, his voice roughening.

"There's no justice in torture," Lisette retorted angrily.

"So you think me capable of that, too," he said with sudden quiet bitterness. "I had thought these past days you were coming to know me better." He turned away and strode over to the window, staring through the narrow split. "Come here."

Lisette approached warily, feeling strangely guilty.

"You see those soldiers out there?" Raverre asked. "They're searching for a bow." He glanced down at her. "When faced with two conflicting stories I deal in hard evidence, my lady."

She couldn't meet his eyes, her anger fading. "And if you find it?"

"Then there's every chance that man knows something about the robbery, unless he can prove otherwise by producing a master who can vouch for him. Any ideas?"

This abrupt question, coming on top of too many ideas, flustered Lisette immediately. "There is another manor," she blurted out. Then gazed up at Raverre in dismay.

The only man to whom the shepherd might belong was a neighbouring Thegn. A very old man who had been a lifelong friend of her father, he had often expressed his view that William's claim was legitimate, and had even fallen out over this question with his only son, Leofwin, who had been killed with Harold, as far as anyone knew. But would Raverre believe that?

Her eyes pleading, she finished in a breathless rush, "But the Thegn is an old, sick man. He could not have ordered that robbery. He's never even taken up arms against William."

"Where is this place?" he demanded, his voice hard.

"Oh, please, he wouldn't—"

"Where?" he roared suddenly, losing patience under the stinging lash of her doubt.

Lisette flinched. "About fifteen miles to the north," she faltered. "His name is Godric." Then, as Raverre turned without another word and opened the door, Lisette felt anger return. "And I am not yet your wife," she flung after him.

Several hours later a definite air of constraint hung over the hall.

Raverre sat frowning at the bow lying on the table before him as if it might hold the answers he hadn't received from Godric. Everyone else seemed uneasily aware of their lord's displeasure. Even Gilbert looked unusually stern.

Lisette watched in silence as the shepherd was marched out to the guard-room between four soldiers. Father Edwin brought up the rear. After passing sentence of death Raverre had told the priest to hear the man's confession. No amount of questioning had made the Saxon divulge any information about the missing gold, but when he had been confronted with the bow his own words had convicted him of firing the arrow at Raverre. From that moment his death had been certain.

Wondering why Raverre had insisted she be present, Lisette rose from the table.

Raverre was instantly on his feet. Lisette had to make a conscious effort not to flinch away from his overpowering aura of strength, but he saw her almost imperceptible movement and took her hand in a gentle clasp. She could easily have escaped it, and wondered why she didn't.

"Your friend Godric sent you a message," Raverre said as they walked across the hall. "He hopes you continue in good health, and your sisters also. And would like to see you again if it can be arranged."

Was she supposed to pretend that their previous clash had never taken place? "'Twas kind of him to remember us," she whispered.

Raverre sent her a quick glance as they mounted the stairs. "His own health is not good, but he seemed coherent enough and certainly no conspirator. In fact he intends to swear allegiance to William. I've promised to send for him when William visits us."

"Oh?"

Raverre stopped at the solar door. "The trial upset you," he murmured. "But you had to see that justice was done. The man had every chance to defend himself and refused. You realise what I'll have to do now?"

"Aye," she said curtly, beginning to open the door. Raverre clamped a hand over her wrist.

"Hate me if you must," he said very low. "But promise me you'll stay inside tomorrow morning."

Lisette raised a surprised face. He had sounded almost...regretful.

Raverre met her eyes steadily. "You shouldn't have to witness more violent death. You're haunted enough."

In utter astonishment Lisette watched him stride away down the gallery.

She was still wondering how Raverre had known of her demons of memory the following afternoon as she sat stitching by the fire in the hall, vaguely listening to Marjory's familiar scolding.

"The felon was no more a shepherd than I am. He deserved to hang. Can we have rogues wandering the countryside, loosing off arrows at all and sundry?"

"No, Marjory."

"Well, at least you agree." Marjory shifted her frown to Catherine. "And where have you been, miss?"

"In the stable. Bertrand is back with the loveliest mares I've— Ah, here he is now."

Lisette looked up with a warm smile of welcome, which wavered slightly at the sight of Raverre entering the hall with Bertrand. Did he think she hated him when he'd had no choice but to hang the Saxon? Her father would have done the same, and a lot sooner. Not knowing how to tell him this, she now felt awkward in his presence.

As Raverre set down a heavy chest he caught Lisette's shy glance and smiled at her.

"See, my lady, what Bertrand has brought back from Winchester." He flung back the lid.

"Blessed Saints!" ejaculated Marjory. "I do believe the man has purchased from every stall at St Giles's Fair."

"Oh, do look, Lisette," cried Catherine, delving her hands into the chest. "New linen, warm wool for winter gowns, lengths of lapin and sable trimming. We shall look so fine. And here is a girdle of silver links."

Unable to resist such feminine delights, Lisette glanced down as Raverre lifted out a length of the finest blue silk. He shook it out to reveal a gown of delicate workmanship.

"Here, my lady." He held out the garment to Lisette. "You must have a new gown for our wedding tomorrow."

"Tomorrow?" she repeated, dismayed, her interest in the clothes evaporating.

Raverre held her wide-eyed gaze. "Bertrand tells me there is talk in Winchester of rebellion in the north. If I have to leave I want your position here secured."

Still dazed by Raverre's announcement, Lisette slowly reached out to take the gown. The blue silk whispered, rippling and sliding through her fingers like flowing water.

"'Twas brought from the Holy Land by a Knight for his daughter," explained Bertrand, cheerfully unaware of any undercurrents. "But the lass up and entered a convent before her father returned, and he'd no one else on whom to bestow it, so I purchased it from him.''

"You have an eye for colour, Bertrand," murmured Raverre. "It matches my lady's eyes exactly."

Lisette looked up at him. Raverre smiled that slow, beguiling smile that brought warmth leaping to his eyes. "But there's more."

"Oh, Lisette," burst out Catherine. "I was coming to tell you. The sweetest, daintiest bay mares, with matching white stars on their foreheads and—"

Raverre laughed indulgently at Catherine's transports. "Catherine would have ridden off there and then," he told Lisette. "But I persuaded her to wait until you could come with us." He took Lisette's hand and raised it to his lips. "Would you like that, sweet lady?" he asked against her soft palm.

Tingling heat shot straight up Lisette's arm. Shaken, she opened her mouth to refuse. Then caught Catherine's pleading eyes.

"Very well," Lisette found herself agreeing weakly. She knew she was blushing hotly. The feel of Raverre's mouth against her palm made her legs turn to water. She would be lucky to stay on a horse. Oh, why did that formidable charm have such an unsettling effect when she knew Raverre was only teasing her?

This puzzling question occupied Lisette's mind as she guided her horse up the steep path leading to a plateau high above the forest.

The gusting wind caught both horses and riders, snatching their breath away, tossing silky manes and tails. The river was a mere silver thread far below them, tumbling through the rocky gorge to emerge, stately and serene again, into the forest. Far to the north-west the mountains of Wales loomed dark and forbidding.

"See how this lovely creature tosses her head against the wind, making her mane fly," called Catherine. "Just like that long-haired star we saw flying across the sky the year of King William's coming."

Lisette shuddered, remembering it was also the year her father had ridden off to battle and his death. Many had said the fiery comet had presaged disaster. William, of course, had taken the star's direction towards England as a favourable omen.

"Perhaps you could name her Flying Star," she said somewhat absently.

Catherine hailed this suggestion with delight, but Raverre brought Lanzelet up closer to Lisette.

"What troubles you, sweetheart?" he asked softly, reaching across the small space between the horses and laying a strong hand over hers.

Lisette snatched her hand away. "I think I'll name mine Viking Princess," she said hurriedly to her sister as the mare lifted her nose to snuff the wind.

"She certainly carries herself like one," agreed Catherine.

"Very appropriate," growled Raverre's sardonic voice in Lisette's ear. "Are we discussing the horse still, or her mistress?"

Lisette refused to look at him. He had flustered her enough for one day. Calm civility, she told herself firmly.

"You can see for miles across the forest," she announced unnecessarily. "King Edward used to hunt here, you know."

Raverre gave her a thoughtful look. "William also, when he manages to have a little leisure. Hunting is his favourite pastime."

"Why, that makes him sound quite human," said Catherine wonderingly.

Raverre smiled at her. "Of course he's human. Did you picture some kind of monster? Complete with a tail and horns perhaps?"

Catherine blushed guiltily, having done just that.

Raverre glanced at Lisette. "Surely you don't believe such tales any more?"

"A man does not need a tail or horns to be a monster," she answered coolly, moving her horse away from him.

"Will you ever stop fighting me?" he demanded, a rush of frustration giving the question an unexpected edge. "Or do I have to wait until you meet William and judge for yourself?"

Lisette laughed suddenly at the exasperation in his voice, her spirits lifting at this evidence that she could disturb him also. It was strange that she only felt really alive when she was fighting him. Except for the other day in the stable—

Lisette threw her hood back impatiently, letting her hair fly out in a dark cloud behind her, revelling in the feeling of freedom the wind evoked. She wanted to be free. Free of the disturbing thoughts that had plagued her lately. Free of the constant fear that she could lose more than her home and her independence.

Raverre caught his breath at her look of wild, untamed beauty, feeling desire rip through him as he sensed the un-awakened passion within her.

As if she felt his intense stare, Lisette turned her head, her own eyes widening as she saw the urgent hunger in Raverre's. She quickly pulled her hood forward again, hiding her face and retreating instantly behind a wall of wary reserve.

Catherine's exclamation was a welcome diversion.

"Look!" she cried, pointing across to the golden forest below them.

Alert to the slightest hint of danger from force of habit,

Raverre swung round, reaching for his sword, then relaxed as a flock of pheasants took to the air in panic-stricken flight, their harsh cries reaching them on the wind.

"There must be something prowling about over there," he remarked idly. "A fox perhaps. Come, we'd better be on our way before the wind turns colder."

"There might be a den," replied Catherine as they started back. "There are caves not far from where the birds are settling. Do you remember the fox cub we found there as children, Lisette?"

Lisette looked at her sister sharply, but Catherine chattered unconcernedly to Raverre. In seconds their voices faded into the background as Lisette's thoughts churned furiously.

Missing gold, the mention of long-forgotten caves, that sudden appearance of an unknown Saxon, seemingly from nowhere, and the fact that Godric had never received definite word of his son's death on the bloody battlefield at Hastings—all came together to settle into a picture that was extremely disquieting.

Lisette shook her head as though to clear it of her startled suspicions. Godric's son, Leofwin, had been a childhood playmate. He had spent several weeks at a time with them, under Alaric's tutelage, the two older children allowing the younger Lisette and Catherine to tag along with them and occasionally join in their games of damsels in distress and knightly rescuers. Eventually Enide and Leofwin had been betrothed, and Leofwin had ridden off to war.

The caves, deep in the forest and a relic of the ironworks of Roman times, had been a favourite haunt. Lisette had not thought of them for years, but was it possible that Leofwin had returned secretly, and was now using the spot as a safe refuge from which to conduct forays against the Normans in the district?

But why? Leofwin could not hope to do much alone, or with a small band of men, and surely the rift with his father was not so deep that he could not return openly to his home?

Yet, try as she might, she could not believe the startled flight of pheasants had been caused by a poacher or predatory fox. Poaching went on, of course, but not at a time when every available serf was engaged in the autumn harvest and would be missed. Also, predators, whether they be of the two- or four-legged variety, usually moved under cover of darkness. But a man desperate for food…

Lisette frowned worriedly. She could do nothing about her suspicions at the moment, however, and had to be content with making a resolution to ride through the forest alone as soon as she could escape Raverre's close watch. As it was, her long silence had already made him send her several penetrating glances, Lisette realised, coming back to the present to see the fields of the manor stretching before them, peaceful and welcoming in the soft grey stillness of the late afternoon. They were almost home and she could remember nothing of the ride.

As they trotted sedately past the church Lisette saw Father Edwin waving from the porch and, on impulse, reined in Princess outside the wicker gate leading to the graveyard.

"I would speak with Father Edwin a moment," she explained, at Raverre's questioning look. "About tomorrow," she added, hoping he would think the wedding had been the cause of her preoccupation.

He nodded after a second's hesitation and dismounted, intending to lift Lisette down, but she forestalled him, springing gracefully to the ground.

"I'll take the mare," he said, "and come back for you when I've seen Catherine safely indoors."

"There's no need," Lisette answered hurriedly. "Father Edwin will escort me."

Raverre gave her another long, unsmiling stare, but then mounted Lanzelet again without a word. Lisette watched as she and Catherine rode towards the manor. Had that been a flicker of hurt in Raverre's eyes just before he had turned away? No, impossible. And yet—

"God's greetings, my lady," piped Father Edwin beside her. "So I am to marry you tomorrow."

Lisette turned with a start, remembering her purpose in stopping. "Good day, Father." She hesitated, frowning, wondering how to put the question.

"There is something…?" Father Edwin paused discreetly.

"Aye, Father. It concerns the shepherd."

"Ah, Tostig. Poor unrepentant creature." Father Edwin crossed himself and shook his head.

"I know you may not betray the seal of the Confessional, Father," persevered Lisette. "But did the man say anything you could repeat to me? Mention of a master perhaps?"

"Nary a word, my lady. Nor during his Confession, such as it was. 'Twould not help you even if I repeated it word for word. A lost soul indeed, held fast by the Evil One."

Father Edwin seemed inclined to gloomy contemplation of his failure to extract proper repentance from the shepherd, but Lisette's thoughtful silence eventually bestirred him to speak again.

"My Lord Raverre has already asked me this same question, my lady. I wish I could have answered differently, for he is a good man. Your father would have liked him, I think, if they had not been on opposing sides in a conflict I pray God will soon be done."

This idea had not occurred to Lisette before, but Father

Edwin prattled on, distracting her, and it slipped from her mind as she refused his offer of escort back to the manor.

"I would sit by my mother's grave for a moment," she explained, and Father Edwin saw her off with a cheerful wave.

He might not have been so content had he heard Lisette's whispered words as she crouched in the soft grass where her mother lay at peace. By rights a proper tomb should have been erected in the church, but, with no stonemason on the estate at the time of her father's death, a simple grave had become the final resting place of both her parents.

At least it was consecrated ground, she thought gratefully, and sent up a quick prayer for the repose of her parents' souls.

"Oh, sweet Lady Mother," she whispered, "am I doing wrong? I am about to be married to one who is your enemy and mine. How do I know 'twas not he who delivered the fatal blow to my father? And since then, how many of our people has he killed or caused to be driven from their homes? And yet, dear God in Heaven, what else can I do? I have thought and thought." She bowed her head, mentally exhausted by the constant questioning and emotional struggle, and stayed so for a long time.

When she finally rose to her feet Lisette was surprised to find that twilight was falling, and the tiny graveyard looked still and mysterious in the half-light. A twig cracked behind her and she whirled with a frightened gasp, to see Raverre detach himself from the shadows of the trees by the road and come towards her.

Ignorance of how long he had been watching her, possibly a witness to her grief, didn't improve Lisette's mood. She could feel the wetness of tears on her cheeks, and yet she hadn't even been aware of crying.

Irrationally blaming him for that as well, she flared defensively, "You didn't have to come looking for me as if you feared I might run away."

Raverre ignored the tone and came up to her. "'Tis getting dark; there are other dangers beside human ones, you know."

"Human dangers are the only ones I fear," Lisette said significantly, backing away a pace or two. "See here—" gesturing to the grave at her feet "—is where my parents lie before their time. And for what? A crown, squabbled over by selfish humans who think only of themselves."

"There would have been no need of fighting if Harold had been true to his oath to support William's claim. William has only taken what was his by right."

"By right!" she exclaimed. "How dare you say so? He had no right."

"He had the right granted by the Pope, for one," Raverre countered. "Such things as a consecrated Papal banner are not given lightly. Also a bull of excommunication against Harold for breaking a vow made on sacred relics—"

"A vow made under duress!" Lisette interrupted angrily. "And achieved by trickery. William must have known his claim was not strong, to resort to such methods. He has no English blood, and there are others more nearly related to the old royal house."

"Aye," he agreed, his voice taking on a sarcastic note as he became annoyed at her persistence. "A child not much older than Catherine. That would have been a great asset to the country. Did you see any rallying to his banner after William entered London? Of course not! Edgar swore fealty to William along with many another. As your own father would have done, had he lived."

"He would never have done so!" she exclaimed hotly, stamping a little foot in her agitation.

"By the Holy Rood, let us have an end to this once and for all," Raverre growled impatiently, taking Lisette by the shoulders and giving her a little shake. "Your father was part-Norman himself, and don't try to tell me otherwise," he ordered as Lisette opened her mouth to protest. "My God, Girl, I only have to look at yonder castle to see where his ancestors came from. There were only three other such strongholds in the whole country before William came, garrisoned by Normans put there by King Edward. You even know a little of the language, so don't keep telling me of your pure Saxon blood. I know better."

Furious at being unable to deny this, she flashed, "At least my blood is legitimate, which is more than can be said for your precious William. He is base. No wonder he behaves so. What else could one expect from a low-born bastard?"

Raverre's face darkened, and he shook Lisette again, harder this time. "If you value your soft skin," he threatened, his voice rough, "you won't even whisper such a thing before William. He has had men maimed, and even killed for it before, and the fact that you are a woman won't save you."

"No," she scorned, recklessly ignoring the increasing anger on his face. "I wouldn't expect it to, when I know he beat the Queen for having the courage to speak the truth."

"I'm beginning to think a beating wouldn't do you any harm as well," Raverre muttered, wondering how the argument had become heated so quickly. "If I'd done it earlier this ridiculous conversation wouldn't even be taking place!"

"Go ahead, then!" was her defiant answer. She wrenched out of his hold and stepped back, eyes flashing.

Lisette knew she was courting danger, but couldn't seem

to stop herself. Dimly realising that anger would protect her against the other emotions torturing the edges of her mind, she deliberately fed her rage. She wanted to despise Raverre for what he was! Fight him! Hate him! Not…

"Why should you behave differently from any other Norman barbarian?" she taunted bitterly.

This didn't have quite the effect she expected. Raverre burst out laughing.

"You know I haven't behaved like a barbarian, you little shrew," he chided. Then his eyes gleamed wickedly. "But if that's what you would prefer I dare say I could oblige you."

This provocative remark and his laughter proved too much. Incoherent with rage, Lisette swung her arm up and slapped him across the face before he had any warning.

She was instantly aghast at what she had done, but before she could speak Raverre hauled her against him with a grip that made Lisette fear her bones would break at any moment.

"You little vixen," he ground out, his own temper swiftly fuelled by the bitter scorn in her voice and frustrated desire. "I can see I've been too patient with you, my lady. So you think me no better than a barbarian, do you? Then, by God, I'll show you a barbarian!"

Swiftly transferring her wrists to one hand, he held her face up to his with the other. Then, before Lisette had time to draw breath, Raverre's mouth crushed hers, kissing her with a ruthless anger that fired her own again.

Unable to struggle against the iron strength of the arms imprisoning her, Lisette kicked out at his legs, eventually landing a blow hard enough to make Raverre step back on the uneven ground to avoid her. She immediately renewed her attempts to escape, throwing them both off balance, but even as the earth rose dizzily to meet her, Raverre twisted, taking the brunt of the fall.

Half dazed by the force with which they landed, and the stinging of her mouth where her lips had been cut, Lisette barely realised that Raverre still held her before he rolled, using his weight to subdue her.

"Now," he said, glaring down at her, "are you ready to calm down?"

With a cry of mingled pain and rage Lisette lashed out with her arms, only to have her wrists captured again. She turned her head and tried to bite him.

"Stop it, you little fool," Raverre grated. "You'll hurt yourself."

"You're the one who's hurting me," she cried, writhing beneath him as she tried to free her arms.

"Damn it, stop that! You don't know what you're doing. Christ!" The last exclamation was smothered against her lips as Raverre brought his mouth down hard on hers again.

When he finally raised his head Lisette had stopped fighting. Her breast heaved as she struggled to catch her breath. She could feel the threatening pressure of his desire against her body.

"Now do you know what you're doing to me?" he rasped. "If you provoked another man like this you'd find yourself raped."

The brutal statement made her flinch. "If you think I'm going to marry you after this you're wrong," she choked.

Raverre went still. Lisette saw the intent in his eyes even before he spoke.

"Then I'll just have to make sure of you," he said with cold menace. "I didn't want it like this, but you're not going to find it so easy to break your promise, my lady." His long legs parted hers with frightening ease, and his free hand lowered to her breast.

A whimper of pure terror escaped her.

"Don't worry," he said bitterly against her mouth. "I'm not going to be rough with you, even if you are as false as any woman. But after tonight you'll know you belong to me."

The quiet tone was threatening, but Lisette grabbed on to the hope that his anger seemed to have died.

"If you take me here," she gasped, fighting to draw breath against the fear gripping her throat, "over my mother's grave, you'll be no better than the brutes who put her there!"

Raverre gave a mirthless laugh, the bitter note more pronounced. "Then your opinion of me shouldn't change, should it?" His hand swept her gown up to her thighs.

Lisette barely heard him. The distant roaring in her ears grew louder, and rushing wings of blackness swept over her. As the forceful weight of Raverre's body drove the breath from her lungs she lost consciousness, going limp beneath him.

Chapter Six

It took Raverre a full minute to realise that Lisette was no longer fighting him. When the knowledge finally penetrated the red mist of bitter rage aroused by her threat, and he drew back to see her lying senseless, her limbs spread-eagled in the grass, ice-cold fear washed over him.

He searched for her heartbeat with a hand that shook, only partially relieved to feel the uneven fluttering in her breast, and to know that Lisette had merely fainted. She seemed so small and fragile that for a sickening instant Raverre thought the uncontrolled strength he had used to subdue her might have been sufficient to end her life.

As sanity returned Raverre quickly swung the mantle off his shoulders. Wrapping the warm garment around her unconscious form, he gathered Lisette into his arms. Then, whispering words of reassurance and love, barely aware of what he was saying, he began to murmur soothingly as she stirred against him, willing his voice to stay soft and even.

Lisette returned slowly to her senses, to find herself still in Raverre's arms, and began to struggle weakly. Then his deep voice penetrated the confusion in her dazed mind and, though too distraught to understand the words, she was calmed by the tone. With shuddering relief she realised that

Raverre was no longer the terrifying stranger she had provoked so blindly. She tried to speak, but her throat seemed to have closed up and she could not utter a word, trembling uncontrollably in his arms for several minutes before he helped her to stand.

"Come," he said, his own voice sounding strained, "they'll be wondering where we are—it must be almost suppertime. Can you walk alone? It will arouse comment if I carry you."

"Aye," Lisette managed in barely above a whisper. She felt as if her legs would not take her more than one step before collapsing beneath her.

However, she did begin to feel stronger as Raverre guided her along the road and through the gates. By the time they reached the outer stairway Lisette started to feel more herself, and, realising she wore Raverre's mantle, put up a shaky hand to return the garment.

She would have spoken then, but he laid a gentle finger over her lips, and guided her silently around the stairway and into the empty guard-room, closing the door behind them.

The room was dark and cold. "Wait," he said as Lisette hesitated by the door.

Raverre quickly lit one of the rush sconces on the wall, and came back to her, seeing for the first time her torn lip and the dark shadows beneath her eyes. He had never asked any man's forgiveness in his life, let alone a woman's, but, looking into Lisette's eyes at that moment, Raverre would have done anything to remove the hurt he saw there.

"I'm sorry," he said abruptly, awkwardly. Then as her swollen lip quivered he took her in his arms, cradling her close, but ready to release her if she wished it. "Forgive me," he murmured more naturally, closing his eyes as his mouth caressed her hair. "You were right, I would have been no better than the men you spoke of."

She shouldn't let him hold her like this, Lisette thought. Only minutes ago Raverre's powerful body had made her terrifyingly aware of her helplessness compared to his superior muscular strength. And yet now she only wanted to stay in those same strong arms, resting her head on his broad shoulders and holding on to a suddenly peaceful feeling of having found a safe harbour after weeks on a storm-tossed sea. She was too exhausted, however, to puzzle over this conflict, and besides, she too had an apology to make.

Lisette drew gently out of his embrace. "'Twas not your doing," she said very low, "I was at fault. What I said to you, I regret. 'Twas untrue and unjust. I know you are not like them. You have shown me nothing but courtesy when you could have been so different. I didn't mean—" She took a deep breath. "I promise I will be a dutiful wife, my lord."

Raverre took her hands in a light clasp. "Dutiful?" he repeated, smiling faintly at her fervent tone.

"Aye," Lisette insisted, determined to make amends. "I do know my duty. I remember my mother telling Enide."

"What did she tell Enide?" he questioned gently, brushing a stray lock of hair from her cheek.

Lisette drew in another deep breath, like an obedient child about to recite a lesson learned by heart. She fixed her gaze on Raverre's tunic.

"That men are different from women and a husband's carnal nature must be tolerated. 'Tis a wife's duty to submit, no matter...no matter how unpleasant...she may find..."

She faltered, her fears returning twofold at the memory of her mother speaking of a distasteful duty. And there had been love between her parents. Without love, surely it must be terrible.

Raverre smiled crookedly. "And now you think you've just seen undisputed evidence of a man's carnal nature," he said. "God, I wish—" He glanced away, then back again, gazing earnestly into her face as Lisette looked up, surprised at his hesitation.

"I suppose 'twould be useless for me to tell you of a woman's carnal nature, as you put it? I prefer to call it desire."

Lisette looked shocked. "Ladies don't have such desires," she protested. She thought of the last half-hour and shuddered. "I couldn't imagine any woman enjoying... wanting...*that!*"

"Not that," Raverre said swiftly, gently cupping her face with warm hands. "This. No, sweet, don't shrink away. Let me show you how it should be. How it will be."

His mouth brushed hers, then he drew back immediately, smiling into her eyes. Her face showed wariness, but she didn't pull away. Raverre lowered his head again.

Lisette felt the gentle touch of his mouth. On her temple, in a series of tiny kisses across her cheekbone and down to the corner of her mouth. Her eyes drifted closed. She should protest. This same man had almost taken her in anger. But it was so sweet. She'd never known such warm sweetness. She felt weak again. But this time it was not the weakness of forced submission; rather a willing, melting surrender.

Raverre repeated the delicate caresses on the other side of her face, coming near her mouth, but never touching it. And then, unthinking, instinctively, Lisette turned her face slightly and their lips met in a kiss of heart-stopping tenderness. She felt the briefest touch of Raverre's tongue lightly caress her bruised mouth, then he was straightening away from her.

"There," he said huskily as her eyes flew open, dark and wondering. "You see? Was there anything to fear in my kisses?"

"No, but..."

He smiled." And you liked them."

This was too much to confess, but Lisette blushed. "I have said I will be dutiful," she stammered. "What more do you want? You are forcing me to wed you...you have taken my home...we are enemies."

"No," Raverre denied instantly. His eyes hardened. "Don't start that again. I am no enemy of yours. Your home was lost to you when your father swore for Harold, but by marrying me you will regain it. You do not lose by our bargain, my lady."

Lisette edged to the door. "I will keep my promise to wed you," she whispered, "but there can be no more than a bargain between us."

She had reached the doorway and was halfway through it, when Raverre spoke again.

"I wouldn't have forced you." The words were clipped and harsh. "I know you'll keep your promise."

Lisette hesitated. Then, glancing back with a timid smile, she slipped into the night.

Cool, pearly grey fingers of dawn crept over the horizon, heralding her wedding-day.

Unable to sleep, Lisette had been crouched in the window embrasure for hours, wrapped in a new red woollen cloak Bertrand had brought from Winchester. Paid for by Raverre, she reminded herself. It was another item on the account she owed him.

The improvements to the manor she could argue away—

they were to Raverre's advantage, after all. But by marrying her and sending Enide to the Church's protection he had forfeited two possibly valuable alliances. And, apart from that, he was supporting all of them from his own funds until the manor became fully self-sufficient again.

Of course, there were advantages to him also in marrying her. Lisette tried to concentrate on those, because if she didn't she would think about the way she had behaved last night. But the memories kept coming back.

Of herself lashing out at Raverre like a wild creature, threatening to break her vow to marry him. Lisette wondered if that demented girl had really been her. She had behaved as one possessed by demons. And why? Because she had wanted to despise Raverre and couldn't? Because she wanted to fight him and needed a reason? Even in his anger, he still hadn't given her real cause for hatred.

He had used his strength to subdue her, but the bruises on her body he had been provoked into inflicting. Lisette knew there were plenty of men who would have beaten her unmercifully in answer to such provocation, and not apologised for it later.

She huddled further into the cloak at the memory of Raverre's tenderness in the guard-room. And later. At supper he had seen her hand shake on the wine cup and had steadied it with his own. His gentle concern had almost brought her to the brink of tears, and she had clenched her teeth until her jaw ached, determined not to shame herself any further.

And nor would she shame herself by betraying how nervous the thought of becoming Raverre's wife made her. She would be dutiful if it killed her. At this inconvenient moment she remembered how her mother had died, broken and bleeding, after being raped and beaten by Norman soldiers.

"Lisette? Are you feeling all right?"

It was Enide, looking worried, her fair hair tousled from sleep. With a start Lisette realised that full daylight had come while she'd been so engrossed in her thoughts.

Catherine was sitting up in the big bed, rubbing her eyes and yawning. Marjory grumbled at the cold air blowing in through the shutters Lisette had opened. Just another morning.

If only it were.

Lisette summoned up a smile. If nothing else, her sister would be safe. Already Enide looked more animated than she had for months, knowing she was to be permitted to retire to the cloister.

"I was wondering how our mother felt on her wedding-day," she improvised.

"Relieved to get out of that fever-ridden swamp the Celts had retreated to, I imagine," said Marjory tartly. "And, if you must open the shutters before a decent time of day, at least put on some warm clothes."

Lisette couldn't help laughing. "Oh, Marjory, what would we ever do without your good sense?" she cried, flinging her arms about her old nurse.

"Tush," returned Marjory sternly. But she stroked Lisette's cheek lovingly, her gaze softening. "Your mother told me she sat up to watch the dawn, and wondered if her husband would ever come to love her as she loved him. As she found later, he already adored her." Marjory smiled complacently. "You and Raverre are not so different, I think."

Lisette's mouth fell open. She was quite unable to speak, however. Taking advantage of having had the last word for once, Marjory steered her favourite nurseling over to a stool.

"Now, sit and let me comb out your hair. I ordered hot

water and the tub to be brought first thing, and here is a bowl of freshly perfumed soap. We shall have you bathed and scented, and as pampered as any new bride should be.''

Marjory was true to her word. When Raverre finally saw his bride enter the churchyard on Bertrand's arm his breath caught at her beauty.

Her dark hair had been left loose and hung to her waist in a shining bronze cloud, threaded with autumn daisies. The blue silk gown, made in the Norman fashion, clung to her still girlish figure, outlining her small breasts and slender waist, before flaring below her hips to fall in graceful folds to the ground. Marjory had stitched a trim of dark sable fur at the hem and around the full sleeves to add a touch of luxury, and a heavy girdle of chased silver, set with garnets, gave her a look of delicate fragility.

Lisette saw the crowd of churls and soldiers, heard the appreciative murmurs paying tribute to her beauty, but they seemed to remain at a hazy distance. She felt as though she watched another girl walking along the road and through the wicker gate.

And she still clung to that cool, protective distance as she stepped into the porch entrance of the church, where Raverre awaited her.

So, she was now a Norman's lady, Lisette told herself, gazing over the hall from her seat at the high table.

The ceremony was over. The feasting was over. People were gathering in their accustomed groups, exchanging gossip, and some of the younger folk had started an extremely noisy game of hoodman blind. Lisette saw a timid Edgith coaxed into the game by a young, fresh-faced soldier who hovered over her protectively.

This is the beginning of a Norman England, she realised suddenly. A stronger England perhaps. The notion startled her, but she couldn't erase it. I'm tired, she thought. But she was feeling more at ease now after several draughts of wine and very little food.

She wasn't the only one. A burst of loud laughter made Lisette glance up to see Gilbert dancing about with a harp, his actions becoming more and more suggestive of an ardent suitor pursuing a most reluctant maiden.

Raverre grinned, but turned to Lisette. "I think perhaps your sisters should retire. This feast is about to become most unsuited to delicate maidenly sensibilities."

Catherine giggled. "Don't worry, Alain," she advised cheekily. "Saxons are the most hardened drinkers in the world. You should have seen some of my father's celebrations."

"I dare say," he answered, with a shrewd glance from her flushed countenance to the empty drinking horn in her hand. "But I doubt if *you* stayed until everyone fell asleep where they sat. Be off with you before I have Marjory after me for corrupting her chicks."

He stood and held out a hand to Lisette, drawing her up beside him. "Come, sweetheart, 'tis time we retired also."

Lisette blushed wildly, barely managing to bid goodnight to her sisters with any coherence as she and Raverre were surrounded by jostling well-wishers. Robust advice on how to keep a husband—or wife— content in the marriage bed was laughingly shouted out from all sides.

Dazed by the noisy confusion, Lisette shrank against Raverre. Instantly she was swept up into his arms and cradled against his chest. Quite unconsciously she clasped her arms about his neck, hiding her face against his tunic.

"Don't be alarmed," he murmured in her ear. "'Tis only fun." He strode towards the solar, shouldering the door closed on the boisterous, applauding crowd.

There was blissful silence. The air felt wonderfully cool

after the close, smoky atmosphere in the hall. Lisette wondered why Raverre hadn't moved from the door.

"You can look now," he said, laughter in his voice. "We're alone."

Wishing she could hide her face until the night was over, Lisette looked. The first thing to meet her gaze was Raverre's amused face. But behind the smile in his eyes a glittering elation burned. Lisette's heart began to race.

Trying to hide her nervousness, she glanced about the room. The solar had been transformed. Newly acquired tapestries, with a distinctly Norman look about them, softened the chilly appearance of the stone walls. A table and chair occupied the space between the two window embrasures, and two solid chests flanked the fireplace.

A fat candle burned in solitary splendour atop its iron spike, and more light was cast by the wall sconces. There was even a thick sheepskin rug on the floor, and Lisette was illogically relieved to see a prie-dieu in the corner by the bed.

Naturally she hadn't believed those rumours that Normans were the spawn of the Devil, but it was comforting nevertheless to see proof of it. Then her gaze fell on the newly constructed bed, with its bearskin cover turned back and a fresh linen sheet laid over the straw mattress. Thoughts of comfort fled.

Seeing her eyes skitter nervously away from the bed, Raverre strode forward to set Lisette down by the fire.

"I expect the solar looks somewhat different to you," he remarked with deliberate casualness, moving back to the door to drop a wooden bar into the brackets on either side. It landed with what, to Lisette, sounded like an ominous thud.

Why hadn't anyone told her what she was supposed to do now? Did a dutiful wife just blithely throw off her clothes and climb into bed like some willing sacrifice? Lisette suddenly remembered Raverre's fiercely burning passion when he had kissed her in the stable, and how helpless she had felt in the churchyard in the face of his overwhelming strength. She decided she could put off being dutiful for a few moments longer.

Starting to shiver, she moved closer to the fireplace and sat down on the small stool there, holding her hands to the warmth.

"It does look different," she agreed. Was conversation proper at a time like this? "But I like it. The tapestries are very good."

"My mother did them," Raverre replied, striding over to the windows and fastening the wooden shutters. "There. Warmer now, sweet?" He returned to the fireplace, hunkering down on his heels with his back to Lisette and reaching for a small jug.

She hadn't noticed it before, but now Lisette breathed in the spicy aroma of mulled wine.

"I must try to send my parents word of our marriage," Raverre commented. "My father would like to know our line will continue here in England."

"They won't mind that you've married a Saxon?" Lisette queried cautiously.

Raverre grinned at her over his shoulder as he held the dark liquid close to the flames, swirling the wine jug gently with his wrist. "My mother will be so overjoyed to know I'm married that it wouldn't matter if you were Saxon, Dane or Saracen. I've been the despair of her for years."

Oh, dear, she was starting to like him again, Lisette thought. When those blue eyes smiled with such male wickedness it was impossible not to smile back. And he was being so kind, letting her get used to being alone with him in the quiet privacy of the solar.

She thought of all the other occasions when he had shown her gentleness, even understanding, and tried to banish her fears. Then Raverre rose to his feet, immediately looming over her. Lisette's heart jumped, but he merely crossed to the table and poured some wine into a drinking horn.

"I had this mulled earlier, and it's been keeping warm here by the fire." Raverre came back to Lisette and handed her the drinking horn.

She had already drunk a lot of wine this evening, Lisette remembered, but on the other hand the fresh air in the solar had now blown away her slight dizziness, so perhaps a bit more would help.

Unable to meet the intense look in Raverre's eyes, Lisette grabbed the drinking horn and tilted it to her mouth far too quickly. Warm wine splashed her nose, and what managed to find her mouth went down the wrong way. Lisette choked.

Raverre rescued the drink and placed it on the hearth, then took her hands, drawing her to her feet. "There's no need to be so afraid," he murmured, wiping wine drops away with his fingers. "I'm not going to hurt you."

Lisette looked up. He was so big. She barely reached his shoulder. "You're not?" she quavered doubtfully.

One corner of Raverre's mouth quirked in a wry smile. He hadn't expected to spend his wedding-night explaining to his wife what she should have heard from another female.

He caressed her cheek with his knuckles. "Sweetheart, I'll be very careful with you, but the first time..." His mouth lowered to hers. "If I hurt you it will only be for a moment, I swear." Their lips met.

Lisette had no real time to absorb his words before she was caught up in the sweetness of Raverre's kiss. He had kissed her in passion and in anger, and she had managed to resist both, but this gentle seduction of her senses threatened to make her forget her fear, forget their bargain, forget everything except a gradually more insistent need to respond.

Before she could, however, Raverre suddenly released her mouth. Sweeping her off her feet, he carried Lisette to the bed and sat her down on the bearskin. Then he knelt and drew off her soft leather shoes.

"God's bones, your feet are like ice!" he exclaimed, chafing them briskly.

It seemed such a commonplace, practical thing to do that Lisette felt herself relax a little. Her eyes wandered to the fair head so close to her. In the light his hair shone like gold. Unable to resist wondering how it would feel, she put out a timid hand and touched him. His hair felt soft.

Raverre glanced up quickly and Lisette snatched her hand back, flushing.

He rose and propped one knee on the bed beside her, capturing her face between his hands. "Don't be afraid to touch me, Lisette," he said softly.

Her name, spoken in that deep, husky voice, sent a strangely pleasurable shiver through her. One long-fingered hand began to thread through her hair. A daisy fluttered to the floor.

"See? It feels good, doesn't it? Your hair feels like silk, almost as soft as your skin." Another daisy fell into Lisette's lap. Raverre's soft voice murmured reassuringly as he continued to remove the flowers. "These looked very pretty today, but I fear they will be sadly squashed if they stay where they are."

Suddenly he nuzzled the side of her throat, his lips caressing through the silky strands of hair. "Your scent reminds me of a rose garden I once saw in Aquitaine. 'Twas beautiful, but empty.'' He drew back to gaze into her eyes. His had darkened to slate. ''Now I can picture you there, as soft and lovely as one of the roses.''

The huskily murmured words were as seductive as the caress of his mouth, Lisette thought hazily. Her head fell back under the growing pressure of his kisses and the sweet weakness she had known before began to flow through her limbs.

Without knowing how, she found herself lying across the bed, encircled in Raverre's arms, his mouth gentle on hers as he brushed the tiniest of kisses across her lips. Her heart fluttered wildly. It wasn't enough. She wanted…

Her lips parted. Instantly he accepted the silent invitation, deepening the kiss until all her senses seemed filled with him. The feel of his mouth, the gentle invasion of his tongue, the sweet taste of wine, the clean masculine scent of him. The unfamiliar touch of his hand against the bare skin of her shoulder.

Lisette's eyes flew open. He had unfastened her gown. She gasped in shock as his mouth left hers, and his eyes shifted, gazing into anxious blue depths for several long seconds.

''Would you rather undress yourself?'' he asked gently.

Lisette nodded quickly. She couldn't speak. Would he be angry?

''Such big eyes,'' he said, smiling down at her. ''It's all right, my shy little bride. ''The smile turned devilish. ''This time.''

Dropping a quick kiss on her lips, Raverre rose from the bed. Lisette sat up slowly, one hand holding her gown in place. She was grateful for Raverre's understanding, but did he expect her to undress while he watched? Suddenly the room seemed far too brightly lit.

Then, as though in answer to the unconscious appeal in

her eyes, Raverre circled the room, snuffing out the sconce
lights. He even doused the candle which normally burned
day and night. Blessed darkness fell over the solar, broken
only by the flickering of the rapidly dying fire.

Lisette hurriedly pulled off the blue gown and her shift.
Letting them fall in a silken heap to the floor, she leapt into
bed, pulling the bearskin up to her chin. Only then did she
risk a glance at Raverre.

He stood with his back to her, stripping off his tunic and
undershirt. Corded muscles flexed across his shoulders and
back as he flung the garments aside. His arms were strongly
sinewed, and when he turned the same powerful ripple of
muscle showed across his chest and flat stomach. The firelight flickered over his skin, burnishing it, and his gold hair
fell across his brow in ruffled disorder, softening the hard
planes of his face.

He's beautiful, thought Lisette, startled. She had never
realised a man could be considered beautiful, but Raverre
was. A beautiful male animal in the prime of his strength
and power. She was suddenly acutely aware of her own
slender softness, her femininity.

He sat on the edge of the bed, unwinding the thongs from
his boots and leggings. Lisette hurriedly averted her gaze,
sliding down in the bed until the bearskin covered her to
the eyes. When Raverre turned to climb in next to her she
saw his teeth gleam in an irrepressible smile. He peeled the
bearskin back a few inches, drawing Lisette close to him.

She was immediately enveloped by heat, her senses spinning in a dizzying whirlpool of fear, shyness and the sheer
physical presence of Raverre's naked body leaning over
hers.

He was so close that she could feel the violent pounding
of his heart, the knotted tension in his whole body. Could
feel how much he wanted her, and yet his hands were warm

and gentle as they stroked her hair, spreading it over the linen pillow until it framed her face like a dark halo.

"My beautiful wife," he murmured. "Mine." He bent to kiss her, his hand sweeping in a long caress down the side of her body and up to rest just below her breast.

Lisette trembled. She had never felt so vulnerable.

"I'm only going to touch you," he whispered. "Don't be afraid. I'll be so gentle with you, my love."

Lisette dimly remembered her resolve not to betray her fear. Somehow it no longer mattered.

"I...I feel so strange," she stammered in a tiny voice. "Not really afraid, but...we scarcely know...two weeks ago I didn't even..." Oh, how could she ever explain?

A flash of tender protectiveness went through Raverre. He hung on to it, knowing it was the only thing preventing him from burying himself in her, possessing her until she could never be apart from him again. He knew he would lose her completely if he frightened her, nor could he bear the thought of hurting her.

"I know, little one, I know," he murmured reassuringly. "You don't know how you find yourself flying in the arms of your enemy."

"Aye," she gasped thankfully. "Oh, please don't be angry. I will try to—"

"Shhh." His hand lightly stroked her breast.

Lisette made a small sound of shock at the intimate caress. Her hands came up to push against his arms, but instead she felt herself gripping Raverre's shoulders as waves of heat seemed to dissolve her vague feeling of outrage. Suddenly his touch was no longer alien, an intrusion. It felt right.

The tremors shaking her body increased. Confusion and apprehension fought with tremulously awakening desire.

Raverre held her close. "Don't fight me, sweetheart. Just

for tonight, forget about Norman and Saxon. Here, between us two, there's no need for conquest or surrender, but only a man and a maid.'' His voice deepened to a low, husky murmur that Lisette heard in the deepest part of her heart. ''Trust me, darling. For tonight, let yourself trust me.''

She was his. Though there had been no word of love spoken between them, Lisette knew she belonged to Raverre on some deep, primitive level that lay beyond words.

And the knowledge frightened her intensely. Far more than the simple fear of the unknown she had felt earlier.

Had Raverre taken her roughly, or even carelessly, she could have escaped this sense of belonging, could have remained apart from him, only yielding her body. But no lover could have been more patient with her innocence, more passionately tender. She had barely felt the brief, stinging pain at the moment of his possession, so utterly overwhelming had been the sensation of becoming one with him.

Raverre had held her so tightly, rigidly still while her body had struggled to adjust to his, that she had felt totally surrounded, enveloped by him. And then he had moved.

Lisette stirred in Raverre's arms, and he reached down to pull up the bearskin, cocooning them in its dark warmth. He nestled Lisette against his side, holding her securely in his arms.

''Are you hurting, sweetheart?'' His voice was a soft growl in the darkness.

Lisette considered the question. She was aware of a slight unfamiliar soreness inside, but deeper still a restless ache was making itself felt. It made her want—

Then, even as she questioned, the ache slipped away. She could not hold on to the feeling; its memory eluded her.

''No, you did not hurt me,'' she said. Then, as though compelled by the warm intimacy of the moment, added in a voice that was still uncertain, faintly questioning, "'Twas not…distasteful."

Raverre brushed her cheek in a tender caress. "It will be better next time, love. 'Twas too new for you tonight—" he gave a soft laugh "—and I wanted you too much. Next time there'll only be pleasure, I promise."

That was it, Lisette realised, eyes wide open and staring into the dark. That feeling. An elusive promise of pleasure, and completeness with another, such as she had never known. And there, also, lay the danger, lay the threat she had sensed from the very moment of seeing Raverre.

Instinctively Lisette thrust the thought away. "I wonder why my mother told Enide…" she began, saying the first thing that came into her head.

"Enide is not like you, sweetheart," he answered. "Even before your mother's death, for her 'twould be no more than a wifely duty." Feeling the sudden tension in her body, Raverre bit off his next words, cursing himself.

She was not ready to face the passion within herself, though he knew it was there. He had seen it directed at him in anger, but to have it directed at him in love he would have to move slowly, until Lisette no longer saw him as an enemy.

Turning on his side, Raverre gathered Lisette against the comforting warmth of his body. "Go to sleep now, little wife," he murmured into her hair. "I'll keep you safe."

Lisette remained silent, but as she heard Raverre's breathing deepened into slumber her mind continued to question for long hours afterwards; until weariness finally overtook her as the first pale light of dawn crept over the misty countryside.

The fire had been lit, and someone had brought her clothes from the tower room. Her simple homespun gowns hung from a rod across one corner of the solar, alongside

Raverre's tunics and his long dark blue mantle. She was alone.

Lisette sat up, her eyes resting thoughtfully on her wedding gown, still lying in a silken puddle on the floor, and the wilted daisies scattered by the bed.

He is no longer my enemy.

The words flashed into Lisette's mind and refused to be banished. She tried to deny them, but the questions kept coming. Would an enemy have soothed her fears last night? Or gently coaxed her past her shyness? Would an enemy have held her so protectively afterwards that she felt as though nothing could ever harm her again?

Suddenly restless, Lisette climbed from the bed and flung open the shutters. Bright daylight streamed into the room with a rush of cool morning air. She had slept quite late.

Her linen shifts lay folded on the table. Lisette slipped one over her head. Had Raverre placed them there? she wondered, tying the ribbons at the neck. The thought of his big hands touching the delicate garments brought warmth to her face, and was immediately followed by the memory of those same hands caressing her body. Strong hands, slightly calloused, and yet his touch had been so gentle. The warmth spread as far as her toes.

"'Tis the fire which is so hot," Lisette grumbled, conscious of a sudden urge to know the touch of his hands again, now that she was no longer afraid.

'Tis only curiosity, she scolded herself. And look where curiosity had led before. To a confrontation with male desires that she hadn't been able to control. Of course, she hadn't exactly been in control last night either, she remembered uneasily. Raverre had been the one in command of both of them. Recalling the tensely leashed power in the hard muscles beneath her hands, Lisette realised for the first time how truly formidable had been his control.

It meant nothing, she told herself sternly. If Raverre had married Enide he would have treated her as patiently. But then why did she recall so vividly the incredible feeling of oneness with him—such closeness—the beckoning promise of unimagined delight?

She hurriedly reminded herself that Raverre had taken over her home. For the first time, it did no good. Her inherent honesty argued that it had been granted to him after victory in honourable battle. Such things had happened from time immemorial.

And while she was being honest, Lisette thought, she might as well admit that her churls' loss of freedom had its more positive side. It *was* a relief to know the manor was constantly protected, that the harvest would be gathered safely, that men would be available for the wood-carrying in November, and that even the poorest serf would enjoy the free logs and bonfire which followed.

And, on a more personal level, she knew Raverre was honourable and just. He had been kind to her sisters, and as for herself—

Lisette grabbed the nearest gown and pulled it on. She was back at the start of the argument. But if Raverre was no longer her enemy, then what?

How could she forget that her parents had died at the hands of Norman soldiers? No matter what she thought of Raverre, how could she forget that he was still one of them? An invader? A conqueror? And how could she willingly lie with such a man, except when she must keep her side of their agreement? An agreement, Lisette reminded herself sternly, into which he had forced her.

She began to feel better. Raverre had virtually blackmailed her into marrying him; there was no argument about *that*. Well, she would hold to their bargain, but that would be all. Last night she had been unsure and afraid, and Raverre had been kind. No wonder she felt drawn to him. But he had only married her for practical reasons, after all. She would be dutiful, but distant.

Dragging a bone comb ruthlessly through her tangled hair, Lisette continued to expound along these lines. She had finally succeeded in quelling a nagging little voice that kept asking why she should need to be so determined, when the door opened and Raverre appeared.

Slamming the door behind him, he reached Lisette in three long strides, swung her up into his arms and kissed her warmly on the mouth. Her resolve tottered.

Setting her down again, he said teasingly, "Well, I see you are no worse for being married, sweet lady. How do you find yourself this morning? Hungry? I am come to tell you that dinner is on the table and awaiting. And about time—I could eat an ox whole."

Lisette sank back on to the chair by the table, wondering why her legs felt so shaky. "I must just braid my hair," she managed, but her fingers were all thumbs. The braid was going to be hopelessly loose; it would probably fall apart at the first puff of wind.

Suddenly Raverre's hands covered hers. "I think you need some help," he murmured, a smile in his voice.

Lisette glanced at him over her shoulder, surprised laughter bubbling up through her nervousness. "You?" she asked incredulously.

He grinned down at her. "Oh, I have other skills besides fighting." He propped a plate of beaten copper on the table and turned her face toward it. "Let me show you."

Two seconds later Lisette realised Raverre's intent. Ignoring her squeak of protest, with deft fingers he quickly unravelled the braid, spreading her hair over her shoulders. Her hands came up to stop him.

His eyes capturing hers in the mirror, Raverre gently

returned her hands to her lap. "Wait," he instructed. "I haven't finished."

There was a quick flash of light as he carefully lowered a gold circlet to Lisette's head. Her lips parted in surprise. It was the most exquisite thing she had ever seen. Beautifully crafted, the delicate band was engraved with dragons, whose precious sapphire eyes reflected the colour of Lisette's own. Raverre adjusted the circlet so the dragons' glowing eyes met above the centre of her brow.

"Where did that come from?" she managed weakly.

"Wales, judging by the dragons, but just lately Winchester."

Lisette had to smile. "You know that's not what I meant."

He grinned. That wicked male grin that was totally irresistible. "I've been keeping it for you. Your bride-gift, my lady." Raverre drew Lisette to her feet, wrapping his arms around her. Their eyes met in the mirror. "Do you like it?"

Lisette gazed wide-eyed at their reflections. The circlet was the loveliest piece of jewellery she had ever owned, but that was not what held her attention.

How tiny and fragile she appeared against Raverre's powerful frame, and how devastatingly handsome he looked with the morning light slanting sharply across his cheekbones, touching his firm mouth. His eyes were lowered. Following their direction, Lisette saw the telltale pulse beating in her throat.

"'Tis very beautiful," she whispered.

His arms tightened gently. "So are you," he said huskily. "That circlet makes you look like a pagan Celtic princess." His gaze lifted again to hers.

Dizziness washed over Lisette. She was mesmerised by the suddenly smouldering look in Raverre's eyes. She couldn't move, couldn't breathe. His eyes were burning her. If he had looked at her like this last night she would have died of fright. She still might if she didn't do something, say something.

"I…I really…should wear a coif…now I'm married," she whispered breathlessly.

"I know," he agreed, but he made no move to release her. One hand caressed her silky hair. "You can cover this during the day." He turned her to face him. "But not yet…not yet." His mouth came down on hers in a kiss of absolute possession.

A wild thrill of excitement shot through Lisette's entire body. If Raverre hadn't been holding her so tightly she would have fallen. She could do nothing to stop herself sagging against him, could not stop her arms from clinging to him as if he was her only support.

Still kissing her, Raverre shifted his hold. Lisette found herself swept off her feet and carried to the bed. Releasing her mouth, Raverre flung back the bearskin, and went absolutely still. Confused, Lisette looked around, her eyes falling to the small bloodstain on the sheet.

Reality rushed back with a vengeance. Blushing hotly, she glanced away. "Put me down. Please," she begged, unable to look at him.

Raverre lowered her to the floor, but he captured her face, his eyes now searching troubled.

"Did I hurt you so badly," he asked urgently. "Oh, sweetheart. I'm sorry."

His concern completely undermined what was left of her defences.

"'Twas only a slight hurt," she whispered, feeling strangely impelled to reassure him. "Truly I barely noticed…" Lisette faltered, blushing again at the expression that flashed into his eyes. How could she be distant and dutiful when he looked at her like that?

Then, as his mouth lowered again, she panicked. "They'll be waiting for us in the hall," she quavered.

Raverre hesitated. Then, with a swiftness that left her gasping, he picked Lisette up and deposited her on the bed, flinging himself down beside her and throwing an arm across her as she went to leap up.

"Oh, no," he said softly, leaning over her, his eyes fixed on her face with glittering intensity. "I have you now, my lovely wife, and I intend to hold you. For the rest of our lives."

Lisette gazed up at him, wondering what she was meant to say to this possessive statement. It seemed safer to stay silent. She doubted if she could speak anyway, because the only words she could think of were distant and dutiful. She kept repeating them over and over to herself as though they were a magic incantation which would protect her.

She didn't want to ask why she needed protection.

"You're still afraid of me," Raverre murmured, stroking her cheek with his knuckles. "I'll never hurt you again, love, I swear it."

He'd misunderstood her panic, Lisette realised thankfully. But before she could speak he pressed his mouth gently to the fluttering pulse in her throat.

"Your heart is beating like a trapped bird's," he said softly. "Relax, sweet." He raised his head, puzzled. "You were less—"

Deliverance came in the form of a knock at the door.

Raverre flicked a glance across the room. "Our dinner must be getting cold," he remarked, slanting a wry smile down at Lisette. "Wouldn't you think they'd know better than to—?"

The knock came again.

Muttering something under his breath, Raverre swung himself off the bed. He strode over to the door and yanked it open. *"What?"*

Gilbert and Siward both stepped back in a hurry.

"Sorry, sir," apologised Gilbert, recovering first. "But I thought you should know. A band of serfs turned up in the village just now. Siward says they're asking for shelter."

"Wonderful timing," growled Raverre. He looked a question at Siward.

"Five men, my lord," the blacksmith elaborated. "They say their master has fled. They've been living in the forest, but they have women and children who will not survive another winter in the open. The leader says they're willing to swear fealty to you. I have him out in the bailey."

"Very well, bring him in. I'll see him shortly." Raverre started to close the door. "Feed them," he added curtly. The door slammed.

Gilbert and Siward looked at each other. "I think I'll go hunting this afternoon," announced Gilbert. "And if I were you, Siward, I'd find plenty of work to do elsewhere for the rest of the day."

"We won't see those two for the rest of the day," remarked Raverre, turning to Lisette.

He gave a somewhat reluctant smile when he saw that she had lost no time in leaving the bed. Her hair was now arranged in the most haphazard braid he had ever seen, and she was replacing the circlet over a white linen coif. Then she turned, and the wary relief on her face wiped the smile from his own.

There was a long, uncomfortable silence. Finally Raverre turned and held open the door.

"Come, my lady," he said, his voice very cool. "Dinner awaits."

* * *

Harness jingled. Horses stamped, snorting cloudy breaths into the frosty air. The wind blew coldly, bending the bare branches of the trees standing sentinel along the road. Far to the west storm clouds were gathering in a slowly eddying grey mass.

And Raverre was angry with her.

Since yesterday he had scarcely addressed two words to her. Lisette had retired early, falling into a surprisingly deep sleep, and if she hadn't seen the indentation left by Raverre's head on the pillow next to her she would not have known that he had shared her bed last night.

Lisette eyed her husband as he issued instructions to the soldiers accompanying Enide and three serfs to Romsey. The serfs had been chosen for Enide's comfort and security—Alfrida to see to her needs, and two men to accompany the girl back to Ambray. Raverre trusted them to return, Lisette realised. Why did that realisation make her feel worse? Feel this sudden need to tell him—?

Lisette stopped her thoughts, concentrating fiercely on the farewell between her sisters. With the usual buoyancy of youth Catherine looked as cheerful as if she were merely seeing Enide off on a short jaunt, instead of parting with her forever.

Annoyed at her own tearful emotions, Lisette embraced her older sister briskly. Enide drew back to look into Lisette's face.

"It should be I standing in your place, I know," she began in a low voice. She went on quickly as Lisette made to protest. "No, please hear me. I had not the courage, though I have long known that your husband would not treat a woman harshly.

"Oh, Lisette, forgive me! I shall pray every day that you find the happiness you deserve with him, that I have not done you a terrible wrong. And do not judge Raverre too hardly. He is sending a dowry with me so I may not be taken in on sufferance. Few men would do as much, when he has already permitted me to retire to the cloister.''

Lisette felt tears well in her eyes. She blinked them rapidly away, embracing her sister. ''There is nought to forgive, dearest sister. Go with God and be content.''

Enide turned away quickly, and in a flurry of mounting riders and shouted farewells they were through the gates, disappearing down the road in a slowly subsiding cloud of dust.

''Well, that's one less for you to worry about,'' muttered Raverre behind her.

Lisette turned from her contemplation of the empty road. ''I didn't see Enide as a burden,'' she protested, guiltily remembering the times she had felt impatient with her sister. ''She suffered terribly.''

''No much more than you,'' Raverre stated bluntly. ''You might not have witnessed the attack, as she did, but you still saw the results. Bertrand told me your mother died later in your arms. And then you had to cope with the other deaths and sack of the manor.''

''I...''

''Do you think I don't know why you're so afraid of me—that you feared I would treat you as brutally?''

''No, I didn't—''

''I think Enide would have thrown herself from the tower rather than marry a Norman for the sake of her people. I hope she realises how fortunate she is in her sister.''

''No, you mustn't be so hard. Enide couldn't help—''

''Being weak.''

Was she never to get a word in? ''I wasn't going to say—''

''Do you wish 'twas yourself riding away to a life of

dedication to God?'' he asked suddenly, his gaze intent on her face.

Lisette looked away towards the road. A gust of wind sent a pile of dead leaves dancing in twirling abandon after the riders. She recognised the absolute truth of her answer before she spoke.

''No, I have never wanted that. Even when I thought it the only alternative to—''

''Marriage to me,'' he finished for her grimly.

Lisette gazed up at Raverre, confused by the rather bleak look on his face. She felt an inexplicable urge to say that marriage to him was what she now wanted. But, unwilling to do so far down a path whose destination lay shrouded in a fog of jumbled emotions and unknown consequences, she could only shake her head, clutching gratefully at Enide's words.

''I must thank you, my lord, for providing my sister with a dowry,'' she said, faltering a little as he continued to look so stern and cold. '''Twas a great kindness.''

The coldness disappeared instantly, to be replaced by such raging anger that Lisette stepped back involuntarily as Raverre's eyes went violent.

''Damn it, I don't want your gratitude!'' he snapped harshly, before turning and striding away, aggression in every line of his body.

And he stayed angry. Remaining aloof whenever their paths crossed during the day, retiring hours after Lisette and leaving her bed before she awoke. He made no attempt to claim a husband's rights, and after several days of being ignored Lisette was dismayed to find that duty had given way to longing.

A longing to be close to him that was achingly increased whenever she awoke in the night to find that, despite Raverre's puzzling behaviour, he held her tightly in his arms while he slept.

Did he know? Did he mean to hold her so possessively? Not knowing how to approach him when he continued so cold, nor even fully understanding that her own emotions were changing, Lisette struggled to prevent herself betraying her distress at the loss of the fragile companionship they had sometimes shared before their marriage.

And Raverre, tormented by the suspicion that, by taking her body before he had won her heart, she would only feel polite gratitude and duty towards him, kept his distance, treating Lisette with a cold courtesy that withered at the outset any attempt she might have made to reconcile her guilt and respond to him.

Lisette pondered over a depressing future indeed as she lingered over a substantial supper of venison stew three evenings later. Raverre had thrown a meaty bone to Finn, but the dog now turned his head towards the door as one of the men-at-arms ushered a young Norman soldier into the hall. While the man paced down the length of the room Lisette had plenty of time to notice that he had ridden long and hard; his face was lined with weariness and the dust of the road lay thick on his clothes.

Raverre and Richard de Somrey, whose men were on guard duty at the manor, had suspended their conversation at first sight of the visitor, and Raverre rose to his feet as the young man reached the table. Barely acknowledging the girls with a slight bow, he addressed Raverre in a hoarse, breathless voice, swaying with the effort of remaining upright until his message was safely delivered.

"My lord, I am Ralf de Pictou, squire in the army of our lord King, and bring you greetings from William and news that will make unpleasant hearing but must be told."

"Take your time, de Pictou," recommended Raverre

firmly, having had plenty of experience with over-eager young men burdened with a responsible errand. "A few moments to catch your breath will make no difference, whether the news be ill or not."

De Pictou steadied himself with an obvious effort.

"My lord, ill news indeed, for young Edgar the Atheling is now forsworn, and has escaped from the King's custody. Together with his mother and sister, he has taken refuge with King Malcolm of Scotland. There is rumour abroad that a marriage has been arranged between Malcolm and the Saxon princess, but 'tis not known for sure."

A startled murmur swept the hall at this announcement and some of the men leapt to their feet, but the messenger continued without a pause.

"Also, that traitor Morcar of Northumbria has broken his vows to William, and is busy stirring up a rebellion in the Midlands with the new Earl, Gospatric—another Englishman, God rot them all, who bought his Earldom from William and now has the effrontery to turn his hand against his benefactor.

"The King has sent me to warn you of his coming. He intends to personally direct the campaign against these traitors and will be travelling north as soon as he has seen all settled here on the borders."

"Then he will not be far behind you," decided Raverre, looking grim at the news. "William moves fast. Even with the whole court at his back, he'll be here in two days.

"We'll make all ready tomorrow," he announced in a louder tone for the benefit of his listening men. "To meet whatever need of men and arms the King may have."

Gesturing for them to resume their seats, he looked thoughtfully down at his guest. "But for the moment you must sit and take food." Raverre eyed the younger man shrewdly. "When did you last eat, my friend?"

Ralf swayed tiredly again and shrugged. "I ate something as I rode. To say truth, my lord, I barely remember it. And tomorrow I must be off again to warn the Earl of Hereford at Eywas Harold."

"No matter. You will have proper food and rest tonight at least."

He turned to Lisette, but she had already sent a serf hurrying to the kitchen to bring more hot food and, as their guest. seated himself thankfully between Raverre and de Somery, she gestured to Edric to bring the finger basin so that Ralf could wash his hands.

She didn't dare catch Raverre's eye. After her brave talk of Saxon nobility she was now faced with the turncoat activities of two of the country's once most powerful Earls. For if Morcar had betrayed William's trust then it was fairly safe to assume that his brother, Edwin, Earl of Mercia, would not hesitate to join him. The only possible plea she could make on their behalf would be the one King Harold had used—that their oaths of allegiance had been extracted under duress.

Clasping her hands tightly together in her lap for courage, she leaned forward and ventured an innocuous question while Raverre waited for Ralf to appease some of his hunger.

"Sir, my Lord Raverre spoke of the court. Do you know if the Queen and her ladies will be travelling with the army?"

"Aye," Ralf answered briefly, his mouth full. He turned and looked at Lisette directly for the first time, suddenly aware that a lady who looked as if she had stepped out of a book of romantic poems had addressed him, and that he had answered in a rather surly fashion.

His eyes widened and a handful of bread halted halfway

to his mouth as he took in Lisette's lovely face, framed by her white coif.

He was speedily brought back to earth by Raverre.

"In that case, I look forward to presenting my wife and her sister to the King *and* the Queen," he said conversationally, but with a hint of steel in his voice.

Ralf flushed hotly as he realised that he had been staring at his host's lady like a bumbling yokel. But, emboldened by the downcast look on her face at her husband's tone, he dared to enlarge on his answer.

"You will be pleased to see other ladies with whom to exchange gossip no doubt, madam. Queen Matilda intends to accompany the King to York, where she will no doubt have her lying-in."

"The Queen is with child?" Lisette asked, interest in this snippet of information making her forget her nervousness at displeasing Raverre.

However, he also seemed interested, and began to question Ralf closely about the court, and then the activities of the army, thereby ousting Lisette effectively from the conversation.

She sat back and glared at his unresponsive left shoulder, but could not think of another opening that would lead to the information she hoped for. Catherine, however, had no such qualms. Listening intently to the discussion between the men when they returned to the subject of the Saxon Earls, she seized the first opportunity to question young Ralf herself.

"Do you think, sir, that my Lord Morcar and the Prince were perhaps scoffed at in William's court? Or ill-treated perhaps, to have fled to Scotland?" she asked innocently, not wishing to believe that her countrymen could have behaved so dishonourably without good reason.

De Somery gave a derisive snort, but Ralf answered politely enough, although he directed his response to Lisette rather than Catherine.

"Not at all, my lady. Quite the contrary. When the Atheling and his company landed in Normandy with William last year they were fêted and made much of; respected for their learning and noble appearance, and treated with all courtesy and the honour due to their rank. And William brought them back to England with him, even allowing them to return to their estates. No, 'tis undisguised treachery on their part," he finished more angrily.

The girls exchanged dismayed glances, but Raverre, sensing their disquiet, softened the blow by remarking, "Edgar won't be much of a problem. I warrant the boy will come running back to William's heels when he grows tired of the Scottish court. Malcolm, too, will need more incentive than the promise of Edgar's sister in marriage to antagonise William. Border skirmishes are more his style, not a confrontation with the whole Norman army. 'Tis Morcar and Edwin who need to be taught a lesson—they surrendered to William of their own accord, remember."

"Aye," growled de Somery. "Those two weanling Earls have never met William in battle. They need a taste of Norman warfare."

The dour knight sounded so gratified at this prospect that Lisette almost expected him to lick his lips in anticipation.

If de Somery's attitude echoed the King's, she quaked at the thought of the lesson the Earls were likely to be taught, but Ralf apparently thought William would be more inclined to be lenient.

"We didn't expect him to execute his own half-brother, even after the trouble Odo stirred up within the army," he said after remarking on the King's behaviour. "But we did think he would be imprisoned at least. However, all William did was send the Bishop back to Normandy, and still

in a position of some authority. William's mercy to his
enemies is becoming something of a byword. Even the
common folk are not treated hardly. Take the case of the
butcher—''

He caught sight of de Somery's expression, which clearly
mirrored his desire to get on with talk of war. "But I weary
you with such irrelevant tales."

"Oh, no," protested Lisette, not seeing Raverre's quick
frown in her eagerness to hear news of the outside world.
"Please do tell us, sir. We have not had any visitors for so
long."

Ralf flushed with gratified pleasure at being so eagerly
addressed by such a beautiful lady. Sending her a glowing
look, he launched enthusiastically into his tale.

"Well, my lady, it came about when the butcher who
supplied the court, one Siegbert, sold the panterer bad meat.
Fortunately the man realised the stuff was unfit to be eaten
and went straight to the King to complain, thinking the
butcher might have intended some deliberate harm. But apparently he was only interested in making the most money
for the least value." In spite of his indignation, Ralf began
to laugh.

"The punishment was fitting at least, if some thought it
too mild. The rogue was put in the pillory and the foul stuff
burnt under his nose. He could not move his head, of
course, and his grimaces were something to behold, I can
tell you. The crowd enjoyed the sight, in any event, and
added to the wretch's discomfort with their jeers. 'Twas
more like a show of mummery than a penalty, but I swear
he won't try to cheat his customers again."

Even Raverre smiled in appreciation of the story. Lisette,
relieved that he didn't seem to be angry with her for wishing to hear it, rose from the table.

"An amusing tale, sir," she said, smiling warmly at Ralf,

whose chest swelled visibly. "Thank you for indulging a female's curiosity. But you will no doubt have much to talk about with my lord, and we ladies shall only be in the way," she added gracefully, preparing to retire with Catherine.

"Must you go indeed, my lady?" asked Ralf, looking crestfallen at the thought of losing such a charming audience. "There are many more tales of town life which—"

But Raverre had also risen, and slanted a cool look down at the younger man.

"My lady will have a busy day or two ahead of her, and you, sir, will have to leave in the early morning to reach the Earl of Hereford with William's message," he stated unequivocally. "There is still much I would like to discuss with you, so the ladies do well to retire early."

Ralf was abashed, but couldn't resist pressing an ardent kiss on to Lisette's hand as she wished him Godspeed, or a lingering look as Raverre escorted her to the solar. Barely giving her time for the briefest of goodnights to her sister, he handed Lisette through the door.

"It will be late when I join you, my lady," he said tersely. "Sleep well." And, turning away before she could answer, he strode back to the table without another glance.

Lisette closed the solar door with something of a snap. Really! What had she done now? she wondered crossly, not recognising that Raverre's behaviour sprang from jealousy. Not having had the slightest intention of attracting young Ralf, nor even noticing his reaction to her interest, so eager had she been to hear news of life outside their own small community, Lisette could only surmise that her husband's cavalier treatment of her this evening was just part of his recent change of heart.

The lowering suspicion that Raverre felt he no longer needed to give her any extraordinary degree of attention now they were married could not be ignored. Wistfully remembering the times when he had teased her or tried to coax her into a better understanding of him, and forgetting that she had repulsed any warmer advances, Lisette felt miserably on the verge of tears. Only her scornful dislike of such feminine weakness prevented her from giving way to them as she prepared for bed.

Chapter Seven

Several hours later Lisette awoke to the sound of thunder growling overhead. The ominous storm clouds hovering in the west over the past few days seemed finally to have come to a head directly above them.

A brilliant flash of lightning illuminated the room, followed seconds later by a cacophony of thunder claps which almost shook the solid foundations of the castle. In the glaring light Lisette saw that she had forgotten to fasten the shutters across the window.

With a quick glance at Raverre she slipped from the bed, meaning to remedy her oversight. However, the scene that met her eyes as she glanced outside made her pause, spellbound.

The countryside lay in dense blackness, but the darkness of the upper sky was lifted by the eerie moonlight which showed through the violent, constant shifting of the clouds as they streamed across the sky like galloping wraiths, their voices the shrieking of the wind, lightning the spur driving them on.

''The Wild Hunt,'' Lisette whispered, awed, unaware that Raverre, also awakened by the storm, had come up behind her.

"Hunt?" he questioned, making her jump.

As Lisette turned he wrapped his cloak about her shoulders, and she clutched gratefully at its warmth. So enraptured had she been by the war of elements outside that she had quite forgotten that she was standing totally naked in the cold draught.

"The Wild Hunt," Lisette repeated, still gazing out at the sky. "The souls of the damned, riding through the storm. Don't you hear them?"

A flash of tenderness went through Raverre at the solemn conviction in her voice. He wrapped his arms about her and pulled her back against the solid strength of his body.

"'Tis only a storm," he murmured, his breath stirring her hair.

"Oh, no!" she persisted fervently. "Why, even monks have seen them. Holy men! They've told of seeing ghostly hunters riding their black deer through the sky, and of hearing the blasts of their horns."

He did seem to have heard some similar tale, remembered Raverre vaguely, but, though he was a true son of the Church, he was also much too practical a man to believe in such superstitions as phantom riders whenever a storm struck.

Intending to reassure her, he tipped Lisette's face up to his, and was instantly still, reassurance forgotten, as a flash of lightning lit up her expression.

She was not afraid, he realised at once, his heart beginning to pound, but excited. A responsive surge of desire went through him as his gaze took in her shining eyes and softly parted lips. The cool draught lifted her hair slightly and he remembered how she had looked on the cliff-top—burningly, intensely alive.

Driven by passionate instinct, all rational thought forgotten, Raverre's hand moved convulsively to grip Lisette's hair. Holding her still, he took her mouth in a searing, invading kiss that caused her own lightning to flash through her body, igniting every nerve-end.

When he felt her instant response in the soft yielding of her body as she seemed to melt against him Raverre tore his cloak from her and lifted Lisette into his arms, pressing their naked flesh together as if he would absorb her into himself. He reached the bed in two long strides, hot desire slicing through him again at the soft moan of longing which came from her throat when his weight followed her down to the mattress.

Taken completely unawares by the unexpected fierceness of Raverre's embrace, Lisette could only surrender helplessly. The drugging pressure of his mouth, the sure, possessive touch of his hands swept her beyond thought. The small voice at the back of her mind, telling her she would regret this in the morning, was silenced beneath the cascade of sensations bursting through the barriers she had imposed on her own passionate nature.

She was unable to stop herself from pressing against Raverre as tumultuous waves of pleasure broke over her again and again, unable to stop her hands from probing the hard muscles of his back, feeling them tense under her caresses as he fought for control, the urgent movements of her body beneath his driving him to the edge of insanity.

"Dear God," he whispered against her breast. "I love you. Lisette…Lisette…I love you."

But the hoarsely muttered words were in Norman and Lisette only heard the urgent male desire in his voice. She responded to it instinctively, her own aching need becoming more insistent as she abandoned herself totally to Raverre's mouth and hands.

Then she felt him move over her, gathering her into his arms. Her heart raced wildly in breathless anticipation as he parted her legs with his own. She could feel his breath short and fast against her cheek, but he held back.

"Lisette, say my name."

"What?" Oh, why was he waiting?

"You've never said it. Say my name." His voice was rough, tense with restraint, but the compelling demand reached her.

"Alain?" she whispered, confused, but willing to give him what he wanted if he would only satisfy the throbbing ache inside her. And then she repeated it more surely, longingly, "Oh, Alain."

With an almost feral growl of triumph he surged forward.

Lisette immediately forgot the tacit admission Raverre had forced from her. This was what she wanted...needed. The heat of him—the hard strength of his arms—the unleashed male hunger that burned away resistance and left the utterly consuming need to be joined with him. One heart...one body...one soul. And then she was swept into a spiralling whirlwind of pleasure so intense that Lisette cried out, ceasing to think at all.

Raverre felt the tremors shaking her body, heard her cry of completion, and his control shattered instantly. He was pulled violently into the fiery whirlwind with her. Lost in her...possessing her...possessed.

She was retreating from him. He could feel it. Feel tension replace the languid softness of her body as she lay beneath him. And he didn't know how to stop it. He didn't even want to relinquish his possessive hold, but he knew his weight must be crushing her.

Slowly, reluctantly, Raverre rolled to the side, turning Lisette into the circle of his arms. Stroking damp tendrils of hair from her face with a hand that shook slightly, he tried to see her face. But just as their own wild storm had passed, bathing them in a trembling aftermath, so too had the tumult outside, and the night was still and dark again.

Damn it, he wouldn't let her retreat now. He would never be able to leave her alone after tonight, despite his intention to wait until he'd won Lisette's love before taking her again. Under the goad of hot jealousy aroused by de Pictou's interest in her that intention had dissolved like snow in the spring thaw.

And if he had to use his power to arouse the passionate response Lisette had just given him then he'd do it, if it would make her love him. But he wouldn't damage her pride, Raverre vowed silently as he heard her take in a shuddering breath. She needed time. Time to admit she had wanted him as much as he wanted her.

Raverre held Lisette closer, stroking her hair gently. "Go to sleep, love," he murmured. "And don't regret this." He kissed her with devastating tenderness. "Don't ever regret this."

Aye, sleep, Lisette told herself. Don't think. Don't think at all. The morning and its inevitable recriminations would come soon enough.

"'Twas the storm, for sure."

"Aye," agreed Lisette firmly. She and Catherine were in the garden, repairing the ravages of the night before. "After all, people do behave strangely when under the influences of nature's forces. Remember that poor woman who ran amok in the village last year at the full of the moon? Tearing her hair and scratching her face and screaming that the Normans were really demons from hell who were going to devour us all?"

Catherine stared at her sister in bewildered astonishment. "Holy St Elizabeth save you, Lisette. What has that to do with the damage to the garden?"

Lisette flushed hotly, quickly bending over a flattened lavender bush. "Well…nought…but…" She let the sentence die away.

She really was losing her mind. She hadn't even been listening to Catherine's chatter, but had been wholly occupied in convincing herself that the primitive elements of nature had touched off an answering chord within herself last night. How else could she explain her wanton response to Raverre?

"I think we've finished here," she said hurriedly. "And I have to speak to Wat."

"Lisette, are you feeling quite—?"

"I'm perfectly well, sweet sister. Come, there's still much to do."

"Well, there are plenty of serfs to do it," observed Catherine practically as they rounded the corner of the tower. "I'm going to watch the huts being built."

"Huts?"

"Aye. Didn't you hear Raverre say we needed two or three huts to house some of the guests? Look, they've started already."

Lisette glanced across the bailey. Against the sheltered north wall, men were erecting the framework of a small beehive-shaped cruck, attempting to bend one of the oak branches which would form the curved walls and roof. Some rather impious language wafted across the open space towards the girls as one of the men lost his grip and the branch sprang smartly upright again.

Then Lisette noticed Raverre. He had stripped to his leggings, and now lent his formidable strength to the task of bending the solid branch. The sunlight caressed his fair hair and the play of muscles across his broad shoulders, and Lisette instantly remembered the feel of both beneath her hands the night before. The sudden sharp stab of desire she experienced to touch him again startled her. Then Raverre turned and their eyes met.

"You go on," Lisette said breathlessly to Catherine. "I've forgotten the herbs Wat asked me to bring him."

Wheeling about, she fled back to the garden, appalled that the sight of Raverre half-naked had made her weak with longing to lie in his arms again.

What was happening to her? She had woken this morning to find herself alone again, and had been shocked at the pang of disappointment that had lanced through her. And now this. One look from him and she melted inside. How could she have such feelings for a man who was showing only too clearly that he had married her for the sake of expediency? Why did she have to wonder what it would be like if Raverre loved her? It shouldn't matter. She didn't love him. She didn't!

"Good morning."

At the sound of the deep, husky voice behind her Lisette froze. She could not face him. She couldn't bear it if he was cold again. Or, worse, triumphant. Did he think he had conquered her heart, despite her brave words that first night at supper? She had to salvage her pride. She would not surrender so easily. Raverre had overwhelmed her last night, but she had only yielded her body. Not her mind. Not her heart.

Her brain in total confusion, Lisette grabbed the willow basket she had left on the wall. Kneeling, she blindly grasped a bunch of thyme and pulled. The entire plant came away in her hand.

She glared at the inoffensive herb in vexation, which quickly turned to dismay as Raverre took the plant from her, tossed it into the basket and brought her upright with a strong grip on her arms. Shifting his hands to Lisette's waist, he lifted her to sit on the wall, trapping her between his braced arms.

Through her indignation at this demonstration of easy masculine strength, she was conscious of relief that he'd donned his tunic again.

"Good morning," Raverre repeated. His voice was soft, but Lisette saw the determined gleam in his ice-blue eyes.

"Good morning," she whispered back, helpless under that compelling demand.

Immediately the ice melted into shimmering warmth. "Should I warn the King that his dinner is going to be highly spiced?" he asked with a smile that was totally irresistible.

Lisette's thoughts of salvaged pride promptly flew out of her head. She smiled shyly back at him.

Raverre leaned forward, his hands still resting on the wall, and pressed a gentle, sensuous kiss to her mouth, which immediately set her insides fluttering. But before Lisette could give in to the desire to return the slight pressure of his lips he drew back to gaze into her eyes.

Lisette's lashes fluttered down in confusion. He didn't seem to be triumphant at her utter lack of resistance to him, she thought. Rather, there had been a strangely searching look in his eyes. But what did he seek? And why?

With an abruptness that made Lisette's eyes fly back to his face Raverre straightened.

"I came to tell you that I must ride to Godric to inform him of William's coming. You will be pleased to see the old man, I expect."

Both voice and expression were calm, but there was something in the forced stillness of his body that gave Lisette an impression of precarious control. It made her nervous.

"Aye, but…must you go yourself, my lord?"

Raverre's eyes blazed with sudden light. "I'll return to-day, sweetheart. Do you think I would let you spend the night alone?"

Hot colour flooded Lisette's cheeks. Holy Saints, what had made her say that?

Unable to look at him, she stammered, "I…I mean…'tis a long ride, and if the King should arrive…"

"William won't be here until tomorrow," Raverre answered, watching her like a hawk. In fact, Lisette realised with a shiver, she was beginning to feel distinctly hunted.

"I go myself as a courtesy to Godric," he added, still not taking his eyes from her. "But I'll take some men should Godric decide to postpone the journey until tomorrow; he is an old man and may wish for a stronger escort than a few serfs. Let us hope he is in reasonable health, as I think 'twould put his mind at rest to swear allegiance to William. He told me that he and your father often argued about who would be better for England—William or Harold. And I believe he fell out with his son over the same question."

Lisette nodded in uneasy agreement, but couldn't resist saying, "My father chose Harold because he was English and had been elected by the Witan and King Edward."

"An unfortunate choice, as it turned out," Raverre commented. "William also claimed that Edward promised him the crown of England, and he is too direct a man to lie about such things." His voice hardened slightly. "And, since we're on the subject, I ask you not to anger William by arguing Harold's lost cause or bringing up the King's bastard blood. For your own safety, Lisette, if not for my sake."

"But you are his friend," she pointed out, wondering how far Raverre would go to ensure she didn't antagonise his King. "Would William punish his friend's wife for her loyalty to her people, or for stating the truth if he is so honest himself?''

Raverre shrugged. ''Tis difficult to say. William is usually even-tempered and he appreciates loyalty, but his mother's origins are a sore point with him. You would have to know more of his earlier life to understand. He has had to get used to discarding friends who seemed to betray him.''

He hesitated a moment, then took her hands. ''You probably won't want to hear this,'' he warned softly, ''but your father would have sworn to William after Harold was killed. Both Godric and Father Edwin have said as much. I would have told you sooner, but I thought it likely you wouldn't believe me. Now, however, you have to know if it will obtain me your promise to be careful.''

Feeling outnumbered and outmanoeuvred, Lisette promised. There was not much else she could do when Raverre spoke so convincingly and at the same time held her with that compelling gaze. She was rewarded with the warm, intimate smile he had given her before, but, feeling that this time he was using his considerable charm to manipulate her, she refused to respond. Pulling her hands away, Lisette jumped down from the wall. She felt oddly hurt.

''I must see things put to rights inside,'' she said curtly. ''You will not be shamed before your King, my lord.''

''Last night you called me Alain,'' Raverre murmured before he could stop himself.

He saw Lisette go still. Then his heart leapt as he watched her lips silently form his name. Taking a quick step forward, he reached for her…a moment too late.

Lisette had fled.

The minute Raverre rode out of sight on his way to Godric's manor, Lisette acted. All through an interminable dinner she had been making plans as the realisation had dawned on her that here was the only opportunity she might have to investigate the caves in the forest.

Raverre would be gone for several hours, and, although some might think it strange for the lady of the manor to go riding when they were expecting visitors, she was confident that her serfs would not ask questions. The Normans were another matter entirely, and Lisette set her mind to thinking of a plausible tale that would satisfy whoever was on duty at the gate.

First she would need protection. Preferably unsuspecting, silent protection, so she enlisted Oswy's help. That presented no difficulties. It seemed perfectly logical to his simple mind that he should escort his mistress, since she was going to visit his mother, and he happily saddled up Lisette's horse to be ready whenever she wished to leave.

Catherine was next. That, too, was easy. Knowing how her sister would receive an invitation to call on a respectable cottar's wife who had known her since she was an infant, and would bemoan her hoydenish behaviour at great length, Lisette issued it. Catherine declined with haste, only too happy to be asked to direct the house carls in binding up fresh rush lights for every sconce in the castle, and completely forgetting to ask why Lisette felt it necessary to pay such a visit now.

Marjory was supervising the laying of clean linen on the beds and generally keeping an eye on things in the kitchen, much to its master's annoyance. Overhearing an acrimonious debate about the merits of using larks in a pie as opposed to pigeons, Lisette was confident that Marjory would be kept well occupied for some time.

Luck, almost deserted her, however, when she led Viking Princess to the mounting block and saw, with a sinking heart, that Richard de Somery was speaking to the soldiers at the gate. By his casual attitude he looked as if he had all the time in the world to stand talking to his men, and Lisette knew she couldn't afford to wait until he had business elsewhere.

Relying on her father's oft-expressed theory that a confident attitude carried the day, she rode boldly up to the gate, Oswy by her side. As she expected, de Somery halted her with an enquiry about her purpose in riding out, politely enough but determined upon an answer.

"I go to visit Oswy's mother, sir," she answered composedly. "To ask for her help at the castle while our visitors are here."

"Can the lad not go by himself?" questioned de Somery. To his credit, the man's concern was mainly for Lisette's safety while Raverre was absent from the manor, but she turned her haughtiest look on him.

"I dare say he could, but I consider it a courtesy to go myself," she stated, borrowing Raverre's words. "Besides," she added, lowering her voice, "he may not deliver my message correctly and I want all to go well during the King's visit."

De Somery could find no fault with this. After eyeing Oswy, who was gazing dreamily off into the distance, he nodded acquiescence.

"Very well, my lady. But I know my lord would wish you to take some men as escort. That young fellow may be big enough, but he's none too quick in his reasoning."

"Nonsense!" she remonstrated briskly. "Oswy is all the protection I need on our own land. My errand will only take a short time, *if* I am permitted to start immediately," she glanced pointedly at his hand, which still held her horse's bridle.

Not a man to be easily intimidated, however, de Somery stood his ground. "Do I have your word to return before dusk, then, my lady?" he insisted.

"Of course," Lisette answered, fervently hoping she could keep her promise. The very thought of Raverre's reaction should he return home to find her missing was enough to add complete conviction to her tone. "I have no wish to be out riding after dark, I assure you."

After a tense moment of contemplation de Somery nodded and stepped back, obviously not entirely satisfied, but unable to think of a valid reason to order Lisette to abandon her errand.

Keeping her face impassive, she trotted through the gates, Oswy obediently keeping pace at her stirrup.

As soon as they were out of sight of the manor Lisette changed direction. Fervently praying she would have enough time to search the caves and carry out her hastily manufactured errand, she urged Viking Princess to a faster pace, but one which Oswy could match, not stopping until they reached a spinney in the depths of the forest without hindrance.

There Lisette left Oswy guarding her horse, and slipped through the trees. The forest here was thickly wooded and dim in the fading afternoon light. She would have to hurry. Though Raverre would not return until after dark, she must be back at the manor herself before nightfall or a hue and cry would begin.

De Somery had still looked as if he doubted her flimsy story, and Lisette suspected he had only let her go because he had not received any specific order to keep her inside the castle walls. That would not stop him, however, from instigating a search should she not return in good time for supper.

Freeing her mantle from a clinging branch and stepping carefully over a tangle of impeding roots, Lisette sped onwards, hoping her memory would not lead her astray. It had been years since she had played here, peopling the caves and the wood with magical creatures and heroic knights. Remembering her girlish dreams of one particular handsome knight who would rescue her from some un-named terror, fall instantly in love with her, and spirit her away to everlasting happiness with him, she was annoyed to find herself picturing Raverre in that role.

Resolutely suppressing the thought, she brought her wandering mind back to the present. A flurry of wings above her head made her jump and she scolded herself for her nervousness. There was no reason to be afraid. Oswy was only a short distance away, though the density of trees made her feel as if she were quite alone, it was still daylight, and she had given up imagining nameless terrors long ago.

Had the caves been this far from the spinney? She could not remember and, pausing, anxiously peered about, wondering if she had passed by them unnoticing. No, surely that gnarled old oak looked familiar, with its thick cloak of moss spreading along its roots and up the immense trunk.

Moving faster now as memory rushed back, Lisette took a straight line from the mossy side of the ancient tree, and was rewarded moments later by the pile of rocks which marked the entrance to the old Roman ironworks.

It was not surprising that Raverre's men had not mentioned the caves, Lisette realised as she approached. Over the years the hanging branches of the surrounding trees had encroached on the entrance, and even to a keen eye the haphazard pile of rocks merely had the appearance of a simple cairn erected by some long-forgotten tribe.

Lisette pushed her way through the almost leafless branches, ignoring the scratches her hands received, and felt her way along the ancient stones until her searching fingers slid into the crevice which she knew led into the several chambers excavated by the efficient Romans.

She hesitated, suddenly nervous at the thought of leaving the comparative light of the forest. What if her instinct was wrong and some other fugitive, unknown and threatening, had taken refuge in this lonely, forbidding place?

Leofwin had a comfortable home to return to, after all, even if he had disagreed with his father as to which side to take. When she stopped to think Lisette could not imagine why Leofwin would choose to stay in a cave at all, let alone for any length of time, and she began to feel rather foolish for risking possible danger or Raverre's wrath should he ever find out what she was doing.

Then she recalled the sniper and steeled herself. She had not come this far only to draw back now. If Leofwin was here and she could persuade him to return home then she would do so. And she would also have to explain what had happened to Enide.

Squaring her shoulders, Lisette squeezed through the crevice, stopping just inside the first small chamber as inky blackness embraced her, and cursing herself for not thinking to bring a candle.

The caves were much darker than she remembered, but then years ago the entrance had been fully exposed, and they had only played in the full light of midday.

Lisette took a shaky breath and called into the sombre gloom, "Leofwin?"

Her voice sounded tremulous and hesitant in the extreme. Mentally giving herself an impatient shake, she called more loudly, "Leofwin, are you there? 'Tis Lisette."

Dark silence pressed about her for what seemed like several minutes, and Lisette was about to slide thankfully back into the daylight, when a footfall sounded. A second later faint light flickered against the rock wall ahead of her.

Her heart thumping violently, Lisette watched a hand appear around the angle of a jutting rock.

The hand was followed by its owner, a ragged individual, barely decently covered by his torn clothes, his gaunt, pale face glowering at her through a rough, untrimmed beard and long, shaggy hair. Lisette thought she was about to swoon away for the second time in her life, before she let out a gasp of relief as the apparition came closer, and she recognised the man she was seeking.

Slumping against the side of the rock chamber with relief, she tried to steady her racing pulse.

"Lisette?" the creature questioned cautiously, holding the light higher. "Holy Mother, it really *is* you! Why are you…how did you know?"

"Never mind that now," she answered, swiftly regaining control of herself with the sharp awareness of passing time. However, as her eyes adjusted to the gloom, his pitiful condition distracted her.

"Oh, Leofwin, look at you!" she cried, distressed. "To what lengths have you gone to be living like an animal in a cave, waiting to starve or be captured? Why have you not returned to your father, or sent word to Enide?"

"You think 'tis that easy?" Leofwin asked, his wonder at seeing her quickly changing to harsh bitterness. "There's a price on my head. I've risked all, coming back to this district, but I needed money. I would have had it, too, if those fools hadn't bungled… But never mind that. Tostig was to steal some from my father's manor but the fool has either been caught or deserted me and I dare not wait much longer."

"Then he *was* your man!" Lisette exclaimed, fixing on the one thing that made sense to her. "Oh, Leofwin, don't you see? 'Tis what made me think you might be here, and, if I think of it, others will too. You must go home! Reconcile with your father. He has mourned you as dead these two years—do you think he would not welcome you, forgetting past disputes?''

''Just a minute, Lisette! Never mind my doddering fool of a father, what do you know of Tostig?''

''He is dead,'' she answered baldly, too shaken by his callous description of his parent to choose her words. Had Leofwin said *steal* money from the old man? And what bungling fools? Lisette began to wonder how wise she had been in coming here so impulsively. Was this the boy who had shared those long-ago sunlit days of her childhood, the man her gentle sister had sworn to love?

''How did he die?'' Leofwin asked in a hard voice, bringing her attention back to the present.

''He tried to kill the man who has been granted my father's lands,'' she answered more carefully this time. ''If your own father dies your lands will also be forfeit, Leofwin, but if you return you may yet claim your rightful place.''

''Aye, by swearing fealty to the Norman bastard!'' he retorted angrily. ''Why do you think I'm in hiding, girl? I've been trying to rally our people to rebellion, but the spirit has been beaten out of them. I had hopes of my lords of Northumbria and Mercia, but they were only interested in their own gain, and sided with William. We needed money and would have had it if the idiots I hired hadn't been blinded by that ingot.''

''*You* arranged that robbery?'' gasped Lisette.

Leofwin didn't seem to notice her shock. ''So you know about it. Aye, but the plan went awry. When I saw they'd stolen the gold instead of coin and jewels I thought at first we could take the ingot down river to the Thames and across the Channel to France. The French King has little love for William, and there we could have melted it down. But the others took fright, and Tostig and I couldn't handle it alone. Do you know how much the damn thing weighs? 'Tis still hidden underwater in the Itchen,'' Leofwin finished bitterly.

"But you, Lisette.'' He gave her a hard stare, seeming to realise he might have said more than he should. ''How are you living at Ambray if a Norman Baron now holds the land? I suppose you're ekeing out a living on a miserable strip of land that no one happened to want, like so many others.''

"Not quite,'' she hedged, unwilling after what she had just heard to inform him of the exact nature of her circumstances. ''But Enide. Don't you wish to hear word of her?''

Leofwin gave a harsh laugh. ''Aye, my gentle betrothed,'' he jeered, as if only just remembering. ''Do you think she would be willing to cross the country with me, hiding like escaped slaves, and then take ship for so far a place as Constantinople?''

Lisette flinched from his sarcasm, but could not remain silent.

"But you love Enide,'' she faltered. ''I remember how you argued with my father before he would consent... Did you say Constantinople?''

"I have to leave the country,'' he answered, as if that explained everything. ''Many Thegns have joined the Varangian Guard of the Byzantine Emperor, where, let me tell you, we'll be accorded the respect we deserve! But first I need money and clothing. Some food would not come amiss either. You'll have to bring me some, Lisette.''

She shook her head, but not in bewilderment than refusal. "But—''

"Ah, Enide,'' he remembered. ''Well, you may tell her to consider herself free of me. She is no use without her inheritance. I notice she didn't accompany her little sister, but then she was always the shrinking one of you three, wasn't she?'' His scorn was unmistakable.

''But you loved her!'' insisted Lisette, feeling stupidly repetitive, but unable to reconcile the Leofwin she remembered with the contemptuous stranger before her.

''And you were always the romantic,'' he scoffed. ''Enide was the eldest—your father's heiress, you little fool. Of course I asked for her. But,'' he continued in a thoughtful voice, ''I often wished you had been in her place. You always had twice her spirit and you've grown quite lovely, little playmate. I thought you would, and I had plans. Still, you can hardly carry your lands with you, so your lack of dowry doesn't really matter now.''

Without warning Lisette was conscious of a new danger. She could not name it, but it seemed to hover in the air between them, almost taking tangible form as Leofwin continued to speak, almost to himself.

''You wouldn't hesitate to flee the country with the man you loved, whatever the dangers, would you, my pretty? You used to act out such fantasies, didn't you? In this very place. And what remains for you here? A life of poverty? Slavery to a Norman Baron? Or do you think to retire to watch your beauty fade away in some cloistered nunnery? No, I don't think we can allow that.''

Lisette straightened her spine to its fullest extent. She had to stop this right now.

''Leofwin, listen to me!'' she ordered, her voice an unconscious feminine echo of Raverre's when he was issuing commands. ''Why should you leave England? Surely you don't really wish to—?''

''Haven't you heard a word I said?'' he demanded impatiently. ''If someone blabs about that robbery I'll be outlawed. Unless I can leave the country I might as well be dead.''

"But you know where the ingot is hidden," Lisette argued eagerly. "Don't you see? If it's as valuable as everyone says and 'twas returned you would be pardoned."

"Aye, and penniless, knowing William's liking for wealth and lands—may he rot in hell."

"You won't lose your lands. Your father is going to swear fealty to the King and may be able to intercede for you. Why, even now my husband is on his way to your manor to inform Lord Godric of William's arrival."

Or more likely on his way back by now, she thought to herself, anxiously wondering what time it was.

"The Duke is coming here?" Leofwin queried sharply, his attention momentarily diverted from their argument. "Jesu, what an opportunity. But what can I do about it alone?"

"Don't even think of doing anything!" said Lisette firmly. "Do you imagine for one moment that William travels unprotected? And in this instance most of the army will be with him."

Leofwin's brows rose in interrogation.

"He is mustering soldiers to put down a rebellion in the north," she explained. "So you see how careful you must be. Leofwin, I beg you, go home."

Lisette began to edge towards the entrance, where a reassuring sliver of daylight still showed.

"I must return also," she added, hoping he wouldn't try to detain her. "Before dark."

"Lisette, wait!"

As she hesitated, looking worried, Leofwin put out a hand. His teeth showed in a smile, but the light was too dim for Lisette to see the coldly calculating expression in his eyes.

"I've shocked you with all this talk of robbery, but remember 'twas done for our people. And I'll think about going to my father.''

This sounded so much more like the Leofwin she had known that Lisette smiled at him for the first time. The effect was unfortunate.

His voice and gaze sharpened. "You spoke of a husband. Who?''

"You would not know him," she quickly evaded, foreseeing more precious time wasted in explanations if she named Raverre.

"Tostig told me he had seen a dark-haired lady with a Norman Baron. As thick as thieves, he said, although I found it difficult to believe. Perhaps I was wrong. Who is your husband, Lisette?''

"Please, Leofwin, I can tell you about it another time. I must go before I'm missed! Oswy is waiting for me.''

He hesitated at this, then nodded. "Very well, but first I'll make sure no one is lurking about outside.''

He brushed past her and cautiously eased through the crevice, returning a minute later to the entrance, where Lisette waited, casting an anxious look at the sky.

"All clear," he reported. "Where's your horse?''

"In the spinney," she said hurriedly. "Leofwin, think on what I've said, but if you still wish to leave England I may not see you again, so—''

"We'll see if we meet again or not," he said enigmatically, giving her another hard stare before sliding back through the hanging foliage.

For a moment Lisette could only gaze at the spot where Leofwin had been, wondering at his meaning. Then she felt the chill breeze rustling through the trees as the wood seemed to settle down for the coming night.

Whirling about, Lisette made for the spinney as fast as she could. Apart from the urgency of getting home before de Somery became suspicious, the forest, with its air of eerie mystery as the light dimmed and a barely discernible mist swirled across the ground, was the last place she wanted to be when night fell.

Raverre himself did not return until well after everyone had retired to bed. Thinking Lisette deep in slumber, he stretched out beside her, gathered her into the curve of his body and promptly fell asleep.

Sleep did not come so readily to Lisette. For some time she went over her conversation with Leofwin, worrying about what he might do and still feeling distressed at his involvement in the robbery. She had been so shocked, she recalled, that she had completely forgotten to tell him of Enide's whereabouts, although in view of his attitude this oversight hardly seemed to matter.

And for herself? How could she send to his death a man she had known all her life? She had to give Leofwin time. If he did not come with Godric to the King then she could think again.

Having reached this decision, Lisette felt better. Snuggling down under the bearskin, she allowed her tense muscles to relax. And so protected did she feel lying in Raverre's arms that Leofwin's vague mention of past plans concerning her vanished entirely from her mind.

The following morning all was bustle and activity. Word had come that the King and his retinue were well on the way and would arrive in time for a late dinner.

Serfs were sent scurrying in all directions, making sure every corner of the manor was looking its best. The hall was swept free of old rushes and their accumulated litter before fresh ones were scattered, mixed with herbs to counteract the unavoidable odours of daily life. Raverre's carved chair was polished until the wood gleamed, and Wat's frequently shouted imprecations echoed from the kitchen.

Lisette herself gathered a bouquet of late-autumn blooms from the garden to place in the solar in honour of the Queen, and it was here that Raverre found her, absorbed in the arrangement of the flowers.

"There's really no need for all this fuss," he assured her as she stood back, anxiously surveying her handiwork. "Matilda will be only too pleased to spend a night in the comfort of a civilised manor instead of a tent, or the crude wooden castles William builds as he travels."

He lifted one of Lisette's hands to his lips, intending to take his leave of her to meet William on the road, but paused as his eyes caught the deep scratch across the backs of her fingers.

"And I certainly don't expect you to injure yourself preparing for our guests, my sweet," he scolded gently, obviously assuming she had received the slight hurt in the garden. "Have you a salve to put on this?"

"'Tis only a scratch; there's no need," Lisette murmured, head bent and flushing guiltily. Prevaricating to de Somery was one thing, she now discovered. Having to lie to Raverre, if only by omission, made her feel shamefully deceitful.

When he let her hand fall abruptly her lips parted as the longing to confide in him almost overcame her. Then an image of Leofwin, gaunt and desperate, rose in her mind. How could she betray a man she had called friend? For another day at least she *must* remain silent.

Steeling herself against Lisette's obvious reluctance, Raverre turned her face to his and kissed her briefly on the lips.

"I'll be back soon," he said, more curtly than he had intended. Then, turning with a swirl of his cloak, he disappeared through the door, leaving her wondering anxiously if his brusque tone betokened suspicion.

"'Tis only guilt making you think so, Lisette told herself sternly, and decided to pacify her scruples by behaving like the perfect hostess when William arrived. It would be worth it just to see Raverre's face, she thought with a sudden burst of mischief.

This made her feel so much more like her old self that Lisette willingly joined Catherine on the tower roof an hour later to watch the arrival of King, Court and army.

They easily picked out the King's standard-bearer, the pennons flying from tall wooden staffs, just behind the lead riders.

"Do you think the man riding next to Raverre is the King?" asked Catherine. "See how rich are the trappings on his steed. He doesn't look to be as tall as Alain, but they say he is so strong that no one else can bend his bow."

"Men always tell such tales of Kings," said Lisette sceptically, but watching the riders with interest.

"Goodness, what a number of baggage wagons!" exclaimed Catherine as more lumbering vehicles appeared at the rear of the train. "That one with the drawn curtains must be the Queen's, or maybe the litter behind it. I can see a lady looking out. What a tedious way to travel—I would much rather ride."

"They do look uncomfortable," agreed Lisette. "Come. They've reached the village; we must go down and wait in the bailey."

She took a last look across the stream and saw Raverre glance up as if he sensed their observation. Impulsively Lisette waved, her long sleeve fluttering in the breeze, and he lifted an arm in a return salute before turning to speak to the man at his side, who had obviously seen the exchange.

As they hurried down to the hall Lisette felt a quick rush of gladness to know that Raverre was back. Whether it was his cool leave-taking this morning or merely his absence, she suddenly realised how secure she had come to feel with him there.

There was no time now, however, to wonder why she was so happy to see him return when she had resented his presence so much. Pushing this puzzle to the back of her mind, already overcrowded with unanswered questions, Lisette hurried out to the bailey.

An air of anticipation hung over the compound as serfs and soldiers alike craned to see the man once called William the Bastard, and now called the Conqueror.

Instructing Edric to bring the welcome cup, Lisette and Catherine waited at the foot of the outer stairway as Raverre and William rode in through the gates.

Her first sight of the son of a humble tanner's daughter who had united Normandy and conquered England gave Lisette a brief glimpse of a man above medium height and solidly built, with a face pleasant enough but rather remote and stern, before she sank into a graceful curtsy, eyes lowered.

As she rose, remembering her promise to Raverre to treat William with respect, Lisette offered him the welcome cup, but, aligning herself to her own people, said, "Welcome, sir, to my husband's manor."

If William heard the distinction he gave no sign. He took a deep draught of the mulled wine and handed the cup back to her, saying, "God's greetings, my lady. 'Tis a fair place you have here. We shall be glad to rest a night and to know you better."

Lisette handed the cup to Raverre, giving him a brilliant smile as she did so. He smiled wryly back at her, the wary look in his eyes disappearing.

"You did not exaggerate your lady's beauty, my friend,"

commented William, noticing this byplay. "No wonder you wasted no time in marrying her."

Lisette glanced at Raverre curiously, but her attention was quickly diverted by the commotion announcing the Queen's arrival.

Matilda was alighting from her litter, and William himself went at once to assist her. As he led his wife towards the group by the stairway Lisette thought they made a strange-looking pair.

Matilda was so short that she appeared almost childlike against her much taller husband. Only four feet in height, she was dressed in a burgundy wool gown, chosen more for serviceability than elegance. An over-tunic of soft grey, as plain as the gown, could not fully conceal her pregnancy, which made her look heavy and ungainly, and yet she had the presence only achieved by those of very strong personality.

As Lisette sank into another curtsy she wondered if she had been wrong to wear her blue silk gown. The Queen was obviously as frugal as William was reputed to be, but Matilda greeted her hostess with friendly interest, and Lisette felt her slight awkwardness dissipate in the warmth of the Queen's smile.

Returning the greeting, she ushered Matilda and her ladies into the solar, shyly inviting them to ask for anything they might require.

"My ladies and I will be glad to wash the dirt of the road from our faces," said the Queen, her eyes falling on the bowl of hot water on the table. "Although I must say your English roads are a sight better than the rough tracks we have to endure in Normandy."

Unsure what to answer to this forthright statement, Lisette curtsied slightly and was about to inform Matilda that dinner would be served as soon as their guests were ready, when the door opened and William entered with Raverre.

It was as though a sudden gust of wind had blown into the solar, thought Lisette. For the first time she understood why men, even Saxons, had been drawn to William's cause. The man exuded an air of determination, an implacable will to succeed, that was almost visible.

"Ah!" the King exclaimed, looking about the room approvingly. "This is more what you are used to, is it not, my love?"

His voice was quite harsh, and seemed to ring out in the confines of the solar, used to carrying over distances or above the noise of battle.

"'Tis indeed comfortable here, Alain," he went on, turning to Raverre. "And we shall be happy to repay you with some entertainment at dinner." A piercing gaze was turned on Lisette. "I believe you have no minstrel or bard, my lady."

This man would miss nothing, she thought as she confirmed his statement.

"Then 'tis fitting that we have both. My lady *would* bring them with her from Normandy when she joined me," he finished, with a quizzical look at his wife.

"One must have some amenities, even in a foreign land, William," remonstrated Matilda with a calm smile.

"So you say, my dear," he agreed good-naturedly. "You ladies must be amused while we men labour. Isn't that so, my lady?"

"I think after *both* men and women labour they *both* like to be amused, sir," Lisette replied demurely, but with a twinkle in her eyes.

The King gave a delighted guffaw and clapped Raverre on the shoulder.

"You've done well for yourself, Raverre, my friend. A

lady who is quick-witted as well as beautiful is rare indeed.
I wish you joy of her. Just now, however, I see a look in
her eye that betokens housewifely concern. You are thinking that dinner will be spoiling if we do not make haste,
my lady.''

Startled, Lisette could not help laughing at his perspi-
cacity. '''Tis true,'' she confirmed, ''but dinner will await
your pleasure, sir.''

''Then let us away to table, my lady,'' William replied,
offering a gallant arm to her.

By the Rood, thought Raverre, preparing to escort Matilda into the hall, I verily believe she's bewitched even
William. I haven't seen him in such a benign mood for
months. If Lisette did say something he disliked I swear
he'd merely try to convince her otherwise by force of argument alone.

Chapter Eight

Roast suckling pig, baked partridge and the controversial larks in a pie had been devoured with gusto, and washed down with wine, cider and ale. Already replete, dogs squabbled lazily for bones among the rushes. And, fully aware that Raverre was trying to keep an ear tuned to her conversation with William, while forced to present a façade of courtesy to his other guests, Lisette put herself out to charm the King.

In fact it was not a hardship for her. William paid her the compliment of listening carefully to her halting Norman, helping her when she hesitated for the right word, and she was pleasantly surprised to find that he had a good deal of sympathy for the common folk, caught up in a war they had not wanted.

"'Tis why I believe so strongly in our way of life, my lady," he explained earnestly. "Your people might have had the freedom to move from one master to another, or work independently in a town guild, but many are so poor that such a way of life was impossible for them anyway. The great wealth was divided between a scant five or six too-powerful Earls, who behaved like rulers of petty kingdoms. I fear my cousin Edward kept his throne merely through the respect they had for his age and piety. Look at the quarrels that broke out the minute he was dead.

"There was no unity, your land torn apart by ambitious men who were only interested in their own gain. If a country is to keep pace with the rest of the world there must be strength and a common aim and protection of the weak. This is what I see for England. She could be a great nation one day, your Saxon tradition and learning allied to our Norman cohesion and initiative."

William was certainly convincing, Lisette thought, impressed by his argument. But she could not suppress a sigh.

"It seems a pity that such things cannot be brought about without warfare and suffering," she remarked.

"Ahh. You say so because you are a lady and gentle, and shrink from these things. Which is as it should be," he answered, but so charmingly that she could not take offence.

Just then a diversion was caused by the entrance of Wat's masterpiece. A large swan, roasted to a turn, and then restored to the full glory of its plumage by the painstaking pasting on of its feathers. It was borne in on a large platter, ensconced on a sea of fruits and nuts, and caused quite a sensation among the company.

Matilda complimented Lisette on her cook, and the conversation became more general.

Glancing down the length of the hall, Lisette assured herself that her guests were enjoying themselves. Matilda's ladies appeared to be indulging in mild flirtations with some of Raverre's men, the royal couple looked relaxed and pleased, and at the end of the high table Catherine prattled happily away to Gilbert as though she had known him for years instead a few scant weeks.

However, as William clapped his hands to summon a troop of tumblers Lisette caught a glance from Matilda's youngest lady, a pretty girl with dark hair and eyes, which seemed to hold a degree of resentment. Surprised, she stared at the girl more closely, but the other had turned her face away and Lisette thought she must have been mistaken. She did not think the Norman ladies disliked her merely because she was Saxon, for they had followed their Queen's example of civility.

A burst of applause echoed around the hall and drew her attention to the nimble antics of the tumblers as they leapt about the floor and twisted themselves into fearful contortions.

Then one fellow ran forward and began to juggle with a handful of brightly coloured balls, assisted by a tiny furred creature wearing a blue jacket, which caught the balls and tossed them quickly back to its master.

"Oh, the darling little thing," cried Lisette in delight, clapping her hands. Turning shining eyes to Raverre, she asked, "Pray, what is it, my lord?"

"Why, my lady," interposed a husky feminine voice before he could answer, "have you never seen a monkey before? What a dull life you must lead here, I vow!" Matilda's lady-in-waiting finished with a tinkle of scornful laughter.

There was no mistaking the animosity this time. Feeling like an ignorant country bumpkin, Lisette sat back in embarrassment, wondering if Raverre also considered her simple pleasure in the entertainment to be childish and naïve.

Matilda came unexpectedly to her rescue. "Tush, Judith," she scolded. "I warrant my Lady of Raverre has had little time for such frivolity these past several months."

She turned her back on Judith and applauded vigorously as the little monkey climbed nimbly up to its master's shoulder, where it gave the company a quaint bow before being carried out.

Lisette, avoiding Raverre's eye by concentrating on the bard who had come to sit on the floor in front of the high table, also failed to see the languishing gaze Judith cast at her husband. Stung by the Queen's rebuke and Lisette's obvious success with the King, the girl decided she would soon show this rustic Saxon wench how her own more worldly attractions would better suit a Norman Baron. And my Lord Raverre, with his magnificent physique and those piercing ice-blue eyes, was certainly a man worthy of her attention.

The bard was strumming a few random notes on his lute while he waited for his audience to make a choice.

"Would you like to hear a tale of Saxon courage in battle, my lady?" queried William politely.

Upon Lisette's agreeing to this, he signalled to the man to begin, and a hush fell over the hall as the story unfolded of the final stand of the fyrd.

Tears glittered in Lisette's eyes as Harold's personal guard were lauded as the most dauntless of warriors as they stood to the last man, ever ready with their steel in defence of their King, the only movement in their ranks the dropping of the dead.

William had been victorious that day at Hastings, Lisette reflected, but he still granted his fallen enemies respect and honour.

The end of the tale was greeted with polite applause from the Norman company, but Lisette turned impulsively to William, thanking him warmly for allowing her to hear it.

Seeing the King's indulgent pleasure in her unfeigned thanks, Raverre felt a flash of jealousy. Why couldn't Lisette smile so freely at him? he wondered angrily, watching her dimples deepen the corners of her mouth in a way that made him want to drag her into the solar and kiss her senseless. There they were, the two of them, getting on famously on the strength of a few hours' acquaintance, while he—

"Where are your wits gone begging, my friend?" exclaimed William jokingly. "I ask what you would like to hear now my fellow has caught his breath, and all you can do is sit there in a daze. Dreaming of your lovely wife, I doubt not."

Lisette flushed hotly, but fortunately Raverre seemed not to notice. In fact, after he had given William a noncommittal answer, his whole attention now seemed to be centred on Judith, who was speaking animatedly, gesturing with her hands and bringing a smile to his handsome face.

"Why not allow the ladies to hear the saga of Norman settlement in Gaul, sir?" asked Gilbert, seeing Lisette's discomfort and tactfully giving her time to recover.

"A good thought, de Rohan," declared William, nodding to the bard, and settling back in his chair to listen.

Lisette found herself caught up in the saga. It told of one Rolf, son of a noble of Harold Fairhair, King of Norway, who had been banished from the court and had sailed with his followers to the Hebrides—those remote mystical islands off the coast of Scotland. From there they had again set sail in their *drakkars*—the great dragon ships—to Gaul, rowing many miles up the Seine to Jumièges, where they had prepared to attack the cathedral city of Rouen.

Alarmed by the fierce demeanour of the invaders, the people of Jumièges, had begged their Archbishop to negotiate with the Norsemen, offering them no resistance if they would allow the town to remain unscathed. Accepting this, Rolf had entered Rouen as its conqueror.

The Viking war spirit still ran hot in the blood of the victors, however, and for many a year they had plundered the French countryside, defeating every army the King had sent against them, until the long-suffering monarch had finally sued for peace. Promised the title of Count of Normandy if he would become the King's vassal, Rolf had converted to Christianity, married the King's daughter Gisele, and had settled down to rule his domain, his successors becoming Dukes in the course of time.

Lisette enjoyed the romantic ending to the tale, but the high point for the Normans came during the telling of the ceremony of allegiance that made Rolf the French King's bondman. On being ordered to kneel and kiss the King's foot, Rolf had refused point-blank and it had looked as though the whole business was doomed to failure. However, the huge Norseman had solved the problem by grasping the King's foot and lifting it up to his lips to bestow the kiss of allegiance while still remaining upright. The King had promptly been tripped over and had landed flat on his back.

The hall resounded to roars of approval as the bard finished. He retired to recruit his energies with some refreshing draughts of cider, and the feast grew louder as men, inspired by the heroic sagas, thundered out songs of war and adventure.

Lisette became increasingly conscious that Raverre seemed to be ignoring her. And there was little consolation in the fact that he now appeared to restrict his talk to the other men at the table, apparently deaf and blind to the attentions Judith was attempting to bestow upon him.

The wench was certainly doing her best to attract him, Lisette thought indignantly. Look at her, giving him those sidelong glances, and leaning forward so that she was all but falling into his lap.

Deciding that if she couldn't see what was going on she would be less upset, Lisette turned to the Queen, suggesting they walk in the garden for a while as their husbands now seemed to be involved in more serious discussion. Matilda accepted graciously and the ladies withdrew from the hall, but not before Lisette noticed the proprietorial hand Judith placed on Raverre's arm as he and William rose politely.

Compared to her buoyant spirits earlier, she now felt quite low as she and Matilda paced slowly around the small garden. The wind bit keenly, prompting Matilda to remark that she hoped they would be settled in York before winter.

"This would make a comfortable pleasance in the colder months, my lady, if the wall was a little higher," she suggested. "A sheltered spot to sit outside can be a relief after days spent indoors."

Lisette agreed, but the remark didn't make her feel any better. She loved her home and had never noticed any lack of comfort, but now she wondered if it looked small and crude to Raverre, compared to the great fortress keeps across the Channel. And did he think her ignorant and simple, compared to the more experienced Norman ladies?

Self-doubt haunted Lisette for the rest of the day, making her so miserable that she didn't even bother to wonder why she cared about any comparisons Raverre might care to make. Only long force of habit kept her veneer of gracious hostess in place. But by the time she had seen her female guests settled for the night after a supper in the privacy of the solar—the men still occupied in the hall with discussions of war—she was thankful to seek her own bed, where she could sort out her feelings and talk herself into a better frame of mind.

Unfortunately, worse was to come. Lisette remembered, through her preoccupation, that Godric had not put in an appearance. Thinking that he might have arrived late and, too weary to see William tonight, retired to one of the huts reserved for his use, she went outside to investigate.

He had not yet arrived, however, and, wondering if his delay had been caused by Leofwin's appearance, Lisette returned to the hall. She had just started up the stairway to the tower room when a low murmur of voices made her turn her head.

Lady Judith stood in the light of one of the sconces, out of sight of the hall in the screen passage, gazing appealingly up at the man before her. His back was towards Lisette, but there was no mistaking that height or those broad shoulders, and, as Lisette watched, Judith put up her hands to Raverre's chest, lifting her face in unmistakable invitation.

Unable to bear any more, Lisette fled up the stairway and into the tower room, only halting when she saw her sister's look of astonishment at her abrupt entrance.

"Hush, Lisette," admonished Catherine, indicating Marjory, snoring gently on her pallet. "You'll wake Marjory, bouncing into the room like that. What ails you?"

"The stairs were so dark," Lisette explained lamely, not surprised when Catherine continued to look at her strangely.

"I thought Raverre would bring you upstairs," she said. "He was looking for you a few moments ago."

Pain slashed through Lisette at the mention of his name. She walked stiffly over to the bed, wondering if Raverre would indeed seek her out that night.

To her profound relief Catherine turned away and climbed under the blankets on the pallet next to Marjory's, yawning widely, too tired to question further.

"What an exhausting day," she mumbled sleepily. "Goodnight, Lisette."

"Goodnight," Lisette returned, controlling her voice with an effort. Blowing out the candle and removing only her shoes and coif, she curled up in a tight ball on the bed, hugging her arms close to her body as she fought against acknowledging the cause of the sharp pain piercing her heart.

Nothing had prepared her for this, she now realised. Not the loss of her parents or the ravages of war. She had grieved, yes, but the grief had been bearable. Now she felt that if she took her arms away her heart would shatter like brittle glass into a thousand tiny fragments that could never be repaired, and she would die from the agony of it.

Oh, why had she not seen what was happening to her?

She loved Raverre! Had loved him for a long time and had tried to ignore all the signs, so that her love had grown stronger in that dark, secret place in her heart that she had thought to suppress. But you didn't, she berated herself, and now you must bear the torment of loving a man who only sees you as a means to an end, and probably a troublesome one at that.

But he desires me, her heart pleaded. Does that mean nothing?

Less than nothing, her mind told her inexorably. Look how quickly and easily he is beguiled by another woman. One who has more experience in pleasing a man than you will ever have. You have shown him nothing but cold duty, and—as an image of the ungainly figure of the Queen came to mind—do you think he will still want you when you are awkward with child? You fool yourself. The only thing left to you now is your pride. Or do you think to abandon that as well and shame yourself forever?

No, she thought determinedly, staring into the darkness. After what I told him that first night when we met I can only survive this if he never knows how complete his conquest has been. Or, worse, if he felt only pity for me out of kindness.

Shielding the raw, throbbing wound in her heart with this resolve, Lisette carefully added another layer of protection. She would do her utmost to give Raverre a son so that her position as his wife was secure. If he was unfaithful to her she would just have to bear it, but at least she would be able to stay with him.

Cringing at the thought of what Raverre would make of this admission after her determined resistance to him, Lisette lay unmoving in the darkness like a wounded animal, her eyes remaining dry but burning with the abrasive heat of her unshed tears.

So benumbed did she feel that she barely registered Raverre's presence when he entered the room some hours later.

He pulled the curtains closed around the bed for privacy, stripped, and climbed under the covers. Reaching for Lisette, he was surprised to find her lying on top of the bearskin, still fully clothed. Raverre raised himself on one elbow, leaning over her.

''Sweetheart?'' he questioned softly, concern momentarily causing him to forget his earlier jealousy.

How can he call me that after coming from the arms of another woman? she thought.

Raverre drew a caressing hand along her arm, but when she didn't stir Lisette felt him leave the bed. Was he going to spend the remainder of the night elsewhere? she wondered, almost wishing he would. Then she felt the mattress dip when he returned and the light weight of a blanket as he drew the covering over her.

Dear God, don't let him be kind now, she pleaded silently. If Raverre showed her tenderness Lisette knew she would be unable to resist him. Her emotions were so vulnerable, a raw, open wound which ached unbearably, that one gentle word from him and she would turn and fling herself against him, begging him to hold her until she felt whole again.

But the word was not spoken. Raverre, thinking she must be worn out by the stresses of the day and acutely conscious that they were not alone in the small room, lay back, arms folded behind his head.

Frustration gnawed at him as he could see the progress he had made on the night of the storm fast disappearing. This realisation was made all the more bitter after watching her enjoyment of William's players. That was how she must have looked two years ago, carefree, happy—and so beautiful that a man would risk his very soul to win her.

He recalled the impulsive way Lisette had turned to him when she had asked about the juggler's monkey, her face aglow with delighted enquiry. Until that little bitch of a lady-in-waiting had thrown a damper over her. Was that why she had been lying here, still fully clothed? Or—he had to consider it—had she thought to keep him at a distance?

He should have woken her last night. Damn it, he should wake her now, he thought impatiently. God knew, he wanted her so badly that he ached with it. But, with her sister and nurse in the room, what kind of a response did he think he'd get? He wanted a passionate woman, not a frozen statue, and she'd probably hate him forever.

Thank God William had given him that licence to build. Another tower would take care of the question of privacy when the castle was full of guests, and the building of a tower and a proper barbican over the gate would keep him at home for some time. He hadn't even had to mention the subject. The King needed men he could trust to hold the borders for him while he was fighting elsewhere, and those men needed strong fortresses. William had commandeered several men-at-arms and ordered Raverre to stay put.

''I'll take William fitzOsbern north with me,'' the King had said, ''where his propensity for fighting can be put to good use against that short-sighted fool Morcar instead of simple villagers. I need you here in case any threat comes from the west.''

Which was precisely what he had wanted. Although it wasn't doing him much good, he thought, turning restlessly. The move brought him facing Lisette and, although Raverre couldn't see her, the faint aroma of the rose water she used wafted towards him, evoking images of this mouth against her warm, scented flesh. His body hardened instantly.

So much for distracting himself with building plans. Turning over again, Raverre resigned himself to sleeplessness for what was left of the night.

Lisette awoke in the same cramped position in which she had eventually fallen asleep. She wondered tiredly why the light was muted, then her eyes focused on the closed curtains and memory came rushing back, bringing pain in its wake. She turned over abruptly, almost landing in Raverre's arms.

''Good morning,'' he drawled in a deep, caressing voice that sent a shiver of apprehension mingled with longing down her spine.

Lisette gazed back at him in perturbed silence, then thankfully remembered where they were. She was safe enough, she thought, glancing towards the curtains; they weren't alone.

''They've gone,'' Raverre said, correctly interpreting her expression. ''At first light. Tactful of them, wasn't it?''

Alerted by the intent look in his eyes, Lisette leapt from the bed as though propelled from a catapult. Wrenching open the bed curtains, she saw that they were indeed alone, and turned to gaze at Raverre, her eyes wide with consternation.

He sat up, pushing the covers aside, the muscles of his chest and stomach rippling with the movement, and Lisette retreated a couple of paces, averting her gaze in sudden confusion. Since their wedding-night, when she hadn't looked, darkness had hitherto cloaked their nakedness, and she was conscious of an unexpected twinge of curiosity, which brought a blush to her face.

"Coward," he said, still in that soft voice, which now held more than a hint of amusement.

"I am not!" Lisette denied, trying to instil some firmness into her voice and sounding very nervous instead. Forcing herself to meet Raverre's gaze, she tried again. "But I have guests to attend to and—"

"Come here," he interrupted, smiling lazily across at her with those glittering blue eyes.

She was immediately rendered speechless. How could he look at her with such undisguised lust—for that was exactly what it was—when he had been with another woman last night? She could not have been mistaken. She had seen them with her own eyes. It had been almost dawn when he had come to bed, and now he wanted her as well!

A healthy bolt of rage surged through Lisette, making her forget both her unhappiness and last night's resolutions.

"How dare you?" she gasped, turning pale with anger. She felt quick satisfaction at Raverre's look of utter disbelief following her outburst, but his own temper flared just as quickly, dispelling the expression.

"*What?*" he barked, a black scowl descending on his face as he came to his feet. Completely unconcerned by his state of undress, he advanced on Lisette, looking so savage that she hurriedly put the table between them.

Taking hold of the nearest corner, Raverre upended the barrier with one powerful movement of his arm, hurling it out of the way. Ignoring the resounding crash as table and contents fell to the floor, he grabbed Lisette by the shoulders.

"How dare I do what?" he demanded furiously, glaring

down at her. "Dare to lie with my wife? Is that such a felony that you look at me as if I had just committed murder and come to you with blood still on my hands?"

It was an unfortunate choice of words. Lisette had felt herself start to soften towards him as trembling weakness had overcome her at his touch. He was so big and strong that she had longed to melt against the hard warmth of his body and give in to the deliciously primitive thrill that had coursed through her at his violent reaction to her retreat.

His last question, however, effectively brought a rapid return to cold sanity.

"You have murdered!" she accused breathlessly. "Do you deny that you have killed? Do you deny that you have the blood of innocent people on your hands?"

"Of course I deny it!" he roared, further enraged at this unjust charge. "I have never raised my sword against any man except in open battle. My God! I thought we had gone beyond that old argument."

Raverre's hands clenched on her shoulders, starting to shake her, but as her fragile bones quivered under his grip he pushed Lisette away, realising, even in his anger, how easily he could hurt her.

Goaded, however, by sharp pain at her accusation and the thwarted hunger of the past two days, he added bitingly, "My supposed victims didn't appear to worry you the other night."

Lisette flinched. But, as she saw Raverre's face register her pain, desperation made her rally quickly.

"Aye. For a moment I forgot who you are and what you have done. But that will never happen again, I assure you."

"Oh, won't it?" he retorted, angry again. But now the anger had a hard, controlled edge to it, and Lisette sensed danger. Raverre's eyes narrowed in mocking enquiry. "That's a challenge if ever I heard one. Are you sure you wish to take the consequences of throwing down the gauntlet, my lady?''

She would not let him see how nervous this question made her. Shrugging with a show of indifference, Lisette turned her back on him. ''I suggest you get dressed,'' she answered coldly. ''In case you have forgotten, we have guests who—''

Raverre had heard enough. He spun Lisette around, and jerked her against him so hard that the breath left her lungs in a startled gasp. Holding her head still, he brought his mouth down hard on hers, kissing her with a sensual male dominance which aroused every feminine instinct of surrender that she possessed.

Then his free hand began to unfasten her gown with a swift efficiency that told its own tale of his experience, and fury rescued her yet again.

Feeling her yield, Raverre had relaxed his hold, and now Lisette managed to wrench away from him, clutching at the front of her gown as her forceful movement caused it to slip from her shoulders. She had not retreated more than one pace, however, before Raverre recovered fast. Hauling her back into his arms, he pinioned her own by yanking the close-fitting gown down to her waist. Then, hoisting her over his shoulder, he carried Lisette across to the bed and tossed her on to the mattress. A grim smile curled his mouth as he watched her strive to free her arms.

''Shall I help you, sweet wife?'' he asked silkily as she turned and twisted ineffectually, half blinded by her hair as it fell across her face in wild disorder.

Lisette glared up at him, forgetting his nakedness and her embarrassment, forgetting that she had almost given herself up to the demands of that beautiful, hard mouth. At that moment white-hot rage flared so fiercely in her that it cauterised every other emotion.

"Aye, you can help me!" she spat at him. "But only so I can fight you! Or do you prefer to take your women while they're helpless?"

Raverre gave a savage laugh. Bending, he stripped the gown away from her, tossing it to the floor and preventing Lisette's instant scramble for freedom by the sheer force of his body over hers.

"Oh, no," he said with soft menace. "Not this time, my lady."

With Lisette held captive between his arms, his eyes dropped to her fine linen shift, the only flimsy barrier remaining between them. She wondered with defiant fury how Raverre was going to get the shift over her head, ready to fight him every inch of the way, and he smiled grimly again as he saw the determination in her eyes.

"Do you really think a few paltry pieces of clothing will keep me from taking what is mine?" he derided. "My innocent little wife, you have much to learn." And, hooking his fingers into the neck of her shift without any further warning, he ripped the fragile garment from neck to hem.

Lisette cried out in shock, trying to shield herself from his gaze, but Raverre grabbed her hands and pinned them out to the sides, his eyes roaming heatedly over the sweet curves and shadows of her body.

"Mother of God," he breathed, his anger instantly swamped by a surge of desire so violent that he didn't dare move for fear of losing control completely and hurting her with the driving force of his need. She was so delicate. So beautiful. And he needed her with a hunger that was causing him to shake as much as she did. Raverre's mind froze on the thought as he realised how helplessly Lisette was trembling, his eyes flashing to her face.

She had turned away, her eyes tightly shut, her lower lip caught between her teeth, trying to conceal her distress.

Remorse stabbed through him like a dagger, restoring some of his control.

"Don't," he whispered, his voice hoarse. "Don't turn from me, sweetheart. I'm not going to hurt you. I could never hurt you." His mouth lowered to the tender curve of her neck, savouring the warm fragrance of her skin as he pressed hot kisses across her throat and down to her shoulder. The taste of her went to his head like strong wine. He groaned with desperate longing. "You're so lovely. So small and soft. Let me love you, darling—my sweet love— I want you so much."

Lisette heard the words of need and desire, but was deaf to the note of yearning love. Lacerated in quick succession by anger, outraged modesty, fright and her own need, she could bear no more.

"I can't! I can't! Oh, please—" Her voice broke on a despairing sob.

Raverre felt the breath leave his lungs as though he had been hit across the back by a battering-ram. He was incapable of movement for several seconds, his only conscious thought that he had all but told Lisette how much he needed her, how much he loved her, and she had thrown it back in his face.

Unable to bring himself to break down her resistance by force, he sought release from the pain of her rejection with the only other alternative.

Flinging himself off the bed, he threw the blanket over Lisette with a jerky, violent movement that in no way assuaged the agony spearing through him.

"You must pardon me for not knowing you think it shameful to lie with a Norman husband, madam," he grated with biting sarcasm, tormented by the memory of the way she had willingly charmed William and Ralf de Pictou. "Your behaviour last night with the King led me to believe you were more than content with our company. And I must have been mistaken in your response to me a few nights ago. Or perhaps 'twas the thought of that young soldier which aroused your passion.''

''Don't confuse me with your Norman whore,'' Lisette flung back, goaded into a retort by this unfair barb.

Raverre paused in the act of throwing on his clothes. ''What?'' he questioned, his voice dangerous.

Lisette sat up, clutching the blanket.

''That wanton you had last night!'' she cried recklessly. ''Don't bother to deny it. I saw you and the Lady Judith with my own eyes. 'Twas hours before you—''

Her voice was abruptly cut off as Raverre strode forward, reaching down to grip her face with one hand. ''Don't say another word,'' he snarled, his eyes so ferocious that she shrank back in alarm.

''Just so there's no mistake,'' he gritted, his teeth clenched, ''I was with the King most of the night. Whatever you saw obviously didn't include me telling Judith that I already have my hands full with a blind, stubborn little—''

''I may be blind and stubborn,'' Lisette cried angrily, ''but I don't trifle with another woman's husband.''

Raverre released her and strode to the door. ''She may have been a wanton,'' he yelled back, ''but at least she was willing. I was a fool to have pushed her away!'' The door slammed behind him, leaving his parting words to echo in Lisette's brain.

He hadn't been with the Norman girl last night. Raverre might have thrown the words at her in anger, but Lisette recognised the truth when she heard it. Holy Mother, what have I done? she wondered in despair, falling back on the bed. In her frantic snatch for any weapon that would prevent Raverre making love to her in the light of day, when he would see the response she could no longer hide, had she now driven him away altogether?

Turning her face into the goosedown pillow, Lisette gave way to the tears of bitter regret which had burned behind her eyes all night.

Matilda was seated by the window where the morning light fell on the skeins of wool in her lap. As Lisette entered the solar the Queen took another strand of wool from one of her ladies, holding it up to compare the colour. Hearing the door open, she looked up and smiled.

"Good morrow, my lady," she greeted Lisette. "Come. Talk with me while our husbands are occupied with business."

Waving away her woman, who retired to the group of ladies on the other side of the room, Matilda herself drew up a stool and patted it invitingly.

Lisette sat, facing away from the light. "You enjoy tapestry, madam?" she ventured timidly. Still suffering from her raw emotions, she felt more awkward than ever in the face of the Queen's composed dignity. She wondered what, if anything, the two of them could have in common.

"Indeed," Matilda answered, giving the girl by her side a shrewd glance. "I cannot sit with idle hands, and it passes the time pleasantly when I have no household to attend to. The King insisted that I rest this morning. He wants this child safely delivered. It will be our first born in England, another boy if our blessed Mother is kind."

"Then you will not be witnessing the ceremony later?" questioned Lisette, remembering Godric with a guilty start. She wondered if the old man had arrived.

"In truth, my dear, I am happy not to be surrounded by noise and people for a while. Although even another ceremony of allegiance would be preferable to getting back into that extremely uncomfortable litter. But not a word to William, mind. He thinks it gives me a respite from riding, and you know how stubborn husbands are when they think they are doing one a favour.''

This very human observation made Lisette smile, albeit a trifle wanly, and Matilda remarked shrewdly, ''You seem somewhat distraite, my dear.'' She lowered her voice. ''And you've been weeping. Never tell me that Judith's attempts to captivate your husband last night have caused trouble between you?'' She smiled at Lisette's startled expression. ''Never have I seen a man less interested. 'Twas most amusing to watch. Foolish girl.''

''I am not so foolish that I would let him see I was jealous!'' Lisette retorted, hoping devoutly that Raverre hadn't had time to put such a construction on her last angry words. ''Which I wasn't!'' she added unconvincingly, then flushed as she remembered to whom she was speaking.

Matilda chuckled. ''I meant Judith was foolish, silly child. Anyone with a farthing of sense can see your lord has eyes only for you. Well, if 'twas not the antics of my maid that has upset you, what is it?''

She waited a moment, but as Lisette stayed silent, grappling with Matilda's surprising description of Raverre, the Queen continued in her forthright way, ''Your mother is no longer here to advise you, I believe, but perhaps I may be of help.''

An urge to confide in the older woman swept through Lisette as she suddenly recalled the tales she had heard of William's courtship of his wife. Perhaps the Queen *could* help, she thought, rushing impulsively into speech before her courage deserted her.

''Oh, madam, the situation is not as you think. My Lord Raverre forced me to marry him. Not because he cares for me, but to further his own ends, and I thought I hated him for it, for taking my family's home, my people's freedom, but—''

''But now you have fallen in love with him. Is it not so?''

''Aye,'' uttered Lisette, in such a tragic voice that Matilda smiled to herself. Lisette gripped her hands together. ''How can I, after what he has done? And yet he can be kind also, I know that, and now you say he looked only at me last night, though—''

She took a deep breath and tried to sound more coherent. ''If only I knew what to do! Oh, madam, I think you might understand how I feel, for the King was not always so concerned for *your* feelings, and—''

She stopped as Matilda, in her turn, looked startled. Holy Saints, what have I said? Lisette thought, appalled at her indiscretion.

Quickly kneeling at Matilda's feet, she stammered in sudden fright. ''Oh, forgive me, my lady. I should not have said such a thing to you.''

But Matilda merely looked thoughtful. ''So, even old news travels far,'' she mused. Then briskly, ''Get up, child, I am not offended.''

She clapped her hands to gain the attention of her chattering ladies. ''Go into the hall, all of you,'' she ordered, waving them towards the door. ''I would speak privately with my Lady of Raverre.''

They rose obediently and left, with curious glances at Lisette, who had resumed her seat.

''What version of the old tale have you heard, child?'' Matilda asked as the door closed again.

''Why, that the King beat you once,'' Lisette answered cautiously. ''Because you had refused his offer of marriage.''

The Queen smiled, a reminiscent look on her face.

"Well, as far as it goes, you heard truthfully enough. Aye, he beat me." She gazed into the distance as memory took her back to her girlhood. "William had come to my father's court in Flanders to ask for help in subduing his Norman Barons, and after he left he sent a courtier to ask for my hand in marriage. My father was not really in favour of the match. William's position as Duke of Normandy was precarious indeed; he had been surrounded by treachery and deceit most of his life, not knowing whom to trust. A friend today might turn out to be an enemy tomorrow. But my father left the choice up to me."

She smiled wryly at the listening girl. "You know that I refused him?"

Lisette nodded.

"I was young, only fifteen, and unversed in the ways of men. William had seemed so cold to me, so remote, as if he didn't care about me one way or the other. But I had been drawn to the strength in him, and wanted to goad him into a show of feeling. So I sent back a message saying I could never marry one of bastard blood and low-born into the bargain."

Matilda chuckled. "He would probably have beaten me there and then, before my father and the whole court, had he been present, but he had to wait, which fed his anger.

"It happened as I was leaving the church one day with my maid. As we stood there William rode into the square, dismounted, and without uttering a word, set about me with his hands, tearing at my clothes and finally throwing me to the ground before mounting again and riding off. I swear to you, child, I could not believe he had left me there. He could have abducted me, forcing me into a position where I would have to marry him or be shamed, for there was no one to gainsay him. But he didn't, and finally I understood. He still wished to wed me in all honour, but would teach

me who had the stronger whip-hand, and when he sent
again to my father I accepted him. You wonder why, I
suppose.''

Lisette shook her head. ''I think because you loved him
from the beginning, madam. But weren't you angry after
he had treated you so roughly? And in public!''

Even as she spoke, though, Lisette remembered that after
Raverre's attack on her in the graveyard she had not felt
anger, only regret that she had so provoked him. Matilda's
laugh brought her back to the present.

''Of course I was angry. I swore that William would not
come near me again, but as soon as I calmed down I
changed my mind. After all, I had sent him a message
which I knew would anger him beyond reason, and in the
years that followed while we waited for the Pope's dispen-
sation I realised that I loved him.''

She leaned forward and patted Lisette's hand. ''You see,
my dear, we are strong women, you and I, and therefore
we are only truly happy with a man who shows himself as
strong or more so. As William proved to me, earning my
respect, and, I think, as Raverre has done also with you.
Think, child. What would you say to a man who hung about
your skirts, doing nothing but sigh all day, and thrown into
extravagant displays of rapture whenever you deigned to
give him a smile or kind word?''

Lisette grimaced.

''Exactly so. And what did you think of Raverre when
you first saw him? Be honest now.''

''To say truth, Your Grace, I was afraid of the force in
him,'' admitted Lisette. ''But when we were married he
was so…''

Matilda nodded wisely. ''Aye. That union of strength
and tenderness in a man is what most women can only
dream of finding.''

It was true, thought Lisette. Raverre had used his power to take her home and marry her, but his gentleness had conquered her heart. She saw Matilda smile knowingly.

"But he does not love me, and, as if that is not bad enough, I feel so disloyal for loving *him*," Lisette answered, agitatedly wringing her hands again. "I understand what you are saying, my lady, but you at least did not see the King as an enemy of your people."

"No," agreed Matilda, "but why torment yourself with regrets for what cannot be changed? Instead, look towards the time when Norman and Englishman may live side by side, though it may take a generation or two. Who knows, maybe this first child of mine to be born on English soil will take part in such a future? After all, do you see me as an enemy?"

"Oh, no," said Lisette fervently, then gave a shaky laugh.

"You see? We are merely two women, sitting here gossiping about our husbands. And as to Raverre not loving you, what makes you think so?"

"Well, he has never said—"

Matilda tut-tutted in exasperation. "Foolish child. Men are not so easy with words as we women, but you say he treats you with kindness? And, judging by the way he watched you last night, like a dog guarding a bone, I would wager my best cloisonné brooch that he comes eagerly to your bed and is as reluctant to leave it."

Lisette felt herself blushing, but she couldn't help smiling as a tiny bud of hope burgeoned in her wounded spirit. The Queen's words reminded her of the nights she had awoken to find herself in Raverre's arms, and how protected she had felt there.

"That's better," approved Matilda as she saw Lisette's expression brighten. "Put the past behind you, child. Now go and put on that lovely circlet I saw you wearing yesterday and but smile at Raverre. He won't be able to get rid of us fast enough.''

Lisette giggled at the thought of Raverre hustling the King off the premises, but rose with alacrity.

Smiling at her eagerness, Matilda dismissed her, asking Lisette to send her ladies back to the solar.

When Lisette hurried into the hall she sensed at once that something untoward had occurred. Several men were gathered in the room but there was no murmur of conversation. Even Matilda's ladies, standing by the fireplace, were quiet, and the silence hung in the air, ominous, waiting.

As she stepped around the carved oak screen which hid the solar door the first men she saw clearly were Godric and Leofwin. The elderly Thegn and his son were standing before the high table, behind which sat William, with Raverre on his left. All four looked tense and, in Godric's case, anxious.

Lisette motioned to Matilda's ladies, wondering if she also should retire with the other women, but as she hesitated William saw her.

''Ah, my lady,'' he greeted, beckoning imperiously. ''Your arrival is most timely. You have long been acquainted with Lord Godric and his son, I believe.''

''Aye, my lord,'' she replied, and turned to smile warmly at Godric. Her speech of welcome died on her lips, however, as William continued.

''We have weighty matters to consider. Leofwin Godricson stands accused here of rebellion, but now wishes to acknowledge us as his Sovereign. As his father has done of his free will. The son throws himself on our mercy and has proof of his good intent. We are waiting to hear it.''

William leaned over to confer with Raverre in a low voice, and Lisette had a chance to wonder at the change in the King from the previous night's charming indulgent guest to this morning's sternly calculating monarch, before he motioned her to a bench near the table.

"You may stay, madam, in case I need to question you. Firstly, sir—" he addressed Godric, "—we will hear your son and judge on his own words."

"That is fair," answered Godric, bowing and stepping back a pace.

William gestured to Leofwin. "Speak."

"My lord, I heard talk one night of missing gold. 'Twas from a man I chanced to meet in a tavern, a mean place. The fellow was far gone in his ale cup and bragging." Leofwin paused. "He might have been lying."

William's face remained impassive. "Continue."

"I thought myself the wretch was lying when he spoke of great wealth. He looked as mean as the inn itself. But when I scoffed at him he grew angry as only the cup-shotten can and told me where this wealth was hidden. If he spoke truly 'tis there still, tied fast to the supports of the main bridge over the Itchen."

"God's bones, still in Winchester itself," muttered William. He regarded Leofwin thoughtfully. "You didn't consider taking the gold yourself?"

Lisette didn't listen to Leofwin's reply or the interrogation that followed. What was she to do? If she hadn't heard Leofwin's previous story she would have believed his explanation today, but he had omitted all mention of his own involvement. In fear for his life probably. And how could she betray him?

Lisette glanced up to meet Leofwin's intent stare. Though still gaunt and pale, he certainly looked more like his old self, but the memory of his bitter anger drifted uneasily at the edges of her mind. He looked away again to answer another question from William.

Leofwin had not betrayed their earlier meeting, and he had come openly to the King with the knowledge of the ingot's whereabouts. If he was truly reconciled to the Norman invasion she could not destroy him merely to placate her own desire to be rid of the secrets between herself and Raverre.

Risking a glance at her husband's stony countenance, Lisette doubted if he would believe in Leofwin's sincerity should she admit the truth. He still looked so savage that even the thought of smiling at him, as Matilda had suggested, was daunting.

With a start Lisette saw that Leofwin was kneeling before William, giving the oath of allegiance, and realised that he must have been pardoned. The knowledge seemed to decide the issue in her mind, but as Leofwin stood he sent her a glance from under his lashes that stirred a *frisson* of doubt once again.

Then he was bowing in her direction prior to retiring. Lisette looked anxiously at the King.

"'Tis as well you're staying here at Ambray, Alain," William was saying quietly as they watched Leofwin solicitously assist his father from the hall. "You can keep a watch on that young man. He seemed sincere enough, but there's something…"

There certainly is, thought Raverre grimly. He could hardly keep his eyes off Lisette long enough to make his peace with William. Despite the hurt anger that still burned in his veins, however, his innate sense of justice had to acquit her of a similar charge. She had sat with head bent as if divorced form the whole proceedings, and he had found himself wondering what she felt at seeing her friend again. Would she have sought shelter with Leofwin had he returned earlier? Had his appearance made her regret their marriage more than she seemed to already?

Realising the futility of tormenting himself with such questions, Raverre brought his attention back to William. The King was speaking to Lisette.

"So you see why I am more inclined to pardon such men, my lady. They are not felons merely because they chose one side over another, but men who are valuable to the welfare of England and therefore of value to me if they can be won over. My belief has been justified—in this part of the country at least."

Unable to ignore the oblique reference to the Atheling Edgar and the rebellious northern Earls, Lisette ventured, "The people of the Welsh Marches are perhaps more used to Norman rule, sir. There had been Normans here for many years. In truth…" she smiled suddenly as words Raverre would understand came into her mind, feeling the weight of her past conflict lift from her shoulders as she made the confession "…one of my father's ancestors came from Normandy."

Holy Mother of God, fumed Raverre. *I* had to find that out from Bertrand, and even then Lisette would have denied it if she could. She spends a few hours with William and comes out with it as willingly as you please. Why, in God's name, can't she speak to me like this?

Scowling furiously, he looked up, his eyes colliding with Lisette's with a shock that made his heart jolt and then start pounding against his ribs as he realised that she was in fact speaking to him. The actual words were directed to the King, but her eyes gazed, unflinching, into his.

"Is it so indeed?" asked William, interested. He glanced at Raverre's arrested expression. "Then you did not object to marrying one of us?"

"I am proud to be Raverre's lady," Lisette said softly. Her face was suffused with shy colour and her lashes quivered slightly, betraying her nervousness, but she continued to hold his gaze, her dark eyes softly glowing.

Then, as Raverre half rose from his seat, William broke the spell. "Good!" he pronounced, coming to his feet, and, as if his movement released the others in the hall from their hypnotic stillness, there was sudden talk and activity.

Slaves hurried into the solar and emerged with bundles ready to be reloaded into the baggage wagons, William's knights bellowed orders to their pages, and Matilda sallied forth from the solar, accompanied by Catherine. Guiltily realising that she hadn't even noticed her sister that morning, Lisette was recalled to her duties as hostess.

In the bustle of the King's departure she had little time to wonder about the consequences of her statement. Duty kept her and Raverre apart for some time, and it was not until the royal guests were about to leave that she found herself standing next to him.

Acutely conscious of his intent gaze, Lisette knelt before the Queen, impulsively kissing Matilda's hand.

Matilda leaned forward. "I wish you good fortune, child," she whispered, before mounting into her litter.

William was already mounted and waiting for Raverre to join him as escort for part of the way, but when Lisette turned to her husband, expecting the formal salute customary for such public occasion, Raverre clasped her about the waist. Pulling her against him, he lowered his head and kissed her long and hard on the mouth.

His body still bent protectively over hers as he broke the kiss, Raverre looked down into Lisette's eyes, his heart leaping in response to the soft surrender in their depths.

"When I get back..." he said huskily. And, releasing her as abruptly as he had seized her, he strode to Lanzelet, mounted, and rode out through the gate without a backward glance.

Lisette remained standing in the bailey, gazing after the riders until they disappeared past the village. No doubt she looked like a love-struck fool, she thought, but she didn't care. The tentative bud of hope, awakened by the Queen's encouragement, had burst into full bloom at the promise in Raverre's unfinished sentence.

Suppressing a sigh of impatience at the delay before he returned, Lisette turned to see Catherine descending the outer stairway with Leofwin and Godric, who were also preparing to depart.

She sent up a heartfelt prayer of thanks for her sister, and hurried forward, holding out both hands to Godric. He bent to kiss her gallantly on the cheek.

"Sir, I must beg your forgiveness for being absent when you arrived, and my shameful neglect of you since. But you are not leaving, surely? Won't you stay and dine with us and rest for the night before you undertake to return home, and allow us to show you a proper welcome?"

"Nothing would please me more, dear child," he answered, "but I am an old man who can only sleep at ease in his own bed these days. It does my heart good to see you again, however, and mayhap your husband will bring you to visit us soon. For now, he knows I did not intend to tarry once we had seen the King, and will understand that I shall be glad to see a long journey over."

Lisette, noticing the yellowish pallor of the elderly Thegn's face that told of constant illness, could see that Godric was anxious to be gone, not wishing to be laid up with sickness in another man's home, and forbore to persist with her invitation.

She turned to Leofwin and smiled, holding out her hand. "Leofwin, I am so glad to see you here."

"Thanks to you," he answered softly. Then, as Lisette glanced warningly at Catherine, he said more loudly, "Our serfs are waiting with the horses, Father. Why don't you start? You will travel slowly and I shall easily catch you up. I would like to speak with Lisette a moment, but do not wish to delay you.''

''As you please,'' answered the old man, and, bidding farewell to the girls, mounted with Leofwin's help. Flanked by four serfs, he started slowly down the road.

''Why don't you both come with me part of the way?'' suggested Leofwin, turning to Lisette. ''I haven't had a good horse under me for months, and we could enjoy a gallop across the fields before I rejoin my father.''

She hesitated, but Catherine clapped her hands with delight. ''Aye,'' she cried. ''Do let us, Lisette. It will seem so dull indoors now everyone has gone.''

Knowing she was far too restless to settle to some sedentary occupation such as needlework, Lisette allowed herself to be persuaded. A ride would pass the time until Raverre returned, and she was naturally curious to know what had passed between Godric and his son. Memories of the companionable rides they had all shared in the past came to mind, and Lisette put aside her slight feeling of unease at leaving the manor.

By the time they had penetrated about a mile into the forest, Lisette was glad she had come. Letting Catherine ride a little ahead, Leofwin had excused his behaviour at their last meeting on the score of the wretched existence he had been obliged to lead, thinking the estrangement with his father had been too deep to be mended. His apology had been a little terse, that was true, but Lisette, full of excited anticipation, was feeling too happy to be critical.

He had refrained from commenting about her marriage, and had received the news of Enide's retreat to Romsey Abbey with admirable understanding. He still appeared rather grim-visaged, however, only responding briefly and unsmilingly to Catherine's attempts to engage him in conversation, but Lisette concluded that this manner was merely the natural taciturnity engendered by his recent solitary existence, and bade Catherine not to plague him with questions.

"I swear you chatter more than any jackdaw," she said, smiling at her sister. "But I must confess I was grateful for it this morning. Thank you, little sister, for being such an able deputy."

Catherine flushed with pleasure at this praise. "I enjoyed it. The Queen is a most gracious lady, don't you think? And the King is much more…but we can speak of that later," she amended hastily as Leofwin scowled.

"Aye, we should turn back now, Leofwin," suggested Lisette, reining Viking Princess to a halt. "We seem to be a long way from the road."

"Very well," he agreed. "But dismount a moment, Catherine, your saddle girth looks a little slack. I don't want you suffering a fall because of some careless stable lad. Perhaps I'd better check yours as well, Lisette."

"Oswy is usually very careful," said Catherine doubtfully. But, springing to the ground nevertheless, she peered under her horse's belly. "Everything looks secure enough to me."

Leofwin was tying Catherine's horse to a tree. "Does it?" he asked in a voice that held an unusually high note of elation.

Lisette looked at him quickly, a sudden premonition of danger brushing her skin like a cold wind, but before she had time to act Leofwin grasped Catherine's arm.

"Then we can be on our way. Over here!"

"What are you doing?" cried Catherine sharply as Leofwin pulled her across to Lisette.

"Making sure of my future. Now hold your tongue and get on the horse."

"Leofwin, have you lost your mind?" demanded Catherine, ignoring these instructions.

"Catherine! Do as he says!" cried Lisette quickly as Leofwin's expression turned ugly, and she glimpsed the dagger that appeared from its concealment beneath his mantle.

Shocked disbelief at Leofwin's unexpected behaviour seemed to suspend all her faculties while Catherine scrambled up behind her, but she forced back the panic rising in her throat and tried to think. She did not have any idea what Leofwin intended, but calm reason had worked before and might again if he would only listen to her.

"Very wise," he remarked, leading Viking Princess over to his own horse and mounting. He handed the reins back to Lisette.

"We'll travel faster if I don't have to lead you," he informed her, his eyes so cold that she shuddered. "But if you fall back I'll take the reins again, and if you try to turn and run your sister will be the worse for a sword in her back. Do you understand me?"

"Aye," she whispered, and he nodded in satisfaction.

They started off again, Lisette giving her sister's hand a reassuring squeeze as her mind searched for a way to delay their progress, giving Raverre time to catch them.

That he would come after them Lisette had no doubt whatsoever, but it could be several hours before he returned to discover their disappearance, and Leofwin seemed to be leading them deeper into the forest. Raverre would waste precious time searching for them on the road to Godric's manor, and panic churned in her stomach again at the thought of spending the night in Leofwin's company.

They now appeared to be heading in a southerly direction, away from the army to the north, and, remembering his talk of leaving the country, Lisette wondered if Leofwin intended taking ship from one of the nearer ports. But in that case, why take her and Catherine?

Glancing back at Catherine and motioning her to keep silent, Lisette brought Viking Princess up closer to Leofwin's mount.

"Why are you doing this?" she asked in a voice that she strove to keep steady and calm. "You must know we would not inform against you if, as it seems, you do not intend to honour your vow to William.

"Why, Leofwin?" she persisted quietly as he continued to stare stonily ahead. "I want to understand. You could have left England without anyone knowing, except maybe your father. Why go through all that ceremony earlier? At least tell me that much."

"How else was I to get to you, Lisette, my dear?" he asked in a conversational voice that was strangely at variance with the expression in his eyes. "I did warn you earlier, but you chose not to hear. Which I consider rather strange now that I find your husband is indeed the Norman Tostig described to me. You should be grateful to be removed from such a shameful alliance. You say you don't understand me! *I* cannot understand how you could be so disloyal to your people."

"She did it to protect Enide and me!" exclaimed Catherine, unable to bear this criticism of her beloved elder sister in silence. "And besides—"

"Hush, sweet," admonished Lisette as Leofwin turned to glare at the younger girl. "'Tis a convenient marriage for both of us. No more than that," she told him calmly, hoping he would make the assumption that her marriage was in name only.

She did not think Leofwin had witnessed Raverre's embrace in the bailey—he had not appeared outside until some moments later—but he sent her a sardonic look which held a good deal of disbelief.

"Do you think I'm blind? Even if he has not claimed you yet, how long do you think you will keep your precious virtue? Or do you expect honour from a Norman who has waded through the blood of your people to get to you?"

"He has more honour than you will ever possess!" she flashed, her temper momentarily getting the better of her. "He would never break a sacred vow as you have done. Leofwin, have you no fear for your immortal soul? And you will only make matters worse for yourself by taking us. Raverre will come after you and we'll only slow you down."

This was the wrong thing to have said, she realised immediately as Leofwin gave her an ice-cold stare.

"If you do," he stated with deadly quiet, "I'll kill your sister. But I have other plans for you, my pretty creature, and I doubt you would think death preferable to becoming my mistress. And if your husband comes after us I'll kill him also. Then, who knows, I may even marry you?"

He laughed suddenly at her appalled expression. "Didn't you think I meant what I said to you the other day? My little simpleton, still blinded by the fact that I asked for Enide. She would have been easy to dispose of, and then I would have asked for you. I had my plans well laid until the Norman bastard set his foot in England. You still look surprised. Don't you know what that innocent beauty of yours does to a man?"

He laughed again, a high uncontrolled sound that froze Lisette's blood, and she allowed Viking Princess to drop back a pace.

"He has run mad," whispered Catherine behind her, sounding as terrified as Lisette felt. "Lisette, we have to get away. He'll never be able to throw his sword among these trees if we run. We have to try."

"No!" Lisette whispered back emphatically. "He'll catch us easily while Viking Princess is carrying both of us. But—" she thought hard "—if I can persuade Leofwin to dismount on some pretext, you might escape. You'll ride faster alone and I don't think he'll risk losing me to go after you."

"But I can't leave you!" protested Catherine. "He'll kill you!"

"No. You heard what he said. 'Tis you he would kill if he's enraged. I think I am safe enough for the moment, but you must get back to the manor and tell Raverre which way to follow before it's too late."

Even as she spoke, though, Lisette felt qualms shake her. If they went much further before Catherine tried to flee she might lose her way. Both girls knew the countryside around the manor for some miles, but already the woods were taking on an unfamiliar aspect, and when the sun went down there would be other dangers.

If some accident happened to her sister Lisette knew she would never forgive herself. But she had to weigh that risk against the certainty that Leofwin would kill Catherine sooner or later. He had only taken them both because he knew Lisette would not have accompanied him alone.

"The river can't be very far from us," breathed Catherine in Lisette's ear, and even as she spoke the glitter of clear water showed through the bare trees, where the Wye cut a wide path through the forest on its slowly meandering way to the Severn estuary.

Knowing this might be their only opportunity, Lisette halted her mount. Here, at least, Catherine could follow the river until she found herself on more familiar ground.

As Leofwin stopped also, glancing around, she gestured to the smoothly flowing water.

"May we not rest just a moment to drink and water the horses?" she suggested, letting him hear a tremor in her voice. She didn't have to try very hard. It was all she could do to keep her hands steady on the reins at the thought of what they were about to do. She and Catherine could both die right here by the river if their scheme failed.

Leofwin cast a glance up at the clear sky, estimating the time, then nodded. "Aye, but don't take too long, and stay together," he ordered as Lisette slipped from the saddle.

She led Viking Princess to the river, her heart plummeting when Leofwin remained mounted, keeping pace with her until he allowed his own horse to put its head down to drink.

Kneeling down on the bank, Lisette looked up at him. "You may as well take a drink, too, Leofwin," she suggested reasonably. "What can we do? We are only women and unarmed."

He laughed scornfully, but, to her relief, dismounted and joined her. "I admire your calm, my dear," he said, but his tone was unpleasant. "I'm going to enjoy the challenge of breaking it down—when we're alone."

"You will get no pleasure from me," Lisette retorted, rising and moving away from him. His tacit admission that Catherine would not survive much longer hardened her resolve, and she added, "I would rather kill myself than let you touch me."

As she had hoped, at her deliberate provocation Leofwin rose and followed her. The minute he was several paces away from the horses, Catherine acted. Hauling on the reins, she jerked a startled Viking Princess's head up and drove her heels hard into the animal's flanks. Unused to such treatment, Lisette's horse squealed in fright and took off into the trees at a gallop before Leofwin had done more than spin around at the sound of the first startled whinny.

Leofwin immediately sprang for his horse, but Lisette ran after him and grabbed his arm, trying to use all her slight weight to slow him down.

"No!" she cried, hoping that if Catherine got a good start Leofwin would choose to put more distance between himself and the manor.

With a snarl he threw her off, shoving her to the ground and reaching for his reins, but then paused as the echo of hoofbeats rapidly died away and he realised pursuit would be useless. Turning, he strode back to Lisette and hauled her to her feet. A detached part of her mind watched the angry red colour surge into his face. She wondered if she was about to die. He looked wild enough to kill her here and now.

Holding Lisette with one hand to prevent her from falling, Leofwin swung his free arm back and struck her hard once, twice, across the face. Almost losing consciousness from the force of the blows, she only half heard him snarl. "You treacherous bitch!" as he hit her again, before letting her slump to the ground.

Through a swirling mist she watched him retrieve his horse and lead it up to her. Then he pulled her upright again by grabbing a handful of her hair. The sharp pain stung Lisette back to full awareness as Leofwin mounted and hauled her up into the saddle before him. Wheeling the horse, he spurred it in the opposite direction to Catherine's flight.

"You may well wish yourself dead when I've finished with you," he grated with chilling menace. "A man quickly forgets the civilised conduct you're accustomed to after two years of the life I've led. An unpleasant fact from which I shall derive a great deal of enjoyment in teaching you.''

Shaking from the inevitable reaction to what had just passed, still dizzy with the stinging pain of her bruised face, Lisette was unable to answer him. Now that Catherine was safely away, sick fear held her in its cruel grip, clawing at her stomach and sapping her ability to think clearly.

The only constant in her mind was that she would never let Raverre be dishonoured by allowing Leofwin to do the things he was describing in such detail. She would die first. Fortunately for her, this resolve, repeating itself over and over again in her head, prevented her from hearing most of what Leofwin was saying.

Eventually, getting no response from her, he fell silent, and the hours and miles slipped away as he kept the horse to a steady canter.

Chapter Nine

Spurred by the strong human instinct for self-preservation, Lisette at last began to free her mind from the clinging tentacles of panic. How ironic, she thought, that when I had to submit to Raverre's possession I never once thought of death as preferable, but now, faced with the same threat from one of my own people, I would gladly embrace it.

And yet…

The thought of never seeing Raverre again, of never being able to tell him she loved him, of never again knowing the fierce ardour of his embrace, was almost more than she could bear. Somehow, if deliverance didn't appear by nightfall, she would try to gain her freedom before facing the ultimate escape offered by death itself.

Another long hour passed in bleak consideration of such an escape, and Lisette began to wonder if Leofwin intended to ride through the night. He had avoided any sign of human habitation, and she had long since abandoned the hope of enlisting aid from passing travellers or villagers. Now, with sunset not far away, even a lonely shepherd's hut would have been a welcome sight.

Then, as they traversed an open meadow, moving slowly on the tired horse, Lisette, desperately listening for the sounds of rescue, at last heard the thud of hoofs behind them. Lost in his thoughts, Leofwin seemed oblivious, and she was afraid to turn her head in case he was warned.

Holy Mother, let it be Raverre, she prayed as her hands tensed on the saddle.

Judging the distance to the woods on their left in case she needed to seek their shelter, Lisette cautiously moved a little away from Leofwin, ready to jump the instant he realised they were being chased. The movement, slight though it was, penetrated his abstraction, and he frowned down at her.

"Hold still, woman," he growled. "We stop when I say and not before."

As Lisette turned her head to answer him she looked past his shoulder and almost swayed with relief. Raverre at last, but still some distance away and alone. Hoping to distract Leofwin from the growing sounds of pursuit, she said, "The horse will not travel much farther. Are we to spend the night in the open, a prey to any marauding animal?"

"Be silent," he commanded harshly, and she realised he was trying to listen over the sound of her voice.

Turning swiftly in the saddle, he saw Raverre, riding hard, and spurred his own horse to a faster pace. However, the animal was exhausted and barely responded. Leofwin cursed viciously and hauled on the reins, so suddenly that the horse reared, wheeling about. Lisette, seizing her chance, sprang from the saddle while he had his hands full controlling the frightened animal.

She landed hard, falling to the ground, but, unheeding of any bruises, leapt instantly to her feet. Grabbing up the loose folds of her gown, she began to run like a hare back towards Raverre. It was purely instinctive. Forgetting the nearer safety of the trees where Leofwin would find it difficult to follow, she fled to Raverre as any terrified female creature fled to the protection of her more powerful mate.

With a bellow of rage Leofwin immediately spurred after her, and Lisette realised that she could never outrun the horse or reach Raverre before she was recaptured. Then she remembered the woods and swerved wildly to her right, giving Raverre the opportunity he had been hoping for.

As soon as Lisette had jumped from the saddle he had urged Lanzelet to a faster gallop, but then with a pang of chilling fear had seen that he wouldn't be in time to intercept Leofwin's frenzied pursuit of her. There was only one alternative. Pulling Lanzelet to a slithering halt, Raverre drew his short bow and prayed for an opening in the rapidly diminishing gap between Lisette and the man determined to ride her down. He saw her change direction, making for the woods, and fired instantly, aiming at his adversary's horse.

The arrow whizzed past Leofwin's mount, missing its face by less than an inch, and the horse shied violently, unseating his rider. Leofwin rolled several times, but sat up, unhurt. Then, cursing under his breath, he climbed unsteadily to his feet as Lanzelet slithered to a halt.

As Lisette fought to regain her breath, sinking to her knees and gripping her side, Raverre dismounted and advanced slowly towards her. Lisette felt as though she gazed at a stranger. A stranger who moved with leashed menace, watching Leofwin with an expression in his eyes not even his men would have recognised.

She had seen Raverre impatient and angry, even furious, but never like this. Now Lisette saw clearly the terrifying, unstoppable ferocity that was the legacy of his Viking ancestors. He looked ready to commit murder, but he was still controlled, and therefore all the more dangerous.

Raverre reached her side and, without taking his eyes

from Leofwin, asked through clenched teeth, "Has he touched you?"

"No," she gasped. And then, more firmly, "I swear it."

He reached down to help her to stand, still with that cold, deadly gaze fixed on Leofwin, who had drawn his sword and stood waiting for the confrontation he knew could not be avoided.

"Wait here," Raverre said briefly, taking his own sword from its sheath on Lanzelet's saddle.

Lisette still held his arm. "Take care," she whispered, "he has lost all reason, I think. He will not fight fairly, my lord."

Raverre glanced down in quick surprise at her warning and saw, for the first time, the livid bruise across her cheek. His eyes narrowed, and an expression of such ruthless savagery crossed his face as his control slipped for a moment that Lisette gasped, stepping back.

"Fair or no, he won't live long enough to profit by anything he may choose to do," Raverre ground out in a voice she barely recognised as his. He moved away from her to the centre of the meadow, circling around to keep the westering sun out of his eyes. Leofwin followed.

Lisette watched, praying desperately, as the two men suddenly came together in a simultaneous attack which sent a vicious echo ringing into the stillness of the late afternoon.

They were fairly evenly matched. What Leofwin lacked in Raverre's great strength and reach he made up with a sure swiftness of movement that seemed to escape his opponent's blows by a hair's breadth, and enabled him to retaliate in kind, both men swinging their great two-handed swords with lethal intent, their breathing audible with the tremendous effort. Had they been jousting it would have been an interesting competition. But this was in earnest. To the death. And it gradually became obvious that Leofwin, blinded by his insane rage and the frustration of his plans, would tire before Raverre, who fought with a disciplined fury that few adversaries could have survived.

Blind rage had its own strength, however, and was not so easily defeated. Lisette gave a hastily smothered scream as Leofwin's blade suddenly flashed under Raverre's guard, slashing his left arm across his wrist. Blood gushed from the wound, but Raverre fought on, unheeding, sending his opponent reeling backwards under a series of tremendous blows that finally sent Leofwin to the ground.

Raverre leapt back. "Get up," he ordered curtly, ignoring the blood that continued to spurt from his wrist.

Lisette pressed her hands against her mouth in an attempt not to cry out again as Leofwin struggled to his feet and returned to the attack.

Raverre now seemed to keep him at bay with almost insolent ease, a contemptuous smile on his lips as he tormented Leofwin, playing with him as a cat did a mouse before the kill. Not attacking, but letting Leofwin feed his own rage at not being able to again wound his enemy, or finish him. The Saxon's face now had the desperate look of a man who saw his own death approaching, inexorable, inevitable. He was tiring quickly, but there was fight in him yet, and finally Raverre knew he would have to end it, or risk Lisette's life by collapsing through loss of blood.

Changing his tactics with a suddenness that took Leofwin by surprise, Raverre launched into an attack that unleashed the full strength of his fury. Slashing relentlessly at the man he had sworn to kill, forcing him backwards with every blow, he sent Leofwin's sword flying through the air to land several yards away. Leofwin's hand went instantly to his dagger, but he froze as Raverre's sword-point rested against his throat.

''You should have thought twice before you abducted my wife, Godricson,'' he bit out, shortening his arm for the final thrust.

''Maybe so, but I've had her first!'' Leofwin hissed maliciously.

Raverre's arm stayed. His eyes went the colour of ice and his mouth curled in a deadly smile. ''Not so, Saxon. She's mine. She was always mine. She always will be.''

He watched as Leofwin's face registered the absolute certainty in his voice. Raverre laughed.

At the sound of his opponent's derision, Leofwin's face shattered into raging insanity. Lips drawn back from his teeth in a snarl of pure hatred, he pulled his dagger, but Raverre was quicker.

His sword entered Leofwin's throat with a thrust that drove it to the spine, and the two men stood frozen for a moment. Then Leofwin crumpled forward, death freezing the snarl on his face into a ghastly mask.

Raverre pulled his sword free and stepped back, breathing deeply and swaying slightly as dizziness washed over him. He was suddenly acutely aware of the silence and the slight chill in the air that warned of the coming night, and turned his head as Lisette flew towards him, tears of mingled fright and relief running down her face.

She slowed her pace as Raverre remained still, making no move towards her. Then, gathering all her courage, she stepped forward and took his hand, instantly feeling the warm stickiness of his blood.

All lesser worries fled. ''Your arm! Oh, my lord, why did you go on fighting? You could have killed him a hundred times instead of letting your wound bleed so.''

Raverre looked down vaguely at the blood, which continued to spurt from the ugly wound. '''Tis not as bad as it looks,'' he murmured, and promptly staggered against her, his weight bearing Lisette to the ground with him as he sank into unconsciousness.

"Oh, God!" she cried, momentarily panicked, then pulled herself together. This was no time for feminine hysterics. She had to stop the bleeding.

Hurriedly lifting her gown, Lisette pulled at the hem of her shift until it tore and she had a wide strip to use as a bandage. As she peeled back Raverre's sleeve to expose the long gash he stirred.

"Tie a knot tightly above the elbow," he instructed softly. "As tight as you can make it. Then bind my wrist."

Not wasting words, Lisette set about following his instructions, pulling the knot tight with her capable little hands and pressing a pad of cloth hard over the place on his wrist where the blood still seeped. Though now, she was relieved to see, it came sluggishly instead of the steady spurts that had weakened him.

Raverre watched her face as she worked, his eyes skimming over the tear-stained and bruised cheek nearest him.

"I wanted to make him suffer for that," he said, lifting his other hand to her face.

"I spoke truly, my lord," she said meeting his eyes steadily. "No matter what Leofwin said, this—" she touched her cheek "—was all he did."

"I know," he said, but his face was tense, his eyes searching. "I had to kill him," he went on, a strangely desperate note in his voice. "He was your friend, but I killed him."

"I know," Lisette answered, as he had done. "Leofwin was insane. You had to kill him as one would kill a rabid animal."

Raverre seemed to relax a little and his eyes closed again. "Is it still bleeding?"

"Just a little."

''My men are following,'' he told her when Lisette had finished tying a firm strip of cloth around the pad on his wrist. She held his arm against her breast, keeping the pressure firm. ''We split up, hoping to find you sooner, but some of them should be here shortly.'' He felt the faintness creep on him again, and fought against it. ''If they are not here by nightfall take Lanzelet and ride for the castle.''

''No!'' she exclaimed. ''I will not leave you.''

''You'll do as I say,'' he commanded abruptly, reaching up to grip her arm.

''I will not leave you,'' Lisette repeated emphatically. ''But, if I help you, we can both mount Lanzelet. He will have to go slowly, but we will at least come up with your men sooner and—''

''You'd never be able to take my weight if I lose my sense,'' Raverre interrupted and, as if to prove his point, slipped into unconsciousness, his hand falling from her arm. Lisette looked about her in despair.

The sun slipped below the horizon even as she watched it, and she cast a worried glance at the shadowy woods. Come nightfall there would be wolves, she knew, and, though it was unlikely they would attack a human at this season of the year, they might be drawn by the scent of blood and the corpse, lying exposed in the grass. Lisette looked back at Raverre, holding his arm closer, her hand starting to become numb with the pressure she was still exerting on his wrist.

''Don't die!'' she ordered fiercely. ''Don't die!''

Leaning forward, she stroked the sweat-darkened hair from his brow with her free hand, letting it lie for a moment against his cheek. He felt slightly cool, and she wondered if she should get his cloak from Lanzelet's saddle to keep him warm, but dared not release her hold in case the bleeding started again. As she watched him Lisette felt her heart fill with such love for Raverre that she wondered how she could have remained ignorant of her feelings for so long.

If he lives, she vowed, I will tell him. I don't care if he loves me not, if he only pursued me for his own honour. Oh, blessed Mother in Heaven, please let him live. I love him so.

Suppressing a sob, she bent over him, whispering, "Oh, my love, my lord, you *must* live."

She stopped with a sudden shock as she saw that Raverre's eyes were open. But as she took a shaky breath he said, "Call Lanzelet, then, and we'll try your plan. He'll stand quietly enough." And Lisette realised he had no recollection of the time that had elapsed since her suggestion.

It took them three attempts, but eventually Raverre managed to stand upright long enough to get into the saddle. Lisette mounted in front of him, bracing herself to take his weight against her back, as she nudged Lanzelet into a slow walk.

Raverre passed his good arm about her waist, pressing his hand into the saddle to take some of his weight off Lisette.

"At least I've stopped bleeding like a stuck pig," he murmured in her ear. "But the gash will have to be cauterised."

Lisette's stomach clenched at the thought of a treatment that was more like torture than cure.

"Maybe not," she said, thinking she would try anything rather than see Raverre's flesh seared by a hot iron. "If the cut is clean it can be stitched. Bertrand knows how. He saw it done in Spain when he travelled with my father, and once when a slave cut his hand in the kitchen Bertrand sewed the edges together. When it had healed there was only a thin line to show for it."

Raverre leaned more heavily on her as his senses swam. "Cauterising is quicker."

"But it does so much damage to the surrounding flesh, especially if left to clumsy hands," she argued. "And I know how to make you sleep while your arm would be stitched, so there wouldn't be any pain."

Raverre was silent for so long that Lisette thought he had swooned away again, but after a while he said, "Keep talking to me, sweetheart. How can you make a person sleep?"

"You need hemlock, opium, mulberry juice, hyoscyamus, ivy, mandragora and lettuce. The mixture is dried on a sponge and moistened. Then the patient inhales it and falls asleep."

"Does he wake up again?" Raverre demanded with a touch of humour.

"Aye, by fennel juice applied to the nostrils."

"Sounds disgusting," he said, the words slurring together.

But even as he seemed to slump against her, Lanzelet gave a soft whinny, and Lisette's straining ears caught the sounds of hoofs almost immediately afterwards. Peering into the rapidly deepening twilight, she saw several riders, their Norman clothing easily recognisable, and released a long breath of relief.

Gilbert reached them first, flinging himself out of the saddle almost before his horse had plunged to a stop.

"My lady, thank the Saints you are safe! But Alain—" He broke off suddenly as Raverre swayed.

"You must dismount, my lady. Quickly, while I have him!"

Lisette slid thankfully to the ground.

"He was wounded in the arm. Oh, Gilbert, he has lost so much blood. I have bandaged it, but he fought for so long with it bleeding terribly, and it will take hours yet to get him home..."

Her voice broke on a sob, and leaving Raverre to the other men who had come up with them, Gilbert gripped her hands.

"Do not give way now, my lady," he said firmly. "We shall do well enough. I have seen Raverre take deeper wounds than this scratch and survive. He is strong; 'tis merely loss of blood that has made him lose his senses, but that shall soon be remedied. I should think he will recover his wits before we are halfway home. Now, if you will allow me to help you on to my horse, we shall be on our way."

These bracing words made the helpless, sickening feeling of panic recede again, and Lisette nodded. Stumbling slightly with the chill and stiffness in her body, she began to feel her bruises and was glad to be gently lifted into the saddle of a tall chestnut, and to wait as Raverre was made secure by the man who mounted behind him. She was thankful to leave it all to Gilbert's capable direction, and could see why Raverre had so much trust in his young knight.

He strode over to her. "We must ride slowly, my lady, but you may go ahead with some of the men. You can trust them to keep you from harm, and the sooner you are safe home, the better. The others will be anxious."

"Catherine!" she uttered, conscience-stricken. "Oh, how could I have forgotten? Is she safe?"

"Safe, and back at the castle under Bertrand's escort by now," Gilbert replied reassuringly. He smiled unexpectedly. "She came up with us on the road to Godric's manor, where some of the serfs thought you may have been taken, riding like a wild creature from a Norse legend. I verily believe she would have ridden with us but that Raverre sent her back home. She has a great deal of courage for one so young,'' he finished admiringly.

"Aye,'' Lisette agreed thankfully. Then, as he would have mounted, she stayed him with a gesture. "Gilbert, we cannot leave Leofwin's body for the wolves. Base though his actions were, they were also the actions of a man out of his mind with madness, and his father has done nothing wrong. Let him at least have his son's body returned for Christian burial. After all, I am unharmed but for a bruise or two,'' she added coaxingly.

Gilbert hesitated, wondering what Raverre would say to this, but he wasn't proof against Lisette's pleading eyes.

"Very well, my lady,'' he said reluctantly, and gave the order for some of the men to go back for Leofwin, and for his body to be taken to Godric.

"The responsibility is mine,'' she assured Gilbert as they started and he came up to ride with her. "I will answer to my lord if need be.''

"You could do no wrong in his eyes, my lady,'' was his surprising reply to this.

Lisette looked at him in quick enquiry, but Gilbert refused to say more, and wheeled his horse away to ensure that his captain and friend was secure and not losing more life-blood.

It was almost morning when they filed wearily into the bailey, and the torches at the gate were burning low in their sconces. Lisette had refused to go on ahead, but, overcome with exhaustion, had finally agreed to ride double with Gilbert, and had been half asleep for the last few miles. She also fell into Bertrand's arms, but anxiety for Raverre, who had drifted in and out of consciousness during the long night, kept her from letting Marjory lead her away to her bed.

"I must see him tended to,'' she insisted, swaying

against Bertrand as serfs came running to carry Raverre into the hall. "Bertrand, don't let them use a hot iron on him."

"What you must do is rest," scolded Marjory. "You can nurse him all you like tomorrow, but now you will probably swoon with hunger and exhaustion, and then be in the way."

Lisette would have protested at this brutal truth, but Bertrand, having taken a look at Raverre's arm, agreed with Marjory. "Mistress Marjory speaks wisely, my lady," he told her. "I can stitch the arm, but 'tis not a sight for your eyes. The best thing you can do is rest. The manor needs you while my lord is unable to command."

"I will rest when my lord has had the proper care," Lisette protested. "After last year, do you think I will swoon at the sight of a cut arm? Who do you think bound it up? Now, no more of such foolish arguments. Marjory, fetch me food and have a pallet set up in the solar, so I may be near Raverre."

As they hesitated Lisette sensed victory. She smiled suddenly at their mutinous faces. "Besides, you want to hear what happened, don't you?"

Lisette pulled the bearskin over her sleeping husband, carefully avoiding his injured arm. He stirred slightly but did not waken, and she went to sit in the window embrasure, where she could watch him in comfort.

Resting her head against the wall, she sighed wearily. For a day and a night Raverre had slept, only waking when she tended his arm or coaxed him to take some nourishment. At first she had been frightened by his utter stillness as he lay in the bed. He had barely seemed to breathe, and to see such a big, powerful man so helpless had torn at her heart. But Bertrand had assured her it was the deep sleep of healing, and Bertrand had been right. Lisette's vigil had been rewarded in the early hours of the morning.

She had been changing the bandage on Raverre's arm when he had opened his eyes and looked straight at her, his vivid blue gaze disconcertingly aware. Feeling her heartbeat quicken under his steady regard, Lisette had bent her head and concentrated on applying the healing salve of her own making as gently as possible, knowing the slightest touch must be painful. Bertrand might have congratulated himself on a neat piece of sewing, but she looked at the bruised skin where the needle had entered and almost felt the pain in her own body.

As she had wrapped a protective covering over the wound a faint smile had come into Raverre's eyes. "You said I might need one of your brews one day," he had reminded her softly.

Feeling suddenly shy in the intimate atmosphere of the dim, quiet room, Lisette had only smiled back in answer, but, unable to resist touching him, laid her hand on his brow to check for fever. Raverre had brought his right hand up to clasp hers.

"Stay with me," he had murmured, his eyes beginning to close again. And the unexpected vulnerability in his voice had restored her powers of speech.

"For the rest of our lives," she had quoted softly, remembering his words on the morning after their wedding.

She had not been sure if Raverre had heard her, for he had turned his head and fallen into sleep again, but this time the sleep had been more natural.

Since then he had woken several times to eat a little and to drink the warmed milk mixed with wine that Lisette kept ready. And each time as he had fallen back into slumber he had murmured, "Stay with me."

As she watched the regular rise and fall of his chest, and

let her eyes roam over the strong lines of his handsome face, softened now in sleep, Lisette felt so much tenderness for him that the emotion threatened to overwhelm her. In the past Raverre had frightened her, angered her, and forced a physical response from her—all violent emotions in their way, over which she'd had little control. Raverre had been the one in command, self-possessed, contained.

But now this giant of a man who had faced undaunted the Danes of the fyrd swinging their battleaxes with terrifying accuracy, who had undertaken to settle in a land still hostile to his face, and who had never seemed to depend on anyone other than himself, had shown that he needed her.

The sound of the door opening interrupted Lisette's reflections and she looked up to see Gilbert enter quietly, carrying a tray, which he set down on the table.

Glancing at Raverre, he said, ''Marjory said I might see Alain for a moment if I made myself useful by bringing in your supper, my lady. How is he?''

Lisette smiled and rose. ''Much better,'' she said, amused to see how ill at ease he looked. Gilbert had probably gazed on the most hideous scenes of battle carnage without flinching, she thought, but, like most men, was as helpless as a babe when it came to nursing.

''There is no sign of fever,'' she assured him, ''and the wound is clean. It should heal quickly, thanks to Bertrand.''

''Aye,'' Gilbert answered. ''Though I must say I was doubtful at the time. There we were, wasting time arguing, some of the men all for using a tried and true method and Bertrand saying that if he didn't get started he wouldn't have a patient to work on. I know the Moors have used stitching on wounds for years, but *I'd* never seen it done, and Raverre was no help, lying there senseless. If you hadn't told the men you'd hold them responsible to the King if Raverre died I don't know where we'd have been.''

''What an interesting scene I missed,'' said an amused voice from the bed, and they both jumped, spinning around.

Lisette moved quickly across the room as Raverre began to sit up.

''No, no! You must lie still,'' she admonished, placing her hand lightly on his chest just as he came upright.

At the contact of her palm against his warm skin they both froze, staring into each other's eyes. Lisette felt as if every faculty became suspended. She was barely conscious of breathing as she gazed into the blue depths so close to her, their expression as searching as her own.

''Gilbert,'' said Raverre softly, his eyes never leaving Lisette's, ''go and count the weapons in the armoury.''

Gilbert grinned in quick comprehension and, convinced of his friend's recovery, left the room in double-quick time.

As if the closing of the door released her from the strange spell of Raverre's gaze, Lisette snatched her hand back, flushing slightly. However, her legs were shaking so much that she didn't dare try to step away from the bed.

''You must rest,'' she said faintly. She had felt so confident while he had been asleep, but now, faced with what appeared to be the full return of his senses, shyness overcame her again.

''I've been resting,'' Raverre answered inarguably, propping himself against the end of the bed. ''Now that the room has stopped spinning around my head I feel a great deal better. Or I would if I could eat something more substantial than that pap you've been forcing down me all day.''

Lisette couldn't help smiling at the aggrieved note in his voice. He sounded like a disgruntled little boy, she thought, feeling some composure return.

She found she was able to walk quite calmly over to the table. "Well, you may have some bread with your broth, if you like, and a slice or two of meat. But not too much," she scolded, as if he were in truth the child her imagination had conjured up.

She glanced up, still amused at the thought, and her shaky composure, disintegrated instantly. Raverre was still watching her, and the expression in his eyes was all adult male.

"Come and sit down," he invited, his voice lowering to that soft growl which seemed to come from deep in his throat.

Her heart starting to race, Lisette armed herself with the tray and complied, placing the meal between them. Raverre gave her a quizzical look, but began to eat.

"There's enough for two," he pointed out when she didn't follow his example.

"I'm not hungry," she said. She would never be able to get any food past the nervous lump in her throat. She could hardly speak. All she really wanted to do was reach out her hand and touch him again, to reassure herself that he was warm and alive.

Raverre finished his meal and went to place the tray on the floor, but the movement pulled his left arm and he paused, grimacing slightly. Glad of the excuse to move away from the bed, Lisette returned the tray to the table.

"Do the stitches pain you very much?" she asked, hating the thought of him suffering.

"Not as much as the memory of you leaping from that horse," he said rather grimly. "You could have broken your neck!"

Lisette rearranged the tray with intense concentration. "Are you very angry?" she managed.

"That depends," he returned, his expression suddenly

probing. There was a thoughtful pause. "Why did you do it?"

"I...I didn't want Leofwin to have an advantage over you once he saw you were so close. He was already dishonoured, so I knew he would not meekly let you kill him without a fight." She sent Raverre a quick, nervous glance. "He could have used me to disarm you, and I thought, whatever you felt for me, you wouldn't risk my life."

"Whatever I felt for you?" he questioned, his voice suddenly so rough that she looked up in surprise. "Lisette, come here."

Oh, the temptation of the strong male demand in his voice. But there were still secrets between them. Lisette gripped her hands together.

"I have a confession to make first," she said desperately.

Raverre eyed her anxious expression and his brows rose. He leaned back against the bedpost again, propping one arm over a raised knee and tilting his head in amused enquiry.

"Well? What dreadful sin have you committed?" he asked indulgently.

Oh, would he still smile at her like that when he learned how she had gone looking for Leofwin?

"The other day wasn't the first time I had seen Leofwin," Lisette admitted in a rush. Unable to face the sudden frown in his eyes, she dropped her own. "'Twas the sniper—"

"What of him?"

"You searched for others and found nothing, but I remembered some caves deep in the forest where we all played as children, and when you went to Godric I decided to look for myself."

She thought Raverre drew in his breath sharply and looked up, but whatever emotion he felt was hidden beneath half-lowered lids, and as her glance dropped to his other hand, clenched on the bearskin, he deliberately relaxed his fingers. Keeping her gaze fixed on his hand, she said simply, ''He was there.''

''What happened?'' Raverre asked, his tone revealing nothing more than mild curiosity.

Relieved that no outburst of rage had been forthcoming, Lisette ventured to look at him again. Raverre's face was expressionless, but a muscle quivered in his jaw once and was stilled.

''We talked. I had only half expected Leofwin to be there,''she explained, ''but when Godric denied knowing that shepherd I could think of no one else who would need to hide in these parts. Then he told me about planning the robbery, though others had carried it out, and I begged him to return home, to confess and make his peace with the King. Oh, my lord, I wanted to tell you, but I thought to give him time to surrender.''

''And after you spoke he let you go without hindrance?''

''Aye.''

There was an ominous silence.

''I swear it!'' Lisette added vehemently when Raverre didn't say anything. ''Leofwin didn't know of my marriage then. We were only together a short time. I had to get back here before dark and—''

''I believe you,'' he interrupted softly, and she went limp with relief.

Then he exploded. ''God's blood!'' he roared, abandoning his relaxed façade. ''He could have killed you! Reckless little fool! I could strangle you myself for taking such a risk.''

An echo of his voice reached the hall. The door opened and a serf looked nervously into the room.

''Get out!'' bellowed Raverre. The door was closed hurriedly. "What in God's name is a serf doing right outside our door?" he demanded, but in a less wrathful tone.

"In case I need anything during the night," she faltered.

"Get rid of him," he snapped. His eyes closed and his head fell back against the bedpost. Lisette, seeing the look of weariness that passed over his face, decided it would be wiser to obey.

"You mustn't tire yourself," she said, after complying with his order. Somehow the knowledge that Raverre had not fully regained his strength calmed her nerves, and she came back to stand by the bed.

"Don't forget I had known Leofwin all my life," she explained reasonably. "He had been like a brother to me, and I wanted to help him. There was no danger from him...or so I thought until he started speaking in that strange way," she mused, remembering.

Raverre's eyes snapped open, their expression grim. "Oh, so he was strange even then, was he?" he asked sardonically. "And yet you and Catherine still went off with him. I might have known you'd do something rash the minute my back was turned, but I didn't expect you to risk your life twice over!"

"I'm sorry," she placated, hanging her head.

At his derisive, "Hrmmph," Lisette felt her old spirit revive.

"How could I see anything wrong in his asking us to accompany him for a while?" she demanded indignantly. "You saw for yourself that he swore allegiance to the King, and he even begged my forgiveness for his earlier behaviour. What was I supposed to do?"

"Stay here and wait for me!" he shot back.

"Well, I would have," she retorted crossly, "but I was too impatient and excited to just sit and...wait."

The last word came out as a whispered breath as Lisette

realised what she had just said. Raverre's whole body seemed to stiffen. His eyes fixed on her face with a look of such glittering intensity that she took a nervous step back, not sure whether his stare betokened anger. But when he flung off the covers to come after her she rushed forward again.

"No! You mustn't get up. You're not strong enough yet."

Snaking his good arm around her waist, Raverre fell back on the bed, taking Lisette down with him. She landed sprawled over his massive chest, gazing wide-eyed into the twin blue flames of his eyes.

"I know," he said, with a devilish grin. "And you wouldn't fight a wounded man, would you?"

"Oh, your arm!" she exclaimed

"To hell with my arm. Look at me!"

Unable to obey this peremptory command while she was lying all over him, Lisette looked at her fingers instead as they softened their hold on his shoulders. The temptation to let her palm lower to his chest, to savour the feel of hard muscle, warm skin and curling hair, was too strong to resist.

"Alain," she whispered.

"Oh, God, sweetheart, come here!" With a ragged sound deep in his throat Raverre moved his hand to Lisette's head, bringing her mouth down to his.

Her body went soft against him, melting with heated longing, and he groaned again into her mouth, deepening the kiss until Lisette forgot her shyness and kissed him back for the first time. Her mouth opened over his in exquisite surrender, letting him feel the love she had repressed for so long.

Raverre broke the kiss abruptly, pressing Lisette's head into his shoulder and rolling her on to the bed so she was held protectively against his side. Still submerged in the sensual spell their kiss had woven, she murmured a soft protest, and he held her closer.

"I know, sweetheart. I need you too." His lips stroked across the soft tendrils feathering her brow, and Lisette felt his mouth curve in a smile.

"Tell me you love me," he murmured, trying to see into her eyes. But, feeling vulnerable, when Raverre himself had only mentioned need, she tucked her face into his shoulder.

"You must know I do," she whispered, feeling the ripple of the powerful muscle under her cheek.

Raverre held her for a moment in silence, then spoke suddenly in a voice which held such anguish that Lisette looked up again.

"Dear God, do you know what I thought when I got back here to find you gone?"

She shook her head, her eyes widening at the expression of remembered pain in his.

"I thought you had taken my parting words as a threat, and could no longer bear to live as my wife." His voice dropped to barely above a whisper. "After what happened that morning…you were afraid I would force you. And then later you were so quiet while Leofwin was here. I wondered what you were thinking about at the time, and when you disappeared I thought I knew."

"Oh, no," she said, lifting a hand to touch his face.

After hearing the tormented note in his voice Lisette could no longer doubt Raverre's feelings, and, loosed from the bonds of uncertainty and constraint, her own love illuminated her face with a radiance that caused him to catch his breath as the glowing warmth reached out to him.

"Lisette," he murmured. "Tell me."

"I love you," she said, her voice very clear and soft. "Oh, Alain, I love you."

"At last!" Raverre growled in fierce triumph, catching

Lisette in a one-armed embrace, which nevertheless threatened to crack her ribs.

But, instantly realising how strongly he gripped her, he relaxed his possessive hold a little and his voice held a more tender note as he murmured, "I love you so much, Lisette. You don't know how long I've waited to hear you say that."

"You love me," she repeated wonderingly, savouring the words.

"From the first moment of seeing you," he affirmed, smiling down at her. "You looked so small and fragile and yet so defiant, and all I could think of was how much I wanted to make you love me."

"I think I did even then," Lisette admitted. "When I saw you for the first time I thought you looked like one of the Viking warriors my father used to tell us about. So tall and fierce and strong. You were the hero of all my dreams, and yet I was afraid."

"I know," he groaned, remembering. "And all I seemed to do was give you reason to fear me. I was so desperate for you, Lisette. I'd never felt like that about any woman before, but with you…" He gave a self-mocking laugh. "I only had to be near you and I lost all control, driving you away."

She shook her head. "You didn't drive me away. 'Twas myself I feared. I was afraid to love you, to have such feelings for one I thought was an enemy."

"I have never been an enemy of yours, sweetheart. I tried to tell you that, but all you seemed to do was resent my presence. If you only knew how often I wished we had met differently. And then when I thought you had run away with a man who was Saxon and a friend, one whom perhaps you loved, I almost wished we'd never met at all."

"And yet you came after me? Even thinking I might love another?"

Lisette felt every muscle in Raverre's body become rigid with primitive aggression. "Do you think I would let another man touch you?" he demanded roughly. "You belong to me. Even at the risk of making you hate me, I would have brought you back. I'll never let you go, Lisette. Never!"

I would have called that Norman arrogance and resented it a few weeks ago, she thought, smiling inwardly, but now she thrilled to the fierce possessiveness in Raverre's voice.

"Besides," he went on, his eyes gentling with softer emotion, "after that first shock, when I began to think clearly, I knew you couldn't possibly do anything dishonourable. You had made a vow, and even if you didn't love me I knew you would never break it willingly."

"I do love you," she whispered. "I belong to you. I thought you had understood what I meant by my answer to the King the other morning." She peeped up at him through her lashes. "Even though you were still angry with me."

"I wasn't angry," he replied, holding her close again. "Not really. 'Twas the only way I could get out of the room that morning without begging you to let me make love to you. I wanted you so much. I kept remembering the night of the storm when you were suddenly so sweet and yielding. God—" he pressed his mouth to hers in a quick, ardent caress "—you don't know what your response that night did to me. I had such hopes that you might at last be coming to care for me, only to find later that you couldn't seem to bear me near you."

"I didn't mean it like that," Lisette cried softly, snuggling closer in remorse for the pain which, even now, echoed in his voice as he remembered the agony of her rejection. "I was such a coward. I thought you had only married me for convenience and I was afraid that if you...if we..."

"Made love," he supplied, his voice very deep and tender with amusement at her shy hesitation.

"Aye." Lisette pretended to frown. "Don't laugh at me. I was afraid I would betray how much I loved you when you only desired my body and not my heart."

"My sweet love, don't you remember what I said to you the first night when we sat at supper together? Your heart *was* the prize I longed for."

Raverre kissed the frown away, then drew back with a devilish twinkle.

"However," he added wickedly, "your delectable little body would turn a monk from his path of chastity."

Lisette blushed fierily, and Raverre moved his mouth across the warmth in her cheek. "I adore you when you look so innocent and shy," he murmured, laughing softly. "You don't know yet what that does to me. Especially when I know of the fire beneath your shyness."

His words stirred an uncomfortable memory. Leofwin had said almost the same thing, Lisette remembered uneasily. Did all men see something in her which she herself had never suspected? Raverre sensed her reaction immediately.

"What is it?" he asked sharply, drawing back to look at her face. "I've upset you."

"No," she assured quickly. "But Leofwin said something—" Lisette struggled to remember the words "—about what innocence does to a man." She looked at him, troubled. "What does it do to you?"

"It makes me want to love you," Raverre replied instantly, looking deeply into her eyes. "In every way I can. To cherish you, care for you, protect you with my life if need be."

Lisette gave a sigh of pure happiness, which quickly

changed to a tiny sound of feminine excitement when Raverre suddenly raised himself on his good arm, leaning over her. He was so much bigger than her that Lisette felt herself tremble in thrilling anticipation of his strength, knowing it was leashed by his tenderness.

"And it makes me want you more than my next breath," he growled softly, beginning to unfasten her gown.

"But your arm…" It was a very half-hearted protest.

Raverre smiled that wicked, utterly irresistible smile. "We'll improvise," he murmured huskily, lowering his mouth to hers.

The last thing Lisette saw clearly before Raverre swept her into a swirling vortex of exquisite sensation was the expression of passionate love in his glittering blue eyes.

A long time later Lisette stirred in Raverre's arms.

"You make me feel so…I don't know…wild, I think," she whispered, wondering if she ought to be shocked at the abandoned response Raverre had drawn from her.

"Good," he growled, a smile in his voice. "Because the instincts you arouse in me aren't exactly civilised either. I've never wanted anyone so much in my life." Suddenly his voice held a note of concern. "I wasn't too rough with you, was I, sweetheart?"

"Never," she murmured, brushing a kiss against his shoulder. "My gentle conqueror."

Raverre laughed softly, sleepy male satisfaction in the sound.

"I love you," he said, kissing her tenderly. "Whatever happens in the future between our people, always remember that."

"Always," Lisette answered from the heart. "As I will love you."

Chapter Ten

Early summer, 1071

Lisette sat down in her favourite corner of the garden, carefully laying the snugly wrapped infant on the ground beside her and settling her back comfortably against the stone wall. Lifting her face to the sun, she closed her eyes, a smile of contentment deepening the corners of her mouth as she savoured the memory of last night's passionate reunion with Raverre. He had been gone five long months and she had missed him every minute of that time.

Her mind went back to the arrival of the King's messenger the previous year, bringing news of a major rebellion led by a Lincolnshire Thegn known as Hereward the Wake. The man had chosen his time well to conduct sudden raids against the nearer Norman settlements.

That Easter of 1070 William had finally disbanded the army. The northern Earls had surrendered and been pardoned after two insurrections, the last of which had been brutally crushed when the King had finally lost patience.

Almost insane with rage, William had ordered such wholesale destruction of the north that the entire countryside was now a barren waste. No crops grew, no cattle grazed, and those people who had survived the savagery of the army had fled. His action had been a blot on an otherwise brilliant and noble career and Lisette had thanked God that Raverre had not taken any part in the "Harrying of the North", as it had come to be known.

However, when Hereward had gathered what few rebels remained and retreated into a secret camp in the fastness of the marshes surrounding the Isle of Ely, William had called for men and arms from those of his Barons and Knights who had settled in England. Hearing that Earls Morcar and Edwin had once again joined forces against him, the King had sworn that there would be no more pardons.

Raverre had had to answer the call to arms, leaving Lisette expecting their first child. He had hoped the rebellion would be put down quickly, but the months had dragged on, his son had been born, and Lisette had heard nothing until a messenger had arrived with the welcome news that Raverre was on his way home.

A serf had been keeping watch on the road all that week, and Lisette had been waiting in the bailey as Raverre and his men had ridden in under the barbican. She had been shaking so much with excitement that Catherine, with one look at Raverre's face as he had stridden towards them, had rapidly removed the welcome cup from her hand. Lisette hadn't even noticed its disappearance as Raverre had taken her hands in a painfully hard grip, staring down into her face as if he didn't quite believe she was standing before him in the flesh.

Her speech of welcome was forgotten as she had gazed longingly up at him, wishing the etiquette governing public greetings didn't prevent her from flinging herself at him.

Raverre had had no such inhibitions. Releasing her

hands, he had swept Lisette into his arms, holding her against his heart, his face buried in her silky, fragrant hair.

They had clasped each other tightly in the close, wordless communication of lovers. So intense had been their silent embrace that some of Raverre's soldiers had turned away, as though they gazed on something not meant for the eyes of other men. Then, recollecting himself, Raverre had set Lisette back on her feet and swept her into the hall, where Marjory had been waiting with a squalling bundle.

"Your son, my lord," Lisette had announced softly, her dark eyes glowing with love and pride. "We had him baptised William Geoffrey for the King and your father, if it please you."

Raverre had smiled into her eyes. "It pleases me very well, my love." And, taking the child, he held him up to the men, who had crowded into the hall after them. "A sturdy son for the house of Raverre," he had announced, and a resounding cheer had rung to the rafters.

The plaintive wail piercing the quiet of the garden brought Lisette back to the present moment with a start. Picking up the baby, she quickly loosened her gown and guided the hungry little mouth to her breast, shielding the child from the sun with her shawl. The wonder she felt at nursing Raverre's child filled her heart every time she held the tiny baby in her arms. So absorbed was she in the sweet bonding that Raverre, coming into the garden in search of her, was able to watch them unheard for several minutes.

Then as he moved his shadow fell over Lisette, and she looked up, her face lighting with all the love he had once longed to see there. Sitting down beside her, he said softly, "Motherhood suits you, my lovely wife, but should you not have a wet-nurse?"

"I like it," she answered, smiling up at him. "Besides, the Queen told me that when Prince Henry was born she insisted on nursing him herself, and look how he has thrived.''

Raverre caressed her cheek with his hand. ''So long as you don't tire yourself, sweet. At least you won't have the manor to worry about now that Gilbert and I are back.'' He stretched out beside her. ''Ah, 'tis good to be home, I vow.''

Until the next time, Lisette thought with a sudden pang. Raverre saw the worry in her face.

''I'll not leave you again, love,'' he reassured her. ''When duty calls me from home I want you with me. There won't be any question of danger. All England is William's now. Did you hear nothing of what happened?''

''No. We thought the King might pardon Morcar yet again in his penitence for what happened in the north. And I swear I never thought to hear myself say this, but, until the man is killed, how will there ever be any peace in England?''

''He is not dead, but imprisoned,'' answered Raverre. ''For life this time. The man's a fool. He could have kept his lands, held his high position under William, and prospered. But no! He has to keep us kicking our heels around the dampest swamp you can ever imagine for the better part of a year. If it hadn't been for one of the monks on the island betraying the secret path to Hereward's stronghold, I swear we'd be there still.''

''And Hereward himself?''

''He escaped during the fighting, but has now surrendered to William and had his lands restored. The fellow was acquiring quite a reputation for heroism—William knows there is little glory in killing such a man, better to win him over. As for Edwin, Morcar's brother, he was slain by his own men, trying to escape to Scotland.''

''The Atheling is still there, is he not?''

"Aye. William says Edgar is welcome to Malcolm's court. He bears the boy no ill will. 'Twas William's intention to rule through Earls of English birth as well as Norman. The Saxon courts of law remain unchanged and he always admired Saxon craftsmen and learning, but, thanks to all the rebellions, 'tis no longer possible.

"However," he continued on a lighter note, "William intends that young imp, Henry, to be reared here in England, so at least one of his sons will be more English than Norman, even if he's unlikely to come to the throne with three older brothers before him. And, speaking of family matters, my love, I have had an offer of marriage for Catherine."

Lisette carefully settled the baby. "Oh?" she questioned cautiously.

"From Gilbert." Raverre grinned at her obvious relief. "Did you really think I would give your sister in marriage to a stranger who did not care for her?"

"'Twould be common enough," she admitted, "but I know how fond you are of her and Gilbert. I'm so glad he has shown his feelings for her. She has been quite in despair these past months, hearing no word from him."

"He felt she was still too young last year, though he loved her then. However, I believe she managed to convince him of her newfound maturity last night after we had retired. The poor fellow didn't stand a chance. What was I to do but give them my blessing?"

He smiled across at Lisette, already anticipating her reaction to his next statement. "As well as deeding him Godric's manor. I thought you would like them near enough to visit often."

He got his reward when Lisette flung herself into his arms, her face aglow with happiness. Raverre wrapped her in a tight embrace, his eyes a vivid blue as they roamed over her delicate features, framed by the curtain of her dark hair.

"You are the most wonderful man in the world!" she exclaimed joyously.

"And despite being a Norman, too," he stated with smug satisfaction. He dodged the swipe Lisette laughingly aimed at him, catching hold of her hand and bringing it to his lips. "'Twas the practical thing to do, love. The manor has been standing empty since the old man died, and William granted me the land, and—"

"I still think you are wonderful," she interrupted firmly. "And I missed you so much," she added softly, laying her head on his shoulder, revelling in the strength of his arms.

Approaching footsteps intruded on her lazy contentment and Lisette raised her head, but Raverre tightened his hold, refusing to release her.

"Fine goings on!" declared Marjory, coming upon them in her search for her infant charge.

"Most valued Marjory," Raverre said, grinning up at her unrepentantly. "Have I thanked you yet for taking such good care of my wife and son?"

"Aye," snapped Marjory, refusing to be placated. "'Tis as well someone is around to keep things running smoothly. There is Catherine, having nothing better to do this morning than sit gazing at that impudent rascal de Rohan. And he is as bad. And now I find my lady with her hair hanging loose and sporting in the garden like any farm lass and her swain."

"Sweet Marjory, would you begrudge a weary soldier the solace of a loving wife and a sunny garden?" Raverre winked at Lisette.

Marjory saw the wink and frowned direfully. She bent to pick up the happily gurgling baby. "Come, my little lordling,'' she crooned. ''You shall sleep in your proper place, though others may forget their dignity.''

Little William stared up at her solemnly for a moment and then yawned hugely in answer. Raverre began to laugh.

''You are outnumbered, Marjory,'' he told her. ''Retreat is the only defence.''

Marjory stalked towards the gate, muttering to herself. ''Just like his father,'' they heard her say. It wasn't a compliment.

''I should hope so,'' murmured Raverre wickedly, determined to have the last word.

''Oh, hush,'' pleaded Lisette, trying not to laugh. ''She'll be disapproving for days now, and you know we can't do without her.''

''I know I can't do without you,'' he replied, letting his fingers play through the bronze cloud of her hair. ''Have I told you yet how much I love you?''

She dimpled at him. ''Several times last night,'' she began, counting on her fingers. ''And again this morning when you gave me that set of garnet veil pins and then refused to let me wear them because you wanted to see my hair loose, thereby bringing Marjory's wrath down upon me.''

''It reminds me of the first time I saw you,'' he explained, and kissed her.

When they reluctantly drew apart both were breathless.

''Perhaps we also should retire to our proper place, my sweet lady,'' Raverre suggested, springing to his feet and helping Lisette up.

Hand in hand, they strolled towards the hall. At the top of the stairway Raverre paused and looked out across the bailey and through the gate to the fields, lying golden and peaceful under the summer sun.

''Thank God all the fighting is done,'' he murmured.

"This land is too beautiful to be stained forever by the blood of its people. Our sons should inherit peace and prosperity, not war and privation."

"Perhaps they will," Lisette answered softly, seeing in their own happiness the promise of the unity and strength William of Normandy had dreamed of for England. "Perhaps they will."

* * * * *

Madselin's Choice

by

Elizabeth Henshall

Elizabeth Henshall is married with two young sons and lives in Cheshire. Following a degree in French and German, she had a variety of jobs before deciding to give up office life. A year in Germany teaching English convinced her that this was certainly more exhausting! She now teaches French and German at a local secondary school and finds her life is indeed very busy. Fascinated in particular by local history, Elizabeth enjoys writing and researching with wine at hand.

Chapter One

"Seize him!"

Madselin was surprised at how harsh her words sounded as they rang out across the copse. No doubt years of living under Alice's pitiless regime had taken its toll on her in more ways than one. Drawing her thick coney-lined cloak about her against the raw gusts of October wind, she turned to her guards.

"Well?" she uttered with rising indignation. "Don't just stand there. Take him."

Her Norman guards did not wait to be told a second time and hurried to do her bidding. Much to her surprise the poacher remained where he was, lowering his bow with what seemed like faint irritation. He made no attempt to escape, merely watching her approach with a bold stare.

Slightly ruffled by his arrogant manners, Madselin pursed her lips and returned his appraisal. Tall as she was for a woman, her head barely reached the man's broad shoulders. Long, unkempt fair hair framed a lean, weather-beaten face, which was covered in stubble. Cold as the winter grey skies, the peasant's eyes glared down

at her with unmistakable annoyance as the guards took
hold of his arms.

"Take the Saxon peasant with us to the bailey. Sir
Richard will deal with him."

As the man opened his mouth in protest, Madselin
raised her hand to halt his words. "Hold your tongue. I
have neither the means nor inclination to understand your
guttural gibberish. Sir Richard may have that pleasure."

The man's eyes glittered almost silver under the fast-
darkening afternoon sky, but Madselin was glad that he
made no further attempt to speak. If all the peasants in
this wet, cold, godforsaken land were as surly and as ill-
mannered as this, no wonder her kinsman was forever
quelling insurrections.

A few streaks of rain across her face reminded her that
she still had some way to go before reaching the safety
of Sir Richard's bailey. The deep, wild Forest of Bowland was no place for a traveller after nightfall. Wolves
roamed freely in this isolated northern outpost of William
Rufus's kingdom. Madselin shuddered. She would be
glad to be gone from this barbaric land.

"We must hurry." Her words were addressed to the
guards. "Set him to walk behind the mule. I'll not be
delayed by a Saxon."

The guards pushed the man through the undergrowth
to another clearing where the rough outline of the northern road was visible. There stood a group of horses and
one beleaguered mule, clearly labouring under the weight
of the travel bags. By its side, a small, rotund figure huddled in a dark cloak stamped heavily on the ground, muttering indistinctly to herself.

"Emma! We are done and ready to go." Madselin
hurried over to her ageing maid. The poor woman had
suffered greatly over these past few weeks on the journey

north and she doubted if Emma could carry on much longer. Tough though she was, at forty years Emma was not young.

"About time, too," came the querulous retort. "A body could die of cold before you lit a fire." Emma raised her pinched white face from the folds of her travel-stained cloak, pulled her hood close round her ears and lumbered towards her uncomplaining horse.

Madselin stared after Emma, her mouth twisting in a wry smile. The woman was impossible. It was Emma who had insisted on accompanying her, despite all Madselin's well-founded reasons for wanting her to remain in her brother's manor in Normandy. She had relented only when it became clear that Emma would suffer from Alice's cruelty if Madselin were not there to protect her.

Sighing heavily, she turned to find the tall peasant staring at her in a most insolent manner, almost as if he understood what had been going on. Despite the fact that he had been tied to the mule, he stood proud and erect with such self-possession that it caused Madselin a moment's doubt.

A keen howl suddenly rent the air and froze her blood. It had come from some distance hence, but only a fool would linger in a spot like this. Shouting her orders, Madselin mounted her horse gracefully with the aid of a fallen trunk and the party headed north once more.

From time to time, Madselin glanced back at the captive peasant, but he walked easily and she could discern little discomfort in his long stride. His cloak, she noticed, was lighter and shorter than theirs. Like his boots and his breeches, it was also mud-spattered and torn.

Just as the thick cloudbank rolled over the last of the daylight, a shout from the scout ahead caused Madselin to send up a prayer of thanks. At last they had arrived.

Breathing a sigh of relief, she trotted on to the bend in the road where the scout awaited his orders. Not far beyond, like a bright jewel in the dark, lay the stone-built keep held by Sir Richard d'Aveyron. Torch flames lit every corner, offering welcome and warmth to the cold, weary travellers.

The scout galloped ahead to warn the guards of their arrival whilst Madselin made a vain attempt to brush some of the dust from her cloak and restore her appearance. She knew that the wind had torn her dark hair from the tight braids into an unruly bird's nest—little short of a miracle could do aught about it. Madselin would be needing more than one miracle tonight.

"Left your brother's demesne? Are you witless, girl?" Sir Richard d'Aveyron's handsome, swarthy face had turned almost red with apoplexy.

Madselin faced him calmly, deciding that it would be best to ignore his last reference to her status. They were the same age yet, whereas he was one of the King's favoured barons, she was being tongue-lashed for displaying the same mettle.

"Nay," she returned quietly, ignoring the sea of interested faces turned in her direction. It was most rare for Sir Richard to lose his temper. "I have not run away at all, but I have no doubt my sister-in-marriage is likely to see my journey in that light."

Calmed somewhat by the soft, reasonable tone of her voice, Sir Richard grunted at the mention of Alice de Breuville. Alice had been a beauty, and he himself had not been averse to her frail, delicate charms, the white-gold hair and her seductive green eyes. But over the past five years of her marriage to Robert de Breuville, Alice had turned into a spiteful shrew who had made Madselin's life a misery.

He gulped down a mouthful of the sweet red wine he favoured before turning back to face his cousin. "I received word from Robert some days back. He is convinced you are about to dishonour the family name."

Madselin stared stonily at Richard. "Alice wanted me to marry Goddefroi de Grantmesnil." Her arms crept about her slender frame in protection. "He is old, cruel and has already killed off three wives." Madselin's chin rose a little in her defence. "Nor has he ever produced any children."

Richard gave a weary sigh. Domestic trivia irritated him. He was a soldier. "He is of noble blood, Madselin. Your duty…"

"My duty?" she interrupted. "Would you wish to lie with that stinking heap of flesh?" The deep flush of her cheeks betrayed her true anger. Richard d'Aveyron drank deeply from the silver goblet before eyeing his cousin thoughtfully.

"So," he said after a moment or two, "I take it you have a desire to marry, but not the Sire de Grantmesnil?"

Madselin looked up at him warily. When Richard was quiet, he was at his most dangerous.

"Aye."

"He must also be young, kind and lusty?"

Madselin nodded slowly, a frown creasing her brow.

"Tell me," asked Richard quietly, "do you have a candidate in mind?"

She held her breath. Had Alice sent word about Hugh, too? And yet, this might be her only chance. Her only one to choose.

"I had always hoped that Hugh and I might…"

"Hugh?" D'Aveyron raked his memory.

"Hugh de Montchalon," she supplied. "His father's land marches with ours."

There was silence as Richard digested this piece of information. "Is he perhaps a younger landless son?" Richard's dark eyes bored into her with cynicism born of experience.

Madselin's shoulder's drooped. "Aye, but he is hoping to gain some property soon."

"He is younger than you," came the harsh reply. "Do you not think he might prefer a more...biddable maid?"

Had not Alice said as much a million times over? Was it not that very taunt that had caused her finally to search out the head of her family and gain his permission?

"Six and twenty is not so very old and I have been patient these last eight years whilst my brother dithered over my future. His interests were paramount."

Eight years? Had it really been that long? His mind flitted back to a moment that seemed etched forever in his memory. He remembered her as a beautiful bride of eighteen, her heart torn to pieces by what to Madselin had been the senseless act of a Saxon mercenary.

Madselin sat down on a wooden seat, weariness overcoming her. "Please," she whispered. "I am begging you not to send me back to Alice."

Staring at her face, Richard noticed for the first time the telltale lines of strain about her mouth and her eyes. She was tired and overwrought and he needed time to think on this.

He bent to kiss her on the brow. "We'll talk further about this on the morrow. What we need is some food and drink."

Madselin nodded slowly. What she truly wanted was a hot tub of water and a soft mattress. Her recent experience of England did not give her much hope.

Richard d'Aveyron's lands had been granted courtesy of Roger de Poictou, one of King William's most feared barons. Brother of the notoriously cruel and traitorous Robert de Belleme of Montgomery, de Poictou had been implicated in the rebellions that swept England during 1088.

Most of Rufus's barons owned lands in Normandy and England and many believed their other lord, Duke Robert of Normandy, should have received England's crown before Rufus. With the help of his loyal men and the English army, Rufus had crushed the rebellions, but had deemed it prudent to treat the majority of his barons leniently.

For this reason, de Poictou had retained his lands, although his activities were viewed with extreme suspicion. De Poictou's north-west lands stretched from the border with Scotland down to the foothills of the Pennines and played a vital role as a guard against the destructive nature of their Scottish enemies.

The responsibility of safeguarding the northern borderlands rested on d'Aveyron's broad shoulders and he chose his tenant knights with care. Treachery amongst the greedy, self-serving Normans was a problem that William the Conqueror had had to contend with and one that now kept William Rufus ever on his guard.

Life amid the never-ending, cold, wet forests, snow-covered peaks of the long hills and treacherous coastal marshlands was hard and lonely. His men were of necessity gritty, tenacious and tough, their women likewise. But his duties lay not only in England. The king was locked in endless fighting with his elder brother, Robert of Normandy. The demands on his barons' coffers and on their knights' service were consequently high.

Madselin gazed around the richly furnished feasting

hall, dazzled by the unexpected display of colour and
finery. Beeswax candles hissed and fluttered in the
draughts caused by the servants carrying in numerous
platters of meats, pies and other tasty morsels.

Richard did not stint on luxury, it seemed. Bundles of
dried herbs were strewn amid the rushes on the floor and
hung from the ceiling rafters to scent the air. The top
table was covered in a snow-white tablecloth and boasted
several wine goblets of fine silverware and an exquisite
silver cellar filled with crumbly salt.

She shared a deep trencher with her cousin who plied
her with several choice slices of roast pork, chicken and
succulent kid. But, although polite, Richard was distant.
His mind was clearly on other things. It would seem that
she had been very lucky to find him at his keep.

"Tell me, de Vaillant—" Richard leaned across Madselin to address her neighbour "—have you any more
information about Orvell? He's been a thorn in my side
for too long."

Ivo de Vaillant was a small, stocky man of middle
years with a shock of thick black hair and very broad
shoulders. Keen brown eyes stared out intently beneath
shaggy black brows. He was, she decided, the surliest
man she had ever met. The knight shook his head before
burping loudly. Madselin's cheeks flamed red. Such uncouth manners! He was, however, apparently oblivious
to her haughty stare.

"Not yet." His voice was almost a growl, and Madselin noticed that his massive hands sported a pelt of
black hair. "I've heard rumours that the Scots are on the
move. No more than that."

He slurped noisily from the delicate goblet before wiping his mouth with a filthy sleeve. Clearly his very ruddy
complexion owed much to his drinking habits. Reaching

across Madselin, de Vaillant helped himself to a chicken and began to tear it into smaller joints before stuffing them into his mouth.

Oblivious to the appalling manners of his man, Richard d'Aveyron nodded silently. "Any plans?" he demanded curtly.

With obvious relish, Ivo de Vaillant licked his greasy fingers before rubbing them clumsily across the front of his woollen tunic. Madselin shuddered. "I'll take some men along the coast, but Isabella won't hear of me being away after All Hallows."

Madselin digested this piece of information with incredulity. "Isabella is your wife?" she asked faintly. She could not imagine anyone telling him what to do.

The brown eyes bored into her before returning to his trencher. "Aye. A good woman. Always nervous when she's near her time." His thick features had softened a little and Madselin perceived that, beneath his coarse exterior, Ivo de Vaillant was a man who regarded his wife with some affection.

"How many children do you have, Sir Ivo?"

"This will be the tenth," he said gruffly and without hesitation. "The good Lord has seen fit to bless us."

"Let's hope this one's a girl, then, Ivo."

Madselin looked up to see the laughing blue eyes of Albert Mallet on her neighbour. "Nine boys are enough for any one man, surely?"

Ivo de Vaillant merely grunted good-naturedly before pouring more of Richard's red wine down his throat. Madselin permitted herself a smile. It would appear that Ivo de Vaillant was not the ogre she first thought him to be.

It was not until Richard bemoaned the lack of good

venison at their table that Madselin finally remembered the poacher she had caught.

"Here? You caught a poacher?" Richard stared at her as if she were mad. "The peasants hereabouts are so scared they'd never dare. I have to see this one for myself." Ordering the prisoner to be brought to him, Richard rose to stand closer to the fire.

From the look of the peasant, he had spent an uncomfortable few hours outside in the rain. A twinge of conscience overcame Madselin until she caught sight of the man's eyes. Mutinous was the only word for them. Banishing any weakness of spirit, Madselin held his glare for what seemed like an age. His temper, she decided, was not at all downtrodden.

Despite his wet clothing, the man walked with all the assurance and arrogance of a knight. Tall and well built, she noticed how the eyes of the women slid over his body. His profile was that of a confident man, not at all like the cowed villeins on her brother's demesne.

"Edwin?" Richard's outraged voice boomed across the dais as he stared at the peasant.

"My lord." The words were uttered in perfect Norman French with a calm designed to aggravate and irritate. Madselin could feel the blush stealing over her cheeks. She could do no more than stare dumbly at him. This was not likely to end well for her.

"Do we starve you, Edwin? You had only to ask for more!" Madselin could tell instantly that Richard's jovial bantering was misplaced and that the man had truly had enough.

"I see you are acquainted." Her voice was aimed at both men but her eyes were trained on the accused.

Once more she felt the full blast of his contempt.

"I take it, lady, that I am now permitted to speak?"

The blush turned into a deep, burning red. She could only managed a brief nod of her head in reply.

Sensing at last the awkwardness of the situation, Richard unsheathed his hunting knife and hurried to cut Edwin's bonds. Within seconds he had a goblet of fine wine thrust into his hands and was ushered closer to the fire.

"It was merely target practice, my lord. The lady chose to believe it was poaching."

Madselin's eyes were riveted on the rushes at her feet. It was true she had not thought to look for evidence, but any fool could make up that excuse. "You said naught in your defence. I took you to be a peasant. That is not so difficult to believe."

"Only a fool would enter the forest in finery," he countered, his grey eyes flinty in the firelight. "And if you remember aright, my lady, you forbade me to speak."

She was grateful at least that he did not repeat her exact words. "Then it surprises me that the guards said naught when you were brought in."

"The guards are not likely to question the word of a Norman lady over that of a mere peasant."

"Enough." Richard's stern voice cut through their anger. "Edwin, this is my kinswoman, Madselin de Breuville. Edwin Elwardson is a crack archer from Cheshire. I would hope, Madselin, that you can repair the damage done to Edwin's pride."

"My apologies, sir. I hope you did not suffer too badly." The words sounded prim and insincere, but Madselin did feel a pang of conscience. She could not look him in the eye.

Edwin Elwardson's eyes flickered over her with nothing less than contempt. "I hope, my lord, that you give me fair warning when you next expect a visit from your kinswomen?''

Richard gave a shout of laughter and clapped the man on the back. Madselin shot him a look of distaste. ''Aye, but for now you're in need of a hot tub and warm meat. Go to my chamber and I'll send in my squire to tend you.''

Edwin merely nodded; he certainly did not bear the look of a man who was grateful for such care. Madselin pursed her lips.

''Who is that dreadful man?'' Madselin whispered to Richard as she watched Edwin Elwardson's broad back disappear through the archway.

''A godsend,'' came the thoughtful reply. ''An honest man who does as he's bid without question. Best archer I've ever seen.'' Richard smiled ruefully. ''How we conquered the likes of him I'll never know.''

Madselin shrugged her shoulders. ''I found him most surly and arrogant.''

''Perhaps, dear Madselin, if you were less impulsive, you might have fewer regrets?''

Madselin looked up at her cousin sharply. ''If that was a veiled reference to my journey here, Richard, then the sentiments were misplaced. This was no impulse. It took me months to summon up the courage to leave.''

D'Aveyron placed his goblet carefully on the table. ''And no doubt it took every ounce of ingenuity you possess to have foiled Alice.''

As Madselin was about to speak, Richard raised his hand. ''No more. You are tired and in need of your bed. Gaston will show you to the ladies' quarters. When my wife has finished her duties, she will attend you.''

She was dismissed.

* * *

"Well, my lady. We're here now." Emma attempted further reparations to her mistress's hair with an apparent sense of relief. "Though the accommodation leaves a lot to be desired."

They were sitting on roughly hewn stools before a meagre fire, Emma pulling the silver-traced comb through Madselin's hair as she had done for the past twenty-six years. Despite thick woollen sleeping robes, both women were acutely aware of the chilling draughts that swept their quarters.

Madselin smiled to herself wearily. "What would we be doing now if we were back in Normandy? I can't remember the last time I was sitting idly before a fire."

Emma snorted at the very thought. "I've no wish to criticise, my lady, but Lady Alice uses you a deal too much. Your father, God bless his soul, would have a fit if he knew what your brother lets her get away with. You're no more than an unpaid skivvy. I know you do it because you love her children, but that doesn't make it right."

Madselin shrugged her shoulders. "If I didn't earn my keep, Alice would have found a way to get rid of me years ago. At least this way I can stay in a home that I love, surrounded by family and friends."

A heavy hand squeezed her shoulder. "Aye. The servants love you for your quiet kindness and thoughtful ways, despite that sharp tongue of yours." Emma gave a wheezy sigh. "We all know how you've suffered since that day, my lady. And the children adore you."

Under the rhythmic motion of the comb working through her long hair, Madselin had closed her eyes and yielded to the comfort it provided. The tension that had been building up for years seemed to ebb away. It felt good to be idle. "I miss the children," she murmured finally. "Especially Mathilde."

"Aye. She's a way with her, that one." Emma smiled fondly at the memory of a three-year-old with blonde curls and shining blue eyes. "'Tis a pity she has a witch for a mother. That child loves you more than she does her ladyship, and that's a fact. It's you she cries for in the night, not Lady Alice."

"Hush, Emma. Alice is a busy woman."

"Not too busy to nag your brother about a betrothal for the poor child."

Madselin's eyes snapped open. This was the first she'd heard of such a thing. Anything that affected the well-being of the children was important to her, and Alice could not always be trusted to have their best interests at heart. "Has aught been decided yet?" Emma always knew what was going on.

Any reply she was about to receive was interrupted by the sudden arrival of a small, plumply pretty woman with thick blonde braids and a knowing pout.

"Greetings Lady Madselin." Her quick green eyes swept over Madselin's serviceable bedrobe with distaste. The sketchy bob she made was bordering on insult, but Madselin was too tired to upbraid her. "My lord begs to know if there is aught I can do for you before you retire?"

Madselin contemplated the fire for a moment, not liking the rather cocksure tone of the woman's voice.

"Thank you…"

"Blanche, Lady Madselin."

"Blanche. I require two cups of spiced wine."

There was no more than the briefest hesitation before she managed to grind out her assent. Just as the woman reached the door, she hesitated and turned back. "Is it true that you took Edwin Elwardson captive?"

Madselin's cheeks began to burn. "It is," she replied calmly, sitting up to adjust the laces on her bedrobe. "I believed him to be poaching. It was an honest error." She looked up to catch the servant's eyes almost gloating with satisfaction.

"About time that man got his comeuppance," she murmured, tossing her flaxen braids over her shoulders. As she left the room, she collided with a small, dark-haired woman whose rich clothes proclaimed her high status.

"Hold your tongue, Blanche. If you have naught good to say, then stay silent." Her repressive tone quelled the insolent look on the servant's face and Blanche scuttled down the hallway. The woman remained at the doorway, frowning at Blanche's retreating back. "That woman will reap the rewards of her own evil tongue one day."

She sighed before turning to Madselin and Emma. "I must apologise for her behaviour, but her head is ruled by a very tempestuous heart." Her rather plain face was transformed by a girlish grin. "She is most distressed that Edwin has not singled her out as the sole object of his affections. It would seem that he prefers to bestow his favours…quite liberally."

Madselin was not quite sure what to make of this particular confidence, but forebore to create any further chaos by voicing her opinions about Edwin Elwardson's loose morals.

"Forgive me for prattling so," the stranger continued quickly. "I am Beatrice, Richard's wife. I'm afraid I missed you earlier because my son was demanding my attention."

"Nothing serious I hope?" Madselin enquired, her interest stirred. There was something very likeable about this plain, warm-hearted woman who did not seem to stop either talking or smiling.

"No. No more than a sore gum, but twelve months is a hard age for a babe. I believe Jordan has already learned the man's knack of gathering as many women about him for comfort as he can manage."

"He must have been watching Edwin Elwardson," Madselin replied tartly.

At that, Beatrice put her hand to her mouth and burst out into a fit of giggles. It was hard not to warm to the woman. "I, too, have suspected that to have been the case."

As she advanced towards them, Madselin could see at closer range the richness of her garments. A close-fitting undertunic of fine blue wool was contrasted with a rich, wine-coloured overgown of heavy velvet. The edges of the gown were trimmed with bands of blue and oversewn with intricate stitchery in gold thread. Madselin blinked up at Beatrice d'Aveyron. This was a woman who dressed for beauty as well as practicality.

"I hope my unexpected arrival has not caused too much inconvenience," Madselin began, knowing that Beatrice was expecting some kind of explanation. "It was necessitated by a matter of utmost urgency."

To her surprise, Beatrice sat on the rushes before the fire and looked up at her expectantly. "If you want my help," she began softly, "you had best explain things carefully to me. Richard is the best of husbands and an excellent soldier, but he does lack…sensitivity." Another warming smile curved her lips.

Madselin frowned. "Forgive my bluntness, but why should you wish to help me? We have never met before."

Indeed, she had not even known that Richard was married until her arrival at his manor.

A slight sigh escaped Beatrice's lips. "Richard has often talked of you with affection and I believe you were ever his favourite kinswoman. He said you were close as children."

Madselin nodded. That had been a long time ago. "But I have not seen him since…" She still could not bring herself to say the words. "For about eight years," she finished rather lamely.

Beatrice stared at her with a look which betokened pity and compassion. She knew, Madselin decided. No doubt the whole world knew. Her next words, however, caused Madselin to look at her more closely.

"I have also conceived a powerful dislike of Alice de Breuville and it would give me great pleasure to cause her inconvenience."

A conspiracy! Madselin smiled back at Beatrice d'Aveyron. She had found a friend. This was indeed a miracle.

Chapter Two

The commotion in the courtyard beneath her window roused Madselin from a fitful sleep.

From the soft tone of the light filtering through the shutters, Madselin estimated that it was very early. She knew that she would not sleep further and slipped from her pallet to the window embrasure, pulling on her bed-robe as she went. A blast of ice-cold air enveloped her as she opened the shutters to look down on to the group of riders assembled in the courtyard.

Huge, muscular destriers pawed the mud impatiently, whilst their riders issued curt orders to d'Aveyron's men-at-arms. From the richness of their armour and garments, Madselin was certain that these were knights from Roger de Poictou's stable and, whatever their purpose, they had caused Richard's men to scatter urgently.

Beyond the palisade, the dark forest was shrouded in mist and low-lying clouds. It looked dangerous, even in the early morning sun. The wind that swept in from the west had a salty tang that caused Madselin a shiver of adventure.

She had seen the sea but once and that had not been a fortunate encounter. The crossing from Normandy to

Pevensey had been marred by heaving grey waves the size of castle walls with white foaming swells that made their small boat lurch from side to side. Her sickness had not abated until her feet touched solid ground.

Mindful of her need to place herself in Richard's favour, Madselin washed and dressed hastily. Just as she was about to leave, a rather pale-faced Beatrice scratched on the door.

"What is wrong, Beatrice?" she demanded quickly. "Is it bad news?"

Beatrice shook her head with a faint smile. "Nay. The only excuse for my whey-faced looks today is a sleepless night with my son. As for our visitors, Madselin, I think you had best come down and break your fast with Richard. I doubt he will be here much longer."

"How so?"

Beatrice rolled her eyes towards the ceiling and sighed wearily. "Roger de Poictou is demanding knight service from his vassals. Richard is to leave this morning and I know not whether he goes to Normandy for the King."

Madselin nodded, torn between her sympathy for Beatrice and her concern that her plans were about to be ruined. "Come then," she smiled, taking Beatrice gently by the arm. "Let us break our fast, and on the way I can tell you of my remedy for sore gums that worked well for my niece."

The hall was in uproar. Weapons and supplies were being packed and readied for loading into carts whilst Richard's men shovelled rye bread and ale down their throats. Meals would be an uncertain business for them from now on. Servants and men-at-arms scuttled through the doors causing several calamitous but non-fatal collisions. The din was awful.

Richard was sitting at his table with the strangers and

several of his house-knights. Compared to the night before, their mood was noticeably subdued and serious. All were aware that if their destination were Normandy, they would not return to their manors before the spring. For some of the younger men, no doubt the promise of adventure would be a welcome relief. For others, the call to arms posed problems of a different nature.

Madselin noticed that Ivo de Vaillant was scowling into his cup and wondered if his thoughts were of his wife. Ale and bread lay untouched before him.

A little apart from the rest sat Edwin Elwardson; it was clear that the only thing on his mind was satisfying his immediate hunger. His appearance, however, was much changed. The blond locks had been pulled into the tight braid favoured by Saxons, revealing to inquisitive eyes a determined but clean-shaven chin.

A plain, serviceable overtunic of midnight blue lent the man an air of nobility that seemed to sit well on his broad shoulders. His eyes were fixed on the food before him, although Madselin was certain that he was aware of everything that was going on around him. Irritated that she was so conscious of the man, she made a determined effort to put him from her mind and followed Beatrice to the dais.

The murmurings immediately ceased once the men noticed their presence and Madselin could feel her colour heighten as she became the target of unwelcome speculation. Her years as an older, unmarried woman had forced her to deal with such attentions quickly and effectively.

Casting a cool and unhurried eye over the assembled group, she treated the men to a look of haughty contempt before sweeping to her place at the table. Knights leaving for war were wont to tumble maids in the stables as a final attempt to stamp themselves over their home possessions, almost as if they were hoping for immortality. Madselin was gratified to note that not one tried to catch her eye.

Richard d'Aveyron stared at her silently and his expression was not at all encouraging. No doubt there were more pressing problems claiming his attention.

Madselin, unable to postpone her fate any longer, took a deep breath and treated him to a dazzling smile. "Well, Richard? Have you made a decision?" She could feel the smile stiffen as Richard remained mute. The bread and ale put before her were ignored as she waited for his response.

"Truly, Madselin, the problem is a vexing one," he said finally. He rubbed at the tender spots on his chin where he had barbered himself too close in his haste. "I do not like to interfere in a family matter which is none of my making." He glanced speculatively at Madselin before reaching to fill his cup with more ale.

Those heavy-lidded brown eyes missed very little despite their sleepy appearance, she decided.

"It would certainly not benefit me to annoy your brother, especially in such uncertain times."

He was going to refuse her. Madselin felt her icy heart thud to the pit of her stomach. Gritting her jaw, she stared unblinkingly at the table. "I beg you, Richard. Alice is bent on marrying me to that old man or sending me to a convent because she hates me. She has always hated me." Her voice was almost a whisper.

"I just want a chance to choose some sort of life of my own, with a kind husband and at least the prospect of children." Fear and anxiety coursed through her bones at the thought of returning to Alice's crowing embrace. "I did the only thing within my power to bring that

about.'' She lifted her head proudly to fix him with suspiciously bright eyes.

The stern set of his face had softened a little. ''Aye,
and it was a foolhardy thing to do.'' Richard cleared his
throat. ''But there is no time left for me to think clearly
on the matter.'' He breathed deeply and rubbed the stiffness from the back of his neck. ''Since crossing the sea
in winter is impossible, you will have to remain on my
lands.''

''But—'' Madselin attempted to interrupt.

''Silence!'' From the harsh tone of his voice, Madselin
knew she could do no more than obey him. ''As you
have proved your courage, then you will make yourself
useful to me.''

Richard gave his wife a quick, sidelong look. ''Isabella
de Vaillant will need a stout-hearted companion whilst
Ivo is away. I have decided that you will deal with her
and her children admirably. If your suitor is as determined as you believe, then a few months longer will
make no difference.''

Madselin's gaze met Richard's in frank comprehension. He had handed her a solution that would not upset
her brother and would allow him some time to think on
the matter.

Madselin knew she ought to be grateful, but the
thought of spending the winter in this cold place made
her balk.

''It seems I have no choice,'' she conceded finally.

The tense look to Richard's face relaxed and he settled
back into his chair. ''I thought you would be pleased.''
He tossed the remaining ale down his throat and then
slammed the cup back onto the trestle.

That appeared to be the prearranged sign since all the
men suddenly moved to stand as one. Beatrice turned to

her husband and pulled him a little to one side away from the bright glare of the braziers. Madselin realised how selfish she had been in claiming his attention. There would be no way of knowing whether Richard would return.

Turning away she caught sight of Ivo de Vaillant's gloomy countenance and wondered if he would welcome the chance to send a few words home to his wife. Deciding to risk his frown, Madselin approached him.

"I am to go to your wife, sir." Her voice did not betray the uncertainty of her feelings. "Would you send word with me?"

Ivo de Vaillant glanced at her briefly as he hefted an oak strongbox onto his shoulders. "I said it all before I left," he replied gruffly. "But it pleases me that she'll have another woman about."

From the way he glared at her, Madselin was not at all sure that he approved of her, but judged it wise to nod agreement.

"Have a care, though, woman. There's strange goings-on out there and few you can trust. Do as Elwardson tells you and you'll be well enough."

Madselin's face drained of all colour. "The Saxon?" she whispered faintly.

"Aye," came the impatient retort. "An honest man for a Saxon." Satisfied that he had bestowed the greatest approbation on Edwin Elwardson's character, de Vaillant lumbered towards the courtyard without a backward glance.

Left feeling firmly put in her place and not a little foolish, Madselin turned her head in Edwin Elwardson's direction and found him actually smiling. The sour scowl he appeared to favour had been replaced by a most engaging smile, displayed, she discovered, for the benefit of the pouting Blanche. Remembering Beatrice's words, the two of them seemed to be well matched and thoroughly deserving of each other.

Suddenly, as if aware of her eyes on him, Edwin turned the full force of his grey eyes on her and Madselin caught her breath. For a moment, their gazes held fast before Blanche jealously demanded his attention.

"Come," said Beatrice, interrupting her thoughts. "Bid the men farewell and then we can make plans." She slid her arm round Madselin's waist and drew her towards the courtyard.

"When must I leave?"

Beatrice, sensing constraint in Madselin's question, smiled gently up at her. "When 'tis most convenient," she decided firmly. "Now come."

Once the horses and carts had clattered out of the bailey, the manor sounded strangely quiet and deserted. Richard had left half his men but they were out of sight. Beatrice surveyed the churned mud, horse dung and puddles with a baleful eye. "Perhaps a turn around my gardens will restore us. There is much to be done, I fear."

Madselin shot her a brief smile. For a woman whose husband had just left for an unknown destination and an uncertain fate, Beatrice d'Aveyron was remarkably calm.

"Does aught grow in this country?" she countered with mock surprise.

A suspicion of a grin twisted Beatrice's lips. "You are too hard on this land, my Lady de Breuville. I confess to being right pleased with my home here." She glanced up at the bright blue sky and drew in a deep calming breath. "A woman can grow to love the place, despite the rain."

Their eyes caught and the two women suddenly burst into laughter.

"You are very fierce in defence of this godforsaken

island. Normandy is your true home, I believe?'' Madselin looked at Beatrice in complete confusion.

Beatrice simply shrugged her slender shoulders and smiled. ''There is a sort of magic here,'' she said airily. ''I find I do not regret my birthplace at all. And there are certainly fewer grasping women waiting to catch my husband's eye.''

Although the comment was made in jest, Madselin was sure that it was spoken from the heart.

As they talked, Beatrice had guided Madselin around the palisade of the bailey and stopped at a small gate. Opening it, she proudly bade Madselin enter a tiny, sunfilled garden which was protected from the worst of the wind by the bailey wall. A rough wooden bench had been erected to catch the sun, and they sat down to make the most of it.

It was peaceful here, thought Madselin, as she too settled back against the wall. Birdsong floated around them and the aromatic scent of herbs calmed her agitated nerves. It reminded her of a soft summer day a long time past.

''I last saw Richard on the morning of my wedding day. Alice was there, but she was very young—just sixteen, I think…'' but then Madselin stopped. After a moment's pause, she began again. ''I doubt if I would have noticed much that day.''

Madselin felt a gentle pressure on her arm.

''Forgive me, Madselin. I had not meant to remind you of that terrible day. We shall not speak more of it.''

Aye, it was still painful, but not as it had been. The grief had dulled over the years and she was trying to put the past behind her. Alice had never made that easy with her constant references to Guy. She shook her head. ''It does me good to talk of such things and I have no wish to forget him. Truly.''

''Well, if you are certain?'' Beatrice shot her an uncertain look.

''How do you know about Alice?'' Madselin began to fiddle with the folds of her tunic.

Beatrice laughed sourly.

''Richard offered for her, but she dismissed him with such arrogance that it took him many years to approach a lady again. She gave him to believe her heart was engaged elsewhere and that marriage to your brother was...convenient.''

For no reason at all, Madselin was certain those words should have meant something. Part of her mind was reaching out to try to piece something together. Beatrice had revealed nothing new about her sister-in-marriage, however. Alice was not known for her discretion.

''That is probably the truth,'' she admitted. ''It was no love match and Robert does not care to hide his mistresses from her.'' She looked across at Beatrice. ''Richard seems most content.''

''Content!'' Beatrice spat out the words. ''Aye, he is content.'' Suddenly she turned to Madselin. ''I don't want him to be content. I want him to desire me with such passion that he can think of nothing else.'' Sighing with frustration and despair, Beatrice threw herself back against the wall with a thud. ''To him I am just...there. Plain, homely Beatrice. I might just as well be his mother!''

Madselin was stunned by this revelation. ''Alice has never known such contentment,'' she said eventually.

Beatrice blushed and turned her head. ''I know you must think me ungrateful, for I have so much. But sometimes...'' Her lips twisted in that wry grin that Madselin was coming to know. "Mayhap I get myself too involved in these old local customs."

Madselin frowned in confusion. "What do you mean?"

"The people here are very isolated. Some of their customs must have their origins in their old pagan beliefs." A blush covered Beatrice's pale cheeks. "Once or twice I have watched what goes on. 'Tis most…revealing."

Madselin stared at her openmouthed. She would never have guessed.

"Isabella de Vaillant is most knowledgeable about these customs." Beatrice flashed her a sidelong glance. "She can be very…enlightening."

The mention of Isabella de Vaillant reminded Madselin of her duty and her smile evaporated. "No doubt we shall pass many a long evening together. I shall endeavour to learn more of this Saxon culture." Her words were uttered with distaste.

"They are not all Saxons—" Beatrice began seriously.

"It matters not," interrupted Madselin. "I have no real interest in these people." She looked at Beatrice. "It is my turn to beg your forgiveness. I do not intend to make this my home."

"Aye, well. Perhaps I have been boring you with my nonsense."

Madselin laid her hand on Beatrice's arm. "Never say so, Beatrice. You are the first friend I have talked to in many long years. I have become rude and surly, that is all."

"Hah! Do not think it!" She looked skywards again. "Isabella de Vaillant will test all your powers of diplomacy, rest assured."

Madselin stared at her. "And I thought Edwin Elwardson was going to be my problem."

"Edwin?" Beatrice looked at her in surprise. "Nay. You mistake the matter. It is only that you got off to a poor start. He is a good man."

"So everyone keeps trying to assure me," Madselin said darkly. "But I mislike his arrogance."

Beatrice looked at her askance. "You think him arrogant?" She thought for a moment. "Well, mayhap we are all just used to his ways. He has been here since before I arrived, and he was very kind to me at the beginning." She smiled, almost to herself. "Had I not been married to Richard, I could quite understand why the women make such fools of themselves over him."

Giving a sigh of impatience, Madselin stared at her. "He is a peasant. How could you even think of...?"

"I have not," retorted Beatrice indignantly. "It's just that..."

"Spare me," came the acid reply. "I truly think you have become too involved with these local customs, Beatrice d'Aveyron. They have addled your wits."

Beatrice smiled broadly at that set down. "I truly think, Lady de Breuville, that you are going to find the next few months interesting."

Madselin gave her a withering look which caused Beatrice to smile even more.

Mayhap there was a certain magic in the air or mayhap it was the smell of the sea on the wind? Madselin knew naught except that she had a sudden desire to escape the confines of the keep and be on her own to think. Just for a little while.

Beatrice received the request as calmly as she faced everything else. "I do not think it wise, for you are new to the land and..."

''You forbid it, then?'' Madselin could not hide the disappointment in her voice.

They were standing in Beatrice's private solar before a roaring fire. Beautiful tapestries adorned the stone walls and the thick, herb-strewn rushes underfoot gave the room a pleasant fragrance.

A chubby-faced child with dark curls and an indomitable will was investigating every inch of the place, followed vigilantly by a red-faced nurse. Several young women chatted as they sewed over on the other side of the solar, and one woman with long dark braids idled over a lute.

Beatrice looked down at Madselin's soft, doe-skin boots and fine woollen gown and raised her dark brows. ''No. I do not forbid it. It would not be my place.'' Her eyes came back to Madselin. ''But I believe it to be ill advised. There is much trouble in this area—not from the local people,'' she added hurriedly. ''Richard suspects some of the barons to the north of treachery with the Scots.''

''Scots?'' Madselin repeated. ''I do not understand. He thinks Normans would betray their own kind?''

Beatrice gave a sour laugh. ''And they do not do the same on their own lands in Normandy? Nay, some think of naught but their own profit, and the Scots are forever trying to slip through the defences.'' She pushed back a stray lock of dark hair.

''With Rufus being so involved in the war against his brother, he has little time to spend here. Flambards, his chancellor, has squeezed us dry with his taxes and for many, the lures offered by the Scots are tempting indeed.''

Madselin listened to this explanation with interest. ''I heard Ivo de Vaillant mention there was some such trou-

ble near his manor,'' she remembered. ''It is serious
then?''

A squeal of discontent from the child momentarily diverted Beatrice's attention. ''Aye,'' she replied finally,
bending down and holding out her arms to her son. Much
to Jordan's delight, his mother swung him high in the air
before settling him in her arms. He began to explore her
face with his pudgy hands.

''Especially now that Richard is absent. Once the Scots
find out that de Poictou has been called for knight service
with most of his men, we will be vulnerable.''

Madselin wandered to the window embrasure and
pushed aside the oiled sheet. Away to the north, beyond
the forest, lay the long hills. It was hard to imagine that
such treachery could lie in so wild a place. Sighing, she
let the sheet flop back and returned to the fire. ''Who is
left in charge, then?'' she demanded curiously.

''Albert Mallet has remained here to guard the demesne,'' Beatrice began, pushing her son's exploring fingers from her nose. ''But the rest...''

A giggling, pink-checked Blanche burst through the
door.

''Blanche! What is the meaning of this?'' Beatrice's
furious countenance caused Blanche's apparent joy to
subside instantly.

''I'm sorry, my lady. Edwin Elwardson is without and
wishes if he might have words with you.'' The blue eyes
were fixed humbly on the ground, but no one could mistake the quickness of the girl's breathing.

''Send him in, Blanche, and then fetch us some wine.''

Blanche made a hasty curtsy and retreated to the door.

''That girl is a disgrace,'' began Madselin. ''How do
you put up with her?''

Beatrice smiled as she handed the child to his nurse. "She is just young and fancies herself in love."

Madselin just raised her brows in scorn. "Then she is a fool. He appears little more than a lecherous peasant."

"My lady." A deep voice behind her caused Madselin to start suddenly and then blush with embarrassment. There was no doubt that he had heard her comment and had known himself to be the subject since he had placed much feeling and emphasis on the word "lady". It was a moment before she realised that the Saxon was addressing Beatrice.

Was she always to be at a disadvantage with this man? If the Saxon had noticed her, he gave no appearance of having done so. Pursing her lips into a tight line, Madselin affected her haughtiest demeanour and carefully stepped further from him. He smelled of bracken, fresh air and horses.

"Edwin." Beatrice greeted him warmly and bade him move closer to the fire. "Have the baggage wains been readied? Do you have what you need?"

Madselin watched almost openmouthed as the Saxon once more summoned up his compelling smile for Beatrice. It revealed even, white teeth and a very attractive countenance. For a Saxon, she reminded herself quickly. Clearly Beatrice was susceptible to a handsome face since she, too, was smiling sweetly.

"Aye, lady." His grey eyes were gentle now for Beatrice. "We'll be ready to leave on the morrow. Is there aught I can do for you before we leave?"

Beatrice looked up at the man speculatively. "Lady de Breuville was asking me if she could ride out for a short while. She has need of exercise before the journey. Would you take her?"

The grey eyes shot to Madselin instantly, but they were

neither smiling nor gentle. "Nay." His flat refusal drew
a gasp of outrage from Madselin.

"What do you mean by 'nay'? I can assure you that I
have no desire to be accompanied by you. One of the
young squires will be more than adequate, I'm sure." She
gave him a challenging stare that brooked no further discussion.

"I'll not have a boy's life wasted for the whim of one
spoiled Norman woman who has nothing better to do."
He stared back, undeterred.

Two spots of red coloured Madselin's cheeks as she
faced the Saxon. "You are the most arrogant, rude,
abominable peasant I have ever come across. I was only
suggesting a ride, not a pillage of the country. There
would be no harm—"

"No harm!" he interrupted loudly. "Woman, we have
lost three men in the forest this last week. There's not
one squire in the manor who would willingly ride out
with you, but none would gainsay you for fear of their
punishment."

The anger drained from her face. "I... I did not know
this," she stuttered quietly. "You had only to explain."

The grey eyes speared her with a bitter glare. "It
would seem, Lady de Breuville, that you are quick to
demand and somewhat slower to ask. I hope that you
display far more patience and tolerance in future, or you
will place other lives at risk."

"So, Saxon, you show your true nature." Madselin
glared at him, her humiliation complete.

"I do no more than ensure the safety of all the people
in this manor," he returned quietly, his anger seemingly
spent. "And as I have command here, I respectfully request that you adhere to my judgement." He lay mean-

ingful emphasis on "respectfully", although from the tone of his voice, respect was clearly lacking.

He had made his feelings on the matter plain. A brief glance at Beatrice gave Madselin no hope of support since her eyes were cast to the ground. "I have no wish to cause hurt to anyone. It was certainly not my intention," she added stiffly. "Although I was given to believe that Albert Mallet was in command."

His eyes bored into her. "Not until I leave, Lady de Breuville. Should you wish to confirm this, I am sure Mallet will be happy to oblige."

After a moment's silence, she deemed it prudent to yield on this matter. "I have misjudged the situation and had no idea I was causing you such problems."

A ghost of a smile fluttered over the Saxon's handsome face. "If you think you have caused me a moment's concern, Lady de Breuville, then you are sadly in error."

Madselin raised her brows in disbelief.

He continued to stare at her, his expression unreadable. "As we are to spend some time in each other's company, I think it sensible if we understand one another. You will obey my commands or you will be returned to your brother's demesne without your kinsman's agreement. I hope I make myself clear?" Their eyes met.

"Perfectly."

Apparently satisfied, Edwin turned to leave but checked himself. "I am sure you would wish me to point out that you err in terms of my origins, Lady de Breuville. It would give me the greatest of pleasure to hear you refer to me as an Angle rather than a Saxon. Nor," he added with a faint smile, "do I come from peasant stock." After the briefest pause, he continued. "We leave at first light. Be ready or we go without you."

So saying, he strode from the room, leaving Madselin staring silently after him. "Insufferable man," she hissed, before snatching at her gown and stomping towards her room. "I will enjoy teaching him some manners."

Chapter Three

Blanche settled herself onto the baggage cart and smiled down at Edwin Elwardson's broad back as he bent to test one of the wheels. No one could be in any doubt as to the lewdness of her expression, thought Madselin with asperity.

"Why is she coming?" Madselin eyed the woman with irritation as she fiddled with her heavy riding gown. Beatrice stood patiently at her side.

"She has a sister who works for Lady Isabella and it seemed churlish to refuse her request."

"There is only one reason she wishes to come with us, and he does not appear to have thwarted her desires."

A slow smile crossed Beatrice's face. "You do Edwin an injustice. He has never appeared to favour any one of them above the rest. It is very likely he will find others. Besides, he has much else to occupy his mind."

"I do not think Blanche is interested in his mind."

After a brief blessing from Beatrice's priest, the party of riders and carts lumbered slowly through the high wooden gates of the manor. Dawn had broken about an hour before and the light was uncertain. Thick clouds had rolled in from the west and there was a smell of rain in the air. The black mood that had enveloped her since she had risen hung round Madselin's shoulders like an ox's yoke and she stared ahead at the sombre forest with apprehension.

As well as the two scouts, six armed guards surrounded the two baggage carts. Edwin Elwardson and a young squire of no more than fifteen summers brought up the rear. Her fears were groundless, but none the less she had taken the Angle's warning of constant danger seriously. This land was awash with outlaws and wild animals, after all.

There were no great forests like this near her home in Normandy. The Vexin was a flat land with lush meadows and slow-moving rivers; it lent itself well to crop growing and cattle rearing. Or at least, she reminded herself, it would if it were not being constantly raided and destroyed. They were ever on the alert for roaming bands of mercenaries who cared not one whit about the land or the lives that they ruined. One of their number had certainly changed her life.

The recent downpours had turned the track into a muddy quagmire, and at times the carts stuck fast. Edwin Elwardson would then direct the men and Madselin noted with surprise how quick they were to do his bidding.

At these times, Madselin would look up and find Blanche's blue eyes fixed on her with a look of intense dislike. Clearly she saw her as some sort of rival for the Angle's affections. How wrong could she be? If she was fool enough to be interested, then the woman was welcome to him. Her affections remained firmly placed elsewhere.

Hugh de Montchalon was courteous and attentive, although several years younger than herself. His cheerful humour had helped to restore her spirits in the dark days after her betrothed was killed just hours before their wedding.

Emma was finding the jolting and shaking of the cart increasingly uncomfortable and Madselin watched her greying face with a sense of growing concern. Her health had been poor since suffering a bout of lung fever last winter, and she tired easily. Travelling had never been Emma's favourite pastime; she preferred a warm fire and a comfortable chair.

Unable to watch her suffer more, Madselin slowed her horse until she was level with Edwin Elwardson. The Angle's expression remained stiff and unresponsive but at least the boy scowled at her.

"I think it would be a good time to rest." Her voice was even and her eyes trained on the track ahead.

The Angle was silent for a moment but even without looking at him, Madselin could feel him bristle at her words.

"It's just that Emma looks most uncomfortable. I do not ask for myself," she added quickly.

Edwin observed the women on the cart. "Is she not well, the old woman?" His voice was curt but not harsh.

Madselin shook her head. "The long journey has been hard for her." Her cheeks flushed as she felt his eyes upon her. "I would ask that she does not suffer because of me and my foolish tongue." Madselin glanced down at the reins in her fingers, glad that the man did not interrupt her. "She has suffered more than enough on my account and I would be most grateful if you could show her some kindness."

"The woman must be a devoted servant indeed."

Uncertain as to whether it was a question or a statement, Madselin turned to stare up at his sober visage. "She is obstinate. I had not planned to bring her with me, but she was fearful of being left with my sister-in-marriage. I could not refuse her. Emma is more like a mother to me.''

His hand rubbed thoughtfully at his shaven chin before addressing her. ''And you? Are you also fearful of your sister-in-marriage?''

Madselin prickled a little at being asked so personal a question that was perhaps closer to the mark than she wished to admit, even to herself. ''We do not deal well together,'' she replied eventually. ''Her anger is usually directed at those least able to defend themselves. Emma has been with me since I was born and I would not willingly see her hurt. I do believe that Alice would hurt her deliberately just to punish me.''

Such an admission of weakness made Madselin feel very vulnerable and she could feel his eyes on her, almost commanding her to look at him.

''I am grateful that you have told me about the woman—your concern for her is welcome. We have need of healthy, loyal women hereabouts and I have no desire to lose Emma through ill use. There is a good spot ahead. We will rest there.'' His tone had lost the hard edge.

''My thanks, Angle.'' Had she heard the man aright? Her eyes flickered over his face and registered his expression of gentle concern.

''The horses need water,'' he replied quickly, before urging his horse into a trot.

As she watched him, Madselin became aware that another pair of eyes were boring into her. Blanche was staring at her with an expression of complete hatred and it made her feel most uncomfortable. Why did Blanche want to see things between them that really were not there? Well, the woman would find out soon enough how little interest in the man she had.

Emma levered her bulk back against the trunk of a large tree and sighed with exhaustion. "I'll not last much longer on that cart, especially if I have to listen to that trollop prating on. It still feels like I'm swaying," she groaned, closing her eyes.

Madselin shot her a look of sympathy. "Here. Eat some of this bread and cheese. You'll feel better."

Blanche picked her way across the muddy clearing from the cart, where she had engaged the young sergeant in animated conversation. Their discussion had been summarily brought to an end by Edwin Elwardson's harsh command, which had the soldier scurrying towards the horses. Blanche's eyes were fixed on the Angle, but he paid her scant attention and she stalked towards Madselin and Emma in a huff.

Madselin, too, found herself watching Edwin Elwardson. He was standing by the cart, checking over the equipment with an experienced eye. He looked, she had to admit, very much in control and seemed unconcerned at the reproachful looks Blanche was now casting in his direction. He was not unattractive.

"We leave when the horses are watered." He paused a moment, patently ignoring Blanche's pouting frown. "If you wish a few moments' privacy in the bushes, go now—I have no desire to wait longer than necessary."

"How long will the journey take?" enquired Madselin, pushing her dark braids behind her shoulders.

His eyes flickered to the sky and narrowed a little. "I hope to arrive at the de Vaillant manor before nightfall. Much depends on how often we stop."

At these words, Madselin looked over at Emma. She had a grey pallor which did not show signs of abating.

The Angle had picked up her concern. "Would you

prefer a horse to the cart?'' His question was directed at Emma with a tone that betokened kindness.

After a moment or two's hesitation, Emma nodded slowly. ''But I'll not have my lady being jolted around instead of me.'' Her brown eyes did not conceal any of her wariness.

He laughed and managed a rueful smile. ''I have not the slightest intention of parting Lady de Breuville from a horse she rates so highly,'' he said, his eyes sliding briefly to Madselin's startled expression. ''But young Raoul seems to think my mount unable to bear me much longer. My horse, I think, would be grateful if you took my place.''

He strode towards the group of soldiers huddled near the horses. Eventually, Madselin rose to shake the crumbs from her gown. ''I'd best go into the forest for a few minutes. I'll not be long.''

''I'll come with you and show you the way.'' Blanche suddenly stood up and pushed back her blonde braids with a tight smile. ''I've been this way before and Edwin does not like the women to remain too close to the men.''

The two made their way through quite some distance of undergrowth, bracken and thick mud. Overhead, the trees towered oppressively and the silence enveloped them. There was a most eerie atmosphere which made Madselin shiver. It was odd not to hear birdsong.

''The best cover is just beyond that large stone,'' said Blanche, pointing a short distance ahead to a thick grey standing stone such as they had passed not far back along the path. ''You go first and I'll keep watch.''

Madselin hurried ahead, somewhat uncertain as to why they needed to go so far, but she had no wish to be disturbed by the men. As she reached the stone, the air about her suddenly seemed to grow colder. Pulling her cloak tightly about her, she noticed that the stone was covered in strange symbols. Her eyes were drawn to the picture in the centre of the stone; it was a man with antlers on his head.

''Hurry!'' hissed Blanche, drawing her attention once more.

Quickly, Madselin slipped behind the stone, but to her dismay she found that the ground dropped steeply. The wet earth gave way beneath her feet and she could not stop herself from slipping further and further down the slope. Losing her footing, she fell and rolled to the bottom of the incline in a jumbled heap. Mud, twigs and bracken covered her from top to toe and Madselin hauled herself to her feet in disgust.

Looking upwards, there was no sign of Blanche although the woman must have heard her cry as she on fell. The wretch had done this on purpose.

More angry than hurt, Madselin looked wildly around. She had fallen into what looked like a wide circle of the upright stones, all bearing the same strange markings as those she had noticed on the one at the top of the slope. Within the circle, the ground had been trampled thoroughly and nothing grew there. The silence seemed to boom in her ears and her heart began to thud uncomfortably.

Picking up her skirts, she ran to the outside of the stone circle and her breathing relaxed a little. Hiding behind a nearby tree, she relieved herself quickly and tried then to restore her appearance. Time was passing though, and she had to get back to the others. The forest was a dangerous place to be lost.

Her ablutions complete, Madselin stared around the surrounding undergrowth. Refusing to give way to panic, she gritted her teeth and began to skirt round the incline to see if she could find a way up.

After several minutes, she noticed some tree roots and strong-looking bushes a few feet up the slope and decided to try them out. Madselin took a few hesitant steps and then grabbed for a root. Slowly she managed to pull herself to her feet. It was a long, drawn-out process but, by sheer willpower and strength, Madselin finally managed to haul herself to the top of the slope.

Blood seeped from the cuts on her hands and her gown was ripped and muddied beyond repair. All she felt was relief, though, and allowed herself a moment's respite.

"Hiding, Lady de Breuville?"

Madselin almost jumped out of her skin at the sound of the Angle's cold voice. Her heart was pumping furiously and she could feel her cheeks burning.

"What do you think you're doing?" she demanded breathlessly. "Are you trying to scare me out of my wits?"

The Angle was no more than a few feet away from her, leaning with his back against the large standing stone. His face bore little sign of concern about her ordeal. In fact, he looked rather amused. "You have the makings of a fine peasant, lady." The grey eyes swept over her ruined appearance.

Madselin glared at him, furious that he would make light of the situation. "You were watching me," she accused.

"Aye. Most instructive." He pushed himself away from the stone and came to stand before her. The hand he offered her was large and square, and she noted the myriad of white nicks across its suntanned back—legacy of swordsmanship borne by most Norman knights.

Madselin ignored the hand and pulled herself to her

feet. The Angle's large hand still wrapped itself around her wrist and pulled her hand closer to his face. "You'll heal," he pronounced eventually after he had examined it carefully.

Madselin snatched her hand back. "Very gratifying. How long were you watching me?"

"Long enough."

Madselin's lips tightened visibly. The man was a true peasant, no matter how much he protested his origins. With her nose in the air, she whipped round and stalked back towards the camp. "I suppose you blame me for wasting precious time," she ground out as she felt rather than saw him just behind her.

Edwin's cool voice reached her from behind. "I warned you about the dangers here. It was foolish indeed to go so far. Death would be a very high price to pay for your modesty, lady."

His words were true but that didn't stop Madselin from feeling unreasonably angry. "Blanche brought me here. I would never have gone so far on my own."

He gave a snort of disbelief. "You strike me as a woman used to making your own decisions. I find it hard to believe you would follow a mere servant rather than trust your own instincts."

"I did not think Blanche was just a 'mere' servant, as you put it," she retorted. "She is most keen to impress us with her…experience."

He gave a heavy sigh. "You make absolutely no sense, woman. Blanche is no more than a servant."

"Then why is she here?" Her eyes blazing, Madselin turned suddenly to face him. Unable to stop himself from walking straight in to her, Edwin grabbed her arms and steadied them both.

For seconds, they remained silently staring at each other. "She asked me," came the simple reply.

"My requests do not appear to achieve so much," she countered.

That brought his breathtaking smile to his lips. "Perhaps it is the manner of the request that counts?"

In this strangely humorous mood, the Angle looked very attractive. That she found him so was most vexing. Her breath caught as he reached out to pluck several curls of bracken from her hair. He could be so unnerving and irritating all at the same time. "You chance much, Angle." Her voice was low and menacing, but it only made his smile broader.

"Less than you, it would seem. Did you know you were wandering round a sacred circle? The gods of old are not supposed to look kindly on strangers tramping round their place of worship." So saying, he released her arms and moved past her. "The others await our return and we must be gone. You have caused me enough delay already."

Madselin watched his retreating back with confusion. He was a very exasperating man. What did he mean by a sacred circle? Shaking her head, she followed the Angle back to the camp.

Within an hour or so of setting off once more, the rain began to lash down with ferocity, and Madselin did indeed begin to wonder whether she had angered the gods of the forest. Emma rode in silence next to Madselin whilst Blanche huddled in the back of the cart. She had declared herself to be far too delicate to walk.

The Angle appeared not to notice the rain. They were now at the front of the party, just ahead of Emma and

Madselin, and it was clear that the Angle had not relented his guard.

Every so often he would stop to listen intently at some unfamiliar noise or disappear into the trees for minutes at a time. Madselin found herself holding her breath when he did this, and only permitted herself another when he returned.

Gradually the forest began to thin as they headed westwards, and the landscape changed. There was no longer a green and amber canopy to protect them from the worst of the rain, and underfoot, the earth became stonier and more difficult to manage.

Flat, straight paths had given way to rough tracks meandering over low, stone-strewn hills. Trees still dotted the way, but even they were no longer the huge yews of the Bowland. The strange white glow from the silver birch trees gave a haunted atmosphere to the land. Gorse bushes and tussocks of thick reeds grew in the marshy low places.

Towards late afternoon, the rain ceased and the direction of the wind changed. The boiling clouds were carried inland, leaving a blue sky cobwebbed with fine white wisps. The wind dried their cloaks and lessened their misery a little. Imperceptibly their spirits lightened too. As they reached the top of the hill their first view of the grey sea spread out before them.

It was a breathtaking sight and Madselin could not help but feel a quickening of her heart as she looked beyond the next thickly wooded valley. Close to the shore on a raised earth promontory stood a small, but weather-ravaged keep built of the grey stone that lay hereabouts. A village of sorts huddled within the protective palisade, its tiny church standing a little apart from the rest of the buildings.

The shoreline beyond was a mass of grassy sand dunes, leading to a long beach covered in pebbles and grey sand.

They stared down at the dark wood that covered the lower part of the hill and beyond. Despite the last warming rays of the sun, there was a brooding atmosphere about the place that made Madselin feel uncomfortable.

"Stay close and keep quiet," came the command.

The Angle was standing close by their horses, his eyes squinting over the land below them. There was a tension about him that Madselin had not seen before. His cloak had been pushed casually back over his shoulders, but the muscles in his neck were taut.

"Do you expect trouble here?" Madselin demanded, her eyes also scanning the area.

He took hold of her bridle and gently rubbed the horse's nose. "Maybe."

She was so close to him now that she could see the lines etched on his face by the sun and the rain. It was impossible to tell how old the man was; most likely close to thirty.

Sensing her scrutiny, Edwin looked across at her. His expression was sombre. "It's probably nothing, but I thought I saw something—a reflection in the sun. There's no point in taking chances, though. I want your word you'll do as I bid."

Madselin gritted her jaw and impatiently pushed back the wisps of hair that had been loosened by the wind. "Aye. You have my word." She was not at all sure why she had agreed to it or that her word would be enough for him. Apparently it was.

"Good. Most likely it's the supplies they're after. If there's trouble, make haste to the manor. Wait for no one." He spoke patiently, almost as if he were talking to a child. Clearly he thought he was dealing with a very simple woman.

"I understand, Angle," she replied tartly. "The Vexin crawls with brigands, too."

Her words seemed to catch his interest. "You come from the Vexin?"

"I have just said so." She was pleased to see his cheeks flush a little. "Do you know it?" A most unlikely event.

"I went there but once." The words were almost incoherent but Madselin could see a change come over him. "Come. We are losing time."

When the attack came, the keep was in sight. They had remained in tight formation, their eyes almost on stalks trying to see through the undergrowth. Every sound made them jump. The first sign of trouble was a startled bird taking flight suddenly, its cry shrill in the silence. It was quickly followed by a swarm of arrows swooping across their path. Their attackers were but silent wraiths flickering amongst the trees.

Madselin felt strangely detached from reality as she watched the drivers of the heavy carts whip their horses to a faster pace, their rough faces white with fear and determination. The rest of the guards closed in around them, their swords drawn. Raoul pulled the screaming Blanche from the lead cart on to his mount and motioned to Madselin and Emma to go with him. He was clearly following his orders to the hilt.

Edwin Elwardson had jumped on to the back of the last cart and was sighting an unseen victim with his bow. The arrow sped through the trees, quickly followed by a second and a third. Suddenly a group of horsemen crashed towards them, swords aloft, and swept through

their defence. There were six of them, but they were
dressed in thick hauberks and dull grey helms. Their
leader was a huge brute with a thick red beard and a loud
raucous voice. His sights were set on Edwin Elwardson.

The Angle was desperately trying to aim his arrows at
the horses so that his men could cut the brigands down
with their swords, but it was an impossible task.

Swords scraped against metal and bone and the
screams that reached Madselin's ears were blood cur-
dling. The lead brigand had reached the cart and was
lunging heavily at Edwin. The Angle had pulled out a
sword and was counter striking with swift, well-aimed
blows. But it wasn't enough. An arrow grazed his upper
sword arm and thick red blood welled rapidly from the
cut. He was weakened now, and the brute was pushing
home his advantage with relentless strength.

Madselin looked round feverishly for a weapon, but all
she could find was a thick branch. It would have to do.
Without thinking, she picked it up, remounted swiftly and
plunged towards the cart. With a mighty heave, she
brought the branch down on the enemy's helmeted skull.
For a second, the man stilled and she was sure he had
felt nothing. Then he just crumpled.

"Get on my horse, Angle," she hissed at Edwin.
"Hurry."

He stared at her, speechless for once, but his face was
getting paler and the blood was pouring from his arm.
Uncertain that he understood, Madselin grabbed at him
and pulled him on the horse before her. He slumped forward.

Without waiting she spurred her horse into a gallop
and headed for the de Vaillant keep.

Chapter Four

Uncertain whether the body laid across her saddle was more alive than dead, Madselin hurtled through the gates of the manor. A party of ten or so armed soldiers had galloped past her in the other direction, intent only on saving the beleaguered guards and carts left in the forest. She pulled her mount to a halt amid a crowd of strange, unfamiliar faces. Unknown hands pulled Edwin's body from her.

"I can't abide women who swoon, so don't disappoint me." A strident voice cut across the fuss and noise, drawing Madselin's attention. No more than a yard from her stood a tall, spare woman enveloped in a thick woollen cloak trimmed in fur. Her regal bearing and swollen belly proclaimed her as Isabella de Vaillant.

Thin, mouse-brown braids framed a face which might have been hewn from the local stone. Nondescript brown eyes raked Madselin from head to toe before the woman turned to several servants and bellowed at them to carry the Angle with care into the keep.

Feeling more like she had been swallowed and then spat out whole, Madselin slipped from her horse and handed the reins to a waiting servant. Her legs felt a little wobbly but there was no way she was going to allow this rude woman the satisfaction of seeing her keel over. She deemed the de Vaillants to be well matched.

They were in the muddied courtyard of a small keep that had been built on several floors. It was certainly far grander than she had been expecting. Stables and kennels skirted the inner courtyard wall and a high wall built against the southern side of the keep perhaps hid a small herb garden. A sudden gust of wind from the north-west billowed up her cloak and she noticed that it was covered in blood.

"Stop wool-gathering and come with me." Isabella's stern command brooked no dissent and Madselin followed her to a heavy oak door.

Isabella stopped before her. She was several inches taller than Madselin and Madselin was forced to look up. "Have you any knowledge of healing, girl?"

Close to, Isabella de Vaillant was younger than she had at first thought. She must be near two score years, but the late pregnancy was clearly taking its toll on her. Deep lines were etched round her mouth and eyes, and there was a greyish pallor which was not quite healthy. Madselin had often helped the midwife and what Isabella de Vaillant needed most right now was rest.

Gathering her courage, Madselin unconsciously squared her shoulders.

"Aye, Lady de Vaillant. I have some skill. If you would direct me to the Angle, I will see to him. You need to lie down for a while."

Their eyes held until the merest glimmer of a smile broke Isabella's stern expression.

"Well, you seem to know what's what. I like that in a woman. I take it you are the de Breuville wench?"

Madselin's lips tightened at such blunt words. "My name is Madselin."

"Good. You will call me Isabella." She paused for a moment, waiting for a spasm to pass. "No. 'Tis nothing." Her smile was wan though, and Madselin did not like to leave her.

"Come with me. I insist you go to your chamber and rest." Madselin took the woman's arm and led her into a broad hall that smelled of beeswax candles and herbs. A young blonde woman with a small child in her arms was close by.

"Take Lady de Vaillant to her chamber. She is in need of rest." The girl nodded and beckoned for help to another woman.

"Here a few minutes and you're already taking over the place. I'm not an invalid, so don't treat me as if I'm like to die. It's only a baby and I've managed nine of them before. Joanna will take you to Edwin."

So saying, Isabella waved her servants away imperiously and moved slowly but most regally towards a doorway at the far end of the hall.

"Can you lead me to him?" asked Madselin of the young blonde woman.

"I'll take you myself. No doubt my sister is with him." She bobbed a curtsy and dropped a kiss on the forehead of her small charge. Madselin surmised then that this was Blanche's sister. Smaller in stature and less brazen by nature, Joanna proved far more cooperative.

They entered a small chamber above the hall. It was lit by several candles and a good fire. There was little in the way of furniture or hangings, but there was no trace of dampness or mustiness. Joanna marched up to the small group of women crowded round the pallet.

"Lady de Vaillant has given orders for Lady de Breu-

ville to tend Edwin. Take Blanche to the kitchens and
the rest of you see to the baggage wains and wounded
when they are brought in.'' The girl's command was
quiet but firm and Madselin was not at all surprised that
the women quickly dispersed. The dark-haired child in
Joanna's arms squirmed and she placed him gently on
the rush-strewn floor. ''Be good, Philippe. We have to
help Edwin.''

The boy turned his dark, serious eyes to the man on
the bed and pointed at him. ''Edin,'' he managed.

Joanna smiled at him proudly. ''Of course it's Edwin.
Now, you play quietly whilst the lady and I help him.''

From the confident way the child was smiling at the
beleaguered Angle, it was clear that Edwin was no
stranger to the de Vaillant keep.

Madselin bent down to look at Edwin's arm and carefully pulled at the blood-stained sleeve of his tunic.

''I'll need hot water, some cloths and a cup of strong
wine,'' she murmured before sitting down at his side.

Joanna nodded and picked up the child before leaving
the chamber.

Edwin opened one eye tentatively. ''Are they all
gone?''

Madselin looked at him askance. ''Aye.''

He pushed himself up into a sitting position, his face
grim. ''Stupid women,'' he muttered querulously, his
eyes checking the room.

''You were shamming!'' Madselin glared at him.

He glared back at her, his lips pursed. ''Not entirely.''
As if to emphasise his pain, the wretched man grimaced
as he tried to move his arm. ''But it does give us the
chance to discuss your disregard of my command. You
gave me your word you would do as I said. It seems I
can no longer trust even that.''

Madselin gasped at his words. "I thought you might have been a little grateful that I stayed to save your hide."

"You gave me your word that you would leave immediately at the first sign of trouble. You could have caused far more problems by being caught." His pale skin was flushed an angry red.

"You said yourself that they were only interested in the baggage." Her eyes glittered with anger.

"That was what I told you. It doesn't mean that was the truth," Edwin exploded. "Have you any idea what they might have done to you?"

"I certainly have a good idea about what might have happened to you had I not remained." She paused to toss her braids back over her shoulders. "That red-bearded brute would have hacked you to pieces if I hadn't hit him."

"You did what?" Edwin grabbed her by the shoulders and was almost shaking her.

"I hit him over the head with a branch." Her voice was controlled once more. Madselin gave him a look of utter disdain before pushing his hands away. "I agree that it was a very foolish action. I should have left him to finish you off."

The blood was beginning to ooze from his wound again, and Edwin flopped back down onto the mattress. "Why didn't you?"

Madselin rose to her feet and walked over to the fire. After a moment or two warming her hands, she removed her stained cloak and tossed it on to the pallet. "Richard gave me reason to think that you were important to his plans and that if aught were to happen to you, the rest of us would be in danger." She returned to the pallet and began to examine the wound once more.

''So it was not some misguided sense of honour?'' he said sullenly.

Madselin flicked her eyes briefly over his face and his disgruntled expression caused her to smile. He was behaving like a child. ''Not at all, Angle,'' she replied lightly. ''It was merely a case of self-preservation.''

The door opened and Joanna entered with several women in tow. Each carried their burden to the pallet and after a quick glance in Edwin's direction, they hurried out once more.

The task of mending the Angle's arm was a simple one and took little time once she and Joanna had removed the blood-caked tunic. Madselin found it difficult to keep her eyes from staring at the expanse of chest before her. His skin was a very beautiful golden colour, enhanced by the glow of the flames, and was very soft to touch.

She was not offended by seeing so much of a man's body, since she had often attended the injured soldiers and knights at her home. Yet this seemed a little different. It was the first time she had seen so beautiful a body. Her cheeks warmed at the direction of her thoughts. Quickly she finished binding his arm.

''Well, Angle. You'll live this time.'' She picked up the basin of water and cloths and handed them to Joanna.

''My thanks, Lady de Breuville,'' he muttered almost mutinously as Joanna left the room.

''Think nothing of it,'' she responded cheerfully, quite enjoying the man's discomfort. ''But as you have lost a lot of blood, I suggest you drink of the wine and then rest. I am certain you will wish to be putting in much target practice on the morrow and you are likely to need all your strength.''

He looked at her silently for a moment and Madselin was sure he wanted to strangle her. Suddenly his expression changed and he smiled at her almost wolfishly. The man looked impossibly handsome in the firelight. "You have the softest touch, Lady de Breuville. I shall be hard put to dream of aught else this night."

Her cheeks burned with the implications. He was a wretch. "I hope you writhe in agony all night, Angle," she spat before marching for the door.

A soft sigh followed her. "And I thought you had suffered a change of heart, lady."

Madselin slammed the door behind her. He would pay for such an insult. Although even as that thought came to her Madselin knew herself to be guilty. Hadn't she touched that skin gently, like a caress?

"Lady de Vaillant will see you now." Joanna smiled at her sympathetically. "It's best to comply immediately. The lady does not like to be kept waiting," she added.

With a heavy sigh, Madselin followed the girl down a narrow corridor to Lady de Vaillant's solar. It was a large room, but stuffy and overheated by the fire and the torch-light. Unconsciously she wiped her brow with the back of her hand.

"You're not ailing, are you?" The accusation was flung at her from the shadows to one side of the fire grate.

"Not at all," Madselin replied tartly. "I find the room hot."

Isabella rose stiffly and stepped into the firelight. Her eyes glittered, almost as if she were enjoying Madselin's bluntness. "I feel the cold."

Madselin surveyed the woman's homely features. The grey pallor had been replaced by a slight flush, but she was not convinced that Isabella was well. "Did you rest?" she asked finally.

"As if I could with all that clattering going on about

me," came the irritable reply. As she spoke, Isabella gestured with her hands and Madselin noticed that the woman had the most beautiful hands she had ever seen. Each of her long, slender fingers were encased with pretty rings which caught the light as Isabella waved her hands in the air.

"I wish to hear what you have to say, Lady de Breuville." The brown eyes were surveying Madselin thoroughly as she spoke. "Sit and share food and wine with me. I doubt you wish to eat in the hall tonight."

Madselin inclined her head in agreement. "I admit I am a little tired."

They sat at a small table near the fire and Isabella poured a large cup of sweet mead for both of them. Warmth coursed through her body, reviving and relaxing. Isabella remained silent for some time whilst a servant filled two thick trenchers with a selection of delicate meats. A manchet of white bread was broken in two and left for the women to share.

Madselin had not realised how hungry she was and ate her food with relish. Isabella did not seem to expect her to make conversation and she supposed that as Ivo de Vaillant was a man of few words, this was how it was with them.

When Isabella had finally waved the servant to clear the table, she poured each of them another cup of the sweet wine.

"You are the daughter of William de Breuville and Adeliza de Quesnay." This was more of a statement than a question.

Madselin just nodded in agreement.

"The eldest daughter?" The woman watched her carefully and Madselin felt quite uncomfortable.

"Aye. I have three younger brothers and two younger

sisters." This questioning was making her feel irritable. "My father died seven years ago and Robert has the estate now."

Isabella nodded her head slowly. "He married that dreadful Cauvin heiress, did he not?"

Despite her irritation, Madselin could not quite prevent her lips from smiling. No one had ever called Alice that before! Still, she should not show such a lack of loyalty before a stranger. "Alice is regarded by many as a very beautiful woman. She has provided my brother with three healthy children."

Her words were received with a scornful snort. "From what I hear, the parentage of the last one is very doubtful."

The strength of the wine was causing Madselin's cheeks to flush. "I will not stay to hear my family insulted," she began hotly and rose. "I find I am most tired and would welcome my bed."

Nobody moved for a moment whilst Isabella observed her keenly. Finally she gave a faint smile and waved away the servants. "Sit down, Madselin. I admire loyalty in people, although," she added with a sigh, "I think it misplaced in Alice de Cauvin."

"De Breuville," Madselin corrected stiffly. She sat down and looked at Isabella's face. The firelight seemed to soften her features a little. "Do you know my family?" she asked, her interest pricked.

"I knew your father. He was a hard man. As for the rest…" She waved her hand dismissively. "I know as much as many others. Gossip travels far these days."

Unsure as to the direction of the conversation, Madselin took another sip of the mead. Its very sweet, rather sickly taste was not much to her liking, but it was soothing. "I thought I had escaped that."

Isabella laughed. "We knew you were coming," she informed her, her fingers smoothing out her gown over her swollen belly.

"How?" Madselin looked at her in surprise.

Isabella shrugged. "We have to know what is happening, otherwise we could find ourselves very effectively taken by surprise. Danger is everywhere."

"Why do you stay?" Madselin watched Isabella rise and stretch her back.

"My husband wishes it," came the simple reply. "And the truth is," she added after a while, "I love this land."

"It's very cold and wet and full of barbaric peasants."

Resuming her seat in front of the fire, Isabella laughed. "Aye, but it grows on you. Now," she began more brusquely, "I want to know why you are here."

"I'm surprised you need to ask," replied Madselin primly.

Her implication was ignored. "I prefer to hear the truth from you."

Despite the woman's blunt ways, there was something quite likeable about Isabella de Vaillant that made Madselin trust her. Her story was quickly told.

Isabella stared at the fire for a few minutes, deep in thought. "You were betrothed once before, I gather. What happened?"

Madselin stiffened. "He died just hours before our wedding."

"Died?"

"Killed, then."

Isabella rubbed at her back. "Unfortunate. Who killed him?"

Madselin rose to stand before the fire. "A Saxon mercenary.'' She almost spat out the words, such hatred did she still feel for the animal who had ruined her life.

"Do you know why?" Isabella looked at her enquiringly. This was something the woman didn't know then.

Madselin shook her head. "At the time, I was too distraught to ask anything. Later on, Robert told me the little he knew. Guy seems to have been butchered for no reason. He was so gentle and kind," she added. "Why should anyone want to kill him on his wedding day?"

"Why, indeed? And this Hugh. Is he a good, honest man?" Isabella stroked her belly in a gentle rhythm.

A vision of Hugh swam before her eyes. He was handsome and cheerful. Was he good and honest? "Of course." For a fleeting second, an odd memory of Hugh laughing rather intimately with Alice flashed before her. It was gone the minute it came, but it unsettled her. "He is greatly concerned for the well-being of all our family."

"I've heard he's a vain popinjay with a sweet tongue. Think you he wants your dowry?"

The words speared Madselin like an arrow. "You go too far, Lady de Vaillant." Madselin rose quickly. "I have need of my bed and would bid you goodnight."

Isabella sighed heavily and pulled herself to her feet. "As you wish." At her silent command, a servant appeared from the shadows. "Follow Anne. Sleep well, Lady Breuville."

Madselin slept soundly, helped no doubt by the two cups of mead poured so generously by Isabella. She woke early to the sound of waves crashing loudly beyond the palisade and seagulls screeching in the wind.

Pushing herself onto her elbows, she looked around the room. It was small but sweet-smelling and comfortable. The stone walls were draped in tapestries and woollen hangings and the window hole was covered by well-fitting shutters. A good fire was roaring in the grate and the empty pallet next to it indicated that Emma was already about.

The wooden door was suddenly pushed aside.

"So you're awake, my lady. And high time, too." Emma was plainly irritated as she stomped around the room.

"What is it, Emma?" Madselin watched her curiously.

"This place is filled with idiots who cannot speak a proper tongue. There's a great Saxon lummox in the courtyard who certainly does not know his place. It's got me quite of a bother and my wits have addled. The Lady de Vaillant is keen for you to join her downstairs as soon as you can, my lady."

Dumbfounded that the normally even-keeled Emma had been wrongfooted by a Saxon, or Angle or whatever, Madselin could only stare at her. Emma scowled at her then, so she leapt out of bed.

Isabella de Vaillant sat near the fire with Edwin Elwardson. His long legs were stretched out before him and he looked very much at his ease.

"Come sit with us, girl." Isabella beckoned her with a gesture that looked more like a command.

From the conciliatory inclination of Isabella's head, Madselin surmised that the words spoken last night were forgotten. Edwin managed a fleeting nod in her direction and she very much doubted if he had spent the night dreaming of her soft touch!

"Edwin tells me you think he needs more target practice," Isabella began, a tight smile on her lips.

"I may have said that." Madselin stiffened. "But it was merely an observation from a novice, of course."

Edwin leaned forward suddenly, placing his forearms

on his thighs. He had decided to ignore her presence. "I'll be taking out a patrol as soon as I can muster the men. We may find something." All pretence of teasing had been put aside and his tone was deadly serious. "Have you any proof that Orvell was behind the attack?"

Isabella shook her head slowly. "Gyrth seemed to think he recalled one of the dead men near Orvell's keep, but naught beyond that. The man is very careful."

Edwin picked up his cup from the table and took a deep draught of the ale. "I doubt if the Scots would act before spring now. Time is on our side, but we must be careful. If Orvell is involved, he'll be keen to rid himself of any problems."

"He knows something is amiss or he'd not have attacked you yesterday." Isabella's loud voice dropped. "I'd lay my life that all the servants are loyal, but there's always the chance that one might be tempted."

Edwin drained the cup and placed it carefully on the table behind him. He turned to Madselin. "Stay close to the keep. You have seen what they can do."

"I am forbidden to leave the keep?" Her voice was very still. "I had hoped to visit the beach."

He stood up and pulled his brown cloak about his shoulders. "I'll take you on the morrow." The Angle left without further words.

Madselin's lips compressed tightly. No doubt he was right to be careful, but his words were insolent.

Isabella had watched them with a gleam in her brown eyes. "Do not gainsay him, Madselin. His pride is sore after yesterday and he thinks himself entirely responsible for the loss of the soldier's life. These things go hard with him."

The oat cakes turned to ashes in her mouth. "He is but an Angle. Why should he feel such duty?" This was not something she could imagine of the man. Surely he was interested only in his own gain?

"He is a man of many facets, Edwin." Isabella fiddled with the rings on her fingers. "He is torn between hatred for the Normans and duty. Revenge and his own gentle nature."

"Gentle? The man is an oaf." Madselin frowned into her ale. Were they discussing the same man? "And if he hates us all so much, why is he here?"

Isabella gripped her stomach, her face drawn. Before Madselin could move closer to help, she had raised her hand to stop her. "Do naught. The babe readies itself, that's all." When the spasm had passed, Isabella sat still for a moment. "His family were killed by a renegade band of Normans, but he was raised by a Norman family with their own children. He had a happy life, it seems."

"Well, that accounts for his French, but hardly his manners." Madselin teased roughly at a mark on her gown with her fingernail.

"He seeks his revenge against the murderers of his family. Where else would he learn about these men? He has spent ten years on their tracks. Do not make the mistake of believing the man simple because he chooses to appear as a peasant." Pushing herself up slowly, Lady Isabella carefully arranged her cloak about her. Madselin lifted her eyes, aware that she was the object of the woman's attention.

"I have never suggested he was simple. Merely that the man is an oaf. There is a difference," Madselin declared with feeling.

"Hmm. Better an honest oaf than a treacherous peacock, perhaps?"

"I know not what you mean." Madselin was beginning to wonder if the damp weather had killed off the woman's wits. She talked in riddles.

Isabella gave her a hard stare before raising one dark eyebrow. "It's time you saw the place for yourself, Lady de Breuville. Come."

Madselin contemplated Isabella's stiff back. Had the woman been referring to Hugh de Montchalon? Hugh was worth ten of Edwin Elwardson; she would be proud to be his wife.

Several grimy-looking children pelted through the puddles in the bailey, splashing and laughing their way to the gate. A cheery sentry allowed them through to the outer Palisade with a few words of their guttural tongue. Madselin sighed. Did everyone speak the peasants' language?

The cold and rain of the day before had been blown away in the night, leaving a blue sky full of fresh promise. A stiff wind blew in from the sea, carrying an exotic cocktail of odours that caused Madselin's spirits to lift. Perhaps she had been hasty in her view about the weather.

Accompanied by more children, several soldiers mounted on sturdy ponies rounded the far wall of the keep. They idled towards the gates and then stopped, huddled in a tight group, the horses stomping impatiently on the muddy ground.

Edwin followed them a few minutes later, astride a magnificent black courser that bore absolutely no resemblance to his tame mount of the previous day. The man himself, however, was dressed simply, as was his way, in his old brown cloak and breeches.

Despite his apparel, Madselin had to admit that he did look every inch like a noble lord. And where had that thought come from? She studied him anew. His back was

straight and strong, his head held proud. Edwin Elwardson was a natural leader who commanded the respect of
his fellow men.

Isabella de Vaillant had proceeded slowly towards the
gate and was joined by several others who obviously
wished to see the patrol leave. Amongst them stood
Joanna, who held a boy of about three years in her arms.
This child was most unlike the little dark-haired Philippe,
who Madselin had learned was Isabella's youngest son.
This one was far more sturdily built, with a thick crop
of blond hair.

As soon as the boy saw Edwin, he held his arms out
to him and Madselin watched, amazed, as the surly Angle
plucked the child from Joanna's arms and threw him in
the air. Squeals of laughter informed the crowd of the
child's complete approval of the action; indeed, he demanded a repeat performance.

Madselin found herself entranced by the sight of the
Angle laughing with the child. It was very clear to her
that there was a special bond between the two. After
glancing at them curiously for a while, she thought she
saw a resemblance between them. They definitely had a
look of each other.

As Edwin handed the boy back to Joanna, she noticed
a look pass between them. Were they lovers? From the
way he smiled at her, it was a strong possibility. The
child could be his.

She had no idea why those thoughts should concern
her at all, but Madselin found that they did. He had not
shown any marked interest in Joanna when they were
attending to his wound, but then that would not be his
way. She realised that instinctively, even though she
hardly knew the man. Madselin was also aware that Edwin seemed far more at ease here than at Richard's keep.

He turned then, almost as if he knew she was watching him and held her eyes for several heartbeats. Within seconds, his attention was claimed by Lady de Vaillant who was no doubt giving him his final orders.

A movement to her right caught her eye and she found herself being scrutinised by a massive giant who was leaning idly by the palisade wall. Taller even than Edwin by at least a head, the man was as wide as he was tall, with thinning blond-grey hair that straggled over his shoulders. He had survived well beyond two score years, but time had taken its toll on his weathered face.

Dismissing her with a snort, the giant thudded across the courtyard towards the patrol. Whoever he was, Madselin had the distinct impression that she had been found wanting.

Chapter Five

When the patrol had left, Isabella had slowly taken Madselin round the tiny village in the outer bailey. For her it had been a matter of great pride that these peasants had seemed cheerful and relatively well nourished. They had certainly appeared happier than those on the de Breuville demesne in Normandy.

When Isabella complained of fatigue and returned to the keep for a rest, Madselin had decided it was time to purge her soul of her recent wrongdoings. The heavy oak door of the church had opened with a loud groan and Madselin had peered in apprehensively. There was no one about, since most of the villagers were about their business, and Madselin ventured in.

As she prayed, Madselin finally became aware of another presence in the church. Turning round, she came face to face with a small man with dark brown hair and twinkling green eyes. Not young, with thick grooves etched between his nose and mouth, the man was watching her with interested eyes. His heavy brown woollen robe proclaimed him to be the priest.

"I beg your pardon, Father," she exclaimed. "I did

not know you were there!'' Madselin hastily scrambled to her feet.

"Lady de Vaillant would never recommend such reverence from a young lady as yourself. I'd be thinking I was doing some good here!'' His rather harsh features broke into a warm smile. "I'm Father Padraig,'' he announced with a strange accent she could not place. "I've been here for the last ten years and I'm still the newcomer. If you need any advice—practical or spiritual— then I'm your man.''

Madselin frowned. "You're not from here?''

"Ireland,'' he replied with a heavy sigh. "It's across the water.''

Madselin only had a vague idea as to where that land might be but knew naught about it. "Do you not wish to return there?'' She liked the man's warm smile and his honest face. He was very different to most priests she had come across.

He laughed then, as if she had said something funny. "And who would guide these lost souls then? Lady Isabella would have a fit if I even suggested it, and that woman has a way of knowing exactly what a man thinks. It's a most unchristian skill she has.'' The last words were uttered with a gloomy shaking of his head, but his tone was rueful rather than resentful. Madselin doubted that he meant anything dreadful by his words.

"They are not of the faith, then?'' she asked, her fears about these people materialising.

There must have been something about the tone of her voice that caused the good man to pause and breathe in deeply through his nose. "I would be honoured if you would accompany me for a while. It's been a long while since I've had a pretty young girl in need of a bit of advice.''

That hadn't answered her question at all, but Madselin was shrewd enough to have realised that Father Padraig was perhaps somewhat deeper than she had at first thought.

As they wandered amongst the villagers' huts, Father Padraig gave her a short history of each family. Basically of Angle stock, the villagers had gradually converted to Christianity many years before the Norsemen came.

"So this is a Christian village, then," Madselin stated, pushing back some strands of hair.

Father Padraig raked his small hands through his hair and smiled ruefully. "Aye," he replied eventually. "But you have to remember, Lady de Breuville, that old habits die hard in an isolated village."

"Do you mean they still worship their old gods?" Madselin widened her eyes. She had heard the stories of the pagans and their dreadful sacrifices. What Norman hadn't?

The priest laughed good-naturedly. "No. But they like to carry on some of the old traditions. It's just their way."

"And you allow these practices?" Madselin cast him a challenging look.

"Sometimes it is best to let things lie," the priest explained carefully. "These people do their duty by me and the rest of their…activities are harmless enough." He smiled at her, his eyes gentle and honest.

"What sort of…activities do they participate in?" she asked. Perhaps she was misjudging the situation.

Father Padraig put his arm across her shoulders and turned her towards the inner courtyard. "Nothing dreadful," he assured her with an amused voice. "They celebrate the changing of the seasons with a bit of dancing and music. There are other times—such as All Hallows—

where they dress up in old masks and costumes. It's just a bit of fun.''

They reached the gate and stopped. ''And Lady de Vaillant allows this?''

''Lady de Vaillant is a very shrewd woman who understands the nature of these people. She is devout and sets a shining example to the villagers, but she feels it would be unwise to prevent them from following harmless traditions.'' His words were uttered in all seriousness, almost as if he were trying to warn Madselin to leave well alone. ''Come, I'll tell you about one of their legends.''

They ended up at the top of the keep. Madselin caught her breath as the strength of the wind almost bowled her over. She drew her cloak close to her body and looked out towards the bay. It swept outwards, curving round in a broad arc of sand as far as the eye could see. Heavy grey waves swirled and crashed down on the rocks near the shore. A few fishing boats bobbed up and down in the distance. The beach was deserted.

''If you look over there—'' Father Padraig pointed inland, towards the forest ''—you'll see a lake in the clearing.''

Madselin screwed up her eyes against the glare of the morning sun. About a mile from the keep, in the middle of a wide clearing, she could see water glinting in the sunlight. ''I see it,'' she shouted into the wind.

''It's called Lhin Dhu. The black lake.''

Madselin turned to him, holding back her hair from her face. ''It doesn't look black.''

''Nay. It's the nature of the water that has earned the name.'' His voice was whipped away in the wind.

''What nature? Is it evil?'' Madselin shivered, not all on account of the freshness of the air.

"Only God can answer that one, my lady." He rubbed his clean-shaven chin with his hand. "But it's said that the lake takes its own revenge on wrongdoers."

Madselin stared at the lake sceptically. "And how would a lake do that?" She did not trouble to hide the doubt in her voice.

"A long time ago, a giant of a Dane led a raiding party in the area and killed several villagers. He drowned in the lake." The words were uttered without emotion, as if he were just relaying facts. But Madselin could swear that the priest believed every word.

"If it were true," she said slowly, "it could just be coincidence." Lots of people drowned since few were able to swim.

The priest smiled good-naturedly. "Maybe…" he hesitated for a moment "…but the villagers believe it."

Madselin sighed. "I doubt I'll be here long enough to consider the matter too much."

Looking across at her, Father Padraig leaned his head to one side. "These things aren't always as simple as you think, child." Then, as if mentally shaking himself from a reverie, he grabbed her shoulder. "It's about time I went to see Lady de Vaillant. She'll be accusing me of turning you away from the Church if I keep you much longer." He chuckled deeply, clearly amused at his own words.

For no good reason that she could think of, a vision of Edwin's stern, humourless face came to her. Perhaps years of vengeful thoughts could twist a good man, too? A thread of irritation stirred her into recognising that Isabella's brief account of Edwin's early life had touched her after all. She put all thoughts of the Angle firmly from her mind.

* * *

"The child is merely young, not an idiot, and I will not have you cooing at him as if he were unable to understand simple French." Isabella glared at an unfortunate young woman who had been attempting to entertain Philippe.

The boy was as dark and swarthy as his father but, at two years of age, was displaying the inquisitive and somewhat arrogant tendencies of his mother. Rather conspiratorially, he gave Isabella a lop-sided grin which displayed two perfectly tiny front teeth, before pulling the girl's unbraided hair. Understandably deflated, the girl retreated to her unfinished sewing near the window.

Two other boys of similar colouring and precocious nature were wrestling on the other side of the room. Madselin remembered Ivo de Vaillant telling her that they had nine children. Momentarily diverted by her appearance, the two boys stared at her before resuming their game. Isabella just smiled indulgently at them. "Charles! Benedict! Go and play your rough games in the stable, not in my solar." Within seconds they had gone.

"Pleased to hear you in fine voice, my lady." Father Padraig moved closer to take her hand and kiss it with more warmth than priests usually display.

"The day I stop shouting, I'll be dead," laughed Lady de Vaillant mirthlessly. "Now." She speared them both with an unwavering eye. "I take it that the good Father has sought to give you a truthful impression of himself?"

Madselin offered a quick smile at the priest, but he seemed more concerned with warming his hands than arguing with Isabella. "A most enlightening experience," she said quietly. That was the truth, of course. "I look forward to seeing the rest of your lands before long."

"You look as if you have been dragged through most of it already."

Suddenly realising how dishevelled she must look, Madselin tried to put her wild hair into some kind of order, but Isabella halted her futile efforts with a brisk wave of her hand. "Leave it. I think I prefer you a little ruffled. Blanche!" Although her voice did not rise to give the command, Blanche appeared from amongst the crowd of women sewing in the corner. "A flagon of wine and cups."

Madselin could see that the brusque order had done little to improve Blanche's expression and the girl stomped off towards the door.

"Blanche doesn't seem to get on with Joanna. Are they not close?"

At the mention of Joanna, Isabella's face softened just a little. "They were, but since Joanna had the child Blanche feels rather...ignored." She gave a dissatisfied sigh. "A little more guidance from the Church wouldn't have gone amiss."

Father Padraig smiled blandly and ignored the raised eyebrow. "The girl has a mind of her own, just like her mother. Blood will out, Lady de Vaillant, as you are always wont to say."

"Well, I certainly wish she was here now." This was accompanied by a heavy thump of a lovely hand on the table before her.

"Where is her mother?" Madselin ventured to ask.

"Dead," came the uncompromising reply. Isabella's shoulders sagged. "Ten years ago. In childbirth," she added more quietly. "She came with me from Normandy on my marriage. I should never have let her get married to that great oaf. She'd still be here if I'd kept my reason."

The priest lowered his head and shook it slowly. "It would have done no good, Isabella, and you know it. Marie and Ulf were set on it." His eyes rested on her with affection. He reached out his hand to her shoulder and gave it a gentle squeeze. "And Ulf has done his best with the girls."

"Who is Ulf?" Madselin felt out of her depth and quite confused.

"The head of the village. A huge great ox of a man with more brawn than brain."

Despite the flattering description, Madselin recognised the man as Emma's lummox.

"Will you listen to yourself, my lady? Sure, Lady de Breuville must think you and Ulf are at each other's throats."

Isabella sniffed. "When I need your advice, I'll ask for it. Now, go about your business whilst I talk to Madselin."

Blanche eventually arrived with the wine and poured the two women a cup each before flouncing out once again. Madselin noticed that Isabella was holding her breath.

"When is your time, my lady?" Her eyes took in the woman's wan face and white lines around her mouth.

"All Hallows, or thereabouts." Slowly, Isabella exhaled. She hesitated before adding, "And I hope this time it's a girl."

"Your husband told me you have nine boys." She looked around for more evidence, but found none.

"There's only Charles, Benedict and Philippe here. William left for Normandy last year as a page, like the others. Alain is almost eighteen and hoping for a knighthood." Her voice had softened considerably and Madselin surmised that Isabella was not as harsh about her sons as she chose to display. "He might be back near Yuletide."

They whiled away several hours in conversation of a similar vein.

A horn outside shattered the peace of the keep. One of the women ran to the window and peered down into the courtyard. "The patrol has returned, my lady."

"Tell Edwin to come up as soon as he is able," Isabella commanded. "And fetch him some ale."

Madselin started to move. She had no desire to be near him.

"Stay. Whatever he has to say will be important. If I am ill or dead, then you have to know the plan." Isabella's brown eyes almost challenged her to disagree, and Madselin sat down again in confusion.

"But I don't..."

Isabella interrupted her swiftly. "Richard is no fool. If anything were to happen to me whilst Ivo is away, he would need to have someone run the place. You have experience."

Madselin could not argue with the logic but it certainly changed her perspective of the whole situation. "I'm sure Edwin..."

"Edwin is a man who knows much about tracking, killing and archery, but very little about running a manor. He'd never be able to control the women. He's far too soft with them. Stop being ridiculous."

Madselin was uncertain whether or not to breathe a sigh of relief when Edwin was announced. He strode in, bringing with him the fresh smell of the forest. He greeted them with his usual nod and gladly accepted the ale Madselin proffered.

She took the opportunity to study him a little more. His skin was flushed and locks of hair had escaped from his braid. Thick mud was splashed on his boots, breeches and cloak. Hugh would never have appeared before ladies in so dreadful a condition.

Not until he had drained the cup did he speak. How like him, she thought disparagingly. "We found some tracks, but it was difficult. The rain last night must have washed most of the signs away." He pushed his cloak over his shoulders and walked to stand before the fire.

He looked weary, she allowed. "Will you sit?" Madselin offered. After all, the man had lost a fair amount of blood with his injury and he had not rested for some time.

Her concern seemed to surprise him, but he accepted her offer. "My thanks," he muttered, eyeing her with suspicion. His expression brought a slight smile to her lips. What on earth did he think she was going to do?

"Orvell?" Isabella's single word of interruption broke their silent communication.

Edwin rubbed his wounded shoulder with a frown. "I think so. Gyrth is watching the manor for a while. His information could prove valuable."

She'd heard the name mentioned before but couldn't place it. "Who is Gyrth?" she asked since no one appeared to be volunteering the information.

"Ulf's son," snapped Isabella, more or less as if she were addressing a simpleton. "Fortunately, he has more brains."

A smile shattered Edwin's taciturn expression and, despite the appalling state of his clothes, Madselin realised that she could see why Blanche felt so jealous. Although he was old—near enough thirty summers—he bore few of the signs of ageing that many Normans seemed to. "He has more charm, that's all."

"Well? What do you plan to do?"

Pulling himself up to a sitting position, Edwin

shrugged. "Nothing for the moment. I don't wish him to know we suspect him. He might make a mistake without being forced, since he's been running unchecked for so long."

"Suspected of what?" Madselin demanded.

Edwin turned to her, his grey eyes as cold as the sea. "Treachery with the Scots." His eyes slid away to stare at the flames. "He also has a liking for manhunts."

Madselin felt cold blood run through her veins and shivered. "Will he attack us again?" Her customary haughtiness had been replaced by genuine interest.

"Nay. But he might try another tack."

"If he comes sniffing round here, I'll show him what we're made of," declared Isabella, her granite cheeks flushing with indignation.

"It might be better if you did not." Edwin inhaled deeply. "If he thinks we suspect naught, he'll want to plan his attack. Take us by surprise."

Isabella shot him a look of disgust. "He's not coming through the portals of this manor." She shifted uncomfortably on her chair; but waved away Madselin's look of concern.

"Let him in," contradicted Edwin firmly. "We might recognise some of his men."

They were both thinking of that red-bearded giant, Madselin was certain. "And what then?"

He grinned at her. "I thought I'd let you loose on them."

Madselin gasped. The surly Angle was displaying a sense of humour, and it was most ill timed. "Be serious," she hissed.

Clearly he found the thought of allowing Madselin to run amok with thick branches most amusing since he was unable to prevent the smile from tugging at the corner of his mouth. His eyes, she noted, were almost blue. This was not a side to his character she hoped to see again. It was most disturbing.

A gentle snoring from Isabella's chair caught their attention. The woman was looking very tired and Madselin did not think she was as well as she tried to make out. Pulling a thick woollen blanket over her, Madselin then turned to Edwin.

"I am worried about her," she confided, catching her lower lip between her teeth. "The pregnancy is not progressing as well as it should. I have some experience in these matters, but I would like a midwife to look at her as soon as possible."

All trace of teasing was gone. "I'll send Agnes to you. She's the old herb woman," he added by way of explanation.

She smiled tentatively. "That would be kind. Thank you."

He stared up at her intently, his grey eyes searing into her. "It's good she's got another woman with her."

Madselin's eyes slid across the room to the gaggle of women chattering in the corner and raised her eyebrows. It hadn't occurred to her that a man like Edwin Elwardson would consider the comforts of women.

He followed her glance and exhaled very expressively before standing. "I meant a lady," he murmured with feeling, before stalking towards the door.

Stunned by his words if not his expression, Madselin could only stare at the closed door. She was not sure that was a compliment of any sort, but the fact that he had said it at all interested her greatly. Sinking down onto his vacated chair, Madselin sighed and picked up some discarded sewing. It was going to be a long winter.

* * *

Agnes was a toothless crone with a weatherbeaten, wrinkled face the colour of brown berries and a body the shape and size of a gnarled stick. Wreathed in a dusty brown tunic, the old woman had surveyed Madselin with silent suspicion.

Despite her unpromising appearance, Agnes dealt with Lady de Vaillant in a manner very similar to the one adopted by Madselin, albeit of course in the local tongue. It certainly proved effective since Isabella grudgingly drank of the foul-smelling potion and promptly fell into a deep sleep. As the concoction was one she recognised from home, Madselin's estimation of Agnes's skill rose.

Judging by the guarded looks the woman was giving Madselin, however, it was obviously not a mutual feeling. She wished she could have communicated more freely with the woman, but the language barrier was just too great.

When Isabella woke up hours later, she looked much improved. Her unhealthy pallor had been replaced by a fresher, brighter countenance. The inquisitive gleam in her eyes, however, remained much the same.

"Have you got a better gown than that one?"

Madselin shrank a little under Isabella's disdainful scrutiny. Her hands smoothed out a few of the creases in defence. "It's a perfectly serviceable gown," she protested.

"Well, it does nothing for you. A brighter colour would look better."

Madselin's chin rose a little. "I see no good reason."

"Don't you? Well, I'll tell you then." Isabella heaved herself up to a sitting position. "All of the villagers will be present tonight and they will be viewing you for the first time."

"I don't quite see…"

"They know that if aught happens to me, you'll be the lady of the manor until Ivo comes home."

"Then they will have to take me as I am." Her voice sounded more defiant than she felt, but Madselin suddenly felt as if she had been transported back to stand before Alice.

However, Isabella seemed to understand. "Very well. Have it your own way."

When she finally graced the great hall, Madselin was feeling somewhat shaky. The thought of those peasants' eyes watching her every move was a most sobering thought. She was used to merging into the background and being obeyed for who she was, not what she was. The sight that greeted her did little for her composure.

Isabella graced the centre of the table, resplendent in turquoise silk and grey coney trimmings. Madselin was glad that she had responded to the criticism of her green kersey and had changed into a gown of heavy rose damask. It was old but well made and Madselin had always felt her best when she wore it. The pink lightened her dark colouring and somehow managed to light up her brown eyes. Simple but effective. She was pleased to see Isabella's mute approval.

On Isabella's left sat the chieftain she now knew to be Ulf, and on her right, Edwin. Much to her disappointment, Madselin found that she was to be seated next to him. She surmised the feeling was mutual, since he barely gave her more than scant attention on her arrival.

The quality of the food was not the best, but it was well spiced and tasty. Potage, chicken and rabbit were not high table fare, but Madselin found herself eating far more than was her custom. Something to do with the air, she was certain.

Isabella was indulging in conversation with Ulf although, observing him closely, Madselin realised that Isabella was doing most of the talking. Ulf merely nodded or grunted.

Edwin was studiously ignoring the adoring eyes of the women which seemed to be centred on him throughout the meal. Despite his apparent ignorance, she was certain that Edwin was finding the whole thing rather an ordeal.

"You look as if you would rather be at an execution," she began conversationally.

He turned his head slowly in her direction as if unsure as to whether her remark was intended for him. "And isn't it?" came the dour reply.

Madselin shrugged. "Not for me."

For some reason, that brought a smile to his lips. "Are you sure?"

She blinked rapidly and listened to the conversations going on around her. None of it made any sense. "Quite sure."

Her smugness was premature.

"Ulf thinks you unsuited to our land and our men. Too haughty and too thin for child-bearing," he said conversationally as he bit into a piece of honey-coated chicken.

After a moment's intake of breath, Madselin rallied. "And why should I be contemplating anything in this land other than escape?" She speared him with her most haughty glare.

His eyes roved over her slowly, lingering over her breasts and bringing a flush to her cheeks. "Too old?" he asked simply before reaching for a handful of bread.

Madselin's mouth compressed into a tight line as she regarded him with utter distaste. "Too clever," she managed between gritted teeth.

He chewed her answer over with the bread before addressing the chieftain in his own tongue. An outburst of laughter from all sides followed. Madselin could barely keep her head up for the shame. "What did you say?" Her anger was barely controlled.

Edwin tossed down a cup of ale before wiping his mouth on his sleeve. "Just what you said."

"Can't you talk to him in French?" Her humiliation was complete.

"No. He doesn't understand."

"Well, he should learn." She slumped back grumpily and drank deeply of her wine.

"This is not Normandy," he pointed out. "And in truth, Ulf has little need of the language since all but you speak his own."

Madselin's cheeks flamed. He had no need to belabour the point. She was not as stupid as he seemed to think.

Fortunately Emma chose to enter the hall at this point and made her way to the table. She sat down opposite Madselin, her face and body rigid.

"Why is he still watching me?" she hissed across the table.

"Who?" asked Madselin, looking round.

"That great Saxon lummox!" Emma gave her a withering look.

"Oh! Ulf? The chieftain?" Madselin stole a glance at him; sure enough, his small puffy eyes were fixed on Emma. The intensity of his gaze was most eloquent.

Emma raised her nose and tossed back her grey braids. "Well, chieftain or not, I'll be having nothing to do with the likes of him!"

So saying, she proceeded to partake of the food on offer, seemingly oblivious as to the state of the chieftain.

Music and laughter continued for another hour or so before people began to drift away. Madselin was very glad when the ordeal was finally over. She had been asked a few simple questions which Edwin had translated, but after a while it became boring for all concerned. Most ended up just conversing with Edwin. She did not like the covert looks he kept giving her either, and felt compelled to express her disapproval by frowning at him.

"Do not look at me so," she muttered eventually.

"How so?" He raised his eyebrows and waited for her explanation.

She opened her mouth and then shut it again as she noticed Ulf staring straight at the pair of them. His frown said it all. "As if I were a…a simpleton." She fiddled with the bread of her trencher, unable to look at him.

He grinned. For a stern, surly man he was developing an irritating habit of smiling. "You seem to have impressed Lady de Vaillant, at least."

She ignored the "at least" for now, but noted how adept he was at changing the subject when it suited him. "I am considered to be efficient and capable. My sister-in-marriage leaves much of the running of the manor to me."

"And what does your sister-in-marriage do?" He sounded genuinely interested.

Madselin found that quite difficult to answer without appearing disloyal. "Alice is most proficient at sewing and prefers to spend her time involved in other such…time-consuming pursuits." It had not come out quite as she had expected and Madselin coloured as her voice trailed off at the end.

"For someone who dislikes Alice, you seem to do much on her behalf, Lady de Breuville."

"I don't do it for Alice," Madselin muttered. "I do it for her children and for my brother." She had realised early on that Alice would not make much of an effort with running the household. At least they could now be sure of tasty food, clean clothes and comfortable rooms. "It isn't hard for me," she added. "It's my home."

Edwin shook his head. "Running a manor successfully requires much effort, lady. I think you are too modest."

Madselin looked up at him, somewhat confused. Aye, there were days when she was bone-tired with running round from early in the morning until she fell into her bed late at night. The only real pleasure she had was spending time with the children. A few grubby kisses meant far more to her than Alice's condescending smile.

Fortunately, Edwin did not seem to have taken her words amiss. After a moment's rather awkward silence, he looked across at Emma and then at Ulf. "Your maid seems to have captured Ulf's attention."

"It is not a mutual feeling, I can assure you," she replied tartly, directing a repressive frown in Ulf's direction.

A heavy sigh escaped the Angle's lips. "Then he will be hell to live with until he gets his way."

Madselin's eyes widened as she realised the implications. "Emma is a devout and God-fearing woman. If I remember aright, she referred to him as a Saxon lummox. That hardly seems in any way encouraging."

"Ulf rarely takes no for an answer," was the reply.

"Well, if he thinks Emma an easy conquest then he will find out we Norman women are clearly made of sterner stuff than the Angle women."

Chapter Six

It was the first time she had ever set foot on a beach and the only thing spoiling her complete joy was the fact that Edwin Elwardson was there too. Madselin could tell that he was observing her from his lookout on the grassy dune behind the sand, but she chose to ignore him.

A sudden desire to break out from her own mental bonds overcame her natural modesty, and Madselin sat down on the pebble-strewn sand and furtively rolled down her thick hose and removed her shoes. With a sharp glance in the Angle's direction, she satisfied herself that he had at least had the grace to look away whilst she adjusted her gown. Somehow, Madselin had known that he would.

The sand felt at once cold, soft and scratchy between her toes. Pulling up her skirts, Madselin headed for the waves. Edwin had brought her to a small, well protected cove that was hemmed on three sides by high dunes. Rocks and pebbles covered the upper part of the cove, followed by patches of coarse dry sand and then the soft wet stuff that squelched so delightfully underfoot.

Feeling like a child, she stood perfectly still in the patchy morning sun and allowed the wind to buffet her in all directions. For a few brief moments, Madselin felt a burst of happiness course through her.

Tentatively, she placed a toe in the grey foam. The water was freezing and Madselin quickly withdrew her whole foot before it was swamped in the next wave. After several attempts, she finally managed to stand in the water long enough to allow her calves to get wet. Looking out into the bay beyond, all she could see was miles of grey, choppy waves that disappeared on the horizon. It was hard to imagine that danger could lurk there.

Turning back suddenly, she saw the dark outline of Edwin's proud, tall body as he stood on the dune looking out to the sea. She was glad that he had let her explore this new experience on her own; he had been content to watch and wait for her, allowing her to wallow in her own thoughts. It had been a very long time since she had been allowed to do anything at all on her own. Alice had seen to that.

As she paddled along the edge of the water, Madselin found it hard to believe that she had set out on her adventure only four weeks before.

She joined Edwin sitting on his grassy dune and carefully arranged her cloak so that she could sit in comfort. She had few enough gowns that she could afford to find patches of mud and grass on them.

''Well?'' he murmured. ''Is this still a terrible, barbaric land?''

His long legs were stretched out before him and he had propped himself up with his elbows. The wind blew strands of his loose hair across his face as he stared out to sea. Madselin arched an eyebrow and sighed.

''No,'' she allowed, waiting for his snort of derision. None came. ''It's very beautiful here. Very…peaceful.''

Madselin wasn't now sure what his reaction to her views would be.

"I like it here, too. It feels like home." His voice was soft, almost a caress.

Madselin was not sure that she had heard aright. The cold-hearted, surly Angle was admitting deep feelings. It was an admission that fascinated her.

"But this is not your home, is it?"

His serious, judgemental eyes narrowed as if he had seen something. "No. My family came from south of this place, in Cheshire."

"Do you miss it?" Unconsciously, Madselin leaned a little closer towards him. It was hard to hear him, the wind was so strong.

"Aye. At times. I left ten years ago."

"Why?"

Edwin drank in the fresh sea air and exhaled slowly before turning to Madselin. They were very close and she could feel her nerves tingling up and down her spine. "I was given my freedom."

"But if you were happy there…?" Madselin frowned. Why would he wish to leave?

Edwin gave a tight smile and pulled at the blades of grass near his fingers. "It was time for me to leave. I had fancied myself in love, but the lady was newly married and there were things I had vowed to do."

"What things?"

He turned and flopped down on his back. She wasn't sure whether he was ignoring the question or just thinking about it. "My family and the villagers had been butchered by a small troop of Norman soldiers a few years after the Conquest. The two men in command instigated the bloodshed and they enjoyed it all. It is a custom of my people that murdered souls be avenged by the living and I vowed I would.'' His voice betrayed no emotion.

''And have you?'' Her words were almost a whisper.

''Not yet,'' came his stark reply. ''One of the murderers still lives.''

Madselin digested this information in silence. Edwin would certainly make a formidable enemy. Even his eyes were frightening. She nodded. ''And do you still love her, this lady?''

He moved his head so that he could look at her without the sun shining in his eyes. ''She is happy with her husband and I am content for her.'' He did not answer her question, but then she had no right to pry.

For a while a companionable silence existed between them and Madselin did not wish to disturb it. Suddenly Edwin sat up and reached for a water-skin. ''Are you thirsty enough for some ale?'' He handed it to her without awaiting her reply.

It was a bitter brew and her facial expression must have informed him of her opinion. ''This is awful,'' she spluttered as she valiantly swallowed the mouthful

Edwin raised his eyebrows and sighed. ''Aye, but it's all there is. No wonder we peasants all look so dangerous.''

It was an attempt at humour. Madselin stared up at him in amazement, and then she smiled. ''Clearly this is Lady de Vaillant's secret recipe for keeping you all under control.''

He smiled back and Madselin suddenly found her heart beating more quickly. Whatever was the matter with her? ''On the other hand,'' she added slowly, ''I could be persuaded to look into the matter. My ale was well regarded by our peasants.'' Now, why on earth did she say that? She had no interest in doing anything for these people.

She wasn't sure, but her words did appear to interest him. "And what form would this persuasion take?" His eyes had an intense look. Clearly the ale was important to him. Madselin smiled softly to herself and sighed. Men didn't differ much after all.

"Regular visits to the beach," she announced after a moment. "Providing it is safe, of course."

Edwin laughed then. He took another swig of the ale and then looked at her. "You're very easy to please, my lady. For a Norman."

His use of her title made her cheeks grow a little warm. "Am I? Alice—my sister-in-marriage—never seemed to think so." She rolled on to her stomach and flicked at the sand on her cloak.

"Alice sounds a most interesting woman." He closed his eyes and placed his hands behind his head.

"Many men seem to agree with you," she retorted without thinking. "She is a very beautiful woman."

She glanced at him and could have sworn that his lips twitched at that rather bitter response.

"But she does not see to the ale?"

Madselin laughed at that. The man was driven purely by very simple needs. She shook her head. "Fortunately not. My sister-in-marriage was not…well trained in the more useful tasks of running a manor."

"And you were," he stated quietly.

"Yes. I was betrothed to a wealthy man and expected naturally to run his manor." Madselin could not keep the sadness from her voice.

"He is dead?" Edwin's eyes remained firmly closed.

"Aye. Murdered."

The crashing of the waves echoed in the silence.

"Did you love him?"

Suddenly embarrassed that she was having so intimate a conversation with an Englishman, Madselin found she could not tell him. "It was a long time ago," she replied briskly.

"And does Alice approve of your latest betrothed?"

It was a strange question that Madselin was loathe to answer. She did not really wish to examine why that was. "No. She does not. Alice wanted me to marry a much older, more suitable man. A widower thrice over."

Edwin sat up, his fair hair fanned about his shoulders. "I cannot imagine what an elderly widower would want with you?"

"Indeed," she responded, more than a little taken aback by his disparagement. "You and Alice would appear to have more in common than I had at first suspected."

His laugh echoed around the dunes and it was most attractive. Despite her ill humour at his reply, Madselin found the corner of her mouth lifting.

"You mistake me, Lady de Breuville. But I have no doubt that an old man would be more interested in a quiet widow, content to spend her days at his side. You do not, in all honesty, strike me as a woman content to sit anywhere quietly."

"No," she conceded. "But it is hard to hold your tongue when you are responsible for so many people, so many things, and then regarded as…" Her hand went to her mouth. What was she saying? "I mean…of course…"

Before she could finish off her sentence, Madselin found herself squashed effectively under Edwin's body.

"Stay down," he hissed. "And say naught. Riders approach."

Her heart thumped loudly as the Angle slid his entire body the length of hers—and presumably more. He felt warm, hard and heavy all at the same time. Never in her life had she been so close to a man. His fresh forest smell enveloped her.

"Can you see them?" she whispered anxiously. It was a desperate attempt to divert her attention from the feel of his body, not to mention her fear.

"Aye," he replied eventually. "If I am not mistaken, they are Orvell's men."

Madselin could feel his breath against her cheek.

Slowly he reached across her to feel for his bow and arrows. She closed her eyes and her fingers dug deep into the sand.

The muttering of deep voices lingered in the distance, but Madselin could not interpret what they were saying. After a while, the sound trailed away and she exhaled slowly.

Edwin did not move. Their legs were entangled and his chest and arms had completely covered her. She ignored the feeling of security he had generated and concentrated on her fear.

"Have they gone?" she demanded in a hiss.

"Aye," came the soft reply in her ear. For a moment, Madselin shivered with the feeling he evoked. Whatever he had done, she had liked it.

Slowly she turned her head to look into his eyes. "Much as I appreciate your protection, I think it would be best if you moved."

His mouth was very close to hers and she could not help but stare at it. Slowly he lifted his chest and turned her to face him. Madselin was suddenly very aware of his hard body and the softening expression in his eyes.

"I was wrong," he murmured, his eyes roving over her face.

"How so?" was all she could manage.

"There is much that an old man could see in you." It was his turn to stare at her mouth.

Their eyes locked and Madselin found herself drowning in the real warmth of his eyes. Had she not seen it before?

Gathering her wits, she smiled at him wryly. "Do you think of your ale, Angle?"

He pushed himself up with a reluctant grin. "I think you are beginning to understand us barbarians after all."

Madselin took his hand and allowed him to pull her to her feet. They had crossed a barrier, and it felt surprisingly good.

"Did you hear what they said?" She pulled her hair from her face and attempted to right her dishevelled headrail.

Edwin shook his head. "Only partly. It was difficult to hear. I was…distracted."

Madselin frowned. "This is not the time to allow your mind to wander," she admonished sternly and strode off in the direction of the manor.

"He is handsome, is he not?" Isabella's bright eyes shone up at her.

Madselin appeared to consider this outrageous suggestion for a while. "Yes, if you like that sort of thing."

For all her weakness, Isabella managed a fairly healthy snort. "If I was ten years younger and unwed, then I would not be wasting my time on some Norman peacock."

Stung, Madselin stared at Isabella in reproach. "Hugh is no peacock. He is handsome and good." It sounded

even to her own ears if she was trying to convince herself.

"Then why is he still unwed?" The button eyes refused to lower, and Madselin attributed her ravings to the
fever.

"Because he is a younger son with three brothers before him." She looked away at the fire. Isabella was being most obtuse. "Think how it will be for Philippe with
eight brothers before him."

Isabella merely sighed and waved her lovely hand.
"That's different."

"Well, I don't see it. Besides, my brother is allowing
me a good manor for my dowry."

"Is he indeed?" Isabella's tone was almost defiant.
"That explains it."

"Explains what?" Madselin glared at the older woman
with unforgiving eyes.

"You want that manor?" Isabella's eyes challenged
hers.

Her cheeks flared. "I couldn't care less about the
manor. It's Hugh I want."

"Why?"

Madselin thought carefully for a moment. He had a
handsome face, an attractive manner and a sensitivity towards others that was not usual in a man. "I like him,"
she said simply. "We deal well together." For some reason, the grip of strong hands and a warm body came into
her mind. She rejected them completely. "Anyway, if
Edwin Elwardson is so worthy, then why is he not wed?"

Isabella raised her hands and then allowed them to
drop. Really, she had the most dramatic ways for so sensible a woman! "He fancies himself in love with Ghislaine de Courcy still. I doubt it's true, of course. Men are
easily persuaded to change their minds."

Exasperated, Madselin raised her voice. "I have no interest in the Angle and I intend to return to Normandy and hope to marry Hugh de Montchalon." Her lips compressed. "Or do you find me wanting?"

"No," said Isabella wearily. "It's not that." Her lips broke their granite expression. "I like you both and I think you suit one another. It would, of course, be very convenient for me if you decided you were suited. That's all."

"He's an Angle peasant," Madselin argued. "We have nothing at all in common."

"He is no peasant. He is of noble Angle stock and I doubt that he will remain impoverished for long. Your kinsman is tardy, that is all. Mark my words, Edwin will be rewarded in the spring."

"You're impossible," replied Madselin with a shake of the head.

Whilst Isabella de Vaillant found her body required increasing amounts of rest, Madselin took on more and more of the running of the manor. True to her word, she instigated her recipe for ale and all the men seemed to be awaiting the new batch with baited breath. All, that is, except Ulf.

The chieftain appeared to have taken Madselin in dislike and, whenever in his vicinity, she tried to ignore him. It wasn't always easy. However, wherever Madselin was, Emma was sure to follow, and Ulf seemed to take this occurrence as God-given. Emma had other ideas.

"Stupid Saxon lummox," she would mutter beneath her breath as he watched her with lust-filled, reproachful eyes. He would draw his thick set body to its impressive height and then leer in what he presumably considered a winning smile. Emma would merely glare at him before returning to the tasks in hand. Madselin was rewarded with the usual scowl as he lumbered on his way.

From the vehemence of the oaths he was uttering, Madselin was not at all sure that Ulf was going to put up with this situation for long.

She noticed that seemingly acquiescent women muttered quietly in that strange language, clearly so that she could not understand if she did hear them. Madselin felt irritation towards them and towards herself. Isabella would have understood them so they would never have done it whilst she was around.

Madselin compressed her lips. Hadn't she always maintained that it was a dreadful tongue and not worthy of her attention? She flushed at her own arrogance. It was no good, she decided. If she was to get anywhere, she would have to learn to speak a few words.

Joanna was happy to oblige. Her eyes twinkled with a rather knowing glance when Madselin made her request. "Exactly who is it you wish to speak to?" she enquired casually.

"Anyone," she snapped. "Did it take you long to learn?"

Joanna shrugged. "Blanche and I were only young when we came to live here. When my mother married Ulf, we lived in the village with the others. It seems like I've always spoken it."

"*Your* mother married Ulf?" Madselin repeated in surprise.

Joanna laughed at her expression, clearly expecting such a response. "He is much gentler than he appears," she teased. The smile quickly gave way to a frown. "I think he is lonely though, and it makes him bad-tempered. Blanche's behaviour does not please him, but he is not sure how to deal with her."

She fleetingly met Madselin's eye and flushed. "She doesn't mean to be bad, lady, but she's had a passion for Edwin for some time."

"Aye, well, perhaps it is about time I discussed the matter with Lady de Vaillant. Blanche is causing too much disruption."

Joanna nodded and turned to go. Just as she reached the door, she turned. "There was…" she began hesitantly. "She gets on well with one of the Norman guards who came here with you."

Madselin inclined her head to think. "Aye, I've seen her talking to one of them quite often. The handsome one with the dark hair?"

Joanna nodded. "Antoine." She smiled timidly, unsure of Madselin's reaction. "He would marry her, I think."

Edwin seemed to absent himself more than ever, clearly aware that he was the focus of the problem. Whenever Blanche was near him, her blue eyes were fixed soulfully on his stern face. If he noticed, Edwin gave no indication but would attempt to escape at the earliest opportunity. Had Madselin not found the situation awkward, she would have found it all very amusing.

One evening, after the meal was finished, Edwin requested a private conversation with Madselin. The solar was quiet and relatively cool after the noise and heat of the great hall, and it was a relief to escape. Madselin waited for him in silence, sensing that he was trying to find the words.

He gave her a tight smile. "There has been a problem…with one of the women," he began hesitantly. "It seems to be getting worse, and I wondered… I wondered…if you might have some advice." Edwin's cheeks were pink with embarrassment and his large frame moved nervously on the hard seat. His strong fingers fiddled with a loose thread on his tunic and a thick swathe of his hair had escaped from its braid to hide half of his lowered face.

Madselin knew that her patient expression was hardly encouraging, but then the problem, of course, was of his own making.

"It's Blanche." His tone betrayed a certain amount of irritation.

"May I ask the nature of the problem?" Madselin smiled benignly in what she hoped was a fair imitation of Alice's most condescending expression.

Edwin lifted his head and pushed his hair back from his face. She could see that he was frowning and his lips were drawn in a tight line. "She will not leave me alone," he said finally.

Their eyes held for a moment, and Madselin was surprised to see in Edwin's normally cold expression something much more human. This was a genuine request for help, and she was not hard enough to refuse him.

She nodded. "What have you said to her?"

His broad shoulders shrugged lightly. "That I cannot marry her and will not take her as my woman. She chooses not to understand me and seems to think I will change my mind."

"Blanche is an attractive woman," Madselin said slowly. "Many men would be flattered by her attention."

He nodded in resignation. "Aye, that's true enough, but I am not free." Edwin's grey eyes stared at her, almost willing her to understand his position.

"Did you ever encourage her to think this was not the case?" she asked. The man had a reputation for womanising and it was clearly well deserved.

"Nay. She always knew that I wished to remain free."

However he put it, his words sounded callous to Madselin. "That's very convenient for you, of course," she retorted tartly. "But it does seem as though you were the main beneficiary of your arrangement." With little thought for Joanna and her child either. Madselin frowned deeper.

"What arrangement?" he asked in a bewildered whisper.

Madselin's cheeks burned. The wretch surely did not think she was going to discuss his seduction of Blanche as if this were the sort of proper conversation ladies had all the time? She glared at him.

"I do not propose to talk about your relationship— proper or otherwise—with Blanche. Her behaviour as a result of your deplorable treatment, understandable though it is, does concern me, however. I suggest that we restrict our discussion to this in future."

Edwin looked at her, his eyes narrowing. "I did not lie with her, if that's what you mean." There was no warmth to his voice now.

"That is not what Blanche says." She stared at him defiantly.

Her words sank in. "So you knew?" He looked at her with flinty eyes, his anger growing.

She lifted her chin, but did not comment. He would draw his own conclusions.

Edwin raked his hand through his hair and shook his head. "Well, Lady de Breuville? Since you have such vast experience at running a manor, have you any advice?"

"Yes." Her tone was crisp. "I have a husband in mind for her, but I require your cooperation."

The anger died in his eyes, to be replaced by curiosity and not a little surprise. "Who?"

"One of the Norman guards. Antoine." Madselin paused as he went through a mental roll-call of the men. "I have spoken with him and with Lady de Vaillant. He is keen to wed Blanche and Lady de Vaillant will allow the match. Joanna assures me that Ulf will present no problem when the time comes." She offered him a tight, superior smile.

If she had expected amazed delight, then Madselin was to be disappointed. A deep frown marred his tanned brow. "And what exactly is my part in this?"

Ignoring his menacing tone, Madselin smoothed out some of the creases in her gown. "In my vast experience," she began, echoing Edwin's sarcastic words, "it is usually best to be quite harsh." She shot him an assessing glance. "Blanche is under the impression that you find my wealth and nobility a real attraction. It might," she hurried on to say as his face darkened, "be a good idea to convince her she is right."

"Nay. I'll have naught to do with Normans." His words were uncompromisingly final.

"I thought you needed assistance?" Madselin's tone was steely. "You need not worry that I shall take any of your overtures seriously, if that is what concerns you."

Edwin stood up and pushed around some of the floor rushes with his toe. As Madselin watched him she was reminded of one of the young pages who was constantly torn between his duty and his desire for adventure.

"You would, of course, need to explain to Joanna."

"Joanna?" His frown deepened.

"Aye. She should know." Madselin was confused by his lack of concern for these women. He truly was a heartless brute.

He rubbed the back of his neck before turning to her and watching her with a strangely intent look. ''I'll do it, but I care not for the plan.''

For someone whose actions had got him into this mess, Edwin seemed very graceless. Madselin rose and was just on the point of telling him so when she found herself roughly pulled against his chest and kissed with a thoroughness she had never before experienced.

Breathless, Madselin pushed herself away from him. His solemn grey eyes were not on her but fixed on a point beyond her shoulder.

Madselin whirled round to find Blanche's white face staring up at her. Just as she was about to utter calming words, she felt a large hand on her shoulder and Edwin came to stand close behind. It was a very eloquent gesture that was not lost on Blanche.

Blanche's jaw gritted tightly as her eyes fixed on the tanned fingers gently stroking Madselin's shoulder. With as much dignity as she could muster, Blanche picked up her gown and marched from the room.

Edwin turned Madselin gently around. Wordlessly he adjusted her headrail that had come awry during their kiss. ''Perhaps you were right,'' he said quietly, his grey eyes roving over her blushing face. ''It could prove a most effective plan.''

Dropping a final soft kiss on her lips, Edwin sauntered casually from the room. Madselin dropped back onto her seat. What had she done?

Chapter Seven

Isabella lay motionless on her bed. Madselin could tell from her laboured breathing that something was amiss although it was obvious she had been dosed heavily with syrup of poppies. Agnes sat quietly at her side in vigil, gently dabbing her colourless face with a damp rag. As soon as Madselin stepped forward, Agnes rose and hobbled towards her. Her narrow, flinty eyes gleamed with a suspicious brightness.

Alarmed to find the usually diffident Agnes so distressed, Madselin tried to form her questions in the Angle tongue. It was very hard, but with help from Isabella's woman and an impressive number of gestures, the two women managed to communicate. Isabella was weak and in pain, and it seemed that the child was not in the right position but wanted to make an early appearance.

Madselin approached Isabella silently and took over wiping her face. The grey streaks under her eyes had become dark smudges and her lips were almost as bloodless as the rest of her face.

Sighing, Madselin looked across the bed at Agnes. There was nothing more she could do for Isabella either and her fate rested in God's hands. Few women came through such an ordeal to nurse their babe. Had not the miller's wife, a strapping mother of six, succumbed to just the same fate last Yuletide? Madselin's eyes roved over her bloated body in pity before turning once more to Agnes.

"Is there no one who can help at all?" she asked quietly. The other woman translated. Agnes sucked on her toothless gums and then slowly nodded her head. Her dry, cracked voice mumbled several words whilst her eyes remained on Isabella's sleeping face.

"She says that there is a woman, although she is not from here. Lady de Vaillant does not approve of her, but Agnes thinks that only her skills can save the lady and her child."

"Where is this woman?" Madselin asked quickly. "Can you take me to her?"

After a few words, the woman turned to Madselin, her expression gloomy. "The woman's name is Bronwen. She lives to the north of here, near Orvell's keep."

Agnes and Madselin stared at each other for a moment and then back at Isabella. "I will see what I can do."

"But my lady…" Isabella's woman grabbed Madselin by the arm "…you cannot go there…"

Madselin shook her arm free. "I will do what has to be done to save two lives." With one last glance at Isabella, Madselin strode from the room.

Edwin was out with the patrol and was not expected back until at least two days hence. He had received a report about strange activities to the north and had gone to investigate. Madselin had noted that there was a look of grim relief etched over his face as he had lead the men through the gates. There was not time enough to send a messenger to him since the matter was urgent.

Two men had been left in charge of affairs at the keep in his absence. Antoine commanded the Norman men-at-arms whilst Ulf concerned himself with the Angle contingent, such as it was. Madselin knew that the only one who could really help her was Ulf.

The church was bitterly cold but the strong smell of burning candles and the lingering smell of rushes and incense were comforting. Father Padraig was kneeling before the tiny altar, his head bent in supplication. Sensing that he was not alone, the priest turned.

"Good morning, Lady Madselin. A willing soul is a rare sight!"

"I am sorry to disappoint you, Father, but I have come to ask your advice. Lady de Vaillant is very ill and Agnes is not hopeful of her survival. Her only hope is a woman called Bronwen who lives to the north of here."

"Aye, I know of her, to be sure," he said uncertainly. "Her skills are well known."

There was a deep frown on his kind face that caused Madselin a moment's hesitation. "But you do not approve of her?"

Father Padraig inhaled deeply, his hands clasped behind his back. He considered Madselin steadily before turning his eyes towards the wooden cross. "She is not of the faith," he said abruptly. There was a pause. "But I daresay her love of gold would ensure her full attention."

Madselin's eyes widened at such assessment. "Not of the faith?" she repeated dumbly. "Is that why Isabella's woman was so against her?" Isabella's piety was of the strictest nature.

The priest nodded. "Aye, to be sure it is. But the good Lord has put her on the earth for a reason and I'm not about to stand in your way if you think she's able to save Lady de Vaillant.''

Madselin nodded. She would have to take the risk. ''Edwin is out on patrol and I will need an escort to get the woman. Ulf does not appear to approve of me and I wondered if you might…help me to persuade him.''

He smiled bleakly. ''You'll not need to persuade the man if it's to help Lady Isabella. But come. I'll explain for you.''

A soft wind gusted around the village huts and brought with it the smell of rain. Madselin stepped carefully around the puddles in the bailey as she and the priest headed for Ulf's abode. Larger than the rest, his hut stood proudly in the centre of the village. A thin trail of smoke threaded its way from the hole in the thatch. After no more than a brief tap at the door, Father Padraig entered the gloom within. Madselin followed warily.

Ulf was sitting before a well-banked fire, his craggy face creased in concentration as he whittled a piece of wood. A pile of roughly hewn arrows lay scattered at his feet, awaiting tips and feathers. Isabella's two young sons, Charles and Benedict, sat close by, watching him with rapt attention. Ulf was clearly their hero.

Ulf's eyes flicked over his visitors for a second before returning to scrutinise the stick in his hand. They were in a lofty room with beautifully carved rafters and a large table. Leather-bound shields and evil-looking spears adorned the walls. Madselin shivered despite the warmth from the fire.

The two men engaged in a desultory-sounding conversation which Madselin found hard to understand. Irritatingly, Ulf tended to mumble his words into his beard. Some parts of their discussion were perhaps best left unintelligible anyway. Every so often, Ulf's blue eyes would settle on her and then move back to his knife. At one point he shook his head slowly and spat viciously into the floor rushes. Bronwen's reputation was well known, it seemed.

Eventually, after several harsh-sounding utterances, Ulf wiped his knife against his thick breeches and placed it carefully in a sheath at his waist. Standing slowly, he turned to Madselin and nodded, muttering a few words which sounded like an agreement.

Madselin managed a brief smile and looked towards the priest. "He'll do it?" she asked hopefully.

"To be sure he will," came the reply. "His bark is far worse than his bite and we'll be safe enough with him."

"We?" Madselin frowned. At this rate there'd be more people traipsing about the land than in the keep.

"Aye. You're not thinking I'd be letting a young innocent girl like yourself go gallivanting around the country without some spiritual support?" Father Padraig looked most put out. "Besides, you might need to persuade Bronwen with more than a bit of gold."

"Oh. I see." She wasn't at all sure that she did see, but the thought of the Father being close by was some relief. "Very well. How long will it take before we can set off?"

After a moment or two of hurried discussion, it appeared that Ulf could gather an escort of his men within a candle notch. Madselin nodded and hurried to the keep. She had much to organise.

Gripping her hood tight round her face, Madselin tried to protect herself from the driving rain strong sea-wind snatched at her cloak and froze her blood as they raced along the coastal path.

After a time, Ulf slowed the pace and turned the party inland towards the forest. The horses' hooves sank deep into the mud as they tramped stoically further north. Beyond the forest, far in the distance, Madselin occasionally caught a glimpse of the towering wild hills whose peaks already boasted a covering of snow.

Father Padraig nodded towards a steep hill about an hour's ride hence. "Bronwen's village lies on the other side of that hill. Let's hope God is with us and she still lives there."

That thought hadn't even crossed her mind. "Is she old?" Madselin realised she knew nothing about this woman either.

The priest shook his head. "Bronwen has a liking for gold, men and usquebaugh. She's left the village many times on account of all of the three."

A delicate flush on her cheeks was the only sign that Madselin had heard the words. No wonder Isabella did not approve! However, it seemed the woman was the only hope. Stiffening her back, Madselin resolved to bring Bronwen back, no matter what.

Straight ahead, at the top of a steep, rocky incline stood a large, grey keep. It menaced the skyline and robbed the valley of its peace. This must be Orvell's keep.

The village was no more than a ragged collection of tumbledown huts huddled around a makeshift-looking church. When they reached the church, Madselin and the priest dismounted, leaving the escort to glower at the three impoverished inhabitants who had gathered about. Feeling very conspicuous, Madselin followed Father Padraig to the very last hut, where, he had been informed by a suspicious old man, Bronwen still resided.

Despite its dark interior, Bronwen's hut boasted several lavish touches. There were beeswax candles instead of the tallow most peasants used, several woollen wall hangings and a handsome, carved stool close to the fire. On the table stood a jug of wine and several cups.

Although grubby, the hut appeared cleaner and sweeter smelling than other such places and Madselin was intrigued. Bronwen was clearly a woman of some standing. At the far end of the hut lay a simple wooden pallet bearing a mattress and soft coverings that Madselin herself would be proud to own. Next to the pallet was a beautiful wooden chest.

"What do you want?" The words were spoken in heavily accented Norman French.

Madselin whirled round to find herself confronted by a tall, slender woman with long dark hair outlined in the doorway. Suspicious brown eyes raked over her and Father Padraig before the woman sauntered inside to the table and poured herself a cup of the wine. Ignoring the deliberate insult, Madselin forced herself to smile.

"We are here to request your assistance." Her gaze did not flinch from the woman's bold stare. "Lady de Vaillant is in need of your skills and Agnes has sent me to see you. You are the only one who can save her and her baby."

The woman had an almost feral look about her, which was enhanced by the soft brown colour of her skin. She walked with the lightness of a cat, moving with fluid grace towards the fire. Still holding the cup of wine, Bronwen sat down on the stool and stared into the fire.

"Why should I help? Isabella de Vaillant has been no friend of mine."

Madselin unlaced a pouch of coins from her kirtle. "I have this for you."

Bronwen glanced across at the offering and flicked her long, unbraided hair back over her shoulders. "I have no need of your gold,'' came the bored reply. ''What is there to spend it on here?'' Her gaze returned to the flames whilst she stretched out and pushed open her cloak. It revealed a red woollen gown tied at the waist with a golden kirtle. Riches indeed for a peasant.

Madselin frowned. She had not expected a blatant refusal of the gold. ''Is there something else that would bring you to the de Vaillant keep?'' she asked finally. Anger would not help, despite her true feelings.

Bronwen's soft laughter filled the hut. It was a beautiful sound, like a young girl's—although Bronwen herself must be of a similar age to herself. ''Have you a handsome, rich man for me? A keep of my own?'' A soft sigh escaped her full lips and Madselin was certain she glimpsed the longings of a very lonely woman.

Madselin shook her head. ''Helping the lady would bring you friendship,'' she ventured.

Her words were greeted with a look of intense scorn. ''What need have I of friendship? Does not every woman around turn to me in their hour of need?''

Father Padraig raked his hand through his dark hair. ''Will you not come to help her, woman?'' His eyes held hers for a moment. In that brief space of time, Madselin caught the change in the atmosphere between them. Something had gripped the both of them and they were pulled along in its wake.

''What goes on here?'' A loud voice addressed them from the door. All three turned at the same time.

''My lord?'' Bronwen's question held a certain edge to it, making it clear that their relationship was more than peasant and master.

The man was tall and very slender. Thick brown hair swept back from a broad brow and hung in waves around his shoulders. The grey locks at his temples softened the

effect of his dark clothing and Madselin estimated his
age at about two score years. His body, however, could
have belonged to a much younger man. There was no
evidence of the over-indulgence in ale, wine and meat so
many of her brother's friends enjoyed. Soft grey eyes
glared at them.

"My lord," managed the priest after a moment's hesitation. He turned to Madselin. "I beg to introduce you
to a guest of Lady de Vaillant. This is Lady de Breuville,
recently arrived from Normandy and kinswoman to Richard d'Aveyron."

White teeth gleamed when he smiled and Madselin
found herself responding in kind. "Henry Orvell, my
lady de Breuville. It is a great pleasure to meet such a
charming visitor in so…unexpected a place." Stepping
forward, he gently lifted her hand to his lips and place a
gentle kiss on her fingertips.

Confusion flooded Madselin. So this handsome,
charming man was the ruthless Henry Orvell? Surely
someone so obviously cultured and gentle could not be
guilty of the crimes Edwin believed him to be? "It is an
honour, my lord." She smiled up at his frankly admiring
eyes. "I hope you do not take offence at our presence
here, but my Lady de Vaillant is in urgent need of Bronwen's help."

Reluctantly he let her hand go and stepped back. Casting no more than a brief glance in Bronwen's direction,
Henry Orvell nodded. "She will go with you. Take whatever you need and keep her as long as is necessary. My
thoughts will remain with Lady de Vaillant this night."

Ignoring Bronwen's gasp of outrage, he indicated to
Madselin that he wished to step outside. Father Padraig
remained inside to help Bronwen. Madselin noticed the
old man still watching them. His eyes followed Orvell

like a hawk. For a moment, she was certain she could see hatred burning there with the fear.

"That is most generous of you, my lord," she said, breathing deeply of the fresh air.

"No. The pleasure is all mine, I assure you. It is not often I get the chance to be of assistance to a beautiful young maiden in distress." His eyes regarded her with amusement. "We are somewhat isolated in this place. Few ladies venture this far."

"Nevertheless, we remain in your debt. Lady de Vaillant is a good woman. There would be much sorrow if aught were to happen to her."

"Just so." Henry Orvell smiled, revealing his perfect teeth. "Father Padraig tells me you are kin to Richard d'Aveyron. What brings you here?" He turned to her and folded his arms across his chest, surveying her carefully.

Madselin hesitated for no more than a few seconds. "I had come to visit Lady de Vaillant since she is needful of another woman at such a time."

Henry said nothing, merely smiling and rubbing his beard with his hand. "It must have been most vexing to find your kinsman leave so suddenly."

"Aye, but I was glad to be of help. I am used to running my brother's manor in Normandy." Madselin brushed a few spots of dust from her cloak. Whatever was the matter with her? Her tongue was running away with her.

"De Breuville? De Breuville?" he murmured the name almost to himself. "The name is most familiar, but I am sure I would remember having met you before."

"Oh, no. I do not recall having met you. You are mistaken," she replied quickly.

He stilled suddenly and looked at her. "Were you once

betrothed to Guy de Chambertin? Forgive me for such a question, but he and I were once very close…''

Madselin could feel her blood change to ice when Orvell mentioned Guy's name. ''Yes,'' she responded in almost a whisper. ''He was killed on our wedding day.''

''Then you are Madselin?'' He moved closer to her and placed a hand gently on her arm. ''Guy used to tell me so much about you.''

''When did you know him?'' Madselin was grateful that her voice sounded close to normal.

''We were together on campaign in the north of England. Many is the night we spent talking of the future.''

Madselin found herself warming to this gentle man who seemed to know much about Guy. He had rarely spoken about his early days on campaign in England. She sighed softly. ''I know so few of his friends,'' she confided. ''It is nice to be able to talk to someone who knew him well.''

''I am sorry,'' he said, his eyes concerned. ''This must be a most distressing conversation for you.''

''Not at all, my lord.'' Madselin smiled. She was certain that Edwin was wrong about him. ''It does me good to talk of him. Guy is not forgotten.''

Orvell inclined his head. ''Then you must be my guest at the keep. When Lady de Vaillant recovers, of course.''

Touched by his sensitivity, Madselin would have liked to have accepted his invitation. ''I'm sorry. Lady de Vaillant insists we stay close to the keep for fear of attack from the Scots. I should not be here now, were it not for the emergency.''

The grey eyes flickered over her once again. ''Aye, well, you can't be too careful.'' He hesitated. ''However, I am not sure Lady de Vaillant is quite correct in her assumptions. The Scots are not our enemy at the moment. I fear the danger lies closer to home.''

''Oh?'' Madselin looked at him askance. ''Who is our enemy if not the Scots?''

Orvell turned to stare up at his keep. ''I am informed that a band of renegade Angles and Saxons plan an insurrection in this area. So far my...investigations have proved fruitless, but I believe they are led by a man who may be known to you.'' He paused to let his words sink in. ''I can prove nothing as yet, but I have eyes and ears in many places.''

''Who is this man?'' Madselin could feel her heart in her throat.

''Edwin Elwardson.''

''Are you sure?'' She could barely get the words out.

He shrugged his broad shoulders. ''Positive. But he is a clever man and will twist events to suit himself. He is most credible and very dangerous.''

Madselin remained silent, trying to make something of this new information. Her mind had gone completely numb.

''I speak to you for your own protection, Lady de Breuville. You must inform no one else or he may escape.''

Bemused by all that he had said, Madselin managed only a nod. Perhaps her first instincts had been right all along?

''When you have no further need of Bronwen, escort her back with the men and visit me.'' His grey eyes were soft and pleading.

''I will try.'' Madselin could only form a weak smile. Her throat was tight and raw, and nausea threatened.

Chapter Eight

It was a measure of his regard for Isabella de Vaillant that Ulf harried them back to the keep before the night clouds had rolled in from the sea. His harsh tongue chided men, women and priest alike if they failed to keep up or do his bidding.

Madselin had been surprised at the man's loyalty since she had not expected it of so uncouth a Saxon. Whatever his reasons, she was grateful to him.

The party audibly sighed with relief as they thundered through the gates of the keep. A babble of voices surged towards them once Ulf had drawn to a halt. Bronwen, who had doubled up behind him, sprang from her imprisonment like a wild cat with a fire on her tail. Ulf had clearly made a strong impression on her.

Madselin watched Bronwen as she stared around her, drinking in the sight of the keep and the strength of the people.

It struck her then that Bronwen was a most dangerous weapon in Henry Orvell's hands, if he was indeed the monster that Edwin believed him to be. He had offered Bronwen's services without a second thought, either because he wanted to help or because he intended to make use of whatever she could find out.

Madselin had spent the hours in the saddle between Orvell's keep and the de Vaillant keep deliberating the problem. How could Guy have befriended a traitor? Henry Orvell had seemed so good and honest that it was truly hard to think him evil. And yet he had named Edwin a traitor in turn.

Madselin rubbed her throbbing head. Despite her hatred of the English race, too many people she did trust held Edwin Elwardson in high esteem. She would have to tread carefully.

Bronwen halted before Isabella's door, almost as if she were afraid to enter. "What will happen to me if she dies?" she demanded, flicking her hair over her shoulder.

Madselin stared at her. "Nothing," she replied indignantly and pushed the door open.

Agnes looked up as they entered the chamber and put her fingers to her lips. At least Isabella was asleep.

The heat from the fire was overwhelming and Bronwen carelessly tossed her fine cloak onto the rushes before moving closer to the bed.

Bronwen murmured a few questions in the local tongue as she gently examined Isabella. Agnes shook her head mostly and sucked on her toothless gums. Madselin surmised that Isabella had not improved.

Pulling back the covers on the bed, the woman placed deft brown fingers on Isabella's swollen belly. Lowering her head to her fingers, she listened to the sounds of the baby for several minutes. Madselin could hear only the fire crackling and the neighing of horses in the bailey.

Slowly, Bronwen righted herself and moved her hands gently over Isabella. Her face was unreadable as she replaced the covers. Without a word, she sauntered to the table and poured herself a goblet of wine. Madselin and Agnes watched her, half-fascinated, half-angry that she could keep them waiting so.

Wiping her mouth with her sleeve, Bronwen turned to face them. "I warn you now that I can do nothing for your lady. She will not live beyond this night and no earthly power can save her." The harsh words echoed round the hot room. Madselin could do no more than stare at her and then at Isabella.

"You lie," she hissed finally. "There must be something you can do."

Eyes darker than her own bored into her. "I can do something for the child, but that depends on you." Bronwen turned to look at the sleeping woman. "Your lady is all but dead. Only her willpower keeps her alive. If I act now, the child may survive."

"What can you do?" Her words came out in a whisper as Madselin felt a surge of frozen blood rush through her.

Isabella murmured something unintelligible, drawing all eyes to her. It was impossible to believe that she was dying.

"The child would never survive the birthing," Bronwen stated simply. She sat down on the edge of the pallet and softly began to wipe Isabella's gaunt face. "To cut the child free now would be the only way it could live."

"That would kill Isabella!" The horror of the situation washed over Madselin. It had to be a lie!

Bronwen picked up Isabella's hand and drew tiny circles on her palm. "There is no other way," she reiterated softly. "It is her fate. You must decide within the hour. Beyond that, they will both be dead."

Isabella's eyelids flickered open. Dull brown eyes turned up to Bronwen and made their assessment before rounding on Madselin. "Save the child," she muttered faintly. "You must save the child."

Drawing closer to Isabella, Madselin took a cold hand in hers. "You will not die, Isabella. You are too strong."

Isabella de Vaillant summoned all her remaining strength to form her granite smile. "The woman is right, Madselin. I order you to save the child." Then, turning to look at Bronwen, she gripped her arm. "I give you my life for hers. You must keep her safe. Stay with her."

For moments their eyes locked and Madselin felt they were in another world. This was something between the two women that excluded all other beings. Yet it did not make any sense to Madselin.

Bronwen, however, seemed to understand perfectly. "Do not make me responsible," she cried out. "I did not want to come." She would have stood, but Isabella still had hold of her arm and gripped it even tighter.

"You cannot refuse," came the implacable reply. "Now send me the priest."

Whilst Father Padraig was closeted with Isabella and Agnes, Madselin took Bronwen to the still room to make the necessary preparations. For all her wild and sluttish appearance, Bronwen was neat and efficient in her dealings with the herbs and potions. Finally, she took a small knife from the leather pouch at her waist and unsheathed it. The blade glimmered in the soft torchlight and Madselin shivered.

"It must be sharp." Bronwen thrust it into the flames of one of the wall torches.

"Can you save her the pain?" Madselin asked quietly, watching the blade in fascination.

The woman's eyes remained on the knife. "Aye. The potion will put her into a deep sleep before her heart stops. It will be quick."

Closing her eyes, Madselin sought to quell the nausea that threatened. When she opened them again, she found Bronwen looking at her. "Where did you learn the skills you have?" she asked eventually. Everyone seemed to have much faith in her, but yet she could not put from her mind those strange reactions that Bronwen provoked in both the priest and Isabella.

With a slight shrug, Bronwen smiled and considered the heated blade before her eyes. "I watched my mother birth ten babes that I can recall. There were others," she added lightly. "When she died, I went to live with an old herbal woman who had learned her skills from her travels. She took me with her and I watched what she did. Eventually, Dunne became too old and people called for me instead."

"What exactly did Isabella mean when she said you must keep the child safe?" Madselin's question seemed suddenly loud in the quiet of the small room.

A small sigh of frustration escaped from Bronwen's pursed lips as she replaced the knife in the sheath. "It is the way of things in these parts. In taking your lady's life to save the child, I am bound to the child by the deed." Their gazes held over the table. "It is time."

Isabella de Vaillant faced death as she had faced all other challenges in her life. When Father Padraig performed the last rites, her eyes glittered with courage and determination, and she insisted on administering the fateful potion herself.

"Courage, Madselin," she whispered softly as she lay suspended between life and sleep, "Trust in Edwin. I want your word on it."

Numb with shock at the speed of events, Madselin could do no more than nod as she gripped Isabella's hand. Isabella, apparently satisfied, closed her eyes for the last time.

Maude de Vaillant entered the world silently as the lifeblood of her mother seeped away. Bronwen plucked the tiny, blood-streaked girl child from Isabella and gently placed her on her mother's still breast. Instinctively, the child seemed to know that Isabella could offer her nothing and she mewled like a new-born kitten for the hands that would give her the warmth she craved.

Almost hesitantly, Bronwen picked her up and looked down into the hazy eyes of Isabella's daughter. It was a moment when the whole world seemed to hold its breath, a moment that few women ever forgot. Maude's innocence and vulnerability wrapped themselves around Bronwen's lonely heart and pulled tight.

"I will keep you safe, child," she murmured as she gently kissed her soft black hair.

Madselin and Agnes watched in openmouthed disbelief as the untamed Bronwen sat quietly in the firelight, crooning softly to Maude. She relinquished the baby only when a wet-nurse was found to provide the nourishment for her that Bronwen could not.

Madselin could not prevent the tears from coursing down her cheeks. Isabella had given her life for her child, yet she would never know that she had given Ivo his much-wanted daughter. Nor would she ever know how beautiful her baby was.

Madselin's heart had melted the moment she saw Maude de Vaillant's vulnerable eyes and crop of black hair. When she held her for the first time, she ached with longing to hold her close for the rest of the night. She had felt the same for Alice's children too. Regretfully,

Madselin had relinquished Maude once more to Bronwen's open arms.

Giving Isabella one last sorrowing look, she thought of the three young boys who were now without a mother. They would have to be told in the morning.

Satisfied that they could do nothing more for Maude, they set about preparing Isabella's body for burial. Despite the pain that she had suffered, Isabella's face was calm and at peace and, in a strange way, Madselin found comfort in that.

When they had finished, Agnes refused to leave. It was her right, she declared in her strange tongue, to watch over her mistress through the dark hours of the night. The brown eyes of the old woman glistened with unshed tears, and Madselin nodded her assent.

She left the room quietly to go in search of Ulf. He would be the best one to tell the boys of their mother's death. They would be able to cry with him far more easily than with a stranger.

Edwin and his patrol returned to the silent keep not long after first light. Ulf's messenger had reached him quickly, but none the less he must have ridden at breakneck speed to have arrived back at such an hour.

He found Madselin sitting before the fire in the hall, her gown still bloodspattered and her face white. As he approached her, Madselin began to stand but he placed a large, strong hand on her shoulder and forced her to remain where she was.

"Ulf told me," he murmured, his grey eyes taking in her grief and her calm. Unpinning his cloak, Edwin turned to pull another stool close to Madselin's and slumped down at her side.

Madselin noticed there were raindrops sparkling in his

hair and resisted the temptation to flick them away. Instead, she busied her fingers with the end of her dishevelled braid. "I know I disobeyed your orders." Her eyes glanced at him quickly, not at all sure of his mood. "But there was no time to delay and I had to…"

Edwin raised his hand to halt her flow of increasingly gabbled words. "You did what I would have expected. There is no need to explain," he said quietly. With deliberate slowness, he placed his hand over hers, almost as if he were afraid to startle her. "Are you all right?"

His question surprised her as much as the comfort she found in his hand. "Aye." Raising her eyes to his, Madselin managed a curt nod. Fanciful though it suddenly seemed, Edwin's strong hands and the way he had placed his long body between her and the rest of the hall made Madselin feel fragile and protected. Imperceptibly, she leaned a little closer towards him and he did not move away.

"There is much to be done. I have no idea why I am just sitting here." Dragging her eyes from his, Madselin attempted to look over his shoulder, but, tall as she was, it proved impossible.

A gentle tug at her braid brought her eyes back to his. "You are tired and upset. Just admit it for once. Go rest for now." He pulled again on her braid as if to emphasise his words. "It's an order, my lady."

His face was so close that Madselin could see every bristle of the thick brown stubble on his face. Suddenly, without warning, he placed a gentle kiss on her lips and then stood up before she could say or do anything. Looking down at her from his great height, Edwin gave her shoulder a squeeze.

Madselin watched him leave, her mind reeling from his gentle treatment of her. This was surely not the same brute who was forever frowning at her or criticising her? It was, however, the same man who had kissed her so thoroughly two days before. Alerted, Madselin scoured the hall. There was no sign of Blanche. The man's behaviour was a complete mystery.

Putting his odd reaction to her to the back of her mind, Madselin rose and hurried to her chamber. She was tired and she was certainly upset. Besides, an order was an order!

Isabella was buried on sacred ground close to the edge of the coastline. It was a sombre, soul-wrenching time which drained Madselin and every member of the village. For all her bluntness and brusque words, Isabella had been respected and loved.

Beatrice had journeyed from her keep, bringing Jordan and a small army of soldiers as escort. Her kind, smiling face had been a welcome relief to Madselin as she struggled to come to terms with Isabella's fate.

"Come, now, Madselin," she soothed, as they sat before the warm fire in the solar. "You did everything humanly possible to save her. Isabella would not want you to blame yourself."

Madselin could only smile grimly. "It all seems so unfair. Isabella was strong and had borne nine sons without any problems. Why should one small daughter have caused her death?" Flicking her damp skirts above her ankles, she stretched her feet towards the hot flames and tried to bring a little warmth into her frozen blood.

Beatrice did the same. "You know," she confided very quietly, "Isabella had sensed that all was not quite right. That was one of the reasons for you being here."

Madselin turned to look at her friend. "She knew? Why did you not say anything?"

When Beatrice finally spoke, her voice was less certain. "She did not wish it and I had no desire to countermand her will. Would you?"

Visions of the strong-minded lady of this wild land floated before Madselin's eyes. Shaking her head, Madselin pushed back some loose strands of hair that had escaped from her braid. "What now, Beatrice? Have you heard from Richard?"

"Nay, but Sir Albert despatched a messenger to him and he will inform Ivo." The heavy sigh escaping her was most eloquent. "It will go hard with him."

The thought of facing Ivo de Vaillant plunged Madselin into deeper distress. He had never seemed a man of gentle manners and she greatly feared his reaction to the news of Bronwen's part in his wife's demise. "It is well that Maude is strong and healthy. At least he will have her to console himself with."

"Aye," conceded Beatrice. "Isabella did say that Ivo would be more than glad to have a daughter, if only because they were running out of relatives and friends who would take on the boys."

Madselin could just imagine Isabella making so wry a comment and smiled in response. They had already farmed out six boys as pages and squires with three more still awaiting their seventh birthdays. She had a vague recollection of Isabella telling her that her eldest son was perhaps coming home over the Yuletide festivities. She would face that event when the time came.

"Have you heard any more news of trouble in the area?" Madselin leaned forward to poke the fire with the iron pole at her feet and then sat back to watch the flames splutter and shoot up.

"Aye. Our scouts have reported much raiding and looting near the border areas, but Sir Albert fears these attacks may just be a cover. By diverting our soldiers, they have more chance of success.'' Beatrice's eyes met Madselin's in a steady gaze. ''What of Edwin?''

Madselin shrugged her shoulders as she sat back. ''The patrols have reported odd things but nothing certain as yet.'' Hesitating, she turned her head towards her friend. ''You do trust him, don't you?''

Beatrice thought for a moment, giving no sign of surprise at such a question. ''Aye. I would leave my son in his care gladly. Richard is always wont to say that Edwin is the most trustworthy of all his vassals, and he does not say that lightly.''

There was a silence whilst Beatrice waited for Madselin's reasoning behind such a question.

''Henry Orvell thinks he is stirring up trouble.''

''Orvell? You have met him?''

''Aye. Bronwen comes from his lands. He ordered her to help Isabella.'' She frowned down at her fingers, which had twisted round a loose thread on her mantle. ''He spoke of Guy. They fought together in England.''

Studying Madselin's tangled fingers, Beatrice was aware of Madselin's confusion. Their friendship was not yet so deep that she could demand to know what had happened, but she guessed that whatever had taken place had affected Madselin greatly. ''He can be very charming when he wishes,'' Beatrice responded carefully. ''Did he give any good reason for such accusations?''

Madselin shook her head. ''He has no proof yet, but believes Edwin to be the leader of some Anglo-Saxon rebels.''

''I see.'' The reply was guarded intentionally to see if it would draw Madselin out further. ''And what do you think?''

Madselin's jaw tightened and she snapped the twisted

thread from the material. "I no longer know what to think. Henry Orvell was a friend of Guy's and I cannot believe he would involve himself with someone less than honest."

"That was a long time ago and people do change, Madselin." Beatrice only voiced Madselin's own concerns, but because she echoed her misgivings she responded with more than a streak of irritation.

"Do you not think I know that?" The sharpness of the retort echoed in the silence of the room. Beatrice remained still. "Yet the last thing Isabella told me to do was to trust Edwin. It was as if she knew what had gone on."

Recognising the emotions that had prompted Madselin's outburst, Beatrice reached out her hand and placed it on Madselin's arm. "Well, then. Just place trust in Isabella's judgement and do not rush into a hasty decision about Orvell. He may be innocent, after all. The rebels could indeed be far cleverer than we imagine."

Madselin looked at the small hand on her arm and smiled. "Aye. It's as well for me that you are sensible, Beatrice."

Beatrice laughed softly. "I thought you were supposed to be the sensible one."

"So did I, but I rather think that Edwin is not of the same opinion." Madselin's humour had been replaced by a rueful sigh. "I have no idea why I even thought to question his motives, but I suppose my feelings towards the English go deep."

Beatrice picked up her cup of spiced wine and sipped at it thoughtfully. "Are you at least talking to Edwin?"

"Talking? Aye." She smiled to herself. "In fact, our relationship has developed apace." In very broad terms,

Madselin explained to Beatrice her plan to rid Edwin of Blanche.

"Do you wish me to take her back?"

Madselin shook her head. "She would never get over it then. No, we agreed to do this and hopefully Blanche will be so involved with her new husband before too long to pay much attention to him."

"Well, if you're sure?"

"Very sure," voiced Madselin, not quite certain why she felt more light-hearted than she had for days.

Beatrice and her men stayed on for several days and she gladly accepted Madselin's invitation to remain for the All Hallow's Eve celebrations. Despite the mourning period, Madselin and Beatrice had felt that the event was too important to cancel. Besides, as Beatrice and Father Padraig pointed out, Isabella had always enjoyed the festivities and would not have wanted them to be missed.

The whole village and manor house busied themselves in preparation. For a day, at least, the grimness and solemnity had lost its cruel grip on them and Madselin could feel the lifting of their spirits.

Catching sight of Bronwen hurrying towards Agnes's hut, Madselin decided she could wait no longer to find out more about Henry Orvell. It was some time before Bronwen returned, Maude gripped tightly in her arms.

Madselin had not seen much of either of them since Isabella's death and the change in Bronwen surprised her. Her hair was still long and wild, but there was a softness to her eyes that had not existed before. Instead of the tight-fitting red robe. Bronwen wore a plain mantle of soft green. It suited her far better. Maude slept contentedly in her arms. Clearly Bronwen suited her, too.

"My lady." She greeted Madselin with her customary

wariness, however, and gripped the baby tighter. It was almost as if she expected her to snatch Maude away, although that made no sense.

"Bronwen, I wonder if we might talk somewhere in private?"

"What about?" Her tone was suspicious, but Madselin supposed she had a right to be wary. Few of the villagers even acknowledged her presence. Only Agnes had shown any interest in her.

"Come to the orchard. No one is about there." Firmly Madselin led her to the orchard on the south side of the keep. It was small but enclosed and they would not be disturbed. They found a wooden bench by one of the old apple trees.

"I wish to ask you some questions."

A strong gust of wind caught Bronwen's long hair and it whipped across her face. Pushing it back, she turned to face Madselin. "About Henry Orvell." It was not a question.

"Aye."

"I have been expecting it." Bronwen stared amongst the trees and along the keep wall. "I'm not sure I have the answers you seek."

"I'll be the judge of that," replied Madselin tightly. Conscious that those words had sounded harsher than she had meant, Madselin reached out to put her finger in Maude's tiny hand. Instinctively, the delicate fingers gripped hers in an iron-strong hold. "What can you tell me of him?"

Bronwen's dark eyes held Madselin's in a cold, intense stare before dropping to watch the baby sleep in her arms. "Henry Orvell is a harsh man if you cross him."

Irritated by her reticence, Madselin frowned. "Most men are."

Bronwen shook her head and looked away into the distance. "He is not like most men. The man is evil."

Alerted by the vehemence of her words, Madselin stared at the woman and child at her side. "How is he evil?" Her words were almost a whisper.

"Orvell cares not how he achieves his own ends. If other people die, he thinks nothing of it. His men follow his example since they are too afraid to do anything else."

It was hard to believe this of the charming man she had met no more than three days before. There was more than a chance Bronwen was lying for some petty revenge. "What did he do to you?" she probed, hoping to catch her out.

"To me? He did not lay a finger on me. He had no need." Bronwen's tone was scathing. "But he had my man torn to pieces by that hound from hell he loves. He was the quarry in a manhunt."

Bronwen's sunkissed face had paled and every muscle in it was taut. Hatred poured from every inch of her.

"Manhunt? What do you mean by manhunt?" Madselin could feel the bile rising in her throat, but she had to know the truth.

"Owain was his scout and afraid of no one. Not even me," she added with a bitter smile. "Orvell and his men had been drinking and had taken it into their heads to go hunting. But this time, they decided it would be more interesting if there was a human quarry." Her cold eyes dropped to Maude, whose face was twitching as she dreamed.

"They hauled one of the village boys in from the bailey, half-dead already from fear. Only Owain stood up to them." Her eyes were shining as she gently stroked Maude's forehead.

"But there were too many of them and none of the villagers would dare lift a finger against their lord. Not even Owain's own father, coward that he is. Orvell released the boy and gave Owain a hundred paces headstart. Orvell laughed as he told me later that Owain nearly made it to Lhin Dhu before the dog ripped him to pieces. Had he made it, the water gods would have saved him."

The silence between them lengthened as Madselin absorbed her words. There was no doubt in her mind that Bronwen was telling the truth and it would explain Orvell's hold over her.

"He even killed the boy later," she added between gritted teeth. "Just so that everyone knew what would happen if they tried to argue with him."

"I am sorry," murmured Madselin, knowing full well how inadequate the words were. "I could not have known." She felt numb. Surely Guy had no idea what sort of a man Henry Orvell was? Perhaps it was as well he had never known. "If you wish to stay here, Bronwen, you are welcome."

A smile twisted her lips. "I have no choice, Lady de Breuville." Gently brushing Maude's soft black down with a finger, Bronwen's eyes roved over the sleeping baby. "Lady de Vaillant demanded my services for the child. I will not leave, but I am sure that Henry Orvell will have something to say about that. He does not give up his possessions easily. You had best tread warily about him, for things are not always as they seem."

They sat in silence for a while, listening to the screeching of the hungry seabirds. "You must hate the Normans," Madselin said eventually.

Bronwen stood up and looked back down at her. "As much as you hate us, my lady." Without a backward glance, Bronwen walked back through the orchard towards the gate.

Madselin was left alone to contemplate those strange words, for she had said nothing to Bronwen about her hatred of the English. Perhaps it just showed in all she said and did.

Chapter Nine

Madselin could not fail to recognise Edwin amid the mêlée of All Hallow's revellers. He was the only one not wearing some sort of mask or costume. Idly making inroads into the ale, Edwin sat in the corner of the feasting hall whilst all around him people chattered loudly. Every so often he would smile to himself as a few of the villagers broke out into song to accompany a rather drunken harpist.

Edwin's very stillness amid the hubbub attracted Madselin's gaze and she found herself wondering more about this enigmatic man. Despite her desire to hate all Englishmen, her instinct was to trust him as Isabella had commanded. Blunt and surly he was, but ever honest.

It was very evident, however, that his lack of charm did not deter some of the women from trying to attract his attention.

All, Madselin noted wryly, were treated to the same tight-lipped indifference, although this did not marry with his reputation for being a womaniser. The sudden and very unexpected memory of his kiss caused her blood to warm inexplicably and Madselin could feel her face turning pink.

To make matters worse, Edwin appeared to have chosen that very minute to glance over in her direction. In order to cover her confusion, she summoned a servant to refill her cup and hastily threw herself into her duties as lady of the keep.

Once the feasting was over, the revellers cleared back the benches so that the dancing could begin.

Amid raucous shouts of encouragement, the musicians burst into action but, despite much clapping and tapping of the feet, no one moved to dance. Madselin was quite at a loss until she suddenly felt a heavy hand on her shoulder.

"I think we are expected to take the first steps." Edwin stood before her, his eyebrows raised in question. "It's a tradition for the lord and lady of the manor to start the dancing. We appear to be…ah…the next best thing."

Glancing around, she realised that most people were watching them. This was not the time to decline. Nodding curtly, Madselin rose gracefully and placed her fingers on his arm. He led her to the centre of the hall and they waited for the music to begin.

As the first note struck, Edwin dispensed with any nicety of manners by grabbing her waist and whirling her round and round in an exhausting jig. Breathless and with her blood pounding in her ears, Madselin could only clutch helplessly at his sleeves.

"For the love of God, Edwin," she hissed into his shoulder. "We're only trying to dance, not run for our lives. Slow down."

She sensed rather than saw his smile. "My dancing is not to your taste, lady?"

"This is not dancing. I would describe it as torture," she gritted through her teeth. "And if you do not slow down, I will be sick."

That earned her another grin, but Madselin was gratified that he did at least take heed of her words. Once they had charged around the hall in a full circle, the more enthusiastic of the revellers joined them and Madselin sighed with relief.

Confident that Edwin would revert to his normal, surly state and return her to her place shortly, she allowed herself to relax a little in his arms. For a large man, he was certainly light on his feet and it had been a very long time since she had taken part in such festivities.

"You adjust well to our customs, Lady de Breuville." His words were murmured so that only she could hear him and Madselin shivered a little at such unsought intimacy. "Perhaps we'll make an Englishwoman of you yet?"

Pushing herself away from him suddenly, Madselin speared him with a haughty glare. "A most unlikely occurrence. I was merely following tradition. Besides," she added with a sniff, "I haven't danced for years."

Edwin's grey eyes roved over her flushed face and grinned. "Too old?" he divined with disheartening accuracy.

Madselin's colour heightened if that was possible. "Alice felt it was undignified for a woman of my years. She preferred me to watch." Madselin caught her breath as Edwin pulled her closer to him and whirled her round again.

"A mistake," he said softly, squeezing her waist in a most familiar manner.

"You've had too much to drink," she accused his ear. "Take me back."

"So you prefer to watch from the side after all. I was sure you had more spirit than that." Edwin's rather endearing grin had subsided into regretful sigh.

"I did not say that." Madselin shot him a vexed look. The man was very trying. "I was merely pointing out…"

"Do you not dance with your betrothed?" he interrupted, his eyes gazing down at her solemnly.

"No" she admitted. It was a sore point, for she would dearly have liked to on many occasions but Hugh did not care for dancing. This was something she would not admit to Edwin. "He is of the same opinion as Alice."

"They seem well suited, your sister-in-marriage and your betrothed."

Ignoring his rather unhelpful comment, Madselin tried vainly to place some distance between her body and his, but Edwin held her fast. "He is not my betrothed yet," she grumbled. "We still await Richard's decision."

With a heartfelt sigh she gave up trying to distance herself from Edwin and looked up at him. His hair was neatly braided and his chin barbered more skilfully than was his habit. Gone, too, were the muddy tunic and breeches he favoured, replaced by a finer, softer tunic of blue edged in red and gold. With so gentle a smile, Edwin did, indeed, look most attractive.

Unconsciously, her fingers slid over the bulging muscles in his arms and she swallowed hard as one of his hands responded in kind by roving over the curve of her hips.

Even though the fire had been damped down a little, the heat in the hall was almost unbearable. The shutters were open to let in some cooling air but all that seemed to do was cause acrid smoke to billow through the hall whenever the wind gusted. Madselin was glad of the excuse to cover her flaming cheeks. "I shall have to sit down or I am afraid you will be left carrying me back," she muttered into his tunic.

"I had not realised you were so wan, lady," he countered quickly with concern. "If you wish me to carry you to your room, I shall be happy to oblige."

Madselin's cheeks flooded with embarrassment as she stared up at him. Had she misinterpreted his meaning or was he genuinely concerned? The wretch gave no indication as to whether he was teasing her or not but she was certain he was aware of the double meaning. "No," she gabbled hastily. "I merely meant that the heat is oppressive. Please do not be concerned since I am noted for my good health."

He removed the offending hand with a wry smile before grinning at her. "Your body has always appeared to be most healthy to me, Lady de Breuville." His grey eyes twinkled down at her as he watched her confusion.

"This is not the time for you to display your tasteless wit, Edwin Elwardson," she hissed at him. Clearly he had drunk far more than she had thought. "I shall forget your strange humour and we shall sit down." So saying, she stalked from the centre of the floor to be followed by Edwin.

Almost hurling herself onto her chair next to Beatrice, Madselin was able to observe the festivities from a position of relative safety. Edwin stood casually at her side as if naught was wrong and that irritated her immensely. Glaring at the dancers, she gradually realised that Edwin's very simple but enthusiastic steps had been but a far cry from those of the others.

"I see Emma has finally succumbed to Ulf's charms," Beatrice observed with raised eyebrows.

Disbelieving her, Madselin's eyes followed the direction of Beatrice's accusing finger. "It looks like he has managed to pour a casket of ale down her throat to achieve it," she responded in concern. "I do believe Emma is drunk."

They watched as Emma careered about the floor, her cheeks red and her eyes merry, before Ulf gently guided her to a seat at the far end of the hall. She confounded all of them by promptly plopping herself onto his lap. Ulf beamed in obvious pleasure at so unexpected a conquest.

Openmouthed at such unlikely behaviour, Madselin was about to go to Emma when a familiar hand at her shoulder prevented her.

"Emma does not look as if she wishes to be rescued," Edwin pointed out.

Pushing his hand from her shoulder, Madselin jumped up and turned to Edwin.

"It is my responsibility to protect her from such things," she argued, staring at him with a frown. "Besides, I have no idea how she is managing any sort of conversation since he speaks no word of French."

That raised a smile from Edwin, who watched her thoughtfully. "Emma is more resourceful than you give her credit for. Her fluency in our barbaric tongue improves daily."

Madselin's eyes narrowed at that barb, but she admitted to herself that she had been neglecting Emma of late.

"If you are that concerned about her, I will watch over her should she go with Ulf to Lhin Dhu, although I cannot promise preserving her virtue if she does not wish it."

Her glittering brown eyes met his grey ones and she saw the humour there. "You do not appear to be in any fit state to help anyone. I shall have to go myself—and besides," she added with a sniff, "it is fitting that I should see these traditions first-hand."

Beatrice stared at her for a moment or two, her eyebrows raised in faint surprise. "You cannot mean that, Madselin?"

"Why not?" Madselin looked at her friend curiously.

"Well…you are not married," she replied quietly. "It is not at all proper for someone like you…"

"I am older than you," Madselin pointed out. "And I am quite aware of what goes on in the forests on feast days. I doubt very much that England is so different to the Vexin."

"Then I suppose I shall have to extend my protection to you as well, Lady de Breuville." Despite Edwin's solemn tone, there was a flush to his cheeks that Madselin could not quite trust and she vowed to keep away from him as far as was possible.

Festivities were interrupted by the loud blare of a hunting horn. A very tall, well-built man dressed in a long green cloak and a hawk's mask leapt onto the high table and slammed a long stick three times into the table. A gruesome horse's skull stared out from the top of the stick.

"Come," he shouted to the cheering crowd. "Let the souling commence."

In the wake of the horse's skull, everyone surged through the doors taking with them burning torches and the yew tree branches that had adorned the hall. Their strange masks gave the procession a very eerie appearance that Madselin had never before seen. Fascinated, she allowed herself to be pulled along with the crowd.

Lhin Dhu was fully deserving of its reputation as a sacred lake. All around the banks grew thick reeds where the sad, dark water lapped mournfully. Cold gusts of wind from the sea sent tiny ripples shivering across its murky surface.

"It's fascinating, don't you think?" Father Padraig had come to stand silently at her side.

She turned to look at him, his green eyes shining in the torchlight, and wondered what he had been like as a young man. "You aren't at all what I am used to, Father. Most of the priests I know would frown darkly on such heathen practices and beseech the wrath of God to smite the perpetrators on the spot."

"Aye, well, I wasn't always a priest," he confessed as his eyes followed the progress of a particularly buxom villager.

"Rest easy, Father. I have no intention of changing their ways."

Father Padraig did not look at her but nodded quietly, his eyes fixed on the village woman. Madselin did notice, however, that his grip on the cross had tightened and she deemed the moment ripe to move on.

On the other side of the lake stood three large stones, similar to the ones she had seen in the forest before. The stick with the horse's skull rested against the largest of these and Madselin found herself drawn to look at it more closely. Unconsciously, she reached out to touch the stone. Etched deep into the stone was the same carving of the horned man she had seen before.

"Do you feel the magic, lady?" Edwin's soft voice behind her made Madselin jump and she pulled back her hand quickly.

"I feel vexed that you keep creeping up behind me," she retorted, unable to keep the waspishness from her voice. "Why do you not dance with Joanna?"

The words had come with no forethought, but all the same, Madselin wondered at their origin.

"Joanna has already found a partner for the night."

Edwin turned to the dancers and nodded to a couple who were closely entwined.

"Does that not upset you?" Madselin asked quietly, wondering at his lack of emotion. He truly did not seem concerned.

"Why should it?" A frown betokened his confusion. "She dances with Gyrth."

As they watched the couple dancing, Madselin recognised Joanna's partner as the tall man who had led the revellers to the lake. The name sounded vaguely familiar. "Gyrth?" she asked eventually.

"Ulf's son and…" he paused significantly "…Joanna's husband."

"Her husband? But I thought…" Well? What had she thought? That Edwin was Joanna's lover and father of her son. "I have not seen him before," she pressed on hastily. "Where has he been?"

Edwin sat down at the base of a stone and leaned back. Staring out at the lake, he picked up several tiny stones and threw them into the water. "Watching the coastline. Searching for information."

Aye, she remembered that she had heard Isabella and Edwin talk about this Gyrth. "Did he find anything out?" Keen to hear, Madselin moved to Edwin's side and sat down.

He turned to look at her, his eyes searching her face. Madselin was most glad that she was shrouded in darkness since he would not see the blush on her cheeks. Why on earth he had this effect on her she had no idea.

"Enough to concern me greatly." There was no humour in his voice now.

"What? Can you tell me?" Inadvertently, Madselin had placed her hand on his arm. She pulled it away quickly.

"Orvell plans to make a treaty with a clan who live just beyond the border. They have been harrying our land for years without much success."

"Why would he make a treaty with them?"

"For their men. Whilst the king and his earls are busy in Normandy, the path is clear for Orvell to take what he wants. In return, he would offer the Scots land, gold or even some rich heiress."

On hearing his last words, Madselin drew her cloak closer to her body. It was very hard to believe that Henry Orvell could commit such treason.

"He suspects you of leading a revolt," Madselin said. "Did you know?"

"Aye." His voice was grim. "But it gladdens my Angle heart to know that you did not believe it."

In the silence that followed, Madselin could almost hear his mind working.

"You did believe him," he said eventually.

"I wanted to," she allowed. "But I could not."

"Well, I suppose I shall have to be content with your honesty at least."

"I am sorry." Madselin placed her hand back on his arm. "I am a naturally suspicious person. Trust does not come easily to me."

Edwin rubbed his face in his hands as if he were tired. "And yet you risked your life once to save mine."

"I was not thinking aright and had clearly forgotten you were an Englishman."

That drew a smile from him. He stood up and offered Madselin his hand. After a moment's hesitation she took it and allowed him to haul her to her feet.

"Have you seen enough?" His chin lifted in the direction of the dancers.

"Aye, although I have been wondering about the horse's skull?"

Edwin turned to pick up the stick, testing its weight in his hands. "It is a symbol of fertility, to ensure a good crop growth next year." He replaced it carefully before turning back to Madselin. "Well, my lady, I had best take you back to the keep unless you are keen to taste my dancing skills again?"

"I think not," she replied with a laugh. "Although I was perhaps somewhat hasty in my criticism earlier this evening. I did…enjoy dancing with you. It has been a long time since I last danced and I think I was just embarrassed." The words were hard to say but she felt she owed it to him.

Her words seemed to have a much greater impact on Edwin than she had thought possible. She could feel his eyes turn on her and could not help her cheeks beginning to burn under his scrutiny. Beyond them, the drums pounded in an age-old rhythm that strangely matched the beating of her heart. Madselin wondered if Edwin could hear it too.

"Perhaps I was too rough?" he began very quietly. "I am used to the village girls and…"

"No. It was not that at all." She could not quite find the courage to look up at him. "I think perhaps I was enjoying myself and I did not want to."

A finger lifted her chin so that she was forced to look up. They were standing so close that Madselin could feel the heat from his body. Strange longings suddenly welled up deep within, and Madselin found it hard not to reach out and touch him. Could it be the magic of the night?

"A Norman enjoying herself in the arms of an Angle?" he teased gently. "Mayhap we ought to test it once again to see if you were right?"

Madselin could feel the heat flood through her body as Edwin slipped his hands around her waist once more. Without waiting for her protest, he pulled her hard against his body and lowered his lips to hers.

Unlike their last kiss, this one was gentle and teasing. His lips were soft and sweet, and tasted of ale, but were irresistible. Gently they coaxed a response from her and Madselin found her hands slipping again over his arms and around his neck. Her body moulded against his, swelling and rejoicing in this forbidden taste of passion. And when had his soft gentle kisses turned so passionate?

Madselin found herself caught up in an embrace so wild that all feelings of control deserted her. Without knowing how, Edwin had pushed her back against the sacred stone for support whilst his hands had begun to slide over her aching body. She in turned had begun to push herself harder against him, wringing a groan from Edwin's hot mouth as his lips brushed gently over the tingling skin below her ear.

"Come into the forest, Madselin," he urged, his hand beginning to stroke the soft curves of her thighs.

His words penetrated her confusion. "Nay," she whispered, pushing him back. "We cannot." How had she allowed this to happen?

"Cannot?" he groaned, his hand stilled on her tingling skin. "Is an Angle lover not good enough?" The bitterness in his voice cut through the air.

"Nay," she replied breathlessly. "'Tis not that."

"Then what is it?" Edwin straightened up and stepped back from her.

"I...I... It is not right," she managed finally, watching his expression in the flickering torchlight.

For a moment his face mirrored his confusion and then

suddenly both of his hands covered her cheeks. "Are you innocent?" he asked incredulously.

Stung at such lack of belief in her virtue, Madselin shook herself free of his hands and pushed him away. "Is that so hard to believe?" Pushing her hair from her face, she tried vainly to bring some order to her appearance. She ignored the pointed silence.

"How old are you?" he asked eventually, his voice no longer passionate nor angry.

"Six and twenty. Why?" Her words sounded harsh in her embarrassment.

Gently he took her hands in his and ignored her attempts to push him away. "You kiss like a woman." Turning each of her hands in his he kissed the centre of her palms and a tingle shot through her disappointed body like a bolt of lightening. "I find it hard to believe that your betrothed has not…" He did not finish the sentence.

"Hugh is a true knight and would not even think of it," she countered with hauteur. He had never kissed her like Edwin either, but she chose not to dwell on that. "I am sure that there are women aplenty who would do as he wished. He would not think of tumbling his wife in the forest."

"Ah," came the maddening reply as he stooped to pick up her discarded mask. "So you would prefer your husband to tumble wenches in the forest rather than yourself?"

Well? Would she? Somehow, Madselin could not imagine herself doing any such thing with Hugh, whether in the forest or a bedchamber for that matter. It just didn't seem quite right. "This is a most improper conversation. Will you take me back to the keep?" It was more of a command than a question, but Edwin forbore to say anything. He passed her the mask in silence and stalked on ahead to the keep.

Madselin stared at his back for a moment before following. His question—or more particularly her reaction to it—disturbed her greatly. Whenever Edwin seemed to talk about Hugh, she began to feel uncomfortable and it annoyed her.

Pulling her cloak close about her, she hurried after Edwin.

Chapter Ten

Madselin stared at the bowl of grey lumpy porridge before her and groaned. Glancing over at the silent, whey-faced Emma, she firmly replaced her spoon in the bowl and went to stand before her. They were attempting to break their fast in Madselin's chamber since the hall was still awash with the remains of the feast. Madselin took her chance and enquired wryly after her maid's health.

"Like I've been kicked in the head by a mule," Emma managed grimly as she significantly placed her chubby fingers over her mouth.

"Do you remember what happened?" Madselin asked speculatively. There was no telling what Emma may or may not remember but she had best tread lightly to begin with.

"Of course I do," came the petulant reply. "I was only drunk, not deprived of my wits."

"What about Ulf?" It was now or never, thought Madselin. She would have to tell her sooner or later so best to get it over with.

"Ulf?" A deep frown stole across Emma's face. "What do you mean?"

"Well," began Madselin doubtfully. "You appeared to...er...see him in a more positive light than before." There really was no easy way to broach this.

"Ye-e-es," allowed Emma somewhat warily. "That is so."

Alerted by her maid's rather hesitant reply, Madselin pressed on. "So you do remember dancing with him? I thought he was a great Saxon lummox?"

"Aye, well, that was before," Emma conceded rather grumpily.

"Before what?" This was most certainly news to Madselin. She stared down at Emma, waiting for a reply.

Emma shrugged her plump, rounded shoulders, but Madselin noticed that there was still a bit of a gleam in her eye. "It was the night Lady Isabella died. You were with her and I was downstairs helping with the young boys as you had asked. The poor things knew that something was up but couldn't find out what it was."

A shadow passed over Emma's face as she thought back to that night. "It was young Charles who did it." Emma's fingers twisted the corner of her tunic. "As soon as Ulf came in the hall, he ran to him and began to cry. Ulf said something to Joanna and nodded." She sniffed as if the memory was still painful.

"Well, he sat down in her chair and called Charles and Benedict to sit on his knees, just like a father would. He told them then, the poor little mites, and the three of them just cried their eyes out together. I'll not forget that sight in a hurry. A huge man like him, not worrying about crying in front of women like us. In the end, we were all crying too."

A lump caught in Madselin's throat at the thought of it. She was glad she had asked Ulf to tell the boys about their mother.

"He is a lonely man, Joanna says." Madselin watched Emma's reaction.

The woman just smiled, a rather soft, secret smile. "Aye, but I reckon I put a bit of a smile on his face last night."

Madselin laughed. "Aye, that's true enough. Although he wasn't smiling when he came back to the hall after taking you out."

Emma sighed and tugged harder at the edge of her tunic. "No. He was probably thinking of her." Her brown eyes glistened with unshed tears.

"Her?" Madselin had not seen him with any other woman.

"His second wife. Marie. She's been dead these past ten years. Every All Hallow's Eve he goes down to that lake with the others and talks to her."

This was definitely a side to Ulf Madselin could never have imagined. "I didn't see him down there."

"You went down there?" Emma whispered in shock. "Why, there's no telling what could happen there."

"Edwin Elwardson was there too. He had offered me his protection."

A most unladylike snort came from Emma's tight lips. "The way that man watches you, I'm surprised you managed to get home at all."

Madselin was prevented from thinking up a suitable reply by a loud scratching at the door. It was Joanna.

"Ulf bade me bring you this," she said quietly to Emma. "He said it would aid recovery." Carefully she placed a pitcher of foul-smelling liquid before Emma and nodded at her in encouragement to drink it. "It does work, once you have been sick," she added with quiet conviction.

Madselin looked at her glowing cheeks and cheery

smile. Clearly Gyrth had a good effect on Joanna. On reflection, it was certainly odd that she could have attributed any such signs of well-being to Edwin. In truth, they rarely passed more than a few words together. It was most odd the tricks a mind could play.

Emma drank the concoction without hesitation. It was several hours before they were able to resume their conversation.

There was no sign of Edwin anywhere in the keep and Madselin heaved a sigh of relief.

The more she had thought about what had happened, the more confused she had become. He had always been overbearing and abrupt with her until that time on the beach. Since then, she noticed, his behaviour had changed. He had smiled at her, even teased her on occasion, and was gentler in his treatment of her.

And what of herself? Had her attitude towards Edwin changed? Aye, she admitted eventually. He was no longer the ruffian peasant in her eyes.

He was a well-respected, trusted steward of her kinsman who commanded a keep with authority and intelligence. The men grumbled at their duties as they would for anyone who demanded vigilance and discipline. No one seemed to resent the fact that Edwin was an Englishman rather than a Norman. No doubt they might think it, but the men wisely kept such thoughts to themselves.

November had dawned cold and grey with the first cock crow. Her feet crunched over the iron-hard earth as she crossed the bailey, the noise echoing loudly in Madselin's head. All Saints' Day was traditionally the day they began preparing for the winter months. Judging by the noise coming from the barns, the slaughter of the herds was well underway and she decided that for now she could not face the stench of fear and fresh blood.

Killing most of the animals at the start of winter was the only way most keeps could survive the long, cold months ahead since they were unable to provide enough food for the animals to last through the winter. All the same, Madselin could not help but feel it was a terrible waste. The beef would be salted carefully in barrels whilst the hides would be made into leather. Nothing went to waste.

The bailey was seemingly awash with women carrying pails of milk or laundry, screeching hens and hounds scavenging amongst the piles of rubbish that had accumulated. Madselin made a mental note to have it cleared away since the stink would be putrid and she loathed the rats that it always drew. A shout from the sentry caused her to stop and turn.

"Riders approach!"

After a moment or two desperately trying to think who the visitors could be, Madselin gave up the struggle and hurried inside the keep. Whoever it was, she had best make sure the hall was in some sort of order and that all the drunkards sleeping off the after-effects were surfed out.

"Henry Orvell requests entrance, my lady." The guard stood to attention as Madselin digested the information. A cold, gnawing pain plucked at her innards.

"How many men are with him?"

The soldier blinked as he mentally added the number. "Six others. All soldiers, my lady."

Nodding her assent, Madselin cast her eye around the hall and found it in a tolerable state. Its very dinginess was oddly comforting. Ordering ale and wine, she went to the hearth and held out her hands before the flames.

Her fingers were ice cold and she was afraid. Much would depend on her handling of the situation.

If the men were to be believed, Orvell was as dangerous as he was charming and if he suspected that she had an inkling of his activities, then he could wreak terrible devastation on the de Vaillant lands. He believed her to be innocent of such knowledge and therefore useful to him, as was Bronwen. Breathing deeply to calm her nerves, Madselin lifted her chin and thought of Isabella.

The heavy door was wrenched open and Henry Orvell strode in, bringing the freshness of the morning air with him.

"Lady de Breuville." He smiled as he reached for her hand and touched her fingers lightly with his lips. His grey eyes watched her carefully as he performed the greeting with effortless grace. Resisting the desire to pull her hand back, Madselin nodded with the haughty acceptance that Alice always used and schooled her lips into a dainty simper.

"This is indeed a surprise and a pleasure, my lord."

His somewhat hawklike expression relaxed at those words, and Orvell offered her a brilliant smile. "The pleasure is all mine, Lady de Breuville." He accepted a cup of wine before removing his cloak and throwing it over the table.

Madselin glanced nervously in the direction of his two men who had planted themselves conspicuously on either side of the door. Her own guards were stationed somewhat laggardly around the hall but appeared more concerned with their throbbing heads than any possible danger from Orvell. She hoped it was just the impression they created. "Perhaps your men would care for some ale?"

Orvell shook his head. "They can wait. It does them

no harm.'' He sipped the rich wine and savoured it slowly before sitting down before the fire. ''I was most sad to learn of Lady de Vaillant's death.''

Despite his disarming smile, Madselin was aware that those grey eyes missed nothing. ''It was very unexpected,'' she replied simply, dropping her gaze to the floor rushes. ''But at least Bronwen was able to save the child.''

Her reference to Bronwen caused Orvell's eyes to flicker but he said nothing. Taking another sip from his wine cup, he nodded silently. There was nothing in his behaviour or expression to cause her concern, but Madselin could feel the tension in him mounting once again.

''Bronwen has indeed been a godsend,'' she remarked carefully. ''Lady de Vaillant expressly requested before her death that she take sole charge of Maude. I had hoped to persuade you to allow Bronwen to remain here.'' Madselin held her breath, unable to discern from the expression on his face exactly what he was thinking.

''Ah.'' That one word was uttered without the slightest inflection. Pushing his dark hair back from his brow, Orvell regarded her intently, his fingertips carefully placed against each other below his chin. Madselin was reminded of one of the stable cats playing with a mouse.

''The baby is much taken with her,'' she felt obliged to offer.

''Then of course she must stay,'' came the bland reply. Inhaling deeply, Orvell flicked carelessly at the soft, rich wool of his tunic. ''However, as Bronwen has skills which can be…shall we say…most valuable, I would require some compensation.''

''Compensation?'' Madselin echoed the word in a whisper. ''What sort of compensation?''

A rather curious smile broke out on his face. ''Rest

easy, my lady. I meant no more than bid you dine at my keep after a day's hunting. My land is well stocked with game and my cooks provide passable fare. Shall we say a week hence?''

"I'm not sure…'' she managed quickly.

"I have some things of Guy's,'' he continued, almost as if he hadn't heard her, although she was certain he had. "You might wish to have them. I know he would have wanted that.''

At the mention of Guy's name, Madselin felt her blood go cold. How could Guy have been involved with such a man? "What sort of things?'' Despite her hesitation, Madselin could not help feeling curious. Anything of Guy's would be precious to her.

"Ah, my lady! That is where I have the upper hand.'' His face was alight with humour and it was almost irresistible. "If I do not tell you, then you will have to come to see for yourself. Guy often mentioned your quick wits and your inquisitive nature.''

Smiling her capitulation, Madselin nodded. "Very well. A week hence.'' After all, he was most unlikely to attempt harm to a Norman lady.

"Good.'' Henry Orvell rose to his feet in one graceful movement. "I shall not detain you further.'' He turned to leave the room. "Perhaps you would bring Bronwen so that she can take her things. I'm sure she needs them.''

"I shall ask her.''

Their eyes held for a moment, before Orvell nodded curtly. As he quit the room, Madselin felt a wave of relief flood through her body. At least he had gone and had made no real fuss about losing Bronwen. Perhaps they had underestimated him? Somehow, she did not think it would be so easy.

Beatrice had left the de Vaillant keep not long after Orvell's departure since she wished to be within her own keep walls before nightfall.

Once her friend had left, Madselin could no longer put off her talk with Blanche and resumed her search in earnest. The girl, however, remained inexplicably elusive. No one had seen her since the early hours of the morning. Madselin eventually gave up with a sigh. There was much to do. Blanche could wait.

Edwin found Madselin in the cellar overseeing the salting of the meat. Trying to take her mind off the meeting with Orvell, Madselin had thrown herself into the most arduous of household tasks. Dust from the salt floated in the stale air and it was hard to breathe. The light from the wall torches barely penetrated the gloom at times.

Just as she had thumped a large leg of beef into the grimy salt box, Madselin felt a hand on her shoulder.

"A word, lady."

Edwin stood behind her, his face grim. There was no gleam in his eye this morning and Madselin half-wondered whether he had also partaken of Ulf's cure. Nodding, she shook the salt from her hands and rubbed them on her gown covering. Several of the women were watching them with intense interest.

"We'll go above." Without waiting for Edwin's reply, she turned and made her way to the solar. Madselin could hear his light steps behind her and knew a certain pleasure in being able to command so easily a man as truculent as Edwin. She doubted, however, that his cooperation had anything to do with her. More like he wished to deliver his own words in private anyway.

Eventually they reached the privacy of Isabella's room. Her unfinished tapestry lay on her chair, cast carelessly

aside as was Isabella's impatient habit. She looked away
from it and turned to face Edwin.

"Well?" To cover her embarrassment, Madselin had
adopted a tone that did not encourage intimacy.

Edwin's grey eyes betrayed nothing. "Gyrth tells me
Orvell came earlier."

"Aye. You were not around so I felt it best to see him
on my own."

"What did he want exactly?" There was a steeliness
about him that made Madselin wary.

"To offer his condolences and to ask about Bronwen."

Edwin's lips formed a tight, bloodless line. "Did you
believe him?"

"I'm not sure," she admitted. That particular question
had dogged her for several hours already and she had not
arrived at any conclusion. "I suspect he was here to see
how the land lies."

Without taking his eyes from her, Edwin considered
the reply. His jaw tightened. "And how does the land
lie?" he asked softly. There was no mistaking his meaning.

"Quiet," she retorted indignantly. "And he invited me
to hunt and dine with him."

"Which you refused," he finished confidently.

"No. I accepted."

The silence between them was charged with tension
and Edwin's narrowed eyes made her nervous. Madselin
had to remind herself that she had done nothing wrong.
"Did he threaten you?" Edwin's tone had an icy quality
that chilled her to the bone.

She shook her head. "He said he had some of Guy's
possessions." Madselin glared at him, discomfited that
he had made her admit such a thing.

"Who is Guy?" His frown deepened even more.

Straightening her back, Madselin lifted her chin. She refused to be cowed by Edwin Elwardson. He was, after all, only an Englishman. "Guy de Chambertin was my betrothed before he was cut down like a dog on our wedding day."

Unexpectedly, Edwin's face drained of colour. He stared hard at her as if viewing her for the first time, his fingers rubbing at his stubbly chin. "Why would Henry Orvell have some of his things?" he asked eventually, his voice quiet and very controlled. There was an intensity in his eyes that Madselin found uncomfortable.

"I believe they were on campaign together in England. Orvell was Guy's commander." His reaction to her words was not at all understandable.

Edwin looked as though he was about to say something, but bit the words back and reached for a cup of wine. That in itself was strange since the man usually drank ale from preference. All the same, he was not acting himself, so Madselin held her tongue and waited.

"Did your betrothed ever mention Orvell?" The wine cup was held before his lips as he awaited her reply.

"Nay. But then I had not seen Guy for years before our wedding. I do not recall him being a guest, although it has been eight years since…"

Edwin gulped the wine down in one and she noticed a little of the red liquid dribble down his chin. The man was not at all himself.

"He is a dangerous man," Edwin said finally, wiping his chin with his sleeve. "It seems very likely that he is the man responsible for killing my family and I would not trust him with a dog. You will not go to his keep, lady. The man is as treacherous as a trapped wolf."

Madselin watched him, sensing his controlled anger and something not unlike anticipation. She doubted that

Orvell was the man who killed Edwin's family. Orvell was far too much a Norman knight—although she had reason to believe his treachery with the Scots.

Her mind whirred on despite herself and she traced the trail of a strange thought. If Orvell had been responsible, then that could mean that Guy…no. It was too absurd. "If you believe that to be the case, then why did you not act earlier?"

Refilling his cup, Edwin swirled the liquid round thoughtfully. "I have no proof beyond recognising him and d'Aveyron will not act on that alone. He has stayed my hand these many months as he doubts the King would view my killing of Orvell on such grounds as anything other than murder. I am willing to pay the price but your kinsman plays a deeper game."

"I don't understand," she said, her tone somewhat softer. It was not often that Edwin spoke of his inner thoughts and she savoured the confidence a little.

With a heavy sigh, Edwin frowned once again at the flames in the hearth. "I am to take him committing an act of treason. That way, Richard can justify Orvell's death by courting Rufus's fear of treason. He has reason to believe the King will be well pleased."

"So," she finished wryly, "your revenge takes second place to my kinsman's desire for favour with the King. I had not thought Richard so blatantly avaricious."

"Your kinsman treads a fine tightrope, Lady de Breuville. His liege-lord is suspected of treason and Rufus will be keeping a careful eye on de Poictou's vassals. D'Aveyron acts not only in his own best interests, but in those of his family and his tenant knights too. I, also, have reason to be grateful for his shrewdness on more than one occasion."

Fascinated, Madselin raised her brow in question but

Edwin shook his head. "I gave him my word I would do as he says."

Madselin remembered Richard telling her that Edwin was one of the few men he could trust to do his bidding to the letter. At the time she had thought that strange, since it did not accord with her own view, and it still did not ring true. He was loyal, she was certain, but capable of independent action none the less.

Edwin carried on, unaware of the nature of her thoughts. "Gyrth has heard a whisper that a small retinue of Scots are due tomorrow eve. They come by boat whilst the moon is low over the channel. I'll arrange a patrol to await their arrival. If we can capture one alive, then we could point more than a finger of suspicion at Orvell." He glanced up at Madselin's white face. "Give me your word that you will not visit Orvell, Lady de Breuville."

Glancing across at the unfinished tapestry, Madselin remembered Isabella's last words to her. Aye, she would trust this strange man. "You have it, Angle," she replied so meekly that his brows lifted almost in question.

He inclined his head in acceptance before allowing his gaze to rake over her. "Do you know your face is covered in salt dust, Madselin?" Without awaiting her reply, Edwin turned to leave the room.

Quickly wiping her cheeks with her grimy hands, Madselin glared at the truth of his words. Why did the man always have the last word? And yet he had allowed her to stand there the whole time with a dusty white face and said nothing at all. Irritated beyond measure, she stalked back to the cellar.

Madselin paused at her sewing and listened to Maude de Vaillant's fierce cries vie with the strains of the harp.

For a tiny baby, she was certainly more than capable of expressing her displeasure loudly.

Madselin stilled for a moment, more concerned for the baby than she cared to admit. Bronwen shushed and caressed Maude gently in the shadowy embrasure of the solar whilst Madselin and Emma sat busy with their mending before the fire.

"The babe is restless tonight, Bronwen. Is she ailing?" The early days were often the most dangerous for the newborn and any discomfort could be the first sign of impending death.

Bronwen looked up and shook her head firmly. "Nay, 'tis either the weather or Morwenna. The woman drank more than her fair share of ale yestereve and I'll wager her milk curdled with all that dancing." Gracefully she stood up and placed Maude across her shoulder, rubbing her back to the rhythm of the harp. "What with her and that Blanche, you've got your hands full."

Madselin ignored the harsh snort that came from Emma's direction. "What about Morwenna? I had thought she was working well as the wetnurse."

Unable to hold her tongue any longer, Emma interrupted. "Aye, until she gets herself with child again. If I'm not mistaken, that won't be very long."

Casting a quelling look at her maid, Madselin turned back to Bronwen. The baby was clutching at her thick braid and snuffled loudly into her tunic. "Are you not pleased with her?" she questioned. There had been little time to oversee Morwenna since Isabella's death and she had thought that since Bronwen had not mentioned it, she was happy with the woman.

Bronwen shrugged her slender shoulders with indifference. "She does what she must, but Emma is right. There is a good chance she will get herself with child soon."

A frown creased Madselin's brow. Aye, she had noticed the priest's interest in her, but other than Emma's caustic words there had been no other indication that he had been dallying with Morwenna. "When did her husband drown?"

"It's been five moons she said," Bronwen replied absently, her lips brushing gently over Maude's soft brow. "She's just lonely," she offered in excuse. "But lying with the priest is no way to find herself another man. Her best chance would be to wait until the spring celebrations. There's many good men around who'd be more than happy to have her tie their hands. She's got two healthy sons and is still young and strong."

Fascinated at such a barbaric method of finding a husband, Madselin mused that perhaps it had its merits. Were it the same for Norman ladies, she would never choose an old man like Goddefroi de Grantmesnil.

Had she the choice, like Morwenna, who indeed would she pick? In a place as wild and treacherous as this, only the strong and the bold survived. It was hard to imagine Hugh pitting his strength against the elements that shaped their lives here. At least, she amended quickly, not for long.

"And that Blanche has been missing since this morning." Emma's censorious tone interrupted her thoughts. "The woman has no morals. That young man of hers has been searching for her everywhere. No doubt she'll turn up when she's good and ready with her nose in the air as if naught was wrong. Leading him a merry dance, she is."

Madselin sighed and rubbed her aching head. "Aye. I'll speak to Father Padraig about marrying her soon. Is he missing, too?" she enquired distractedly, stifling a yawn.

"He was at Lhin Dhu with the others," murmured Bronwen, rocking the now-quiet Maude. She made her way to the wooden crib and bent down to settle the babe amongst the fleeces and blankets that lined it.

Madselin raised her eyes to the woman. "Why were people at Lhin Dhu?" She dry-washed her face with her hands in an effort to wake up.

Bronwen offered her a wry smile as she straightened and walked back towards the fire. "Just adding your Church's approval to our traditional ways. They'd lose us otherwise."

Madselin did no more than raise her brows at this cynical view of the old ways of the villagers versus the religious zeal of the Church. She was coming to realise that perhaps it was better to accommodate than to sweep clean. Besides, she had quite enjoyed herself at the celebrations.

"Did you know that Henry Orvell came?" At last she had broached the subject that had been bothering her most. Bronwen's gaze did not even flicker.

"Aye. What did he want?"

Madselin ignored Emma's hiss of disapproval at such bold questions. She approved of Bronwen's straightforward approach. "To invite me to hunt and dine and to find out if you were coming back."

The silence between them was tense.

"What was your answer?" The woman's tone was cool but Madselin was certain she detected a slight quiver in her voice.

"Yes to the first and no to the second. He did not appear overly concerned," she added as the frown on Bronwen's face deepened.

Bronwen shook her head. "The man goes deep and he has his eye on you. There's something there between you.

A link." She shrugged carelessly before placing her hands before the fire. "It was just a feeling I had, that day you came."

Debating whether or not to divulge this link, she decided to bite her tongue for the time being. There was no need to mention Guy at all and his connection with Henry Orvell was making her uncomfortable. Madselin stood up in a fluid movement. The candles had reduced only a notch or so since they had first retired to the solar.

"I feel in need of a bath," she announced to Emma. "Have the tub and hot water sent to my room. There's no need for you to come too," she added hastily, seeing the startled look on her maid's face. Madselin suspected that Emma had made some sort of secret tryst with Ulf for later on and she had no desire to interrupt their plans. For once she had a yen to be on her own.

Madselin closed her eyes as she lay back against the oiled cloth in the tub. The fragrant scent of herbs and the last of her precious oils enveloped her in a steamy mist that she found most relaxing. The deep ache that had gripped her head for most of the day had lessened as the water lapped over her. Well, it was in fact just a tiny tub with barely much room for sitting in, but it served its purpose.

The latch on the door rattled but Madselin ignored it. A strong gust of wind, no more than that. She carefully removed the damp lock of hair that obscured her view, just to be on the safe side.

"Had I realised how unconcerned you are of your reputation, I would have breached your haven earlier. You are a most difficult woman to pin down."

With a strangled squeak, Madselin sank into safety but

re-emerged, spluttering with indignation. "Get out of here, you…you…"

"Angle?" Edwin offered helpfully, the broad grin on his handsome face indicating clearly how much he was enjoying her discomfiture.

"Barbarian!" Madselin hissed vehemently. "Have you been drinking again?" she accused, eyeing his large, solid body doubtfully.

That question caused a slight flush to his tanned cheeks but she was gratified that he did not come any closer, none the less. Edwin was leaning against the door as nonchalantly as any well-built warrior could, but then he had the upper hand, she reasoned. He was effectively blocking her exit and preventing anyone else from coming in.

As he didn't immediately leap at her, his purpose for sneaking into her room was not apparently as straightforward as she had at first assumed. Her embarrassment subsiding a little, Madselin managed to glare at him in the haughtiest manner she could summon.

"Pray explain why you should wish to pin me down at all, Angle." In echoing his words, Madselin had not at first realised the *double entendre,* but his somewhat amused expression told her that he had.

"Why indeed, lady? A question which has been plaguing me much of the day." He finished the statement with a rather despairing sigh, and Madselin could have sworn there was a certain look of regret in his eyes.

Dismissing any such notion, Madselin glared at him. "What do you want?" she demanded slowly. She felt very alone, exposed and…well…intimate with this great lummox. No! Not lummox! Emma had shown how lummoxes lured a good woman down the wrong path. Barbarian was far more apt. Barbarian. The word echoed round her mind for a moment as Edwin appeared to be mentally preparing what he was about to say.

Now it was her turn to be confused. "For God's sake, Edwin. What is it?" She was not in any frame of mind nor in any kind of position to be trifled with.

His eyes watched her for less than a few seconds but Madselin could see he was not feeling at all perturbed at confronting a fully naked woman in her bath. And then she saw the blood-red colour steal upwards from his neck and he looked away.

Despite her anger and humiliation, Madselin could not help feeling as though she may have been having more of an effect on him than she had at first thought. Fascinated, the germ of an idea gnawed at her.

Sighing loudly, Madselin raised her brows and delicately soaped her arms. "Well," she said in her most matter-of-fact tone, "as you are clearly going to take some time over this, I would be more comfortable before the fire." Gratified at his deepening colour, she continued mercilessly, "You may as well bring me the drying sheet." Her hand waved carelessly in the direction of the vital cloth.

The silence between them grew until she heard his soft footsteps on the rushes.

"Here!" The word was snapped out gruffly and Madselin was relieved to see that he was standing awkwardly with his back to her, the cloth dangling from his outstretched arm.

Slowly, and very daringly, she rose and allowed the water to cascade down over her body before stepping out of the tub and wrapping the cloth carefully around her. Her tangle of still-damp hair was tossed back over her shoulders as Madselin slipped a bedrobe on—she felt a little less naked with two layers on.

Finding herself quite enjoying this somewhat bizarre charade, Madselin turned then to Edwin. He was nearer than she had expected and had to step back a little. A faint flush crept over her own cheeks.

"Well, Angle?" Her voice was a little squeaky. "Have you remembered what was so urgent that you could not wait?"

Those grey eyes missed nothing of her, from the top of her wet, dark brown hair down to her blue-tinged, bare toes. Slowly they took their fill of her, roving upwards once more to her mouth, lingered a while and then returned to her eyes. Madselin was certain that as far as Edwin was concerned she was stark naked.

"No." The word was uttered in a half-groan, bordering on a very intimate whisper. Cold trickles of sweat trailed over her skin as he slowly raised his hand to her face. She was rooted to the spot as his fingers curled around her neck and pulled her across the inches that separated them. "But something else comes to mind."

"Indeed?" Madselin managed, crushed as she was against his chest. The strong, musky scent of him lingered on his tunic as she pressed her fingers vainly against it.

"Can you use a knife or a bow?" He stared down at her from his great height, his expression fathomless.

His question was like a douse of cold water. Strength flooded into her bones and she pushed him away with considerable force. "Of course not," came the confused retort. "I am not a peasant!"

"Hmm." Whether that noise was uttered by way of dissent or distraction, she did not know for sure. "It's time I gave you some lessons then, lady."

"Rest assured, Angle, I have no desire to add those particular skills to my repertoire. My betrothed…"

"Betrothed-to-be," he interrupted with surprising alacrity.

She grimaced her thanks before she continued. "My betrothed-to-be is most appreciative of what I have to offer as a lady."

"Apparently not." The wretch grinned lewdly, his eyes resting on her curves. "He's neither bedded nor wedded you, girl. The man doesn't seem in much of a hurry to me."

Despite her anger, the gibe stung. "It just goes to show how much you know about the meaning of knighthood." Her waspish reply was cut short by his hands pulling her hard against him once more and her mouth covered by those gentle, coaxing lips. Within a heartbeat she was drowning in his passion again.

"You're right, lady," he said somewhat breathlessly. "I know little about Norman knights but I do know some of the ways between men and women." His soft mouth hovered just above hers and Madselin had to school herself not to draw up on tiptoe to respond. "When I first laid eyes on you, I wanted to lie with you there and then on the forest floor and take that haughty smile right off your face."

Outraged at such an idea, Madselin's hand swept towards his face. His hand wrapped around her wrist. "You barbarian!" she spat, her cheeks burning. "You wouldn't have dared."

He laughed and pulled the offending hand down behind her back. "Had you been alone, I would most certainly have tried." The smile faded as the pressure on the base of her spine increased. She could feel every contour of his hard body. "As you can tell," he added wryly, "nothing has changed."

There was indeed clear evidence to support this theory,

and although innocent of what went on between men and women, she was not unknowing. Even as she struggled to free herself, Madselin realised she was fighting a losing battle.

"That's what you get for tempting the devil, lady."

Gulping loudly, Madselin belatedly realised that he was right, but it in no way excused his brutish behaviour. "Let me go," she hissed.

Brows raised, he shook her gently. He was clearly awaiting her apology. Grudgingly she gave it, adding sullenly, "But I did not invite you up here."

Grinning down at her almost impudently, Edwin released his grip on her wrist. "That's true enough, but I reckon we're even now. You achieved what you set out to do," and he glanced ruefully at the area about his waist causing Madselin to blush to her very toes. "And I'll be content to leave with your word you'll practise some…ah…native skills." He uttered those words with the confidence of a victorious man.

"I said no such thing!" Madselin lifted her chin in retort.

"Aye, but you will." His large hand gripped her chin firmly. "Or I shall kiss you again and may not find I can control my…barbaric…nature."

Her lips tightened in anger. "Richard was right," she muttered eventually. "Very well. You have my word."

Satisfied with that, Edwin nodded his head. "Tomorrow, then. Before I leave."

"There really was no need for all this," she grumbled. "You could have simply asked me in the morning."

"Ah, but then I would not have been able to kiss you," he pointed out with a frown.

"That was not your purpose in coming here, surely." The man made no sense.

He sighed in response. "No, but it reminded me of our plan."

"Blanche isn't here."

"Nay, but you're in sore need of practice, lady."

Ignoring so pointed a comment, Madselin shook her head. "If you cannot remember what you sneaked up here for, then I think it best you leave. It would hardly do much for your reputation, being found alone with a Norman."

Edwin's face suddenly became sober, as if she had reminded him at last of his true mission. "Aye, well. As to that, it can wait a while."

He left as suddenly as he appeared, leaving Madselin to stare at the closed door. In truth, no matter how much he irritated her, it was hard to dislike the man when he was in his strange, humorous mood. Sighing, Madselin turned to the bed.

Chapter Eleven

The beach lay windswept and deserted, save for a lone gull pecking with determination at a morsel stranded there by the thrust of the waves. A cold gust of rain blew through every one of the six layers Madselin had put on that morning and she turned, blue-lipped, to face her pitiless torturer.

"I see no good reason for doing this, Angle. You might feel at home here in the wild, freezing cold, but Norman ladies are used to gentler living and warmth. I can assure you that ladies have no such aptitude for fighting. We leave that to men and peasants."

Edwin had planted himself solidly before her, his face seaward and his braids floating a little with the strength of the wind. "Believe me, woman. I've seen a Norman lady do this afore now with my own eyes." Those same grey eyes skimmed over her once again, earning him another glare. "As far as I can tell, your body is not ailing and your eyes…"

She raised her hand impatiently to draw a halt to any further speculation on his part. Edwin appeared to have surveyed her person with a thoroughness that was most unexpected. "I did not say there was anything wrong with me, just the activity." Her teeth began to chatter and she pulled her heavy cloak about her.

"Orvell is a clever man," he explained slowly as if to a rather backward child. "It will do you no harm to learn to protect yourself."

"I thought that was your job?" she pointed out with a superior sniff.

"Aye, but there's always a chance I'll not be there. You are a most difficult woman to…"

"Pin down," she finished tersely. "Aye, you mentioned that, but I have not noticed you having that much difficulty creeping up on me or lurking close by in dark places." Her disgruntled expression caused Edwin to grin.

"I had no idea my presence unsettled you so much."

"Oh?" she uttered in disbelief. "As to that, I would say that your presence is more of an irritation, in fact."

The grin deepened. "Very gratifying," he added.

"Look," Madselin gritted out between clenched teeth. "As you have dragged me outside in this… this…howling gale, could you just get on with it?"

He inclined his head before giving their surroundings a narrow-eyed inspection. They were standing at the edge of the beach since it provided, he pointed out gravely, the softest landing for her. The forest beyond seemed quiet compared to the noisy waves that crashed heavily onto the beach. Edwin then turned back to Madselin and eyed her speculatively.

"You're well built for a woman and probably far stronger than you imagine. Perhaps we should try a few basic moves without a knife first? To get you used to a man's strength." His grin had been replaced by a solemn expression that led Madselin to believe the man was truly serious.

"Whatever you think," she grumbled with a distinct lack of enthusiasm.

"Madselin," came the stern rebuke. "I am trying to be of help to you."

She sighed. "Very well. What will you have me do?"

For at least a candle notch, Edwin proceeded to show Madselin some of the more effective methods of warding off a strong man. Although at first clumsy and unsure, she eventually began to feel more confident. A wave of something akin to pure glee surged through her when she finally managed to floor him with a heavy thud.

"Hah!" she crowed at Edwin's inert body. "It would appear you men have been fooling everyone for years. This is not so difficult." When she received no answer, Madselin looked at him more closely. There was no movement and his eyes remained closed. Panic assailed her and she looked around wildly but could see no form of help.

Kneeling at his side, Madselin gently patted a stubbly cheek. "Edwin? Edwin?" Her voice became louder and she placed her faced directly above his to see if she could detect any signs of breathing. There were none. "Dear God," she whispered. "I've killed him." She just sat there, staring at him in stunned silence, her heart thudding loudly and her fingers gently stroking his cheek.

Suddenly, two strong hands squeezed her arms tight and pulled her full length on top of him. Quickly he rolled over so that she was effectively trapped beneath him. A pair of shining grey eyes blinked down at her.

"I thought you were dead." Her fear had been replaced by a slow-burning anger. "I was just about to send up a prayer of thanks," she hissed.

His nose and mouth were no more than a fingertip above her own and his weight was considerable. There was absolutely no possibility of escape. "Aye, I felt you battering my face with your fingers," he smiled.

Until that point, Madselin had felt relatively safe, but the minute he smiled at her in that certain way he had, her innards turned to water and her limbs refused to co-operate with any command she gave. It was, however, becoming increasingly difficult to breathe. All she could manage was a breathless "Wretch!"

"We men are wily creatures." He pulled her arms above her head and imprisoned them between his fingers. "You should always be prepared for the unexpected, lady. Never assume a man is no threat just because his eyes are closed."

Madselin gaped at him, somewhat chastened by his speed. Well, then. He wasn't the only one who could be wily. "Perhaps this is exactly where I want to be, Angle," she managed a little breathlessly and studied his expression. A tide of red rose gratifyingly up from his neck and he heaved himself a little further away from her nose to look down at her more comfortably.

This small distraction was not quite enough, however. "If you moved a little to the side, I could show you what I had in mind?" Her eyes shone at him with what she hoped was barely concealed excitement and it certainly earned an instant response from her tutor. Edwin shifted on to the sand and let her hands go. As he was reaching for her, Madselin managed to jam her fist in his throat and her foot in his shin before scrabbling to safety.

This time Edwin writhed in agony on the sand. She deduced that this was a more successful ploy than his. "You win," he groaned, before rolling on to his haunches and heaving himself to his feet. "I'll not tumble another Norman lady in a hurry."

Madselin folded her arms and smiled up at him

smugly. She was beginning to enjoy herself. "It was very simple, Angle. I relied on your baser instincts coming to the fore. It would seem you are a most predictable man."

Edwin rubbed vigorously at his throat and shook his head ruefully. "Aye. Ghislaine used to say that."

"Ghislaine?" she enquired, as if she didn't really know.

"Ghislaine de Courcy. My former mistress."

There were two—or possibly three—ways of looking at that statement, but Madselin decided it would perhaps be prudent to concentrate on the "former". "A most astute woman," she murmured. After a brief hesitation, Madselin decided she wanted to know more about this Ghislaine. "Is she pretty?" she asked curiously.

Edwin sat back down on the sand to attend to his leg. "Pretty? Aye, I thought so. Long, wild red hair and dangerous eyes. Skinny." He flickered her a glance. "Younger than you, of course."

Stung, Madselin turned on him furiously. "I asked you if she was pretty, not young," she snapped. "Perhaps our lesson is concluded? If not, I have many pressing concerns back at the keep and would be most grateful if we could finish."

"If you say so, lady." He hauled himself to his feet and produced a small dagger from under his tunic. Its cold blade glimmered menacingly under the stormy grey skies. "Hold it," he commanded.

Taking the weapon into her hand, Madselin knew a shiver of forbidden strength. It felt cold, hard and very dangerous. When she had gripped it comfortably, she looked up at Edwin. "What now?"

Without taking his eyes from hers, Edwin threw off his cloak and pulled up his tunic. Acres of goose-bumped brown flesh stood before her and Madselin felt her own chest constrict as she remembered how soft his skin had felt. He reached for her dagger hand and pulled the point into a spot just above mid-centre. "Aim here. It will kill quickly if you push up hard enough."

He watched her agonised expression with an amused grin on his lips. "You'd best try. It's harder than you think."

Madselin pressed her lips together tightly. What on earth was she doing with a half-naked English man on the beach in the middle of a gale? "I hope," she said repressively, "that I would have attempted something long before my attacker was in a semi-naked state. Even you have a tendency to wear a hauberk when you go out on patrol."

Edwin stiffened. "Aye, but I was just showing you where to aim for. You said you were innocent and I took you at your word. I assumed you have little knowledge of a man's body. Other than a sick one, that is."

"I've learned more than enough for a lifetime since I came across you," she retorted quickly. "Now put your tunic back on before you die of a chill and force me to observe far more of your body than you had intended."

Surprisingly, he obeyed without dissent and Madselin put her speed down to the freshness of the wind.

Lunging, jabbing and ripping were the most important features of using a dagger and although her efforts were competent eventually, Edwin was not happy at her lack of killing instinct.

"For all our differences, Angle, I have surprisingly no real wish to injure you," she observed sardonically.

A look of disbelief wiped the grin from his face. Edwin laughed out loud. "You can't hurt me, woman."

"Then what is the point of this charade?" she ground out. "Obviously there are few men with as magnificent a physique as you, but I assume there must be similarities.''

''Magnificent?'' Disconcerted by Madselin's description of his body, Edwin blushed.

Watching him, she realised he really had no idea of the effect his body could have on a woman. ''Fortunately,'' she continued unabashed, ''your brains are clearly lacking and your body has to compensate where it can.''

Recovering quickly, Edwin frowned. ''Then if that is the case, you should have no fears about being outwitted by me. I suggest,'' he finished menacingly, ''you put it to the test.''

''Fine!''

The contest was over in less time than it took to blow out a candle. Edwin emerged unscathed and Madselin glared at the dagger lying in the sand.

''I've had enough, Angle,'' she muttered disconsolately. ''Take me back.''

He stooped to pick up the weapon. ''Aye.'' His lips smiled at her tone. ''You've done well.''

''For a woman, you mean?'' Madselin raised her brows in question.

''For a Norman lady,'' he corrected, blatantly ignoring her reluctant smile. ''I was right about one thing, though.''

''Oh?''

''That body of yours is very healthy.''

Madselin's cheeks remained red all the way back to the keep.

It had become her recent habit to don her coney-lined cloak before the late meal was served and spend a little time up on the battlements. Standing with her face pointing seawards and her hair blown back by the wind, Madselin had grown to love those solitary moments of pure peace.

Such fragments of time were unknown to her at her own home. At those moments when the world hovered between light and dark, she would feel something close to a deep contentment. No matter how much she at first wished to deny such a ridiculous idea, Madselin gradually came to accept that she no longer hated living there.

Madselin sighed. It would be harder to go home now and she was glad that she had until at least after Yuletide before returning to the Vexin.

The sound of the gong calling the keep dwellers to the meal interrupted her thoughts. Slowly Madselin descended the stone steps, the icy cold almost burning its way through the soft leather soles of her shoes.

Her mind dwelt on the coming ambush and of Edwin and his men who might not return. Her stomach lurched a little. She did not doubt for a minute that the Angle would not give in without a terrible struggle, but in her mind's eye Madselin remembered the face of the red-headed butcher who had led the previous ambush in the forest. Edwin was indeed a marked man and Orvell had made it clear how much he wanted to kill him.

The subject of her thoughts crashed into her as he raced up the steps.

"Oof. You stupid…"

"Angle?" he offered once more, along with his hand.

Madselin straightened up, furiously brushing the dust and dirt from her cloak. "If this is meant to be a further lesson in combat…"

He held his hand to stay her tongue. "Nay. Emma told me where you were and I was afraid you might miss the meal. After all," he added with raised eyebrows, "a healthy woman needs her strength."

Madselin gave him a withering stare. As he was stood two steps below her, they were almost eye to eye. "Are you not afraid I would put your lesson into practice, Angle? I now have the experience to do much damage even to a large man as yourself."

"Hmm," he muttered thoughtfully. "I think I preferred magnificent." He bent his head for a moment as he fumbled at his belt. "Here. Now you can use it, you'd best strap it to your leg. It will be safe enough there," he added wryly.

Under the flickering torchlight, a silver dagger lay on Edwin's outstretched palm. It was not the same one she had used with him that morning. This one was smaller and more intricately patterned. His expression was most solemn.

Speechless, Madselin began to shake her head. "No," she began quietly. "I couldn't take that. It's yours."

His eyes watched her gravely, drinking in her flustered expression. "It was my mother's." His eyes flicked down to the sharp blade. "It has tasted Orvell's blood. She would wish it so," he added.

Touched beyond all measure, Madselin gulped silently and then held out her hand to take the weapon. This one was warm to her touch and very pretty. "Would you not wish to give this to your wife?" Her voice was almost a whisper as she examined the dagger closer to.

"Aye, but I think it an unlikely prospect. I aim to kill Orvell or die in the attempt. My chances of survival are not good either way. The King is not in the habit of allowing natives to murder his barons."

Tears pricked unexpectedly at her eyes and Madselin willed herself to stay in control of her emotions. For all their ruffling of each others feathers, she realised that there was a certain intimacy in it. His death was impossible to contemplate.

She smiled shyly. "Then I accept your kind gift." Their eyes held. "But I cannot take it without you having something of mine." Seeing that he was about to object, Madselin quickly placed a finger gently on his lips.

"It is a custom of my people. Say nothing." Slipping a tiny ring of intertwined gold threads from her finger, her lips twitched in amusement. "It's not very manly, but I would be honoured if you accepted it. My mother gave it to me."

His cheeks burned in pleasure as he placed the ring reverently in his belt pouch. "I shall keep it close."

He looked up at her. "Amongst my people, we have a custom too. When a man bids farewell to a woman, they offer no words. Just a kiss."

"Oh."

It was a chaste, almost brotherly kiss that left Madselin with a raging desire to put her arms around his neck and pull him close. Instead, he did it for her. "That was the custom," he whispered in her ear. "This is for me."

This time, Madselin had absolutely no cause for complaint. He kissed her hard and with a thoroughness that left her completely breathless. If it hadn't been for the noise of the sentry clattering down the stone steps, Madselin could not have been certain that either of them would have been able to stop. As it was, Edwin broke away first. "Perhaps you would accompany me to dinner, Lady de Breuville?"

Madselin could only manage a contrite nod before the interested eyes of the sentry.

The feasting hall looked very festive that evening and Madselin supposed that it was Joanna who had ordered the additional greenery adorning the walls. A wonderful smell of pine and forest invaded the whole room and seemed to have affected everyone. The noise of excited chatter was dreadful.

Food and drink had not been spared and everyone participated with gusto. Well, she noted, at least amongst those who would remain at the keep. The men leaving later appeared to be drinking sparingly of ale. Madselin herself had no stomach for the wine. High up, the shutters rattled with the force of the wind and despite the heat of the room, she felt herself shiver.

Edwin, sitting to her right, had been engaged deep in conversation with Gyrth for much of the time. When there was an apparent lull in their dialogue, Madselin took her chance.

"Have you a plan?" she asked quietly.

Edwin stopped chewing on the mutton bone and looked up at her, slightly askance. "A plan?"

Perhaps he had drunk more than she had thought? "Of attack," she clarified. Madselin noticed that Gyrth had also stopped eating, clearly awaiting Edwin's reply.

"Aye. I have a plan." He continued gnawing the bone. "But I think it best if you know nothing of it."

"So you still don't trust me," she replied huffily and not a little hurt. Madselin pushed her trencher back.

"Aye, I trust you. It's Orvell I don't trust. He has no scruples about hurting women. You're safer not knowing."

Eyeing her somewhat impatiently, he rubbed his chin.

"But someone here has to know what's going on. Isabella would have insisted."

Edwin and Gyrth exchanged looks before staring back down at their ale cups. Seizing her moment, Madselin pressed on. "If Orvell is as clever as you say, then the keep could very well be in danger anyway. The visit yesterday was most likely so that he could find out more about our defences.''

He shifted on his seat before answering that one. She decided Edwin was looking a little perplexed and she could almost hear him thinking to himself. ''Most likely. That's why I've sent two messengers to Mallet at the d'Aveyron keep. He'll send more men.''

''Oh.''

Putting his bone down somewhat regretfully on his trencher, Edwin turned to look at her. ''You'll be well protected, lady. Ulf remains here with enough men to last out until Mallet sends his reinforcements.''

She raised her eyes slowly to his. ''And what happens if they don't arrive? Orvell will have the keep under observation, no doubt. A couple of messengers are not likely to prove difficult to kill.''

''Whatever happens, stay here.'' His eyes flickered to her leg. ''If…if his men find you, use the knife on yourself first. They won't spare you, since you know too much.'' He looked at her steadily. ''Orvell enjoys subjecting people to degradation and pain. God would understand.''

Despite the din all around them, Madselin was sure that the two of them inhabited at that moment a very private world. She suddenly realised just how much she had come to respect his solid, reassuring presence and how much faster her blood ran whenever he was there. Her head moved imperceptibly closer to his. ''You'll take care, Edwin.''

Despite their audience, a large hand crept gently over her much smaller one. It felt warm and strong as his fingers squeezed hers gently. ''I wish you well in your marriage, Madselin. I hope he's a strong man.''

That little piece of humour dispelled the strong emotional pull that Madselin felt for her erstwhile foe and she smiled grudgingly. It was sometimes hard to remember Hugh's face. "My thanks."

A chance remark by one of their neighbours broke the spell and the meal continued with very little further communication between them.

The patrol left not long after when the night clouds had blanketed the land in a blackness that was almost evil. Madselin could see nothing as she watched Edwin and his men melt into the night as they slipped silently from the keep. If Orvell was watching, he made no move. Unsure of what she could do, Madselin made her way to the church. A prayer might help.

An urgent tapping on her shoulder made Madselin jump in surprise. She was kneeling before the altar, concentrating so hard that she had heard no sound behind her. Father Padraig stood there, dripping wet, his face creased with worry. "The guard sent me to you. An old tinker is outside the gate, demanding entry."

Before Madselin could say a word, the priest held his hand up to forestall her. "He says he has news of a young woman that sounds much like Blanche."

Rising quickly, Madselin turned to Father Padraig. "Take me to him."

Despite the raw, wet night the old man was barely covered. Rain dripped from thin, matted strands of grey hair and the rags he wore were thoroughly soaked. His bones were the size and shape of twigs, ready to snap at the first gust of wind.

Clearly exhausted, the old man could barely stand and supported himself against the gate.

"Let him in," she commanded against her better

judgement. Trap or not, she could not allow an old man to die out there. The soldiers had been shooting wolves as target practice for the past few days. If any remaining wolf caught his scent, he'd be dead before they could find anything out.

Once the old man had stumbled through the gate, Father Padraig wrapped his own cloak about his shoulders and Madselin sent a soldier for a bowl of pottage and a loaf of bread. As the man could barely walk, the priest hauled him to his feet and led him to the sentries' hut.

The hut offered little more than protection from the elements and only a little warmth from the brazier, but the man accepted it all with gratitude. At least, Madselin thought he did, but even though her command of the local tongue was improving, it was hard to understand him. His teeth were long gone and as a result, his diction was very sadly lacking. Father Padraig understood.

The priest pinned his fierce eyes on the old man and fired a multitude of questions at him. Thanks to his occasional explanations Madselin was able to follow more or less what the man had to say.

His name was Saer and he came from Orvell's village. The villagers had heard of Edwin's endeavours to take Orvell and they wanted to help. Their lord's cruelty and viciousness were killing them all and it was agreed between them that this would be their chance.

Orvell and his men had left that morning and not returned, having planned a secret meeting with the Scots not far from the de Vaillant keep. Saer had volunteered to run the risk and warn Edwin. It would seem that he was making his way through the forest when he heard someone crying out.

At first he was frightened, thinking it was a boggart or one of the spirits that haunted the place, but as he hurried on, he realised the voice belonged to a woman. A terrified, pitiful wailing that speared him to the heart.

Father Padraig's expressive brows were raised in disbelief at this juncture, but Madselin could see the man was in a world of his own. He was picturing the scenes and reporting it carefully.

The woman had long, blonde hair which was filthy and matted. He could tell from her well-nourished body that she was no simple peasant, but her clothes were in muddy tatters and she was bleeding.

Confused, Madselin demanded to know why he hadn't brought her back with him. Father Padraig hesitated a moment and then asked him. The old man's face drained of colour and he pursed his thin, cracked lips around his toothless gums. He spat out an answer that left the priest staring at him in silence.

"What?" She shook Father Padraig's arm. "What did he say?"

The silence stretched on.

"She's been chained by her neck, beaten to a pulp and left for wolf bait," he replied tonelessly.

"Dear God," she whispered, feeling her blood turn to ice. "Why?"

He ignored the question and spat a barrage of words at the tinker. His response was to shake his head and point a shaky finger in a northerly direction.

"Orvell. He's made use of her and now he's left her to die."

He said a few words to the old man, who nodded and stood shakily on his feet. "I'll get her and the old man will take me to her."

Madselin nodded. "Take Ulf. If it is a trap, he'll be some protection."

"No doubt Orvell did not expect Blanche to be found

so quickly. It can be the only reason the old man survived this far.''

Madselin nodded wearily. ''Go quickly.''

As the three men left the keep, Madselin watched them, wondering exactly what sort of man Henry Orvell could truly be. The man's soul was evil. Heartsore, she rested her forehead on the cold wood of the gate and sent up a prayer for their safety.

Chapter Twelve

The candle had burned down two notches before the sentry called out that strangers approached. Until then, they had all sat in the hall on tenterhooks, not sure of anything save that they could all be in danger. Especially Edwin.

Joanna was sat with her son sleeping in her arms, her face pale and drawn. It was hard to know who she was more concerned for, since Gyrth had gone with Edwin and Blanche, despite their differences, was still her sister. She had said little, answering distractedly in monosyllables, bending occasionally to kiss her son's blond hair.

Bronwen had been strangely quiet as she helped Madselin to prepare salves and ointments that they might need for Blanche if she had survived. A small bed had been made up in Isabella's solar and a pail of hot water steamed by the fire.

Practical as ever, Bronwen had insisted on some usquebaugh being on hand, since that was the only thing that would bring her through the shock. Once everything was readied, there was nothing else left to do save wait.

When the call was heard, they sprang to their feet, speechless, before rushing to the gate. The sentry had identified four strangers, but only three appeared to be moving. The fourth hung limply in Ulf's arms. When they finally staggered through the gate, Madselin put her hand to her mouth and hoped to God she would not be sick.

Blanche was unrecognisable. Her pretty, pouting face was broken and bloody. From the gaping wounds in her scalp it was clear that thick clumps of her hair had been pulled out. Father Padraig had covered her body with his cloak but he had been unable to hide what was left of her mangled feet. They looked as if they had been clubbed until they were no more than a bloody pulp.

Ulf gently carried the girl into the solar. All the while he muttered words in his strange tongue which seemed to have a calming effect on Blanche. Bronwen whispered that he was offering a prayer to the old gods and Madselin decided that it couldn't do any harm.

It might have been better had she died straight away. There wasn't a part of her body that hadn't been beaten or whipped. Her teeth, nose and several ribs were broken and Madselin was not at all sure that one of her eyes would recover. The girl had been subjected to an appalling assault and cruelly left to die slowly and in fear.

Madselin reached for the poppy juice so that Blanche could at least be spared the pain for a while. "No!" shouted Joanna suddenly. Kneeling at her side and gently lifting her head up, Joanna tried to rouse her. "What did you do, Blanche?" she demanded urgently. "Tell me what you did."

Blanche rolled her head from side to side and moaned, trying to push her sister away. Joanna would not go. "What did you do for him to have done this, Blanche?"

One eye blinked rapidly beneath its blue, swollen lid

and her cracked lips moved a little. Joanna moved close
to her mouth.

"Louder, Blanche. Speak louder."

The others shifted uncomfortably, compelled to watch
all the same.

"I told him." The voice was barely more than a broken, hoarse whisper but they all heard it.

"Told him what?"

"About Edwin." Blanche's head drooped to one side,
but Joanna pulled it back again and gently patted her
cheeks. The pain quickly brought the girl round.

"What did you tell him about Edwin?" Joanna demanded.

"About tonight."

Joanna looked up at Madselin. "Dear God. He knows
they'll be there. They don't stand a chance."

"Edwin sent a messenger to Albert Mallet for reinforcements. They may come in time." Madselin picked
up the pail of water and laid it by Joanna.

"Messenger dead." There was no misunderstanding
Blanche's meaning.

Joanna shook Blanche lightly. "Why? In God's name,
Blanche, why did you do it?"

The eye flickered in Madselin's direction and the lips
cracked into the ghost of a smile.

Madselin stared down at her. The girl had done it out
of jealousy. She had gone after Orvell and told him what
she knew of the ambush. All because of her.

"There's no way of telling them now. No one knows
where they are." Madselin's voice was flat and toneless.
It was her fault the men were going to die. She had
thought up that stupid plan and made Blanche think that
she and Edwin were lovers. He had not wanted to, but
she had insisted.

Whilst Joanna administered the usquebaugh and Emma ushered the men from the room, Bronwen drew Madselin to one side. "I know where they will be." Her voice was low and her eyes solemn.

"How?" Madselin looked at Bronwen in amazement. Edwin had refused to tell her but she found it hard to accept he would have told Bronwen.

Bronwen stared at her with bold eyes. "I overheard him talking to Gyrth. Besides, I know this area well enough to work out the most probable landing sites for the Scots. It isn't that hard. Edwin will be close."

A little disconcerted by Bronwen's willing admission, Madselin realised that it was in fact a good job she did tread quietly. "Can you tell me?"

Assessing her for a moment, Bronwen finally shook her head. "You'd never find it in broad daylight, let alone a cloudy night. Besides, you'd be dead before you got there. If the wolves don't get you first, Orvell's men will."

"Well, there has to be a way or we're all in danger. Can you think of anything better?"

The dark eyes glanced at the other occupants of the room. "I might," she said. "But it's still very dangerous."

A deep groan from the bed made Madselin shiver. Why indeed was she wanting to risk her life for these people? They should mean less to her than her own people in the Vexin and they were also English. But her conscience would not let her go. She had created this problem and she would have to do something at least.

Almost as if she knew what Madselin was thinking, Bronwen sighed heavily. "She'll die within the hour. There's no saving her. It's just as well, perhaps."

Anger and helplessness fired through her blood as

Madselin gazed at Blanche's broken body. "Tell me." Her voice was firm and decisive.

"Well," she began, "old Saer could take you. He knows every blade of grass hereabouts." Her eyes glittered down at her and Madselin was certain it stemmed from excitement. Could she trust Bronwen? Was she Orvell's creature after all?

"You know Saer, then?" Madselin asked, her suspicions aroused.

"Aye, although I'm surprised he had the courage to come here. The man's never been keen to cross Orvell."

Frowning, Madselin considered her options. Saer, too, could just be another in Orvell's pay. Just because he brought Blanche back proved absolutely nothing. Orvell could have planned it that way. Inhaling deeply, she looked over at Blanche. Or it could just work. With little more than a brief regret at breaking her word to Edwin, she gave a curt nod. "I'll do it."

It wasn't until Bronwen exhaled loudly in relief that Madselin realised the woman had been holding her breath at all. "What are my chances, do you think?"

Bronwen raised her hand to touch her face. "You have a strong face to match a strong will, lady. I hope your God smiles down on you." With no more than a brief nod, she put her arm in Madselin's and led her to the door. "Come. There's no time left."

If Saer was Orvell's creature, then he was indeed a very wily one. For an old man who had appeared on the point of death not long before, he had achieved a most remarkable recovery.

It could, Madselin supposed, have had something to do with Ulf and the rather threatening words he heaped about the old man just before he lead her through an ancient, unused side door. His black eyes gleamed some-what wickedly in the flickering torchlight before the thin shoulders shrugged their reply.

Ulf grabbed Madselin's shoulder and squeezed it in a gesture she now recognised as that shared by the fighting Englishmen. It signified respect as well as farewell. Clearly she had risen somewhat in his estimation and despite the smile that curved her lips upwards she could also feel the tears pricking her eyes. There was nothing they could say to each other. Ulf stood back to let them pass.

Her companion showed a surprising amount of speed and agility. He was clearly possessed of cat's blood too, since he was the only one who appeared to be able to see the path ahead. There was no moon to light the way.

Scrambling quickly down the steep, rocky path, Saer did not look back to ensure that Madselin was managing to keep up. Obviously, she told herself wryly, he was not used to walking with Norman ladies. Muttering some choice oaths that she had picked up in the keep, Madselin pulled up her skirts and scrabbled after him.

As they reached the lower part of the hill, the sharp stones gave way to muddier earth and malicious gorse bushes that ripped her clothes and her skin to shreds. Saer then began to zigzag his way down with increasing speed until he reached a small clump of alder trees.

Madselin arrived moments later on her backside, her dignity, as well as her cloak, in tatters. Her colourful language caused Saer to offer her a toothless smile. "Not bad for a Norman," he muttered in heavily accented French.

"You speak French?" she accused through gritted teeth.

"Of course," he replied impatiently. "Get down, lady,

or I'll not be answerable to that great ox for your death.'' For an old man he had a surprisingly youthful tone to his threat, but Madselin decided this was not the time to discuss it. ''This way.''

Surprised that they had managed to reach the forest without being attacked, Madselin now realised that the danger here was far greater. The silence about them was as deep and impenetrable as the dark, but she could feel the hairs on her body stand on end. It had naught to do with the cold or the rain.

''The wolves aren't far now,'' came a rasping whisper close to her ear. ''They can smell the girl's blood and they're hungry.''

As if to illustrate the point, one wolf howled loudly and plaintively, causing Madselin's blood to freeze. Saer lifted his head, like a horse smelling the wind, before pulling her swiftly to the left. Whether she trusted him or not, Saer was her only hope of survival and she followed where he led.

Every so often, Saer would pause to listen and, God help her, she could hear it too. Light rustling to their right alerted her to the fact that they were, indeed, being followed.

''Have you a knife, lady?'' Saer's voice was little more than a whisper.

''Aye.''

''Then have it at the ready. The beast is close by.''

With her heart in her throat, Madselin pulled the dagger from the strap round her thigh and ruefully acknowledged that Edwin might have been right. She was not at all confident that his advice could be used against a four-legged attacker, but she would be willing to try. Gripping the dagger until it bit into her fingers, she edged forward with Saer.

"Just one on its own for now. If we can kill it first, we might have a chance."

She was so close to Saer that she could smell his rancid breath and unwashed body, but nevertheless she would have moved closer even still if it were possible. There wasn't a fibre of doubt that this was a trustworthy man. Suddenly his hand grabbed at her arm. It was surprisingly warm and despite the rain felt like parched leather.

"Here it comes. Hold still. If I miss it, aim your knife for its belly."

A pair of yellow eyes now blinked at them a short distance away, waiting patiently. Madselin was feeling sick and faint but determined not to die.

The only sign of the wolf moving was no more than a faint rustle, but Saer was ready. There was no sound bar a growling and then a suppressed yelp. Then silence.

"Saer!" She was terrified to move.

"Aye. I'm still here, lady." The old man crawled back to her, breathless but alive. "A rabid old beast he was," was the only comment he made before urging her on.

Madselin estimated that they had covered another two miles or so before Saer pulled her down again.

"There's someone ahead. Wait there."

She had an uncontrollable urge to drag on his arm and demand he take her with him, but did not actually think it would have any effect on the man. Dutifully she crept behind the trunk of a massive old tree and crouched down to wait. Edwin would have been impressed, she thought, and then wondered if she would ever see him again.

Her eyes were out on stalks and she flinched at every sound until Saer returned a few minutes later. "Hurry, woman," he hissed. "I can see the lights of the boat. They're close by."

Madselin had not even been aware that they were near

the beach, but did not need telling twice. Rising quickly to her feet, she walked headlong into a hawthorn bush. She felt its spikes rip the skin over her cheeks but pushed it aside. This was no time for female hysterics.

Heart hammering, she gripped the dagger even more tightly, although she was certain that she would be frozen to the spot if the worst came to the worst. It did, however, give her a feeling of security. They crept through the undergrowth until ahead of them she could sense rather than see a clearing. The darkness about them had also been changing in quality and somehow seemed lighter.

Madselin had been aware that the forest was thinning out and the tangy smell of the sea was stronger. The wind that edged along the coast caused the trees to sway and creak in an alarming fashion. Madselin clutched at what was left of her cloak.

"Wait here." Without discussing the matter further, Saer disappeared, only to reappear a few seconds later with Edwin.

Although she couldn't tell who it was exactly, the tone of his voice was enough.

"You broke your word." His voice was harsh and uncompromising.

"You're in danger," she hissed at him, half-overjoyed to still find him alive, half-wanting to throttle him for his ungrateful attitude. "Orvell knows you're here."

There was a gratifying silence whilst Edwin absorbed her words.

"Why did you have to come? Saer could have come on his own."

"Saer could easily have been killed. We were attacked by a wolf as it was." The half of her that had been pleased to find him alive was very quickly subsiding into the remaining half.

Muttering several oaths that Madselin had never heard before, Edwin grabbed her arm and pulled her further away from Saer's interested ears.

"When I give you an order, I expect you to obey it, you foolish Norman." He sighed heavily and by the sound of it, he was rubbing his hand over the stubble on his chin.

To her horror, Madselin could feel the tears pricking at her eyes. Angrily she dashed them away with her hand and was just about to tell him exactly what she thought of him when a shadowy figure approached them.

There was a hurried, confused whispering and then the man left quickly.

"The boat's about to land. Now," he tugged at her arm, "wait here and don't make a sound."

"But Orvell will be waiting."

"Aye, but I've a plan. If you hear fighting, wait. No one knows you're here. You'll be able to escape when the light comes. Do you understand me, woman?" He gave her a shake that would cause several bruises to her arm.

"Very well." All tender feelings had vanished, to be replaced by a definite hardening of the heart. "The next time you need rescuing, I shall leave it to God to save your miserable soul."

Her note of absolute sincerity must have roused some finer feelings in the brute since he gave an exasperated sigh before pulling her hard to his chest and squeezing the breath from her. Without another word, he pushed her from him and disappeared into the shadows.

The world was black and silent for several heartbeats before a familiar smell assailed her nostrils.

"Saer?" she whispered.

"Aye, lady. Your man asked me to guard you."

It seemed from his tone that the old man did not particularly see a great deal of merit in this task. He spat on the ground in disgust and settled down on his haunches not far away in the bushes. Madselin crept to her allotted hideaway.

It seemed like hours before the tension was broken by a wild shouting and screaming as if all the spirits of the forest had converged on them. Madselin closed her eyes and prayed hard before realising that was probably a very foolish thing to do. Clutching her knife close to her breast, she almost stabbed herself with it. Saer moved closer as the noise grew louder.

Swords clashed and sparked against each other and inhuman cries rent the air. Madselin sank further into the bushes, terrified. Suddenly, she became aware of a different sound, and she doubted very much that it was human. Frantically she looked around, but Saer was nowhere in sight. Her heart was beating so fast she thought it might burst. The noise, a rustling, rooting sort of sound, was growing closer. Somehow she doubted it was a wolf since she had the impression of a much larger animal. Could it be a boar?

Suddenly the animal bayed. It was a cry born of hunger and hatred and her heart almost stopped. Never had she heard anything like it. A vague memory floated through her mind. ''Hound from hell''. Bronwen had once told her that her husband had been torn to pieces by Henry Orvell's favourite hunting dog. She closed her eyes and prayed, having no desire to stare death in the face.

The stench of wet animal hair and the rank smell of death was accompanied by a snarling fury that made Madselin cower into a tiny ball. The fetid breath turned her stomach over and she gagged behind her tightly clenched fist. Nothing happened.

A quietly evil laugh erupted by her ear, causing Madselin to risk peeping between her hands. Torch aloft, a familiar red-bearded brute of a soldier leered down at her.

It was the man who had tried to kill Edwin in the ambush.

At his feet, within a jaws-length of her face, lay the most monstrous creature she had ever seen.

Chapter Thirteen

"Well, well, Ballor. It would seem the forest has provided you with your next meal after all."

Even in the torchlight, Madselin could see that her captor was a hard-bitten soldier with ice running through his veins. The dog, presumably Ballor, did not take his eyes from her and had clearly understood those words. Although he was held on a tight leash, it would not have taken much for him to break free.

Once the first shock had worn off, Madselin realised how very alone she was. Saer had disappeared and Edwin's men sounded some way off. She pursed her lips tightly together to stop her lips from chattering with fear.

The soldier hunkered down before her and jabbed the torch into the soft earth beside her. His thick arm lunged forward to grip her chin in a jaw-breaking clench.

"Nice soft skin," he commented as his calloused thumb scraped over her cheek. Madselin gritted her teeth and tried to slide back, but the soldier just jerked her towards him in a bone-crushing grip. The stench of male sweat invaded every pore of her body and she squeezed her eyes shut in denial.

"Now, I wonder why a juicy morsel like you is hiding

in the forest at this time of early morning?'' He pulled her white face closer to the torch for an inspection. ''No peasant, are you, girl?'' His lips pulled back in a snarl of a smile. ''You're not worn enough to be a camp follower, though.''

Madselin was too terrified to speak, but it was dawning on her that the dagger was still firmly in her grip and, as yet, hidden in the folds of her cloak. As the soldier's bug eyes stared at her, Madselin knew that the second she made her move if the man didn't kill her the slavering dog would. It still lay there, motionless, but had not taken its eyes from her.

She gulped. The dagger would be best hidden for now. Trying hard not to make any sudden moves, her hand slipped the dagger to the belt at her back. It would be as safe there as anywhere.

''Come with me, woman.'' The man grabbed her arm and pulled her roughly to her feet. Picking up the torch and pulling at the dog's leash, he jerked his head towards the clearing.

Tripping and stumbling with fear, Madselin moved forward. Bodies lay strewn around and she could see a knot of men still fighting for their lives. Swords clashed against swords and shields, horses and men screamed and danced in the swirling darkness of the forest clearing. Strangely detached from reality, Madselin watched in fascination as men lived and died as fate decreed.

''So, what have we here?'' Henry Orvell's gentle voice broke her trance. A tall figure stepped out from the undergrowth. He was almost invisible since she knew he was garbed in his customary black. Her guard lifted the torch to shine a light over her. All she could see of Orvell was the shine of his pearly white teeth in the dark beyond. ''Lady de Breuville? An unexpected pleasure.''

Swallowing, Madselin managed to utter a mannered reply which caused Orvell to chuckle softly. "Guy was really quite a fool, I think."

Madselin stared at him. "Don't even mention his name, you traitor."

Her strangled threat earned her no more than a raised brow as Orvell stepped into the circle of light. "You still sorrow for him, I take it?" he said eventually after examining her cut face.

"He was a good man," she spat at him. "I'm glad he never knew what an evil man you are."

A fist shot out and connected with the side of her face. She crumpled to the ground, dazed and in terrible pain.

"Enough, Fletcher. This is a lady, not one of the whores you're used to dealing with." Despite the warning sound in his voice, Orvell did nothing more. Madselin could almost feel the smile on his face. The man enjoyed seeing her in pain. Swallowing hard, she fought back the tears.

He offered her his hand, but Madselin ignored it and stumbled proudly to her feet. She wobbled violently but concentrated her mind on remaining vertical.

"I take it you found the servant girl? Pity, but it can't be helped." He paused. "She seemed to think that you and the Englishman were...close." His handsome face gazed down at her as his long fingers traced the line of her jaw. Madselin averted her head, dropping her gaze to the ground. "Hmm. Hard to believe, but perhaps I'll put it to the test since the girl was so insistent."

Madselin found herself grabbed from behind by her violent guard and pushed towards the fight. Uncertain as to her fate, she held her head as high and proud as she was able. Not far ahead she could see Edwin at last and she stifled a cry of relief. He wasn't dead yet.

As she watched him lunge, jab and rip, Madselin was filled with renewed respect and something else. Pride? He was truly magnificent in a fight. Quick and deadly, the man's strength was relentless in his grim task.

"Call him!" Orvell murmured at her side.

"No," she hissed.

Orvell sighed and made a sign at her guard. He knelt to unleash the huge dog who was baring its teeth and drooling with hunger. "Ballor has not been fed for days. I allowed him to bite the girl a little and he's keen to taste blood again. He likes to rip a victim's throat, you know, and yours," he added softly, "is a very pretty throat."

Sick to her stomach, Madselin knew she had failed. "Edwin!" she shouted hoarsely. "Edwin."

She was not at all sure that he had heard so thin a cry, but he looked over in her direction. Deftly sliding his sword through the stomach of one of Orvell's men, he uttered a few unintelligible words and moved forward towards the group.

He did not look at Madselin then, but all the same she wished the ground would open up and swallow her.

"Let her go, Orvell. She has brought me to you, so you have no further need of her." His harsh voice cracked the tension.

Sighing heavily, Orvell smiled across at his foe. "I don't actually think that is true, to be honest. I am, of course, most grateful for her interference," and here he paused to bow in Madselin's direction. "But the lady may serve another...ah...useful function in a short while. Much depends on your co-operation, Englishman." The words were spoken as if between two old friends, but the threat was there.

He waved his hand at Edwin's blood-smeared sword.

"I think I would feel much more comfortable if that dangerous weapon were elsewhere."

Frowning, Edwin stabbed it, point down, into the earth before him. It was the only outward sign of his intense frustration and anger. He stood back and waited. The guard leapt forward and searched him for any other weapons. Finding none, he tied Edwin's hands behind his back.

Madselin watched as he submitted silently to the rough handling of the soldier. He had suffered the same fate under her command, too, and she groaned inwardly. The man had been ill-used by Normans and he still stood proudly. If they ever got out of this alive, Madselin made a promise to God that she would make it up to him.

"Get her tied, too, Fletcher. She may be a Norman but I trust her not." Turning sharply to Madselin, his eyes glittered down at her. "You will be tasting my hospitality a little earlier than planned, Lady de Breuville. Unfortunately, the surroundings will be a little less comfortable than my own keep but...I must entertain some visitors who prefer to remain unseen."

The guard took hold of her hands and yanked them behind her. The twine he used to tie her with cut hard into her skin and she winced. Gritting her jaw, she stamped hard on his toes and knew a certain satisfaction in hearing him gasp.

"Not yet, Fletcher!" Orvell's cool voice prevented her guard's immediate retaliation. "You'll have plenty of time for that later. Get the Scots."

Orvell had signalled for his horse and mounted whilst the soldier had disappeared into the undergrowth. He reappeared a few minutes later with five men of unkempt and somewhat frightening appearance.

Silently, the party retreated from the scene of the fighting and headed towards the north-east, deeper into the forest. Orvell's leaving did not seem to have made much difference to the ferocity of the fighting, so Madselin could only assume that he and the men who now accompanied them had not taken part in the foray.

She puzzled over it for a while as she did her best to keep up with the men and the horses, but lack of sleep and fear were beginning to catch up with her.

They numbered fifteen in all, plus the dog, Ballor. Orvell and the Scots had horses, whilst his guards, like Madselin and Edwin, had to travel on foot. The trees and undergrowth prevented any real pace and she was very glad since her strength was ebbing with the day.

For a while she had been able to concentrate on watching Edwin, who strode just ahead of her. If she could maintain his rhythm, she decided she could just about keep up. Tiredness stole through her body and it became harder and harder to concentrate. Finally, her eyelids drooped and she suddenly found herself floundering in the mud.

Edwin was immediately by her side, his grey eyes anxiously examining her. It was the first time he had even acknowledged her existence since their capture, and Madselin offered him a shaky smile.

"I'll be all right," she murmured. "I just tripped."

The red-haired guard pulled her roughly to her feet.

"She's tired, Orvell. You know she'll only hold you up." Edwin's tone was quiet but authoritative and his eyes stared levelly at his captor.

Orvell pulled his horse around to face him. After a moment or two he glanced down at Madselin. "If she can't keep up, then I'll leave her for the wolves." His voice was harsh and uncompromising now.

"Let me carry her."

Madselin jerked her head up and stared at Edwin. "No!" she gasped. "You'd not last long."

He gave a short, bitter laugh. "I don't think I have much longer left anyway."

Orvell shrugged. "Have it your own way." He gestured to the guard to cut her hands loose so that Madselin could grip Edwin's shoulders.

At first her embarrassment was acute. Her legs gripped his waist and her arms wrapped carefully about his neck. Pressing her body close over his back, Madselin could feel the rapid beat of his heart and smell his male scent. She squeezed her eyes closed and whispered gently into his ear that she was sorry. Edwin said nothing.

Dusk was filtering through the trees when they finally came to a halt. The forest had thinned out considerably and the ground was beginning to rise steeply. The higher they went, the more rock they encountered. Edwin's body was labouring under his extra burden and he allowed Madselin to jump down before collapsing in a perspiring heap at her feet.

"He needs some water," she called to the guard imperiously. The soldier stared at her for a minute before leering at her. Picking up the water skin, he drank deeply of it before tossing it back over his shoulder.

Madselin turned back to Edwin. "I'm sorry," she said quietly.

Edwin eyed her almost blankly and shrugged. Closing his eyes, he lay back on the ground and took the chance to rest while he could. She sat down silently at his side. It was a very bleak moment as she realised that Orvell really did mean to kill them.

"Get a move on," grumbled the guard as he sauntered towards them. He jabbed his toe at Edwin's leg but the

Englishman only sighed before hauling himself to his feet.

"Can you walk now?" His grey eyes looked at her steadily as if trying to give her strength.

"Aye," she replied with a weak smile. "I'm sure I can."

It soon became clear that they were headed for a rocky outcrop near the top of the hill. Madselin was grateful for the use of her hands since the guard had not retied them. Edwin was not so lucky. He fell and stumbled frequently on the slippy pebbles underfoot. Henry Orvell, now on foot himself, would stand and gloat as the Englishman fell.

Madselin was prevented from helping him by Orvell himself. "For every hand you give him, Lady de Breuville," he explained, "he will be rewarded by Fletcher's fist. You understand, I take it?"

It was very clear to Madselin exactly how much the man enjoyed humiliating people and hurting them. It made her wonder—just a little—about Guy. Had he really not known about Henry Orvell? She would never know the answer since she had seen so little of Guy before their wedding.

He had spent only a few weeks in Normandy and although he was not far from her, there had been many things he had to take care of. Madselin remembered then how his lack of attention had hurt, but she had brushed it aside at the time. After all, they would have a long time together to become re-acquainted. Alice had goaded her about that, too.

Finally, they reached their destination. Behind the rocky overhang were two large caves. They were well hidden and invisible to the naked eye from below. Over the centuries, the caves would have provided welcome shelter for many people since they were large and relatively dry. For the time being, they were to accommodate Madselin and Edwin too.

The guard shoved them into the smaller cave and they landed in a heap on the floor. Two other guards remained with him, whilst the others were ordered into the next one. Orvell stared down at the two of them coldly. "You will stay here until my friends and I have made our plans. When they have gone I will then be able to devote my entire attention to you." He smiled then as if remembering something pleasant.

"I think," he said slowly, savouring the sound of his own rich voice, "a manhunt would be a good start to the day." His eyes darted to his prisoners, relishing Madselin's look of absolute terror.

"She's a Norman," Edwin spat. "Why kill her? She's comely enough, if a bit stupid. Surely you have other uses for her?"

Orvell laughed. "For her?" He looked at her and then inclined his head in thought. "Well, it's just possible the Scots might be interested…"

Madselin pulled herself to her feet and glared at him. "I'd rather take my chances on the manhunt," she ground out. There didn't seem to be a lot of difference between those Scots and the dog, but at least there was only one of Ballor.

Edwin gritted his jaw but said nothing.

Orvell's face did not show what he was thinking. His expression was bland, almost mask-like. He reached out to lift her jaw with his gloved hand. "Don't worry, Lady de Breuville," came the soft, menacing voice. "I shall have something suitable planned for you. In the meantime, however, I suggest you rest well."

Jerking his head round at the guards, he barked out his

orders before stalking from the cave. The three guards huddled sullenly round the entrance, leaving the two of them in the gloom. Edwin shuffled backwards until he was sitting with his back against the cave wall. Madselin turned on him.

"So," she began quietly. "You think I'm quite stupid, do you?"

Edwin stared up at her. "No," he replied finally. "I think you are very stupid."

"Oh?"

"Aye. If you were clever, you wouldn't be here."

She couldn't fault that logic. "I was trying to help." Her voice had risen a little with fatigue and fear.

"Well, you didn't. You encouraged him." His voice rang out cold and angry. "Every time I suggested he didn't kill you, you interrupt and practically offer yourself on a plate. If I didn't have both of my hands tied, I'd be trying to throttle you myself."

A huge lump had formed in her mouth, and to her horror, Madselin found she couldn't speak. Huge tears splashed down her cheeks. Edwin, she noticed through her tears, simply rolled his eyes to heaven and then sighed. "Sit down here, by me." It was a definite order and Madselin no longer had the strength or the will to resist. At least Edwin looked warm and comfortable. Hesitantly she sat down next to him.

"Sit between my legs and lean back. It'll be warmer."

It was. And she had been right about him being comfortable. Her head relaxed back against his chest until finally, in a haze of fatigue and terror about the next day to come, she could no longer hold back the tears.

Turning away to hide her face, Madselin felt Edwin lean forward as if to gather her to him. As his arms were still tied behind his back, he couldn't manage that, but he wrapped as much of him around her as he could. His face brushed gently against hers. Rocking backwards and forward, he murmured soft words in his strange language into her hair.

She surrendered totally to her fear and her hurt for a while, weeping until she thought her heart would break. Slowly, very slowly, the tears stopped and she calmed down. "I'm s-s-sorry," she stammered into his chest. "I didn't mean to wet you."

He laughed softly at that. "I think that's the least of our worries now, woman."

"Did you know he killed Blanche?" Her tear-stained eyes blinked up at him. It was best that he knew.

Edwin shook his head silently and then lowered it, deep in thought.

Madselin pushed herself away from him a little. "What will happen, do you think?"

He let out his breath and leaned back against the wall. "Orvell is meeting with the Scots and some of the other barons from along the border. Once they have established a plan of action, the Scots and the barons will leave. Orvell will then concentrate on us."

His honesty was welcome, if nothing else, but the truth certainly hurt. "Will he kill us, then?" she whispered.

Edwin looked down at her and trailed his lips gently along the top of her head. "Aye, he cannot afford to let us live. We know too much."

She gulped. "Is there nothing we can do?"

He looked over at the three soldiers who were now playing a game of dice by the entrance of the cave. "Nay." He looked at her then, his grey eyes soft. "Best sleep a while."

"I'm not sure I can," she said in a quiet voice, but

already she could feel her eyes drooping. "But you're very warm, Edwin. Did you know that?"

His lips had dropped to the highly sensitive part of her skin just below her ear. "It has been said once or twice," he murmured wryly.

His voice sent shivers down her spine and she stretched herself against him in response. In truth, he felt a lot more than relaxed and she was glad that they were in a dark spot so he would not be able to see her blush. "What are you thinking?" she asked, feeling his heart beat begin to throb a little harder.

After a few seconds pause, she felt him shrug. "About kissing you," came the muffled reply.

She smiled and fell asleep, wondering if it was true that Edwin did indeed find her quite comely.

"Madselin!" His voice hissed in her ear. "Madselin!"

Slowly she opened her eyes, half-hoping to find that the whole thing had been a dream. Her stiff, cold body reminded her that it was all horribly true. Edwin's stubble rasped strongly against her cheek as she turned to look up at him.

"Unless you are badly deformed, I cannot imagine what is sticking into my stomach. What is it?" His tone was rather grumpy for someone who had been telling her not long before that he wanted to kiss her.

"The knife!" Her eyes opened wide as they stared at each other. How could she have forgotten? Slowly they turned to look at the guards. One was slumped back against the entrance whilst the other two were taking turns to swig from a skin. It smelled very strongly of rough wine.

Carefully, Madselin edged forward and slipped her hands behind her back to retrieve the knife. Once it was firmly within her grip, her hand stole behind Edwin's back to try to cut the twine at his wrists. It was not easy since he was a big man to reach round, but eventually they did manage. From the amount of blood on her hands, Madselin could tell that it was not only the twine that was cut.

She held her breath for a moment or two. ''Now what?''

Edwin didn't move. ''You'll have to distract the two guards,'' he whispered eventually.

They both stared at the two men who were still drinking and dicing. Edwin then eyed Madselin with a withering look. ''You're a woman. These things are supposed to come naturally.''

''That might be true of Englishwomen, but for us Normans, things are different.'' She tossed her hair back over her shoulder in disgust.

Edwin shook his head in disbelief. Then he stopped. Inclining his head towards her, he gazed at her speculatively. ''They might just be drunk enough to make it work.''

''Make what work?'' She looked at him suspiciously, her heart rate speeding up.

He sat up then, pushing himself hard against her, his chin resting on her shoulder. ''The young one, with the dark hair. He keeps looking at you. Go up to him and smile. Get him to kiss you and whilst you're doing that, I'll deal with the one watching. Try to get him to sit with his back to me.''

''I can't do any of that,'' she breathed.

''Madselin,'' he whispered urgently, ''if you don't, we'll die for certain and time is running out.'' A large hand stole around her hips and patted them appreciatively. "Take my word for it. He won't be able to resist. Do you remember what I taught you with the knife?"

She nodded silently, realising that everything depended on her. It would also have to be quiet so that Fletcher didn't wake up.

Madselin rose somewhat unsteadily and made her way to the front of the cave. The fumes from the wine were very strong, enough to make her stomach curdle, at least. Four bleary, bloodshot eyes stared up at her. The young one, blinked, his soft mouth slack from drink.

"Well, well. Decided to join us, lady?" His voice was thick and not a little slurred. Edwin had been right. Chancing a smile, Madselin stepped forward towards the front of the cave.

"I thought a little fresh air might wake me up." She stretched slowly and languorously, knowing full well that the men were watching her. Dropping her eyes to the younger one, who did possess a certain dark attraction, she smiled again.

His blue eyes glinted up at her and his mouth formed a most unbecoming leer. "I can think of a few ways of waking you up, lady," came the coarse reply. His companion merely grunted like a boar and reached for the wineskin.

"Can't think Orvell will bother much if you've tasted the goods," he said amiably. "She'll be dead soon anyway. I'll not mention it and what Fletcher there doesn't see, he won't know. He's drunk enough to sleep through anything."

Madselin gulped in fear. Her suitor, however, appeared to be warming to the idea. Tossing back the last of the wine, he rose rather unsteadily to his feet and wiped his hands on his hauberk. Slowly with his eyes riveted on

Madselin's breasts, he unbuckled his swordbelt and let it drop at his feet.

"Got a fancy for a real man, lady?" he sneered, and reached out to pull her tight to his chest. "Them knights haven't a clue what to do with it, I'll be bound." He wiped his dribbling mouth with his filthy sleeve and Madselin thought she was going to vomit all over him.

"Well—" she managed with what she hoped was a seductive smile "—you're very handsome and strong." Her fingers lifted to touch his greasy black hair. "If I'm to die, then I might as well die happy." Her lips parted a little and she licked them with the tip of her tongue.

The soldier found this all too much. He pulled back her cloak and covered her breasts with his large hands. Madselin stepped back so that she was facing the inside of the cave with a good view of Edwin. The Englishman had not moved and, in fact, appeared to be asleep.

As if on cue, the other soldier glanced over his shoulder. Satisfied that he was asleep, he hunched up over the wineskin and eyed his partner's activities with barely concealed relish. "If she's any good, I might try her myself," he murmured.

The young soldier's hands were now busy pulling up her skirts and pushing her close to the cave wall. They fell in a heap of legs and skirts. Winded under the weight of the man, Madselin took a few moments to get her breath back. Uncertain as to whether she was supposed to be encouraging him or not, she decided that her Norman partner seemed completely oblivious to her needs. Slowly her hand crept up behind her and dislodged the knife.

The soldier was fumbling with his own clothing when Madselin looked up to see the other soldier lurch to his feet, presumably for a better view. Terrified that he would see what she was doing, she began to struggle. That earned her a winey compliment in the ear from her partner. "I like it when you fight back, lady."

She was just about to fight in earnest when she saw a shadow move stealthily behind their audience. A huge brown hand gagged his mouth and she saw his thick body tense, jerk and then sag. Moaning loudly in what she hoped was an enthusiastic response to her partner's bone-jarring grinding of her hips, she pulled the knife from behind her back.

Before she could do anything more, however, the soldier was heaved away from her and subjected to the same treatment as his friend. Madselin saw his eyes open wide in shock and disbelief before death relaxed its grip and they saw for the last time.

Madselin blinked and lay stockstill. Edwin had killed him for her. Never in all her life had she been so close to death.

"Come. We must leave."

She heard his soft words and dragged herself from her torpor. He heaved the soldier off her and laid him so that he looked to be asleep. Wordlessly he pulled her skirts down and offered her his hand. He felt warm and solid to touch.

"You did well, Madselin." He turned her to him and pulled her hard against him. She breathed his scent and put her arms around him before pushing herself back. He was right. They had to go.

Silently they stepped past the sleeping Fletcher and into the daylight.

Chapter Fourteen

They managed to slip silently from their cave and beyond the rocky outcrop without being seen by the other guards. Neither of them exhaled until they had reached the cover of some bushes. Shaking, Madselin looked over Edwin's broad shoulders. Fletcher still slept.

"Will we make it?"

"I doubt it," came the humourless response. "But we're going to try."

Minutes seemed like hours as they made their way down the steep and dangerous hill. Every time they slipped or dislodged a stone, they froze until the moment of danger passed. When they finally reached the bottom of the hill, Edwin looked up at the overcast sky.

"It's still early, but Orvell won't want to be about in daylight. My guess is that he'll be returning to the caves soon to hide the Scots until the light fades." He looked around, assessing the potential dangers before turning to Madselin. "This time, woman, you're to obey me. Do you understand?" He grabbed her arms and shook her a little.

She nodded. This was no game. They were no longer Norman and English, just two people trying to survive.

Her cold fingers stole over his and squeezed gently. "I promise."

He grinned at her, his teeth white against his brown skin. "Takes quite a bit to put you in order, doesn't it?" Without warning, he crushed her to his chest and subjected her to a kiss that left her blood flowing a lot warmer than it had been. "Much better," he murmured against her ear. "Now, woman. Let's go."

"Which way are we going? Back to the keep?"

He shook his head. "They'll expect us to head in that direction. There's a stream a bit further on which heads south-east which we could follow. It runs through the deep part of the forest and out towards the hills. It's dangerous but it might slow Orvell down. If we make it that far, there are several farms in the hills."

"It sounds quicker to head back for the keep," she said a little sceptically. "We might get quite some distance before they discover us missing. Wouldn't it be better to try, at least?"

Her eyes settled on Edwin's dirty, scratched and impossibly handsome face. His stubble seemed to have grown into hedgehog bristles and she rubbed her chin gingerly.

He reached out and touched the raw skin. Before he could say anything, a wild, terrible baying cracked the morning silence of the forest. Its echo seemed to reverberate for minutes. There was no mistaking the cause of it.

"Ballor," she whispered. Wherever that animal was, it didn't sound far enough away for her liking.

Edwin nodded and grabbed her hand.

For a man who had not slept in over a day, who'd fought for his life against a band of bloodthirsty savages, carried a woman on his back for miles uphill and killed

two men, Edwin's energy was very impressive. He pulled
Madselin along with him, dragging her when she begged
him to stop and almost carrying her when her feet refused
to go any further.

They had covered quite a lot of ground before she
heard the steady thudding of hooves. It was no longer an
escape. This was a manhunt.

Terror coursed through her veins as they sped through
the undergrowth and low-hanging trees. She saw nothing
but a flash of greens and browns and the blue of Edwin's
tunic as he ran before her. Fear made her stumble and
fall. Neither spoke.

Suddenly the wild baying erupted right behind her and
Madselin was certain she could smell the hound's breath
as it hurled through the forest almost at her heels. Edwin
stopped and turned, launching himself at the furious beast
even as it leapt at her.

Dog and man fell in rolling, biting, tearing bundle.
Despite his size, Edwin was finding it hard to contain the
animal. It was nothing more than a heaving mass of anger
and hatred, tearing at Edwin's clothes, ripping at his
brown flesh.

"Run!" he grunted as they writhed on the ground.
"Now!"

She couldn't leave him. She could not.

"Stand back." A voice behind her made her jump a
mile.

"Saer!"

"This creature is mine. I've been waiting for my
chance for years." The old man brandished a wicked-
looking knife and he glared at the wild dog doing its best
to kill Edwin. "He killed my son, Owain. Now it's my
turn. No one will ever call me coward again. Tell Bron-

wen.'' The tired eyes blazed with fervour as he watched the struggle. ''Run, now. Orvell isn't far behind.''

She didn't wait to be told again. Tired though they were, her legs carried her faster than she had ever run before. She could hear a crashing behind her and the thudding of a large, heavy body in pursuit. Gulping for air, she headed for the sound of water just ahead. Without thinking, she launched herself into the stream, spraying water everywhere as she ran.

A blood-freezing scream tore through the air. Neither human nor animal, Madselin had no idea what uttered it and hoped to God it wasn't Edwin. She stopped dead and turned.

Edwin was running towards her, his arm motioning her to go on and hide. Dripping wet, her speed was severely hampered. It was not long before Edwin caught up with her. He was gripping his left arm and she could see from the blood seeping through his fingers that he was injured.

''Saer?'' she asked breathlessly.

He shook his head in response and pulled her with him. ''At least he killed the dog before he died. Come on,'' he whispered. ''They're almost on us.''

Ahead of them, the stream widened and Edwin pulled her towards the deepest part. Bullrushes grew in profusion and it was hard to walk at all. ''Sink down and hold on to me.''

That was easier said than done. Her cloak and skirts billowed up around her as the icy water flooded over her. Edwin pulled them down and wrapped himself around her. They floated out until they lay under the shade of a large, overhanging tree and just waited.

Orvell's was the first voice she heard. ''They can't have gone far. Use the spears.''

Edwin pulled her closer to the tree. "Hold on tight. We'll have to go under soon."

She nodded and drew her body as close as she could to his. The water was bitterly cold and had taken her breath away. If they stayed here for much longer, they would surely die of the cold. Clinging to him, Madselin looked into his eyes. "I'm sorry," she whispered. "For everything."

He did no more than smile and draw his arms around her tight. "If we survive this, Lady de Breuville, rest assured I shall make you pay in kind."

His expression was so wicked that she could not prevent a smile cracking her cold lips.

"Boasting, Angle?"

His eyes held hers in a solemn promise before they sank below the surface.

Horses surged through the water and spears rammed down towards the stream's murky bed.

Edwin pushed her further under the roots of the tree, protecting her with his own body. The blades of swords and spears whipped the surface of the water into stirring foam so that Madselin was certain they would be cut to shreds.

Every so often the need to breathe made them rise slowly and take in great gulps of air, but what they saw made them sink quickly. The place appeared to be swarming with Orvell's brutal men, intent on hunting out their prey.

A curious numbness enveloped her body, allowing her to feel nothing other than a desire just to close her eyes and float away. Suddenly Edwin stiffened. She could tell from the way the water was churning that someone on horseback was close by.

With a fierceness borne of self-preservation, Madselin

gripped Edwin until she could squeeze no more strength from her arms. Way above her, she could hear the jingle of a harness and a loud, rough voice bellowing out to an unseen companion. A sword slashed powerfully through the water before its owner turned the horse back to the centre of the stream.

Slowly, very slowly, they floated up the surface. Riders and guards alike were moving on up the stream, leaving the churning mud and broken bullrushes behind them like a scene of devastation.

"Don't move yet," hissed a voice in her ear. "It's too soon."

They stayed immobile for what seemed like hours and their blood, Madselin was convinced, had frozen in their veins. Finally Edwin roused her from her cold stupor and indicated they could get out. That was not so easy as it seemed. Nothing would move. It wasn't until they had managed to rub each other's limbs vigorously that they could move their legs at all.

They dragged themselves through the rushes and squelched heavily to the banks. Madselin attempted to squeeze some of the water from her cloak and skirts, but it was impossible. Edwin pulled his boots off and emptied them. Neither of them said a word, but there was really no need.

Orvell and his men headed towards the de Vaillant keep, as Edwin had guessed they would, whilst Edwin and Madselin made for the hills to the south-east. The next few hours passed in a haze of cold, numb terror. At least that was true for Madselin. It was hard to see what Edwin thought since his face showed no emotion at all. His expression was set, but she doubted it was just because of the chill in his bones.

"If we do manage to get to the farms, what will happen?'' she asked eventually when they sat hidden under some thick bushes. They were huddled together for warmth since Edwin would not even consider making a fire.

Edwin turned his grey, assessing eyes on her. ''I'll try to send word to Mallet about the Scots in the caves and Orvell. With luck they might take them all.''

''And will Mallet have them killed, do you think?'' She picked up a stick and scraped it along the earth.

''No.'' His reply was fierce and immediate. ''I'll kill Orvell.''

''You?'' Madselin jerked her head up to stare at him.

''Aye. I'll offer him combat. Orvell will take it.'' His jaw was tight and a pulse throbbed steadily at his neck.

Madselin's jaw opened. ''He'll kill you.'' She held his eyes, not letting him turn away from her. His were filled with hate and anger.

''Most likely.'' His eyes dropped to the ground and his fingers idly pulled at the grass. ''It doesn't matter.''

But it did matter. ''It matters to me, you foolish Angle.'' There was no trace of a smile in her voice. Just sincere regret.

He looked up at her then, the anger gone, replaced by something much warmer. ''Aye. I'll miss you too.'' The words were spoken so softly that she could barely make them out. ''But he is my fate.''

Their progress was slow but sure as they trudged towards the higher ground that would offer them safety. At every moment Madselin had expected to hear Orvell and his men return for the kill, but as the day wore on their chances of survival increased.

Grey storm clouds gathered overhead, causing her to amend her assessment of their situation. If they did not find cover soon, they would die of cold, exhaustion and exposure. She had also noticed that Edwin's injured arm had begun to bleed again. Stopping briefly to examine it, she tore a long strip of wool from her cloak and bound it carefully.

As she finished tying the ends together, Madselin was aware of his gaze on her.

"I said I'd make an Englishwoman of you," he said with a hint of amusement. He winced a little as he flexed his arm. "You seem perfectly at home here in the cold and wet." He reached out to push strands of her wet hair from her face. "You look like a drowned rat, though."

Madselin glared at him. "That makes me feel so much better," she replied with asperity, shaking his hand away. "And if we don't find shelter soon, I suspect that this will be my permanent resting place."

The forest fell away as they climbed higher. Whilst Edwin appeared to be able to take such effort in his stride, Madselin was finding it very hard to keep up. Breathlessly, she collapsed in a heap behind a large crop of rocks.

"Do you want me to carry you?" Edwin stood before her, his expression perfectly serious.

"No." she snapped irritably. "I want to get rid of these cold wet clothes and sleep."

His eyes left her to gaze over the horizon. "If I remember correctly, there's a small farmholding over the brow of the next hill. Do you think you can make it that far?"

She looked but could see nothing. "If you are lying to me, Angle, I will be your fate." Taking his outstretched hand, she pulled herself wearily to her feet. "Be warned."

Edwin hesitated a moment before turning to her. "I

think it might be a good idea if we told these people we're married.''

She remained stockstill. ''Oh? And why should we tell them that?''

He pushed back her hair and pulled a few stray weeds from her tattered cloak. ''Well, for one thing, farmers always regard strangers suspiciously, especially Norman strangers.'' The emphasis he placed on ''Norman'' lingered in the air between them. ''And for another, you have a somewhat dishevelled appearance that might give them the…ah…wrong impression.''

Placing her hands on her hips, Madselin narrowed her eyes. ''You don't appear completely wholesome either, Edwin Elwardson.''

''No, that's true,'' he replied carefully. ''But it might stop the men trying to…er…find out for certain about your status.'' Satisfied that he had tidied her as much as he could, he placed a filthy finger under her chin and forced her to look up at him. ''Nor do I want to spend the next few hours worrying about you. You'll stay where I can see you.''

She had no intention of arguing with him. The thought of fighting off the attentions of several foreign farmers was the last thing she wanted to do. Staying with Edwin was a small price to pay for peace and sleep. ''Whatever you think best,'' she replied quietly.

Somewhat taken aback by her acquiescence, Edwin continued to stare at her. Then he smiled and placed a heavy arm round her shoulders. ''Good.''

Edwin had not been lying. There was indeed a farming community, living in a collection of homesteads about an hour's walk away. Five or six low wooden buildings lay together within the protection of a stockade and to Madselin's unpractised eye, the village looked very welcoming.

They were greeted at the open gate by a giant of a man who made even Edwin look small. Wild blond hair massed over his shoulders and two faded-blue eyes stared at them suspiciously. Madselin could not help but feel apprehensive as she assessed his ponderous bulk. He and Ulf could have been brothers. From the way he was looking at her, Madselin was very glad she had agreed to Edwin's plan and moved closer to her new ''husband''.

As if they had been married for years, Edwin slung his good arm over her shoulders and gave her a comforting squeeze. The farmer's gaze returned to Edwin, clearly satisfied as to her status.

The two men talked for several minutes in a language that made little sense to her at all. Eventually, the farmer stood back and indicated that they could enter the stockade. Behind them the gates slammed shut and Madselin felt faint with relief. They were safe.

Several curious faces peeped out from doors and windows to examine the newcomers. Most were children and women, dressed in brightly coloured woollen tunics and cloaks.

At the farmer's impatient bidding, Edwin and Madselin followed him to a large farmhouse in the centre of the village. A tall, well-built woman in her forties stood outside the doorway, her blue eyes fastened carefully on the couple. The man and woman exchanged words before the woman stood aside and beckoned them in.

The warmth hit them immediately. A huge fire burned in a stone grate at the far end of the long, very comfortable room. Dried herbs and smoked meats hung from the low wooden rafters and bright woollen hangings covered the walls. Rugs and sheepskin pelts were piled together to form beds and seats close to the fire.

Wonderful smells emanated from an iron pot bubbling by the fire and Madselin could feel her mouth watering. The woman must have guessed as much, since she gently took her arm and lead her to the fire. Edwin was engaged in a serious conversation with the farmer and Madselin guessed that he must have been explaining about Orvell and his men.

Grateful for the warmth, Madselin smiled her thanks at the farmer's wife who waved away her words with the flap of a plump hand. Within minutes of being wrapped in a thick warm blanket, Madselin found a bowl of hot, wholesome pottage thrust into her hands. Edwin sat down next to her, his mouth full of bread.

"What's happening?" she asked quietly, sipping at the food. It tasted heavenly.

"He's sending two men to Mallet to warn him. They lost their horses in a raid by the Scots in the summer, so it will take a while for them to get there. We may as well lie back and rest for a while."

"Does he believe you?" Her eyes flickered up at the farmer and his wife who were talking in low tones by the doorway. Whatever was said seemed to have satisfied the wife, since she returned with a beaming smile and some cups of warm ale.

"About Orvell? Aye." Edwin gulped down his pottage with a look of deep satisfaction on his face. Such praise earned him a wink from the farmer's wife, causing Madselin to assess her hostess a little more carefully.

The woman was perhaps more voluptuous in the way of the large-boned Danes, rather than fat. Close to, she was fine-skinned and attractive with soft silvery hair and dancing blue eyes. It would seem that Edwin had taken her fancy. Madselin smiled to herself at that unlikely thought.

"Osric has no love for Orvell, apparently, and welcomes anyone who wishes to see justice done," continued Edwin, oblivious to Madselin's train of thought. Tossing back his ale, he placed the cup on the table and wiped his mouth on his sleeve. The farmer's wife grabbed the cup and refilled it in seconds.

"If I didn't know better, I'd say she was trying to get you drunk," she observed tartly. Her mouth twitched as she saw his stunned expression. On cue, the farmer's wife, whose name was Frieda, bore down on the hapless Angle and encouraged him to drink up so that she could give him more. Too taken aback to resist, Edwin could only nod and drink. Madselin took pity on him.

Rising gracefully, she went to stand behind Edwin and placed her hands firmly on his shoulders in a proprietary manner. Using very obvious gestures, she managed to convey to Frieda that they were both in great need of a bath and some sleep. Frieda eyed her somewhat warily, but Edwin seemed to have regained his speech and added something that caused a broad smile to split her face. She left the room in a flurry of skirts and hair.

"What did you say?" Madselin enquired, coming to sit at his side.

"I said that we had only just married and you were most keen to display your wifely devotion." He carried on chewing at the bread, avoiding her eyes.

"I see." Her heart started beating faster at the thought of what might be expected of them.

Any further discussion was interrupted by the arrival of a huge wooden bath tub and several brawny boys with steaming buckets of hot water. They all returned on several occasions until Frieda was entirely satisfied that all was well. Clean, dry clothes and blankets were placed carefully on the table and then everyone was ushered out quietly and efficiently. Frieda herself left with a few softly spoken words on her lips.

"What did she say?"

Edwin grinned. "That the tub is big enough for the two of them, so we can enjoy ourselves."

Her cheeks burned at the very thought. "You can leave right now!" she commanded, pulling her tattered clothes more tightly about her.

"We're married!" he protested, smiling at her discomfort. "It wouldn't be right if you threw me out now."

He was enjoying this, but Madselin knew he was right. "Well, you'll have to turn around until I'm done."

"Couldn't we just try it? Together?" The world had gone silent as he spoke the words. There was no mock amusement in his voice, just a quiet entreaty. The fire crackled and shifted.

Madselin was stunned to find herself considering the consequences of such wildly abandoned behaviour. No one need ever know that they had spent a few hours together as man and wife. It was very likely that Edwin would be killed in the morning and it was that thought that stayed with her as she looked at him then.

This Englishman had protected her with his life and made no protest about it all being her fault. She had never met anyone like him before and was unlikely to ever do so again. Marriage to Hugh would be…predictable. She could never envisage life with Edwin being any such thing.

She lowered her head and closed her eyes, not wishing to see the look on his face. "Do you truly wish to?" This was no sudden impulse or whim. It went far, far deeper.

After a stunned silence, gentle fingers slipped around her jaw and turned her face towards him.

"Look at me, Madselin."

Shyly she opened her eyes. His face was still and yet intense. "Aye, I truly wish to. It's only a bath after all. No more than that."

Slowly, very slowly, she moved her face closer to his and their lips met in a soft kiss.

He pulled her to her feet and removed her blankets and cloak. "We'd best not let the water get cold then."

Each removed their own clothes with fumbling, nervous fingers, but it was at least a relief to be rid of the damp things. With her clothes in a puddle at her feet, Madselin turned to Edwin, her face blazing. As she stared at his naked chest, she caught her breath. On a leather thong around his neck lay her gold ring.

"You kept it," she whispered, her fingers reaching out to touch it. His skin was silky soft and burnished copper in the glow of the firelight. In fact, all of his skin was like that. Edwin was beautiful.

As she drew her fingertips over his chest, he shuddered and stopped her with his own hand.

"If you carry on doing that, you foolish Norman, you are not likely to have a bath at all."

It was impossible for him to hide the effect that she was having on him, but still he did not move. Touched by his gentleness, Madselin took his hand and pulled him into the tub.

Frieda was right. There was plenty of room for two. The dirt and grime of the day was gently soaped away with their fear. Gradually they relaxed and leaned against each other, quiet and peaceful in the firelight. As the water cooled, they stepped out of the tub and dried themselves. Madselin pulled on a short chemise before climbing onto a pile of lambswool fleeces and blankets. Edwin crawled in beside her and drew her close. As sleep claimed them, he kissed her damp hair and breathed in her scent. She felt blissfully happy.

Chapter Fifteen

They did not stir until night had fallen and delicious smells from the cooking pot permeated their dreams. At first, Madselin had no idea where she was but the sound of unfamiliar breathing behind her focused her thoughts.

She was pulled hard against him, with Edwin's large body cradling hers. His arm was draped protectively about her and she had absolutely no desire to remove it. Feeling deliciously sinful, Madselin stretched gently and was rewarded with an appreciative squeeze.

Edwin struggled to prop himself up on his elbow and gazed down at her. "You're very comfortable for a Norman," he murmured, his voice a little husky.

She smiled at that and reached to push back a lock of hair. "Comfortable? And just how many Normans have you shared a bed with?" It was very easy to flirt with him like this.

He met her uplifted brow with his steady gaze. "None that I recall."

She shifted round to look up at him properly. "I thought you were a man of great experience?"

"Aye, well, I always thought you were a bit impulsive." He began to trace a path downwards from the top of her arm to her elbow. Even through the soft material of the chemise, Madselin could feel the heat of his fingers.

Facing death together, bathing and sleeping together certainly engendered a sense of intimacy, and Madselin could feel the attraction between them pulling tight. She ran her fingers through his tousled hair. There was a shyness between them as well as a mounting sense of anticipation.

Edwin fixed his grey eyes on her. "Do you remember my threat?" His finger continued its slow path up and down her arm as he spoke. His very touch heated her blood and she was sure he could feel her shudder in response.

Her lips twitched into a smile. "As I recall, you have issued several threats recently. Which particular one did you have in mind?" Madselin turned in towards him so that they were practically touching from chest to toes.

Lowering his head so that his temple brushed her cheek, Edwin breathed gently by her ear. Every hair on her body seemed to stand on end, straining towards him. "I said I would make you pay in kind for using me so abominably."

His words did not seem at all like a threat to Madselin. In fact they were having a very different effect on her body. Every inch of her skin suddenly seemed to crave his touch. "Have you decided on the form this payment should take?" Her voice sounded slightly hoarse.

"Aye." His fingers moved to untie the lace at her neck. Pushing the fabric aside, his lips brushed her skin. Soft and insistent, they sent shivers of desire shooting down her spine. Lower and lower they moved until they reached the full curve of her breast. His mouth closed over her nipple, drawing from her a sharp intake of breath.

Unable to hold back her response, Madselin reached out to pull his head closer to her breasts. She didn't want him to stop.

A loud clattering at the door made them spring guiltily apart. Frieda bustled in, apparently unaware of disturbing them, although Madselin was certain that those blue eyes missed nothing. She had brought warm ale and told them firmly that as soon as they were ready, the rest of the villagers would be pleased to meet them.

Picking up their damp, discarded clothes, the farmer's wife winked broadly at Edwin and then fled into the darkness.

Left alone in the silence, Madselin and Edwin eyed each other warily and then burst into self-conscious laughter.

"I think she came in on purpose," said Madselin, pulling the blanket up over her exposed breasts. "Frieda clearly has doubts as to the validity of our marriage."

Edwin sat up and ran his fingers through his tangled hair. "You don't look obedient enough to be a wife," he muttered rather grumpily. "Not enough proper respect."

She smiled and sat up, clutching the blanket. "Obedience and respect, is it? You drive a very hard bargain, Angle."

He fixed her with glittering eyes and a very seductive smile. "Tonight then, we shall discuss a proper price for my troubles." That seemed to be more of a promise than a threat.

After a few moments of awkwardness, they dressed themselves in the clothes provided by Frieda. Bright and a little on the large side, they were nevertheless comfortable, warm and dry. Madselin tugged the long skirts

up and frowned. "Why do I get the impression that
Frieda doesn't like me?"

Edwin glanced up at her as he pulled on a huge pair
of leather boots. "You're a Norman," he replied in surprise. "What do you expect?" Standing up to try out his
footwear he came to stand in front of her. "Not all the
natives are as long-suffering and patient as me."

Her narrowed eyes met his innocent, wide-eyed gaze.
"There are some natives who don't appear to know their
place," she said darkly. Tossing her thick, black hair over
her shoulders, she stood squarely in front of him.

Edwin bent down suddenly to place a kiss on her forehead. "Aye, well, some of us are very slow learners. Are
you ready?"

She smiled up at him and slipped her hand around his
proffered arm. "I'm not sure this is a good idea, but I
am hungry."

He shook his head regretfully as they reached the door.
"As someone who has hauled you over mountains,
woman, I'm not sure this is a good idea either."

They followed their noses. The delicious smell of
roasting pig and an assortment of other indefinable dishes
came from another home close by the gate. It was similar
in design to Frieda and Osric's house except that it was
perhaps smaller. The inhabitants of the settlement had
clearly been awaiting their arrival for a while and several
of the men grinned with relief as they tentatively stepped
through the door.

Altogether there were about five married couples, five
unmarried men and three young girls. Numerous children
bobbed around the trestle table, but it was impossible to
place any one of them to a family. They all looked very
similar. Tall and rangy in build, the villagers sported

thick blond hair and blue eyes. Their skin was soft but tanned and they spoke with an odd lilt that Madselin found very difficult to understand.

"Danes," whispered Edwin in response to her confusion. "There are several such settlements hereabouts. No one interferes with them much and they prefer to keep it that way. They're very fierce when roused," he added gravely.

The food was delicious. For all that Edwin had complained about her weight, he was very attentive to her needs. Her trencher was never empty and he offered her several tempting morsels from his own.

"If I didn't know any better, Angle, I'd think you were trying very hard to please me." Her eyes stared at him speculatively.

He placed his hand over his heart as if wounded. "You have a very suspicious nature, woman."

"It would seem I'm not the only one." Madselin glanced over in Frieda's direction to find a pair of blue eyes boring into them. Flushing with embarrassment and indignation, Madselin took another sip of the ale. Strong and yet quite sweet, she found it helped her feel more relaxed.

Edwin's hand came to rest gently on top of hers. "Unless you plan to spend the entire night and most of tomorrow in oblivion, I suggest you drink less of the ale. It takes some time to accustom yourself to it."

"Well, it makes me feel less…conspicuous," she observed quietly, reaching for some bread. It was most disconcerting to eat with several pairs of eyes trained on your every move and Madselin was beginning to feel very uncomfortable.

Taking pity on her distress, Edwin patted her hand and then directed a blistering smile at Frieda. They conducted a brief conversation under the suspicious eye of Osric, but the latter seemed to relax a little as some of their neighbours joined in. Madselin was pleased to be ignored for the time being, watching these people carefully for the first signs of anger.

The other women, mainly younger than Frieda although perhaps not quite so attractive, vied with each other to engage Edwin in conversation of sorts. Every so often she would find his eyes flicker towards her and give her thigh a gentle squeeze. She found the whole thing a very enlightening experience.

Far from being the surly peasant she had always accused him of being, Edwin was clearly the possessor of a quick wit and a fair amount of charm. The women and girls would stammer and blush the moment he turned his eyes on them. Even the men laughed at some of the things he said.

After the meal, the villagers cleared the table from the middle of the floor so that the dancing could begin. It was a custom with these people to entertain visitors in such a manner and they all appeared to relish the prospect. With mixed feelings, Madselin realised that she would have to partner Edwin once again but she was given no time to dwell on it.

It was not, however, Edwin who stood up to be her first partner. The huge form of Osric lumbered up to her and gravely held out his hand. Conversation being out of the question, Madselin nodded quickly and found herself propelled to the centre of the floor. Edwin had been captured by Frieda, who was all but dragging him along behind her. The two couples were joined by an assortment of villagers and children.

As the pipes fluted out tunes that set feet tapping, Madselin found herself surprised into enjoying herself. Osric was light on his feet for such a huge man and he man-oeuvred her about the floor with astonishing expertise.

The villagers plunged into the dancing with an unre-strained joy that was infectious, hurling each other across the floor with enthusiasm. What they lacked in finesse, they made up in sheer exuberance. Every so often Mad-selin would catch sight of a red-faced Edwin being whirled around by a determined Frieda.

Once Osric had fulfilled his duty, Madselin found her-self in great demand by the other men, and she assumed this was also the case with Edwin and the women. After several very enjoyable but highly exhausting dances, Madselin retired to a quiet corner to catch her breath.

Glowing with the heat, she leaned back on a cool wall to watch the proceedings. This was the second time she had enjoyed herself like this. Here she was just another visitor and, despite her origins, the people accepted her presence for what it was. They had extended their pro-tection to her as well as to Edwin and she found it a sobering thought.

Having spent eight years hating the English, she real-ised that her anger had been misplaced. For the most part they were just ordinary people trying to survive. Who knows, she thought bleakly, exactly what Guy had done? She knew first hand what Henry Orvell was capable of doing.

She watched Edwin escape from the clutches of an-other bright-eyed villager and collapse by her side against the wall.

"Escaping? Surely not?" Her gaze of wide-eyed in-nocence met his eyes.

"We warriors are no match for Danish women," he replied ruefully. "I'm thinking of asking Frieda and her sisters to join up with my men." He closed his eyes briefly and took some deep breaths. "The Scots wouldn't stand a chance."

They had tacitly refrained from mentioning anything about the Scots or Orvell until now, but it seemed natural to continue. "Are you still planning to fight Orvell?" she asked somewhat hesitantly. His skin was glowing amber in the torchlight and there was a faint sheen of perspiration on his brow.

"Do you think Frieda might do better, then?" he asked drily.

She pursed her lips at this deliberate avoidance of her question. "You are tired and injured," she snapped, staring straight ahead of her. "Orvell is neither."

"Don't tell me you are worried about me, you foolish Norman?" His voice held a note of amusement.

"I am not being foolish. I am being perfectly serious." She folded her arms and refused to look at him. "Why can't you leave Orvell to the King?"

He stared silently across the room at the dancers before finally turning to look at her. "I vowed to avenge my family, and I will."

"Even if he kills you, too?"

"He probably will," Edwin replied soberly. "Orvell is a better swordsman than I am."

There was nothing more she could say to him. His mind was clearly made up. "So this could be your last night alive?" The thought was utterly numbing, but it might at least shock the man into rethinking his position.

Strong fingers reached to grasp her wrist and she could feel the heat from his body flood into hers. It seeped into her veins. "You are tired, Madselin," he said softly. "Rest will make you feel better."

Madselin looked at him then. "I doubt it, but I don't

think I can stay here much longer. Will they be offended if we leave?''

He smiled gently and shook his head. "Wait there and I'll explain."

It was a relief to have left the heat and the noise behind. In contrast, the night was cool and quiet and acted like a soothing balm on her shattered nerves. Edwin walked silently at her side, his expression unreadable.

"You were enjoying yourself," she said apologetically. "You should have stayed. I don't mind if you go back."

He grimaced convincingly. "I think I feel safer with you."

There were several torches burning to light the way. Beyond the wooden palisade, the thickness of the night was overwhelmingly frightening. Madselin imagined Orvell and his men searching for them and shivered.

Edwin put his arm about her shoulders and pulled her close to him as they walked back to Osric's house. "We're safe here. Mallet and his men will find us in the morning." He gave her a small squeeze that made her smile up at him. "Then you'll be able to give the poor man one of your famous tongue-lashings for being so tardy."

"Famous tongue-lashings?" Madselin stopped and shook off his arm, hands on hips. "What do you mean?" she demanded in an outraged tone.

Edwin raised his brows and stared down at her, his eyes glinting in the torchlight. "You know very well what I mean, woman. There isn't a man amongst us who hasn't been subjected to your icy glares and scathing retorts and most of us count ourselves lucky to emerge from the skirmish in one whole piece."

"Oh." She was very glad that he could not see the

deep flush to her cheeks. Was that how she truly seemed to them? "Well…" she lifted her eyes almost defiantly to his "…you all deserved it."

"No doubt," came the dry retort. "Come on," he urged, tugging gently at her arm. "It's been a long day."

Osric and Frieda had apparently given up their home for the night to offer quiet and privacy to their unexpected visitors. Frieda had thoughtfully left ale, bread and some cheese and despite their recent meal, Madselin and Edwin found that they were really quite hungry.

As they brushed the crumbs from their clothes, Madselin glanced over at Edwin. The playful, intimate mood that had gripped them before had been replaced by one that was altogether more reflective and subdued. His mouth was set in a determined line as he stared into the fire.

"Are you thinking about tomorrow?" she asked, pulling her hair from its tight braid. Picking up Frieda's comb, Madselin dragged it slowly through her hair.

"Aye." His head turned briefly in her direction and watched her as she fussed at a tangle. "It's a strange thing," he continued, his gaze returning to the fire. "I've imagined this moment for so long that it hardly seems real."

His words stilled her. It didn't seem real to her either. Edwin was here, with her, alive and strong. They had survived Orvell and his men for now, but he could be dead by tomorrow. Her eyes roved over the familiar planes of his handsome face. She would miss him. More than that. It would be as if she had lost one of her own limbs.

Swallowing hard to remove the growing lump in her throat, Madselin put down the comb. "If you win, what will happen?" she asked.

He rubbed involuntarily at his arm. "An old woman I used to know once told me I would die fighting my greatest enemy. I have no reason to doubt her."

"You plan to do this because of an old woman's prophecy?" she asked incredulously. "Even if it were true, it could mean any number of things." She reached over to him and placed a hand on his arm. "Don't do it, Edwin. I beg of you."

The atmosphere in the room was suddenly charged with an emotion and a tension she could not identify. Edwin blinked slowly and then took a deep breath as if preparing himself for an unpleasant duty.

"Madselin, I think I ought to tell you something about myself that you…"

"I do not wish to hear anything more," she interrupted quickly, placing a forefinger on his lips.

"But you must listen to…"

"No." As she spoke, Madselin knew without a doubt that she had no desire to hear anything more of his past. It would make no difference. "But I have something to say to you." Madselin drew in a deep breath. It would be the hardest thing she had ever said, but it could not keep. Not when he might die in the morning.

"I have had few choices in my life," she began, measuring the words carefully. "But I have one this night. For tonight, I am no one's sister, aunt or chatelaine. I am myself."

Edwin watched her face, his body still, waiting.

"I choose to spend the night in your arms, Edwin Elwardson. If you'll have me." She could not bear to look at him, so great was her embarrassment. The silence in the room was punctuated only by the crackling of the wood burning in the fire.

"Why?" His voice echoed in the silence between

them. Gently he took her hand and pulled it to his heart. "The truth."

Slowly, she raised her eyes to his and smiled tentatively. Edwin was looking far more nervous and apprehensive than she was. "I want you," she said simply.

Without a word, Edwin stood and drew her to her feet. Pulling her hard against him, he framed her face with his fingers. She could feel his heart beating rapidly in time with her own and knew that this was right. "You have a betrothed," he reminded her, his grey eyes searching her face. "He will expect you to be innocent. There might be a child."

Madselin did not look away. "I am not yet betrothed." The prospect of having Edwin's child made her heart leap. "I would be proud to bear your child, Angle."

Edwin smiled at that, but as he gazed down at her the smile faded. Slowly, very slowly, he lowered his lips to hers and closed his eyes. This kiss was a promise.

"I've wanted you since the moment I laid eyes on you, woman." His voice was barely a whisper. "I have no idea why it is like this between us, but I cannot help myself any longer."

This time his kiss was hard and demanding. His hands moved from her face, down over her arms and rested for a moment on her hips. As their passion deepened, he pulled her to him hard. She could not have known how it would affect her.

Edwin wanted her for herself. His body did not lie. That knowledge was an aphrodisiac in itself. Looping her arms around his neck, Madselin pushed herself against him harder. Groaning softly, he pushed her from him until she stood at arm's length.

"Are you sure, Madselin? I mean...I don't think I can be gentle and I don't want to hurt you."

"Edwin," she muttered with a smile. "Be quiet and kiss me again."

That elicited from him the heartstopping smile that made her weak at the knees. He sighed softly and reached for her. "You're a very demanding woman."

They stood together, before the fire, just looking at each other, memorising every feature, every contour. For an experienced man, Edwin's fingers fumbled nervously at her laces as he began to undress her. Madselin watched in fascination as the flush on his cheeks deepened. At last her gown slithered to the ground, leaving Madselin in her chemise. His eyes glowed with suppressed passion as he reached out to touch her hair.

"It's like silk," he whispered, almost shyly. Half closing his eyes, he buried his face in her long tresses and breathed in the soft scent of lavender.

Her fingers found the clasp on his belt and it slithered onto her discarded gown. Pushing Edwin gently back, Madselin went to work on his laces. Never having even attempted such garments before, it took a great deal longer than she expected. Laughing, they finally accomplished the task together. He stepped out of his large boots and pulled off his breeches.

Naked, Edwin was even more beautiful than she could ever have imagined. His skin was soft and glowing in the firelight. Holding her breath, Madselin ran a shaking hand down from the pulse at his throat and across his chest. Edwin was absolutely still, hardly breathing either, as she then pulled her chemise over her head.

The first touch of skin against skin was intensely thrilling and very arousing. Unable to stop herself, Madselin moved her palms slowly over his chest, wondering at his hard strength. "Magnificent," she breathed, placing a soft kiss at the base of his throat.

Any further words she might have uttered were stifled by his lips coming down hard on her own. His hands drew her to his body and they fused, flesh to flesh, as his tongue invaded her mouth.

Suddenly, he lifted her in his arms and carried her to the bed. His face was flushed and his eyes bright with passion. Had she done that to him? He laid her carefully down, sitting back to stare at her.

"Dear God, woman, but you're beautiful. I tried to imagine so many times…"

That caught her by surprise. Madselin raised herself onto one elbow and reached out to touch the thick bristles on his chin. "Oh?" she queried, raising an eyebrow in amusement. "And I was certain that all you ever thought about was escaping from my venomous tongue?" she teased gently.

Edwin had the grace to blush, but pulled her beneath him. "Well, Lady de Breuville, you erred in your supposition. Perhaps I had better show you exactly what I thought of."

He lowered his mouth to her breast and she arched to him. "I think you'd better," she gasped, her eyes closed.

Madselin could not have imagined how it would feel to have him touch her, to have him want her with such powerful urgency. There was not a part of her he did not stroke or kiss, until he burned away every bit of her modesty and her inhibition. Finally, she yielded to his embrace with abandon, returning his kisses with a passion that made him burn.

"Now," he whispered thickly in her ear. "I can wait no longer, Madselin."

Eagerly she opened herself to him. "Don't stop," she urged him.

He speared her to the root with a single thrust that

caused her to moan aloud as pain mingled with a strange satisfaction. Edwin searched her face as he waited for her to catch her breath. His jaw tightened with the effort of holding back, until he could stand it no longer.

"You are mine for tonight, Madselin, and I do not intend to let you forget me. Ever." His words were softly spoken as he pressed her deep into the bed. Taking her wrists, he pinned them above her head before thrusting into her again and again.

Pain and discomfort were quickly replaced by an echoing response that was wild and almost pagan in its sinfulness. This act could never have been sanctioned by her church, she was sure. This was born of the gods of this barbaric land and she welcomed it joyfully.

Every inch of her body tingled and shivered as Edwin lowered his head to suckle at her swollen breasts. Pushing herself hard against him, Madselin rose to meet his every thrust. Suddenly, without warning, a feeling of exquisite pleasure burst forth deep within her and exploded into every part of her body. Hearing her cry out, Edwin pushed himself into her very depths again and again until her moans mingled with his own sigh of release.

The last thing Madselin remembered as they collapsed against each other was the furious music of the pipes and the heat of Edwin's soft skin.

Chapter Sixteen

It wasn't the music that woke Madselin again. It was the heavy pounding of Edwin's heart close to her ear. Still fused together, they had not moved.

Sensing a change in her breathing, Edwin shifted to pull her close to his chest, his arms locking around her. Madselin sighed faintly.

"Did I hurt you?" he murmured into her ear.

She opened her eyes and looked up into his still flushed face. He smiled at her somewhat ruefully.

Madselin made a quick mental inventory of her body. "Not too much," she said, snuggling closer to him and breathing in his faint, musky smell. She felt his lips brush gentle kisses close to her ear and her skin tingled in immediate response.

"That's good," came the muffled reply, as he lowered his lips to the sensitive part of her neck.

Madselin gasped in surprise. "What are you doing, Edwin?" she managed. A large hand moved slowly up her body, lingering over her breast.

"What I've been longing to do since you fell asleep on me," he informed her.

"You want to do it again?" she asked, pulling herself

up to a sitting position. Edwin merely nodded, seemingly bewitched by the sight of her naked body in the firelight.

"This time," he said quietly and persuasively, "I'll be very gentle."

Any tiredness or discomfort disappeared as she saw the desire in his eyes. Her nipples hardened under his gaze and laughed softly. "It doesn't take much to persuade you, woman."

Madselin eyed him speculatively and then reached for him under the blankets. His laugh vanished immediately, to be replaced by a quickly indrawn breath.

"Nor you, it would seem."

Neither spoke for some time.

"Edwin?"

"Mmm?"

"Is it always like this?" Gently, Madselin traced the line of an old scar which ran from his breastbone down to his navel.

He took so long to answer that she thought he had fallen asleep. "No," he said finally. "With other women, all I generally wanted to do was leave or sleep. I'm not sure why it is, but with you, all I want to do is to hear you cry out beneath me. The minute I stop, I just ache to love you again."

She stilled then and looked up at him. "Again?" Narrowing her eyes in mock suspicion, Madselin reached for his ale cup and sniffed it. "Frieda might have given you a potion of some sort."

Grinning, he pulled her to him and kissed her until she was breathless. "Aye, she might. Shall we put it to the test?"

It was Frieda's cheery greeting that woke them shortly after dawn. If she felt any rancour about wasting a love potion on Edwin, she gave no sign of it. Madselin and Edwin struggled to sit up as she busied herself with the fire. The delicious smell of freshly baking bread wafted towards them, reminding the pair how hungry they were.

Uncertain as to the etiquette demanded by such a situation, Madselin gripped the blankets tightly to her and focused her eyes on a spot at the far end of the room. Several huge war axes hung menacingly on the wall. They reminded her of Edwin's future and she found her eyes welling suddenly with tears. A large, solid body enveloped her from behind and a pair of soft lips kissed her gently on her shoulder.

"Regrets, Madselin?" Edwin's tone was bland but it did not fool Madselin.

She shook her head. "Only that we had just one night." Willing away the lump in her throat, she turned to look at him. In the soft morning light, with his thick stubble and his tousled hair, Edwin Elwardson was still magnificent. "You might…?" Her hopeful question was cut short by a long finger on her lips.

"Nay. Don't think it. My death is prophesied. Besides," he added more slowly, "if you knew what I had done, you might not want to spend another night with me."

Madselin sighed. "Whatever it is, Edwin, I cannot believe it to be so awful that I could refuse you that."

They were disturbed by Frieda bringing their pile of dried clothes and dumping them somewhat pointedly on the bed. She and Edwin exchanged a few words before Frieda smiled knowingly and made a hurried exit.

The moment the door banged shut, Edwin dragged Madselin down so that she lay beneath him, pinned down by his weight. His face was no longer smiling and amused. "Mallet is on his way. We have but a short time until he arrives and I must not let him find you like this."

He kissed her with a growing urgency. Placing his forehead on hers, he closed his eyes and held her tight. "You are a part of my soul and have been for years, Madselin. Our fates were bound from the start and I regret only that I have caused you such pain."

"But you have not…"

"Hear me out," he interrupted. "We haven't much time and I won't have your reputation compromised."

His fingers stroked back her hair from her face and his eyes tried to memorise her features. "When I die, know that you hold my heart forever."

Their tears mingled as he kissed her fiercely. He took her then, urgently, stamping his mark on her as she had heard other men did to their women before riding to meet their deaths. No words were spoken, but they cried out loud as their pleasure swept them away to another world.

Minutes later, Edwin stood up and pulled his clothes on hurriedly. He left without another word, picking up a loaf on his way out.

Madselin closed her eyes and tried to will away the inexorable passing of time. Feeling more than a little bruised and battered, but at peace none the less, she determined that whatever happened, she would be with him. Edwin was hers. He had told her so himself.

Clutching that thought to herself, Madselin forced herself from their bed. She washed and dressed with care, wondering if indeed she still looked the same person. Could anyone tell that she was no longer a maid?

Just as she was debating whether or not she could take one of the loaves of bread, Frieda bustled in, her skin flushed with the morning chill. Madselin jumped away from the bread a little guiltily, but Frieda just laughed. A large, warm loaf was shoved into her lap.

Not long after she had eaten her bread, the silence of the early morning was broken by the loud blare of a hunting horn. Frieda wiped her hands on a cloth before rushing to the door, summoning Madselin by gestures and a rapid volley of words.

Albert Mallet was approaching with about twenty guards. The rivets on their hauberks glittered in the early morning sun as they rode steadily towards the village. All the villagers had stopped their chores to watch them from doors or windows. Edwin was standing at the gates with Osric.

Once at the gates, Albert Mallet dismounted hurriedly and clapped Edwin on his back in the manner of friends. As Madselin approached, he stepped forward to greet her with relief etched all over his handsome face.

"My lady. We were pleased to hear of your safe escape from Orvell's men."

She smiled at him. "My thanks, sir. We have been well looked after by Osric and his villagers. I hope that we shall be able to repay their kindness in some way."

Mallet inclined his head. "I shall see to it, lady, but my first concern is to return you to the Lady d'Aveyron. She has been most anxious these past few days."

"And Orvell?" Madselin could not contain the question any longer. "What of him?"

A shadow passed over his blue eyes. "Safe in the de Vaillant dungeon. We caught him close by here late yesterday. He was not far behind you."

Madselin glanced nervously up at Edwin, but he was simply frowning at the ground.

"What of the Scots?" he demanded. "Did you get any of them?"

Albert Mallet shook his head in regret. "Nay, but at least we might get something out of Orvell."

"I doubt it," muttered Edwin, pushing back his unbound hair. He looked at her then. "Come, my lady. You're in need of rest."

The journey back to the de Vaillant keep was arduous because of the need to travel slowly through the forest. Despite the clement weather, Madselin felt cold. Edwin had been as good as his word and had largely ignored her since they left the village. She very much doubted if any of the men could have guessed just how much her reputation had been compromised.

That brought a secret smile to her lips. Aye, and it had been wonderful. Madselin allowed her mind to wander back over their very difficult first meeting. She had thought him a barbaric poacher and all he had wanted to do was kiss her! His expression, if she remembered aright, had not given her that impression though. She could have been forgiven if she had thought murder a more likely possibility.

It was noon before they passed through the gates of the de Vaillant keep. Anxious faces greeted them and the bailey was unnaturally quiet, despite the gathering of many familiar faces. Emma rushed forward, her round, plain face bright with relief.

"Oh, my lady. I'm that glad you're back," she cried, placing her hand on Madselin's leg. "I thought I'd never see you alive again."

"Well," Madselin smiled down at her, "you've Edwin to thank for that. He saved me."

The recipient of her approbation appeared at that moment to lift her from her horse. His hands gripped her waist tightly and she could feel her skin glow where he touched her. Neither spoke, but as her feet met the ground, their eyes held for no more than a few seconds.

She could stand the silence between them no longer. "What will you do first?" she asked, her hand resting on his arm. "You will rest."

Edwin sighed and looked across at Albert Mallet, who was directing the soldiers with significant energy. "Aye. I'll rest. Nothing will happen for a while. Much has yet to be done."

"Send me word," she urged anxiously.

After a moment, he nodded curtly before turning to make his way towards the hall.

Emma shook her head as she watched his retreating form. "I'd never have thought it would be him as saved you, him hating us Normans as he does."

"Some Normans," Madselin corrected, allowing herself a wry smile. "Come. I'm in need of a hot bath and a strong cup of wine."

"Aye, you'll be needing to look your best."

Madselin cast Emma a puzzled look. "Why?"

"There's to be a trial, here at the keep."

The news stunned Madselin. "A trial? But I thought it would just be between Edwin and Orvell."

Emma shook her head most knowledgeably. "Nay, my lady. It's all got to be done right. There's five barons going to listen to his story and they decide what's to be done with him."

Her heart fluttered with anxiety. Perhaps that would mean that Edwin would not have to fight him. "Come, then. We have much to do."

Emma stared at Madselin's bedraggled appearance and sighed.

Three notches of the thick candle had burned away by the time she heard the hunting horn calling everyone to the hall. Bathed, rested and freshly dressed, Madselin now felt able to face Orvell. Calmly, she made her way to the great hall, where the trial of Henry Orvell was to take place.

Despite the late afternoon sun, hundreds of candles were needed to provide enough light for the proceedings to take place. A space in the centre of the hall had been cleared for Orvell, whilst the barons sitting in judgement on him sat at the top table. The lower tables had been pushed back against the walls to allow everyone else to view the trial. A huge fire burned in the grate.

Madselin sat close to the door, which allowed her a good view of Orvell, the barons and, hopefully, Edwin.

She had seen nothing of him since parting with him in the bailey, but he had sent her a small, leather-wrapped package in his stead. It was a tiny, circular brooch of polished silver fashioned in the ancient Angle style. Fastened securely to her cloak, the brooch glistened in the candle light. It was exquisite and she was very proud to display her acceptance of so beautiful a gift.

By the time the barons entered the hall, the villagers had crowded onto the benches and spilled over on to the floor rushes. The hall was hot and smoky and she found it difficult to breathe. Tension was mounting.

Albert Mallet was the only one of the five that Madselin recognised. Clearly he was to represent Richard d'Aveyron. The other four were a surly-looking quartet who did not seem at all pleased to be administering justice in the de Vaillant hall. With a flourish of his hand, Mallet gestured to the guard to have Orvell brought in.

All heads turned to the door to watch Henry Orvell walk slowly to the clearing in the centre of the hall. He came to a halt before the top table and eyed his judges with a bored expression. He did not look his normal, immaculate self. His dark breeches and tunic were covered in dirt and dust, his boots coated in mud and his cloak badly torn. He did not look like a man prepared to face death.

Looking beyond Orvell, Madselin craned her neck to see if she could catch sight of Edwin. She had not seen him, but knew he must be there. On the opposite side of the hall, half-hidden in the shadows, stood the Angle. His blond head towered over the rest of the people about him, but his eyes were riveted on his enemy. There was no doubt in his mind that this was the man who had butchered his family and destroyed his life.

Her attention was then caught by Albert Mallet, rising to address the assembly.

"Henry Orvell is accused of treason and my Lords FitzNeville, de Montmorency, Vernon and Stanlegh are to dispense justice on behalf of the King." A faint murmur whispered through the crowd, but Orvell remained impassive.

Mallet's handsome face stared stonily at the accused. "What say you to this charge, Orvell?"

A smile curved his lips and Henry Orvell shook his head in disbelief. "You know as well as I that I am innocent of all charges." His soft, persuasive voice carried across the hall. "I believe, in fact, that I am the victim in this sorry tale."

The five judges viewed this strange accusation with hard-faced disbelief and the tension in Madselin eased a little. These men did not have a sympathetic air about them and it seemed most unlikely that they would spend much time agonising over sending Orvell to his death. Few barons cared much beyond their own lands and position. Ridding the land of another was in their own best interests.

"Explain yourself," drawled the smallest of the judges. His fat jowls quivered as his pudgy fingers rubbed over a stubbly chin. Dark, beady eyes glared out at the prisoner from beneath bushy brows, but Orvell seemed unconcerned. He merely inclined his head in graceful acceptance.

"I have always been a loyal servant to the King—both Kings—and have been duly rewarded for my services," he replied, eyeing his accuser boldly. Sweeping his cloak over his shoulder, Orvell then turned to stare at another of his judges. "I came here with William of Normandy, as did you, Vernon. Times were hard then, were they not?"

The man he addressed nodded reluctantly. Vernon sniffed loudly and wiped his nose on a rather grubby sleeve. "Men change in twenty years, Orvell," he muttered somewhat incoherently before drinking deep of the wine cup.

"Maybe so. I was young then, perhaps more foolhardy, but a good commander all the same. We held our ground and kept the Englishmen down. It was dirty work but I followed the King's orders." Orvell turned his eyes to another of the men before him. "De Montmorency can vouch for that. We joined forces on occasion."

All eyes fastened then on the tallest of the five, and the eldest. Spare and harsh, de Montmorency's expression was one of complete indifference. Wisps of grey hair clung to his shiny scalp as he scratched at them. "Aye. The King was pleased with your results. He described the methods you used as very…'thorough.'"

"He gave me lands which required a harsh and trustworthy master in return," replied Orvell sourly. "The

Scots have been hammering at my door ever since and it would be foolish indeed to betray the King's trust.''

''Aye, foolish indeed,'' echoed de Montmorency. ''But lucrative.''

Orvell shrugged his shoulders carelessly at that. ''True. However, I may be many things, but stupid is not one of them.''

Madselin noticed that he glanced in Edwin's direction but could not see Orvell's expression. Edwin just stared unblinkingly at him.

''Get on with it, Orvell,'' growled Vernon, his coarse, bulbous features somehow thickening in the torchlight.

''When the Conqueror died and Rufus became King, the Scots grew more restless. They became bolder and sent more raiding parties to cross my land. It was hard to keep them back since we are so scattered here.'' Orvell raised his brows as if demanding an answer to a question.

Only de Montmorency replied by way of a grunt. The rest continued to glare at Orvell with growing distaste. Although she felt no pity for Orvell, Madselin was glad it was not her before these harsh men.

Orvell sighed. ''It was clear that more devious methods would be required to defeat the Scots, so I offered them peace at a price.''

The barons shuffled in their seats at this and looked at each other with self-satisfied smirks. ''A lucrative one?'' asked Vernon with a sneer.

''To find out their plans only,'' came the stiff reply. ''Killing off a few Scots every day achieves little, but the King would be pleased to capture a few of their leaders. Or a prince?''

The silence in the hall was deafening. There was no doubt in anyone's mind that William Rufus would indeed be most keen to get his hand on a Scottish prince. Certainly one that was organising raids on his lands. The barons lost their sneers then, and stared at Orvell with renewed interest.

Madselin realised she had been holding her breath and slowly breathed in again. It was too clever and Orvell was too devious. They could not believe him.

"Apparently," continued Orvell, "I was not the first to try to make a pact with them. They were very wary of my intentions, but over a period of time I gained ground."

"And why did you not mention these plans to d'Aveyron?" Vernon eyed him suspiciously.

"Too dangerous. The Scots had already indicated that another was already in their pay and I did not want to kindle suspicion. It had to be kept secret."

"Convenient," muttered the smaller baron with the dark eyes.

Ignoring that gibe, Orvell turned to look at Mallet. "D'Aveyron's suspicions about me were helpful to my cause. The Scots heard the rumours and began to trust me. I was close to discovering who was behind the raiding when d'Aveyron made his mistake."

Albert Mallet inhaled loudly. "Richard d'Aveyron is no fool, Orvell. He never trusted you."

Orvell merely shook his head. "He was mistaken. He trusted the wrong man."

Those words caused a buzz of murmuring around the room. Madselin shifted on the bench, her stomach churning. A loud bang from the top table silenced them all.

"So the accused becomes the accuser?" De Montmorency's eyes stared at Orvell harshly. "And who is this man?"

Madselin held her breath as Orvell swivelled on his

heels and pointed directly at Edwin Elwardson. "That Englishman is the true traitor."

A spontaneous outburst of chattering amongst the crowd forced another bang on the table from Albert Mallet. "Silence," he ordered loudly. Edwin did not move nor change his expression. He continued to stare woodenly at Orvell, clearly unsurprised by his accusation.

"Richard d'Aveyron is a shrewd judge of character," Mallet's icy words echoed around the hall. "He trusted Edwin Elwardson with good reason. He may be an Englishman, but he is loyal, trustworthy and honest."

Orvell's face remained impassive in the face of this support. "Aye, to d'Aveyron, and have you ever wondered why?"

Madselin suddenly looked up at Edwin and found his eyes pinned on her. There was longing and sorrow burning almost from the very depths of his soul and it was awful to behold.

"Edwin Elwardson killed a Norman noble, in revenge for the death of his family. Richard d'Aveyron has shielded him ever since."

Madselin could feel her throat constrict as she stared over at Edwin. His eyes were closed.

"Who was this Norman?" asked de Montmorency.

"Guy de Chambertin. He campaigned with me in the north of England. Elwardson sought him out and murdered him on his wedding day."

The blood drained from Madselin's face. She had never guessed for a minute that Edwin had killed Guy. "*You* killed him?" she whispered. "You killed Guy?"

Edwin did nothing more than nod, guilt set deep in his eyes. That was the last thing she saw before the buzzing in her head exploded and Madselin slipped into the welcoming dark of oblivion.

Chapter Seventeen

"Wake up, my lady!"

Emma's pleading suffused her consciousness and Madselin opened her eyes. She was no longer in the hall but lying on the bed in her own room.

"Did he really kill Guy?" Madselin remembered her last coherent thought before she had fainted.

Another face appeared next to Emma's. Edwin loomed large and frowning far above her. The silence between them lengthened until Emma tutted loudly.

"No doubt the pair of you have much to say to each other, so I'll leave you be for a while. And no upsetting her further, Angle," she admonished Edwin with a wag of her finger.

Edwin did no more than nod curtly. It was not until Emma had left the room that he sat down lightly at her side.

"Did you?" she repeated, knowing the answer but needing to hear it from his lips anyway.

"Aye."

He said nothing more in explanation but just sat and waited for her questions. Madselin struggled to sit up.

"Why did you not tell me yourself? You must have known."

Taking a deep breath, Edwin nodded. "Aye, I've known since that day at the beach when you told me his name. I tried to tell you last night, but you would not allow me to. Although," he admitted with a shrug, "I did not try too hard."

Madselin said nothing but stared at him, willing him to continue.

"I did not try hard enough since I knew you would hate me then. God forgive me, Madselin, but I could not bear to see you hate me. It was wrong, I know, but I just wanted to spend one night of happiness with you and take it to my death."

She shook her head, unwilling to believe that the man she had come to know as honest and trustworthy had not only butchered her betrothed, but had not told her the truth. His deception speared her to the core.

"I could forgive you many things, Edwin Elwardson, but I cannot forgive you for this. Had you told me and allowed me the choice, I might have been able to love you anyway. As it is, you took from me by deception what was given to you freely in love."

Edwin bent his head. "Aye." Then he looked up at her and gazed at her fiercely. "But I regret not one moment of it, Madselin de Breuville. For one night we loved each other. It was all we could ever have and although I regret the deception, I cannot ever regret what happened."

He stood up quickly "I will not stay to hurt you further." His grey eyes lingered over her face, softening a little, and her heart felt as though it would burst with the pain. "I love you," he murmured before turning quickly and leaving.

The empty room felt cold and Madselin flopped back against the bolster. "I loved you too," she whispered after him, "but I cannot forgive you this." Yet what did it matter? Edwin planned to die anyway and he had snatched at the only straw offered him. Groaning, she turned into the bolster and wept bitterly until there were no more tears.

Oblivious to the passing of time, Madselin stared into the flames of the fire. She had no idea how long Edwin had been gone. It could have been hours or minutes, but it felt like years. She would never see him again and her heart was breaking, just as it had eight years before. And yet this time, everything seemed even worse.

In truth, she had known Guy little, other than as this handsome knight who was charming and so very amusing. When he died, she had mourned the life she thought they might have had as much as the man himself. But Edwin was very different. They had argued, clashed and stalked their way through the past weeks. They had loved for one night. She thought she had known him.

A lump formed in her throat and tears began to spill onto the blanket as Father Padraig suddenly appeared before her.

"I'm s-s-sorry," she managed. "I-I-I didn't h-hear you."

"No," came the soft reply. "It doesn't surprise me."

Madselin sniffed loudly in an attempt to stop crying, but it didn't work. The priest offered her a clean-looking rag and sat down at the bottom of the bed. "So?" he began firmly. "Have you anything you want to talk to me about?" His dark eyes watched her carefully as she wiped her eyes and blew her nose.

Madselin looked at him rather warily. "In what capacity? As a priest, do you mean?"

"In any capacity at all," he replied. "It can help to talk to someone. I may be more understanding of life than you expect."

There was a catch to his voice that made Madselin look at him more carefully. Maybe she had been wrong to judge the priest so quickly. Her mind flitted back to her rather cutting comments over his interest in Morwenna, and she winced ruefully.

"He killed Guy," she said quietly. "And ruined my life."

Father Padraig nodded, his mouth pursed tightly. "That would be very hard to forgive. Did he tell you why?"

"He believed Guy to have been one of the Normans who butchered his family."

The priest sighed heavily and looked at her. "That would be very hard to forgive too, don't you think?"

Madselin's fingers began to fiddle with the edging of the blanket. "But he waited years to do it. And then killed him on the morning of our wedding."

"And now?" he prompted gently.

"Now? Now I find I'm in love with the man that killed my betrothed and yet I can't help hating him, too. It makes no sense." Madselin screwed up her fingers tight and fought back another bout of tears.

"Human nature is a strange thing," said Father Padraig. "In my experience, people do tend to want most those things they can't have. The reality is usually somewhat different."

Frowning, Madselin looked up at him for enlightenment. Now he was making no sense.

''How well did you know your betrothed?'' he asked patiently.

''Since I was a child although, as Guy was much older than me, I did not see much of him. He was away in England a great deal.''

''Would you have been happy with this man, do you think?'' The dark eyes pierced her with their intensity.

Madselin shrugged. ''I shall never know.''

''I see. And this man you are hoping to marry on your return to the Vexin? What of him?''

''Hugh?'' She had forgotten about him completely. Well? What about Hugh? These past few weeks, she had rarely thought of him at all. Compared to Edwin, Madselin realised that he was good-natured but shallow, and she knew deep down that she would not be at all happy with him. ''I'm not sure. But I doubt he has ever lied to me.''

''If he had told you the truth, would you have forgiven Edwin, do you think?''

And that was the nub of the matter. He had killed Guy and she had hated the man that had done that for the last eight years. Closing her eyes, she shook her head. ''God forgive me, Father, for I don't know.'' Had Edwin not used that very same plea not long before?

Father Padraig smiled at her wanly. ''I had best tell you, then, that Orvell has been found guilty. Edwin offered him trial by sword. They fight at the lake shortly.''

''How long is left?'' Madselin asked, the blood draining from her again. Despite the fact that she could not forgive him, and should by rights hate him, the thought of his death struck her to the core.

''Half a candle notch, no more,'' he replied. ''Do you wish to go?''

Her heart was thudding heavily as she drew back the blankets. "Will you take me?"

Torches were staked around the lakeside, just as they had been on All Hallows Eve. The flames leapt and danced in the breeze coming in from the sea, lending a very eerie quality to the assembled crowd. Streaks of pink mingled with the grey of the sky, announcing that night was on its way.

Pulling her cloak tightly to her, Madselin stumbled on the uneven ground as she made her way to the edge of the sacred lake. Father Padraig guided her firmly towards the front where she could see what was happening.

The five judges were stood solemnly before the sacred stones, watching the two combatants prepare themselves for their duel. If Orvell was fearful, he did not show it. In fact, thought Madselin, he appeared much relieved. He had pushed back his cloak and was brandishing a broadsword of particularly evil appearance. Edwin remained as still as one of the sacred stones, his face grim with concentration.

At Mallet's command the fighting began. Someone in the crowd began a haunting melody on the pipes as the two men launched at each other with their weapons. The tune, she knew, was supposed to summon the spirits of the sacred lake and chase away the foreign oppressor.

Edwin began well, thrusting his great sword down and then slashing across as she had seen him do so often in practice. Orvell was agile and knew what was coming. Smaller in build and lighter than Edwin, his cunning and expertise had not been exaggerated.

Instinctively concentrating on Edwin's weakened arm, Orvell pressed home his advantage remorselessly. Dodg-

ng and moving, Orvell thrust and lunged with a determination that was as unexpected as it was effective.

Despite her anger at Edwin's betrayal, Madselin could
not help but watch Orvell's every move like a hawk. The
man was fighting like a demon and Edwin was not doing
much to stop him. He looked as if he were more determined to die.

His last words echoed in her head. "I will not stay to
hurt you further," he had said. "I love you." At that
moment, Orvell parried a heavy thrust from Edwin and
then spun round to slash deep across the Englishman's
chest.

Knocked back by the strength of the sally and the pain,
Edwin stumbled to his knees. The crowd drew in its col-
lective breath as Orvell swept his sword down. Whether
or not it was the spirits of the lake or just good fortune,
the music faltered and Madselin's gasp of his name carried across to Edwin.

Almost as if he heard her, he glanced across and his
expression changed. He lifted his sword with renewed
strength and stopped the Norman's sword from taking his
head. In a fluid movement, Edwin jumped to his feet and
bore down on the smaller Norman with a vigour that had
been missing before.

Madselin's heart was in her mouth. Whatever she felt
for the Englishman, she did not want him to die. Nor, it
seemed, did the spirits of the lake.

Edwin was fighting the Norman so that Orvell was
forced towards the reeds at the edge of the lake. Orvell
still knew no fear. Sweat ran down his brow as he kept
the Englishman's sword from drawing blood, but he, too,
was tiring.

Whether it was the reeds or the Norman's clumsy foot-
hold, Orvell suddenly faltered and fell to his knees. If

they were expecting instant death, the crowd was to be disappointed. Edwin stood back to wait for his enemy to rise.

That gesture of chivalry was lost on no one, least of all Orvell. "Your father did exactly the same, Englishman. It cost him his life," hissed the Norman with vicious intent. Those words did what nothing else could. Edwin launched himself at Orvell, his face wreathed in hatred and anger. It was exactly what the Norman wanted. Stepping neatly aside, Orvell caught Edwin on his weak arm and the blood welled instantly.

Madselin gasped audibly as Edwin groaned, his arm hanging limply at his side. Grinning from ear to ear, Orvell raised his arms in a death blow. As he stepped forward, however, his feet must have caught in some reeds and he tripped heavily. Falling headlong before the Englishman, Orvell sank below the surface of the lake.

Despite the water reaching no higher than their knees, the Norman did not rise. Edwin stood back, but made no move to kill him.

Albert Mallet rushed forward and pulled Orvell from the water. The side of his head was smashed into a bloody pulp. He had hit his head against a jagged stone lying just below the surface.

"Henry Orvell was guilty. God has decided."

From the murmurs around her, Madselin could tell that the villagers thought differently. "The gods decided and took him for their own," came the whisper. "The lake claimed his black soul." Madselin closed her eyes, both in relief and pain. Aye, he had survived Orvell's sword but she could never be with him even though he lived. The pain was wrenching her heart in two.

Almost as if he could hear her agony, Edwin lifted his

eyes to hers. A faint smile crossed his lips before he turned to leave. Madselin watched him. She could not do it. She could not call to him. The feelings were too raw.

Caring arms wrapped around her as her tears splashed to the cold earth.

Chapter Eighteen

"Well, Madselin? Are you ready?" Beatrice's gentle voice roused her from her contemplation of the wild land beyond the palisade. The deep snows of Yuletide had melted with the coming of the spring and Madselin could almost smell the new life beginning to emerge. She smiled, remembering how much she had hated this barbaric land at first.

"Aye. I'll see him." She drew back from the open shutters in Beatrice's solar and turned to look at her friend. "Is Richard in a good mood?"

"As much as he ever is these days," came the rueful reply. Beatrice looked up from her sewing and raised her brows in despair. "I've hardly seen him myself since he returned."

Richard and his men had ridden through the gates of the keep towards the middle of January and over the two weeks since then had spent most of it visiting his vassals. William Rufus, concerned about the treachery of Orvell, had ordered all his barons to be vigilant in patrolling the northern borderlands.

Richard had been anxious to comply with his King's

orders and had returned from one such visit only the night before, with a request to see Madselin that morning.

Under Beatrice's careful watch, Madselin had recovered from her ordeals. The scars that were left were hidden deep within and Madselin doubted that those would ever heal. She would not allow herself to think of Edwin. Yuletide had passed quietly, Madselin having relinquished the de Vaillant keep to Ivo's eldest son.

Alain de Vaillant had returned to find his mother dead and his father still away with his lord, but accepted his lot with a resignation that reminded her greatly of Ivo himself. Madselin's immediate usefulness clearly at an end, Beatrice had insisted that she keep her company instead. Now that Richard was back, he would decide whether or not she would be able to marry Hugh.

Her kinsman was waiting for her in a small room off the great hall. Two chairs stood before a bright fire, whilst Richard paced the room.

"Madselin!" He greeted her with an affectionate kiss on her cheek. "It pleases me to see you looking so well. I had thought you found our land somewhat…tedious."

His dark eyes watched her carefully as though looking for some special sign.

She smiled at him. "I admit to finding your land far more hospitable than I could ever have imagined. And far more…adventurous."

Richard laughed. "I am greatly cheered that your humour at least is restored." As if his own words reminded him of something far more serious, Richard gestured at the chairs, inviting her to sit.

"You did not ask me here to talk about my humour, I take it?" she asked softly.

Pursing his lips tightly, Richard shook his head. He sighed heavily. "There's no easy way of telling you this and perhaps I should have done so before, but I believe I owe you the truth.''

Frowning, Madselin looked at him. "I have no idea what you are talking about. Pray explain.''

He rubbed his thick black stubble with his fingers. "Had I told you all this years ago, I might have saved you much heartache and unpleasantness. Things might have turned out differently for you but I believed I was right in holding my tongue eight years ago.

"I never liked Guy de Chambertin,'' he began somewhat hesitantly. "He was…cruel and I was not happy at the prospect of your wedding him. Your father was adamant though, since it was a good match.''

Madselin stared at him. This was something she had never expected to hear from Richard. "Go on,'' she said faintly.

"Did you know he had made Alice his mistress not long before your wedding?''

Ice swept through her veins. "Alice?'' she repeated dumbly. "Alice, my sister-in-marriage?''

"Aye. She was but sixteen and very determined to have her own way.''

Madselin remained silent, so he continued. "I saw what happened to Guy on the morning of your wedding day. He had spent the night with Alice and was late. I have no doubt,'' he said with distaste, "that this was done expressly. I think Alice believed he would change his mind about marrying you even then. As he was slipping back through the bailey, Edwin stopped him.''

Madselin placed her hand over her open mouth but made no sound.

"He asked him if he was the de Chambertin who had raped and butchered his sister. Guy just laughed and told him exactly what he had done to her—and many others like her—and enjoyed it. There were so many apparently, that he had no idea who Edwin's sister really was, but he did not deny it.'' Richard shook his head in disbelief.

Sickness washed over her. This could not be Guy. It could not. ''Why would you say such a thing?'' she whispered. ''Guy was good and kind.''

''Nay,'' said Richard adamantly. ''He was not. He had always been cruel and liked to hurt people. Especially women. If you want proof, I have no doubt there would be many from his estate who would tell you his true character.'' He sighed, raking his hair with his fingers.

''Edwin challenged him and Guy accepted. There was no butchery. Edwin won the fight and killed him fairly. I knew what would happen if Edwin was arrested, so I hid him and brought him back to England with me.''

''So you knew all the time? Then why did you let me go with him to the de Vaillant keep?'' She stared at him in confusion.

''I thought you would have forgotten Guy, what with wanting to marry Hugh. How could I know anything like this would happen?''

''Did you know of Henry Orvell's part in all this?'' Madselin gripped the chair until her fingers went white.

''Only that I believed him a spy. Edwin could not prove that Orvell was the man he had been searching for all these years.''

For several minutes they remained silent together. Finally, Madselin looked at him. ''I thank you for telling me the truth. At least I can put those false memories of Guy behind me and begin a new life.'' There was no reason for her to doubt Richard's words. Indeed, they confirmed several strange memories that had nagged her over the years. Especially concerning Alice. Was that why she had always hated Madselin? Because of Guy?

As for Edwin, how did she feel about him now? Perhaps he had withheld the truth from her to save her misery? She had often thought over the past weeks how loyal he had been to his family, if nothing else.

Now that she knew the truth about Guy, her unhappiness deepened. She had treated Edwin badly, preferring to believe in a Norman she knew little of rather than an Angle she respected and loved. It would be better for all of them if she returned to the Vexin and made her marriage with Hugh.

"Tell me, Richard. Have you decided about my marriage to Hugh yet?"

"Ah." Richard heaved himself to his feet and stood before the fire warming his hands. Finally he turned to face her. "William Rufus was pleased with Edwin's part in Orvell's capture and offered him a reward."

"I'm sorry," began Madselin, "but I don't see what this has to do with me?"

"He asked only that you be given a choice in the matter of your husband."

Her hand floated to her temple in disbelief. He could have asked for anything, but he had thought only of her. Despite her lack of trust in him, he wanted still to make her happy. Madselin fought back the lump in her throat.

"The King was impressed by his gesture, so much so that he granted the request and gave Edwin Orvell's keep anyway."

"Edwin is up here? I thought he had gone..." Her voice trailed away. She had thought him gone back to Cheshire, perhaps to see his old love. Knowing that he was close by was hard to bear.

"Aye. This happened a few weeks ago. Edwin is at the de Vaillant keep, helping Ivo and Alain with the border patrols. I will knight him there two days hence." He paused to peer carefully at Madselin's white face. "Rufus sent for Hugh."

Madselin sat up with a jolt. "Hugh? Hugh is here?"

Richard shook his head. "We expect him any day now. I thought you would prefer to be...prepared. You might wish to think things over in the light of what I have told you."

Madselin lowered her head. "What do you mean by that?"

Richard turned his head away, clearly embarrassed by what he was about to say. "I have no idea what went on between you and Edwin, but whatever it was certainly had a deep effect on him. He is not himself." Richard glanced at Madselin. "He is a good man and were you to think of accepting him, I—as head of the family— would welcome the match. So would Rufus, I daresay."

After a moment's pause, he continued. "You are both sensible adults, for all I have said on that subject, and were there to be...er...consequences of your time together, I am certain that Edwin would be more than happy to bear responsibility."

Madselin's cheeks burned. "No. That will not be necessary." How could she even consider asking for Edwin? He would never forgive her for her lack of trust and she could not blame him. He was a proud man and she was not worthy of him.

Richard came to her then and took her hand. "Then think about it carefully, Madselin. Even if you cannot take Edwin, there are others here if you wish to stay. You have a choice now."

"You mean you wish me to reconsider marrying Hugh?" She raised her brow in question.

Richard kissed her hand lightly. "Aye."

If Emma missed Ulf, she had given no sign of it. On occasions Madselin would find her staring into the distance with a dreamy look in her eyes, but would leap into action the minute she thought anyone was watching her.

"Do you look forward to returning home, Emma?" she had asked her once.

"My home is with you, my lady." Emma's plain face would smile at her gently. "That is my choice."

Had the woman made more fuss about leaving the de Vaillant keep, or even the country, Madselin would have understood. As it was, knowing that she would perhaps be depriving Emma of happiness, was far more upsetting.

"You know that you only have to say, Emma. If you wish to stay here, I will understand. Don't feel you have to return with me."

Emma had pursed her lips tightly and remained quiet for a moment or two. "It's no good, my lady. I could never leave you. Ulf knows how I feel and we have said our goodbyes. I think it best this way."

Nothing more had been said between them, but Emma was noticeably subdued. Madselin determined she would speak to Beatrice about the problem. Her decision, however, was delayed by the arrival of a large party the next afternoon.

"Madselin!" Beatrice huffed as she ran up the stone steps that lead to the solar. "He's here!"

Jerking her head up, Madselin's fingers froze midstitch. "Hugh?" Her heart began to pound until she was sure everyone could hear it. "He's really here?" Despite the fact that she had thought of nothing else since Richard had told her, it was still a shock to know he was finally here. A lump formed in her throat and her hands suddenly became unusually clammy.

"Aye." Beatrice's face was pink with the unaccustomed effort. "But I don't think he's alone."

Beatrice's prediction turned out to be accurate. No doubt overwhelmed by a potential family member being summoned by Rufus, Robert and Alice had taken it upon themselves to accompany Hugh. Madselin's heart sank when she saw Alice's graceful figure alight from the litter. Hugh remained doggedly at her side, allowing Alice to clutch at his sleeve and simper blatantly.

Something inside of Madselin died at that moment, seeing them together and knowing how it would be. Had she really thought it possible to be happy? The larger figure of her brother stalked up to Alice and snatched away her hand, placing it firmly on his own arm. He then lead her towards the steps, with Hugh trailing somewhat aimlessly behind.

Madselin stepped forward. "Robert. Alice. This is a very unexpected pleasure." She bent forward to kiss each of them on the cheek. Robert managed a rueful grin and pulled her to him in an awkward embrace. It had been years since he'd tried it, after all. "Aye. It's good to see you again, Madselin." Stepping back from her, he smiled broadly. "This barbaric land seems to suit you."

Alice's cold green eyes swept over her. "You do indeed look most at home." Despite the bitter chill of the wind, Alice's nose and cheeks looked prettily pink and glowing. Her pale beauty was enchanting and she was well aware of it. "But we have missed you greatly," came the soft rebuke. "It is to be hoped you will return with us immediately." There was no mistaking the deeper irritation in Alice's voice.

Madselin's jaw tightened but she smiled stiffly, her eyes going beyond Robert and Alice. Hugh. Smaller than she remembered, he was still handsome. A little ostentatious, perhaps, in a rich red cloak lined with coney skins, but it suited his dark colouring. His hair fell in soft waves about his face and shining, brown eyes swept over her with a proprietorial air that she had never noticed before.

She had the feeling he did not approve of her plain but eminently practical gown of dark blue wool. Aware that the cold weather did not enhance her own looks, she smiled at him nervously.

"My Lady de Breuville. I am most glad to see you once more." His fingers were white, Madselin realised quite irrelevantly. Long, white and delicate, they reached for her own and carried them to his lips for a brief kiss.

"Hugh. I cannot tell you how pleased I am to see you." Somehow everything was just so awkward, so wrong, that Madselin wanted to run away. Perhaps all they needed was some time to themselves, but they were surrounded by people who expected far more than they were able to give at that moment. "Come meet my kinsman."

Once the introductions were completed, Madselin accompanied Alice to her room whilst Robert and Hugh were ushered away by Albert Mallet.

Alice swept through the door of the room and gave the plain walls and prettily embroidered bed linen scant attention. Throwing her gloves carelessly on to the bed, she turned to face Madselin. All traces of pretence were gone.

"So. You have what you want, finally." Her voice was harsh and contrasted most strangely with her soft prettiness.

Madselin frowned. "I'm not sure I know what you mean, Alice. Do you mean Hugh?"

Irritation flickered across the younger woman's face.

"Hugh? Do you think you could ever hold a man like Hugh?" She gave Madselin's sensible gown a dismissive glance before walking to the embrasure to watch her baggage being unpacked. "He is very…accommodating, to be sure. But," she smiled sweetly at Madselin over her shoulder, "that was not what I meant."

Pushing the shutter to, Alice strolled around the room until she stood once more before Madselin. "You have the attention of the King."

"The King?" echoed Madselin in confusion. "I have never wished for that." Had Alice gone deranged in her absence? The woman was making no sense at all.

Alice shook her head slowly. "Your innocent acts never fooled me for a moment, Madselin. I knew you sought power and riches. At home you would be the pious sister, all welcoming, kind, organised and efficient, but I saw the way you tried to attract the eyes of the men. Once you had lost Guy, all you ever wanted was to find another rich husband."

"You err greatly in your supposition, Alice. Perhaps a drink might restore your wits?" Madselin took a step back, but was prevented by Alice's strong grip on her wrist.

"I loved Guy, you know." Her eyes were shining in the firelight. "He hated you. He knew you only wanted him for his estate."

Shaking her hand free of Alice, Madselin gave Alice a pitying look. "Guy hated all women, Alice. That much I have learned."

"Guy loved me. He spent the night before your wedding with me and he was late because he tarried with me. I would have been his mistress even after your marriage. He promised me that."

Madselin shook her head. "I have no idea why you

are telling me this, Alice. I know about you and Guy. Is that not enough?''

Alice stared at her with barely concealed hatred. ''You always looked down on me, always treated me as if I were no more than dirt underfoot. He would have married you because your family connections were better, but he chose me to warm his bed, not you.''

She turned to flop down on the bed. ''And when I married Robert, I had the perfect opportunity to show you how it felt to always be second. Yet even then, you were able to make me feel stupid and silly.''

''So that was why you tried to marry me off to the old man?''

Alice eyed her with dislike. ''Yes,'' she hissed. ''It made me feel better to think of you bedding with that disgusting old man. He only wanted you for your paltry manor.''

Only the sound of the fire crackling disturbed the silence.

''And now you can have Hugh, too. Except that he is already mine.'' Alice's bitterness welled up from deep within as her pretty face drew itself into a mask of hatred. ''He loves me as I loved Guy. I shall make you pay a high price for this marriage since his only wish is to be near me. You, at least, can offer him that.''

Madselin stepped back. Her mind was reeling from such an outpouring of hatred. Never had she suspected Alice of such deep emotions. Whatever she was about to say was interrupted by Robert stepping into the room.

''Well,'' she managed, walking towards the door, ''I am sure you will need to rest and refresh yourselves after such a tiring journey. We will meet again at dinner.''

If Robert had overheard any of their conversation, he gave no indication of it. ''I admit to being in need of some time alone with my wife,'' he responded lightly. ''We have had little privacy over the past few weeks.''

''If you have all you need, then I shall leave you.'' Madselin had taken no more than two steps, when Robert reached out to grab her arm.

''You'll find Hugh in the hall. He is hoping to see you before dinner, I think.'' Robert's blue eyes studied his sister carefully before turning to stare at the pale face of his wife.

Shutting the door quietly, Madselin heard Robert's softly menacing voice. ''Up to your nasty games again, my dear? Do you know what I shall do if I find you once more with that ambitious little upstart?'' Was that how Robert viewed Hugh? Did everyone know about Alice and Hugh? Not wishing to hear any more of Robert's opinions on Hugh, she shivered and made her way along the cold stone corridor.

Madselin was not at all sure that she wanted to see Hugh. She thought she had. Hugh had seemed so safe, so kind, so uncomplicated. There would be no cause for worry with him. She doubted they would argue much since Hugh—as Alice had so clearly pointed out—was a most accommodating man. It would seem, however, that she had misjudged him too.

Bracing herself, Madselin decided that she would have to face the man, nevertheless. Alice might well have lied; there would be nothing new in that, after all. With her resolve strengthened, Madselin made her way to the great hall.

Hugh was sitting before the fire, a cup of wine in his hand. Stretched out almost full length, he looked very much at ease and Madselin felt some of her own tension dissipate. There were few servants about at this time and to all intents and purposes, they were on their own.

"Would you like to take a turn in the garden, Hugh?" she asked quietly as she came to his side.

He looked up, his dark eyes soft and bright. "Most gladly, my lady."

My lady. How many times had she heard those two particular words from the mouth of another lover—spoken in very different tones? Harsh, full of sarcasm, amused. Madselin conjured Edwin's face and her composure nearly deserted her. Only a slight gasp escaped her lips. Forgetting Edwin Elwardson was not going to be easy at all.

Hugh stood up and took her arm gently in his. He smiled at the slight tremor that ran through her body. Together they made their way to Beatrice's walled garden. The sun was dying and the air was cold, but at least they had some privacy.

"My lady," Hugh began rather nervously. "Madselin. You must know why I have come here?"

She indicated that they sit on the bench. "Aye. I sought leave from my kinsman for our marriage. I have that choice now from the King."

He nodded, his brown curls bouncing in the wind. Edwin, she reminded herself, had always braided his blond hair, which was far more practical. "And I would consider myself a fortunate man if you still wished for our marriage to take place. I have been patient these many years."

Madselin smiled in acknowledgement, but wondered at the lack of emotion she felt in hearing him say these words. "Do you truly wish this, Hugh?" Perhaps they were in need of getting to know each other again. Talking might help a little.

He shrugged his shoulders dismissively and peered at her curiously. "Do you question it, then? I had thought you wished it too, my lady.'' His handsome face mirrored his hurt. ''On the whole we deal well together and would make a comfortable match.'' Wounded dark eyes stared at her reprovingly. Madselin was reminded of one of Alice's small dogs that forever yapped around her ankles.

Had she expected anything different? His face looked very young and very innocent, although he was only a few years younger than she was. Alice had found in him an easy target. ''And what of Alice?'' she asked quietly. ''Where does she fit in to this 'comfortable' match?''

Unaccustomed to such forthright questions, Hugh seemed genuinely taken aback. ''How do you know about her? Did your brother tell you?''

At least he did not hide the truth. ''Alice told me. She expects to remain as your mistress.''

Hugh had the grace to flush. ''Well, we might be able to come to a sensible arrangement,'' he said eventually, unable to look her in the eye.

''Sensible?'' she queried, wondering at her ability to remain so calm.

He shrugged again in that careless way that was beginning to irritate her. His eyes were fixed on a piece of ground by his feet. For all his protestations about their companionship, Hugh did not seem at all comfortable in her company. Shifting slightly on the bench, his mouth formed a tight smile. ''Well. Something. This is hardly important, Madselin.''

She remembered how he had liked Alice's simpering and girlish laughter. Was that really what he wanted in a woman? ''I see,'' she said abruptly. Aye, she did see. Very well. Madselin withdrew her hand from his arm. ''The hour grows late. We should go in, I think.''

He pulled her to him quickly as she rose to go. ''Well? Is the marriage to take place? I would leave this accursed land as soon as possible." It was a fair question, but not one that suggested a man newly reunited with his lover. Nor could she fault his logic for wishing to leave so quickly since Madselin had felt much the same not four months before. Not now, however.

Madselin hesitated, her eyes studying him carefully. "I need some time to think," she said quietly. "There are other things, that need to be taken care of." She searched wildly for a good reason. "My maid, Emma, has formed an attachment."

"Your maid?" Hugh's dark eyes stared at her uncomprehendingly. "Why concern yourself over her affairs? She'll get over it." Gently he reached out his long white fingers and drew her face to his. His kiss was soft and gentle.

Pulling back, Madselin found her cheeks had flushed and not simply because of his kiss. "I had better go." Turning quickly, she fled to the sanctuary of her own room.

Dinner that night was a trite affair with everyone's eyes turned constantly to Madselin and Hugh. Together they were awkward, their speech stilted and their smiles tight and forced. Had they always been this way? By contrast, whenever Hugh spoke to Alice his eyes shone and his boldness returned, although Madselin could not help but think it shallow.

Alice had been remarkably subdued since coming to the hall. Dressed magnificently in a beautiful silk gown of pale blue, she put all the other women to the shade. However, as she did not wear a cloak, Madselin surmised that the woman must have been feeling very cold. This was, after all, a place where beauty took second place to practicality.

She was beginning to feel some pity for Alice, since all she had to rely on were her looks and a younger lover of little consequence.

Beatrice had said very little either. Every so often, Madselin would notice her eyes flicker in Alice's direction and then towards her husband.

For his part, Richard appeared unmoved by Alice's unexpected appearance in his life. Most of the time, he engaged Robert in discussions concerning the family. If Alice made any contribution, Richard would merely smile politely and then continue. Hardly the actions of a jealous man. Clearly Beatrice also came to the same conclusions and allowed herself to relax a little.

Beatrice had organised music and dancing to celebrate their reunion, but Madselin could have told her that she would not be expected to join in. When the dancing began, Madselin could see Hugh stiffen visibly. She doubted even Beatrice's feelings would override his views.

Beyond the top table, Madselin could not help but notice the cheerful banter of the lower orders and her heart gave a lurch. Normans mixed with Angles and Saxons, much as they had at the de Vaillant keep. Every so often she would catch sight of a blond head or hear a deep laugh that caused her heart to skip a beat.

Conversation with Hugh had become desultory, bordering on difficult and all she longed for was to leave them all. No matter how much she admonished herself, Madselin could not be happy. Was this not what she had wanted but four months ago?

As the dancing became rowdier, Alice suggested that she and Madselin retire. She caught Hugh's look of approval and knew that they could never be happy. Despite the fact that a love of dancing was such a foolish thing, it perhaps went to the heart of a person. Madselin withdrew in silence, glad to be alone.

Madselin blinked up into the warm sunshine and then closed her eyes. The morning was clear and fresh and she had taken the chance to escape into Beatrice's garden to think. She had spent the previous night trying to convince herself that the sensible course of action would be to marry Hugh and return to the Vexin with him.

The truth was that she did not want to leave this land. Nor did she really wish to marry Hugh. There was no alternative though. She could not remain here married to another whilst Edwin was so close. Nor did she wish to retire to a convent. No, perhaps Hugh would learn to love her. Maybe, though, she could help Emma find happiness.

Later on that morning, the whole party would be leaving for the de Vaillant keep to witness Edwin's knighthood and she was very apprehensive. Had there been any way of getting out of this, she would. Richard, however, had insisted and naturally Robert, Alice and Hugh wished to attend as well.

She missed Edwin, damn him. For all his lack of truth, she longed to see him, to touch him, to kiss him. Aye, she admitted wryly, even dance with him. When Hugh had kissed her yesterday, she had known deep down that she could never love him. It had meant nothing to her.

"It's good that the sun shines on so special a day." Beatrice sat down beside her and Madselin opened one eye to greet her.

"How so special?"

Beatrice turned to sit back and push her pale face towards the sun. "Did you not know what today is?"

"You speak in riddles again, Beatrice," she replied irritably. "Truly the damp has addled your wits."

Laughing, Beatrice tugged at Madselin's demure braid for such irreverence. "You foreigners." She sighed. "Today is the one day of the year when the young women of this land may choose their husband. It marks the coming of spring and the beginning of life. Had you not noticed how many of the servants were giggling and wearing special ribbons?"

"No," admitted Madselin. She had been too preoccupied to notice much. "What happens?" Her interest was piqued all the same.

A slow smile curved Beatrice's lips. "The girl entices her chosen partner to a quiet place and then captures him. She binds his wrists with her ribbon and then takes him to the priest. They are then wed according to the custom. Such marriages are supposed to be very favoured."

"Just as well you have a husband already."

"Ah! But you do not, Madselin. Do you not wish to try it out on Hugh?"

Madselin glanced somewhat warily at Beatrice, but she was sitting with her eyes firmly closed.

"No. I think not."

That caught Beatrice's attention. She sat up quickly and opened her eyes. "Do you mean that?"

Grimacing, Madselin nodded. "Aye. But I will marry him. There is nothing else for me."

For a moment or two there was silence. "He told you about Alice, then?"

"Alice told me herself, and Hugh did not deny it," Madselin replied. Pulling the ribbon from her braid, she began to fiddle with her hair. "Do you remember you once told me that you wished to be loved by Richard with such a passion that it made him lose control…?"

A faint blush tinged Beatrice's cheeks. "Aye, I did."

"Well, I found out how that can be."

"Ah," said Beatrice, before closing her eyes and sitting back in the sun once more. "Perhaps I should lend you some new ribbon."

Madselin managed a weak smile. "Edwin would not have me now. My future lies with Hugh." After a brief pause she took Beatrice's hand. "I think Emma might be glad of your ribbon though."

"Ah. I had wondered about that." Beatrice smiled at her friend kindly. "She will not wish to leave you. Is there no way you can stay? We shall all miss you."

Madselin shook her head. "I truly cannot, Beatrice. There is, however, one thing that would ease my heart, Beatrice. It concerns my niece, Mathilde." Madselin tugged at a loose thread on her gown.

"Could you ask Richard to take her in to your keep when she is seven? I know that Alice is already considering Mathilde's betrothal and I do not want to see her married off to some old lecher because of Alice's avarice. I know you would love the child for herself, Beatrice."

Beatrice thought for a moment. "It is too early to consider a match between your niece and Jordan," she said slowly. "But I am sure that Richard would be willing to foster Mathilde." She smiled at Madselin and patted her hand. "I will see what I can do."

Madselin returned the smile. "You are good, Beatrice. At least now I can be certain of saving Mathilde from Alice's poison," she muttered bitterly.

The de Vaillant keep stood dark and proud against the late afternoon sky as Madselin drew her horse to a halt. They had reached the top of the last rise, just as they had done only four months before. This time she felt very different. Her heart gave a leap of excitement as she caught the salty tang of the sea wind in her throat. It was wonderful to see the place again.

"God's teeth," murmured Alice. "I wonder if they've discovered the wheel yet?" She pulled her cloak closer to her shivering body and pouted sullenly. It had been a long, muddy journey and Alice had been very vexed that Richard had refused to allow a litter to carry her. Robert had been forced to ride at her side and neither of them were consequently in a cheerful frame of mind.

"Not very inspiring," added Hugh, frowning down at his mud-spattered clothes. "Perhaps it's just as well I didn't choose to wear something more elegant. Such clothes would have been wasted here, I daresay."

Madselin listened to the pair of them bemoan their fate and was secretly quite pleased that they felt uncomfortable. For the first time in weeks, she smiled as though she truly meant it.

This time, their approach to the keep gates was unimpeded by attack and the party thundered into the bailey with relief etched on their faces. A cheerful crowd had gathered to meet the visitors and Madselin's face lit up with pleasure. Her heart, nevertheless, was thudding unaccountably as she looked about. Edwin was not in sight.

Ivo de Vaillant stepped forward, his face almost hidden by a swathe of black hair. He greeted them all cheerfully enough, although Madselin thought him thinner. Bronwen smiled radiantly two paces behind him, baby Maude clutched possessively to her chest. Madselin fancied Bronwen looked almost cheerful, but dismissed this as a trick of the light.

Alain, his elder son, was still out on patrol but would be back for the ceremony. With no more than a few brief words from Ivo, servants came running to assist his guests dismount and they all headed for the hall.

As she picked up her skirts to avoid the ever-present puddles and dung patches, Madselin was stopped by the grip of a hand.

"Well, my lady. You look much recovered."

She looked up to find Father Padraig standing beside her. His kindly face was beaming with pleasure.

"Aye. I thank you, Father. It's good to see you all again." It was true.

"We are all very pleased that you have come back, my lady. Very pleased indeed." He raised his brows and moved a little closer to speak in confidence. "It has at least stopped Edwin from biting all our heads off."

At the mention of Edwin's name, Madselin could feel the blush steal over her cheeks. "I'm sure Edwin has far more to think about than that."

Father Padraig took hold of her elbow and guided her towards the hall as he spoke. "Perhaps its just the spring. The men are apt to be a bit awkward about now," he sighed.

A huge bellow from the gate caused them to stop in their tracks and turn to see what the commotion was about. Ulf had spotted Emma, bedecked now in colourful ribbons, and was pounding across the bailey to pull her into his arms. Despite the shaking of his head, Father Padraig smiled. "And he's another one who's been hard to please of late."

Joanna and Gyrth waved at her from a distance. It was good to see all these people again and even their strange tongue was a most welcome sound. Madselin had not appreciated just how much she had come to care for them and how important they had all become. The thought of